WOLF TRAP

ALSO BY CONNOR SULLIVAN

Sleeping Bear

WOLF TRAP

A THRILLER

CONNOR SULLIVAN

EMILY BESTLER BOOKS

ATRIA

New York   London   Toronto   Sydney   New Delhi

EMILY
BESTLER
BOOKS

ATRIA

An Imprint of Simon & Schuster, Inc.
1230 Avenue of the Americas
New York, NY 10020

First Emily Bestler Books/Atria Books hardcover edition March 2023

EMILY BESTLER BOOKS/ATRIA BOOKS and colophon are trademarks of Simon & Schuster, Inc.

For information about special discounts for bulk purchases, please contact Simon & Schuster Special Sales at 1-866-506-1949 or business@simonandschuster.com.

The Simon & Schuster Speakers Bureau can bring authors to your live event. For more information or to book an event, contact the Simon & Schuster Speakers Bureau at 1-866-248-3049 or visit our website at www.simonspeakers.com.

Interior design by Kyoko Watanabe

Manufactured in the United States of America

1 3 5 7 9 10 8 6 4 2

Library of Congress Cataloging-in-Publication Data has been applied for.

ISBN 978-1-9821-6642-7
ISBN 978-1-9821-6644-1 (ebook)

For Mariafe

"One seldom recognizes the devil when he's putting his hand on your shoulder . . ."

—ALBERT SPEER

"There are risks and costs to action. But they are far less than the long-range risks of comfortable inaction . . ."

—JOHN F. KENNEDY

PROLOGUE

Eastern Yemen
20 Miles North of Tarim
September 5, 2:33 a.m.

THE IRANIAN MOIS officer Mahmoud Ghorbani tilted his head out of the Saudi AB-212 helicopter's open fuselage, breathed in the cool desert air that whipped his face, and experienced a sense of freedom and purpose that he hadn't felt in decades.

Through his night-vision goggles, he took in the green hue of the craggy desert below as the chopper followed the single-track dirt road south—cutting through the barren Yemeni landscape like a snake.

"We are two minutes out," a deep voice said in Arabic over his head-set. "Are you ready, brother?"

Ghorbani turned his head to the right, gazed at Turki Shahidi, the infamous Saudi government enforcer, and nodded.

Returning his attention to the terrain passing below him, Ghorbani gripped his Kalashnikov and made some last-minute adjustments to his gear.

The first phase of Dark Sun was about to begin—an operation that had been over a year in the making.

He glanced over at Shahidi and thumbed his throat mike. "Make sure all your men have their face masks on. Tell the men and the pilots we will only speak in Farsi from here on out, no more Arabic."

Shahidi nodded, and Ghorbani watched as the man relayed the message, before taking off his own headset, and donning a black ski mask. If this delicate operation was going to succeed, there could be no slipups. Shahidi and his men would need to be able to pass as Iranians.

The Saudi pilots and soldiers who were chosen for this mission were not only Shahidi's most trusted men, but they could speak in passable Farsi, if need be.

Hopefully, it would not come to that.

Ghorbani would be the only person doing the talking.

"One minute out, brother," Shahidi said, in Farsi a few seconds later. "The caravan is just up ahead."

Ghorbani leaned his head back out of the open fuselage and could see the brake lights of a half-dozen vehicles heading south along the dirt road toward the Yemeni town of Tarim.

Turki Shahidi had picked this particular stretch of desert road for the ambush because of its desolateness. For twenty miles in every direction, there was nothing but sand, scrub, and windblown cliffs.

Nobody would hear the gunfire.

Nobody would hear the screams.

Turki Shahidi had planned this operation perfectly—so nobody would see the Saudi coalition helicopters attack their own caravan and free their own prisoners.

The caravan ahead was a prisoner transport and was operated by two dozen Saudi-paid Sudanese guards—most of them children and teenagers.

Shahidi had handpicked the Sudanese guards personally. He'd chosen the ones who were young. Those who were inexperienced with their weapons. Those whose brains and reflexes were dulled by the *khat* in their lips.

After all, this operation was more than just a rescue mission, it was an operation in *deception*—a show for the nine Iranian prisoners they were about to break free.

"Thirty seconds!" Shahidi said, over the headset.

Ghorbani looked to his left and to his right, seeing the two other Saudi AB-212 choppers flying next to them. Both choppers, Ghorbani knew, had six of Shahidi's soldiers within, not to mention the two gunners who manned each chopper's turreted 7.62 mm machine gun hanging out of the open fuselage.

And though he could not see it, a large CH-46 Sea Knight transport helicopter flew at a distance behind them.

"Fifteen seconds!" said Shahidi.

Ghorbani peered straight ahead out of the front windows, the caravan now within a hundred yards.

"Engage target!" Shahidi roared.

The night erupted in pulsating 7.62 mm fire from the two AB-212s—bright tracer rounds pummeled the five Toyota Hiluxes—making sure to avoid the large cargo truck with the canvas topper.

As Ghorbani and Shahidi's gunship hung back, Ghorbani could see the small bodies trying to escape the Hiluxes and return fire, but they were soon chewed up by the 7.62 mms.

The assault took less than a minute.

"Get boots on the ground and secure the area," Shahidi said, when it was finished.

The two other AB-212s landed on either side of the destroyed caravan, and Ghorbani watched as Shahidi's men moved through the vehicles, putting security rounds into the bodies of the Sudanese guards littering the road.

When the area was secure, Shahidi ordered his pilots to land the chopper on the road, and shine its spotlight on the back of the cargo truck.

Ghorbani followed Shahidi as they jumped out of the chopper, then watched as the massive CH-46 Sea Knight transport helicopter landed behind them.

"Tell the pilots to cut their engines," Ghorbani ordered in Farsi to Shahidi.

Shahidi relayed the order, and then Ghorbani walked forward, watching as Shahidi's men opened the canvas flap of the cargo truck and escorted nine shackled men onto the road. Each man wore tattered clothing and had a filthy blackout hood secured over his head.

"Line the prisoners up before me," shouted Ghorbani in Farsi.

Forced to their knees in a line before Ghorbani, a few of the prisoners perked up when they heard their native tongue.

"Now, cut their restraints and take off their hoods."

As Shahidi's men walked up and down the line with bolt cutters, snapping the chains from the prisoners' wrists and ankles, Ghorbani stood tall, still backlit from the chopper's powerful spotlight pointed directly at the prisoners.

When the hoods were removed, the nine men winced at the powerful light shining on them.

"Brothers!" Ghorbani shouted in Farsi. "You are free!"

Nine pairs of eyes now stared at Ghorbani, then around at Shahidi and his men wearing their black BDUs and ski masks.

"Who are you?" one of the men asked.

"You do not recognize me, brother? You do not recognize my voice?"

The man squinted up through the light, then his eyes grew wide. "Colonel Ghorbani?"

"Yes, brother."

The man stood and then saluted.

"There is no need to salute me, brother. It has been a long time since I've been an officer in the Iranian Revolutionary Guard."

"You are a MOIS officer now, an Unknown Soldier of Imam Zaman, are you not?" the man asked.

"I am, brother," Ghorbani replied. "And you are the legendary Quds Force sniper, are you not?"

The man took a deep prideful breath and nodded.

Ordering the rest of the prisoners to stand, Ghorbani stepped to the next man in line. "And you are the gifted engineer, schooled at the University of Tehran?"

"I am."

Ghorbani then turned to the man standing next to the engineer. "And you are the bomb maker, the saboteur?"

The bomb maker smiled.

Ghorbani walked up and down the line of the rescued Iranian Quds Force IRGC soldiers. Each man, other than being one of Iran's most skilled combatants in the arts of sabotage, assassination, and espionage, also possessed a series of specialized skills that Ghorbani found essential for the mission that lay ahead.

In all, there were six accomplished snipers in the group. One engineer, one bomb maker, and one trained pilot—all of whom had been captured by Saudi coalition forces during the proxy war in Yemen.

In the weeks prior, Ghorbani had selected these men from a list of thirty known Quds Force soldiers who the Saudi coalition currently had imprisoned in Yemen. It had been Shahidi who had ordered that these men be put together and then transferred on the caravan this night.

Ghorbani stopped before the pilot and looked into his brown eyes.

"Colonel," the pilot said, indicating the three AB-212 helicopters and the colossal CH-46 Sea Knight, "why are you flying Saudi choppers?"

"It was the idea of your commander, General Soleimani," Ghorbani said, having anticipated the question. "He supplied us with the stolen helicopters so we could fly into Saudi-controlled territory to rescue the nine of you."

Ghorbani then addressed the men. "Brothers! I have been sent here on a mission from Allah, ordered by your commander, General Soleimani. Each of you has been chosen for your particular expertise, your faith in Allah, and your unwavering hatred for the Great Satan and its allies."

Pausing for dramatic effect, Ghorbani then said, "Our mission, if you so choose to join, will be to orchestrate a death blow to America, but I only want the most committed. As you stand before me, you are all free men. Free to return to Iran to be with your families—your wives and children. You have already sacrificed enough and I will not judge you if you decide to return home. But for those who wish to follow me in the path laid out by Allah, to bring the Great Satan to its knees, step forward now!"

All nine men stepped forward without hesitation.

Smiling, Ghorbani said, "Good. Our journey begins immediately."

Ghorbani instructed the nine men to climb aboard the Sea Knight, then ordered Shahidi's men to return to the AB-212s.

As the men hurried to the helicopters, Ghorbani looked over the dozens of dead Sudanese guards lying in the road.

Any other day, it would have upset him to see the dead children, but not this night.

This night, their deaths had a purpose.

As the Sea Knight's twin turboshaft engines roared to life, and its tandem rotors began to whirl, Ghorbani and Shahidi boarded their own AB-212 and donned their headsets.

Lifting into the cool desert air a minute later, Shahidi clapped Ghorbani on the back. "You did it, brother—Dark Sun has officially begun."

"Did you doubt me?" Ghorbani asked.

"I never doubted you, but I didn't expect *all* of them to participate without question."

"That's because they are all true believers; they do not question Allah's will, my friend."

As the helos headed northwest on their two-hour journey to the waiting ship in the Red Sea, Ghorbani envisioned what lay ahead.

Once the men arrived on the ship, they would be split into groups and then given their separate instructions and their new identities. From there, they would begin their long trip into Europe, preparing and hunkering down for months until it was time to strike.

As for Ghorbani, he would be quite busy in the coming weeks. There was a nuclear scientist in Tehran he would need to visit, and a trip to India that they would have to take together.

And when all of that was said and done, the Iranian MOIS officer known as Mahmoud Ghorbani would disappear forever and be reborn anew.

Inshallah.

CHAPTER ONE

THE STORM WAS getting worse.

In the powerful headlights of the Prinoth snowcat, the snow blew sideways, lessening the visibility to only two yards.

Brian Rhome leaned forward in his captain's chair, squinting through the windshield as he eased back on the throttle of the massive machine.

The cat's engine whined in protest, the large, gritted tracks digging into the deep snow, desperately fighting up the hill.

Rhome guessed the snowstorm was throwing four inches of powder onto the mountain every hour and had been doing so for the past four hours. At this rate, Big Sky Ski Resort would be having one of the biggest powder days they'd seen in years.

Rhome flipped on the fog lights.

It was no use. The halogen beams only exacerbated the whiteout and made Rhome's visibility worse.

He swore and brought the machine to a grinding halt.

Leaning over, he grabbed his iPad and brought up the NOAA weather app. The app didn't load. The storm must have blown out the cell towers. Rhome thought back to the weather report he'd heard before his shift. Checking his watch, he saw it was just after 8 p.m. If the report had been correct, the storm was supposed to ease off at any moment, before picking up steam again for the rest of the night.

But in southwest Montana, weather reports were rarely accurate.

Laying the iPad onto the seat next to him, Rhome rubbed at his tired eyes.

During the last four months of working his new job, his body had never gotten used to its new nocturnal habits. He'd go to bed each day at 8 a.m. and rise at 4 p.m., just as the sun was setting behind the Spanish Peaks. By 5 p.m., he'd already have driven up to the resort to start work as the newest snowcat driver of the season.

It was a lonely job, but a job Rhome preferred and had even sought.

After all, what better job was there when one was actively trying to avoid all human contact?

Grabbing the lever that worked the cat's spotlight, Rhome turned the beam left and then right, trying to discern where the hell he was on Big Sky's notoriously steep Elk Park Ridge ski run.

Having grown up doing downhill ski races on this particular slope, Rhome guessed that he was halfway up the piste, most likely a few dozen yards to the right of the seventy-foot Snake Pit Cliff. Driving blind in a snowstorm on this part of the mountain could be suicide.

Rhome keyed his radio to his boss at dispatch.

"This is Cat Two. Jimmy, do you copy?"

Static.

Rhome tried again, "Jimmy, I've got zero viz out here on Elk Park. Any word if there is supposed to be a break in this storm soon?"

Again, static.

Rhome cursed and leaned back in the captain's chair. The wide rearview mirror caught the reflection of his tired, bloodshot eyes, his greasy, unruly black hair and bushy beard.

Rhome jolted away from his reflection.

In the last six months, he'd had trouble looking himself in the eye. So much so, that he'd taken all the mirrors down in his cabin and put them in the shed out back. How could he look at himself? How could he face the man staring back? After what he'd done . . .

Rhome tried to get ahold of Jimmy two more times before giving up.

He was either going to have to hope for a break in the storm soon or make sure he knew exactly where Snake Pit Cliff was in relation to his cat before he carried on.

Reaching for the backpack under his seat, he pulled on his down jacket, gloves, wool hat, and a pair of snow goggles. Cinching a headlamp over his head, he turned on its red light and stepped out into the blizzard.

Instantly, the wind and snow lashed at him.

Reaching back into the cat, Rhome grabbed his hundred-foot climbing rope and tied a knot around the vehicle's winch and the other end around his waist.

He'd heard of too many people getting lost and freezing to death in Montana snowstorms in the past and didn't want to become a statistic.

If he was going to die, he'd do it his own way.

With the rope secured around his waist, Rhome walked sideways across the slope toward where he determined he would run into Snake Pit Cliff.

At nearly six feet tall, and one hundred eighty pounds of solid, lean muscle, Brian Rhome still struggled, his big, powerful legs disappearing up to his thighs as he waded through the powder.

The lights from the snowcat all but swallowed up in the storm behind him, he continued to trudge forward, knowing all too well that the precipice of Snake Pit Cliff could open beneath him at a second's notice. Feeling with his feet, he took ten more cautious steps and then stopped as a sound made his blood turn cold.

Whomp! Whomp!

Rhome froze in his tracks. He knew that sound all too well.

Large masses of shifting snow, like the grinding of tectonic plates.

The prelude to an avalanche.

Standing like a statue, Rhome listened for the thunderous roar and the wave of white, kinetic energy that would surely sweep him away.

For minutes, he stood stock-still, watching as the snowflakes in his headlamp's red beam thrashed about. He knew that any movement, any shifting of his weight could cause his demise.

Dammit, what are you doing? he thought to himself. This was no way to die. This was careless. Stupid. Out of all the dangerous situations—all the hellish war zones he'd experienced in his short life, this was how it was going to end?

A damn avalanche?

For what seemed like an eternity, Rhome focused on his breathing, and eventually noticed that the snowflakes whipping around him were lessening their assault, and a few minutes later, the moon's rays cut through the clouds.

The break in the storm, Rhome thought.

Squinting ahead, and with the aid of the moon, Rhome suddenly realized he had been standing a good five feet from the precipice of Snake Pit Cliff.

He had been correct, earlier, in guessing his snowcat's general location on Elk Park Ridge.

Maybe it was because he stood atop the cliff nearly every night.

As Rhome continued to stare ahead, a violent gust of wind tore at his long beard, the darkness beyond the cliff pulling at him.

Rhome took a step forward.

Then another.

And another.

As he stood on the cliff's edge, a gust of snowflakes swirled downward, disappearing into the abyss below.

The seventy-foot drop into the jagged rocks beneath him would mean a certain, painful death.

It would be so easy.

The fall would take seconds. The rocks below would pummel and pierce his body. If the fall didn't do the trick, the cold quickly would.

Rhome closed his eyes and felt the familiar wave of misery course over him. The pain that had been brewing over these past six months was reaching a critical mass.

Images of that fateful day halfway across the world consumed him. He could hear the agonized yells of his men. The gunfire. The explosions.

But even worse, he could hear the bloodcurdling screams.

Hot tears formed around Rhome's eyes and instantly froze to his eyelids.

A gasping, primal cry expelled from somewhere in his throat and was taken by the wind.

He couldn't go on like this.

How could he live with what he'd done?

What he'd ordered.

Six months of secluding himself in the mountains of his old home, living like a hermit, was getting him nowhere.

Maybe it was time to end it.

On my own terms.

Opening his eyes, Rhome let out another anguished cry and lifted his right leg, so his boot was hanging over the edge.

And then he heard it.

It wasn't the whooshing sound of moving snow. Nor was it the whistle of the wind.

It was a howl.

A series of them actually, coming from below the cliff.

His foot still dangling over the abyss, Rhome nearly toppled in surprise, but he was able to catch himself just in time.

Both feet now firmly planted in the snow, he raised his goggles and squinted down over the cliff's edge.

Rhome watched a pack of nearly two dozen wolves, their eyes illuminated in the moonlight, howling and yipping at the sky.

Rumors had been circulating in town over the past week that the Wapiti Lake wolf pack had made their way out of Yellowstone National Park and were heading in the direction of Big Sky in search for elk. But never in Rhome's wildest dreams did he imagine seeing them at the resort.

As the crescendo of howls died down, and the storm began to pick up again, Rhome saw the pack move toward the woods in search of cover.

Only the biggest wolf stayed behind, his nose pointed skyward, sniffing at the wind.

Then, the predator suddenly turned and stared directly up at Rhome.

Though they were a good two hundred yards away from each other, Rhome felt the hair on the back of his neck stand on end.

The wolf's posture was not aggressive. Nor was it passive.

If anything, the wolf was merely recognizing the smell of another apex predator and communicating without words that there was nothing to fear between them.

As the storm picked up its onslaught, Rhome watched the wolf saunter away from him and disappear with his pack into the forest.

Rhome felt the emotion swell up in his throat again.
He was ashamed how close he had come tonight.
Of all the days, why did he tempt himself this night?
It was too much of a cliché—
Killing himself right before his birthday.

CHAPTER TWO

ORDINARILY, ANGELA BUCHANAN gave little thought to her clothes and appearance.

Still tall and statuesque at forty-seven, the natural beauty had a cadre of handlers who made her wardrobe, makeup, and hairstyle decisions, all of them carefully tested for public reception by private research groups that cost a fortune.

But this evening, Buchanan stood long and still before the three-sided mirror in her expansive closet while Sylvia, her valet, fussed with the fit of the svelte navy-blue gown Angela wore with an understated necklace featuring small ruby, diamond, and sapphire stones that set off the fine lines of her neck and jaw.

The bracelet on the left wrist matched perfectly. So did her earrings. Even her large diamond engagement ring and wedding band complemented the overall look.

"Are you ready for your shoes, ma'am?" Sylvia asked, holding up a pair of gorgeous black brocade high heels.

Normally, Buchanan wore flatter shoes because there was no sense in making herself any taller, but again, this evening was different.

This evening was as much about optics as it was about substance. She wanted her appearance to make a statement, a declaration of bold leadership and personal and political triumph.

She smiled as she came up to her full height in the shoes.

"And there it is," Buchanan said, her green eyes glistening after she tapped a finger against the one wayward strand of steel-gray hair in her hairdo. "There's the look we were going for."

"Almost, ma'am," Sylvia said, coming up behind her with the greenstone pendant on the thin, gold necklace.

"Ah," Buchanan said. "How could I have forgotten?"

Buchanan let Sylvia fasten the necklace around her neck, and then she thumbed the greenstone rock flecked with mica, a sadness sweeping over her. The Papatuanuku pendant, the Maori pendant that symbolized Mother Earth, reflected back at her.

"Ma'am, we are ten minutes away until the first arrivals," a voice said behind Sylvia.

In the mirror, Buchanan caught sight of her White House chief of staff, Katherine Healey. In her early thirties, the younger, and equally well-dressed, woman wore a maroon gown and beamed at Buchanan as she came into the closet, her eyes misting over.

"I'll give you two a moment," Sylvia said, backing out of the closet.

For ten seconds, the two women stared at each other, before Buchanan said, "I'm ready, Katherine. I truly am."

"I know you are, ma'am."

Buchanan felt that familiar tightness in her throat as she continued to stare at the chief of staff in the mirror's reflection. Still thumbing the greenstone pendant, she said, "My only regret is that Bobby isn't here to see this."

"He is in spirit, Madam President."

President Buchanan finally faced the young woman, both of their eyes glistening with emotion.

Healey grabbed Buchanan's hands in hers. "You know what he would have said to you right now, don't you? He'd tell you that you were born for tonight, born for next week in Davos. He'd tell you that this was the moment you'd put your stamp on history—that this was the moment the world would remember you for saving our planet."

Buchanan stared into Healey's blue eyes. At just thirty-three years old, Katherine Healey not only had a law degree and a PhD in political science from Yale, but she'd become one of the youngest White House chiefs of staff ever appointed by a president.

Healey deserved the job.

Five years ago, it had been Katherine Healey who had convinced a virtually no-name Michigan senator to run for the highest office in the land. And it had been Katherine Healey who had launched and successfully run Angela Buchanan's campaign for president.

"I just miss him, Katherine," Buchanan said. "Even in good times like these, I miss him so much."

"I miss him too," Healey replied, giving Buchanan's hands a squeeze.

Angela Buchanan couldn't believe it had been nearly twenty-five years since she had first met her late husband. They'd met at a bar in downtown Manhattan during Buchanan's first year of law school at Columbia. Bobby Buchanan had been with a group of his friends, celebrating his twenty-fourth birthday, when he had looked across the room and locked eyes with her.

It had been love at first sight.

Leaving his friends, Bobby had marched right over to her, introduced himself, and the rest had been history.

Angela had at first been attracted to Bobby's New Zealand accent, his caramel skin, his tall, broad figure, and his boyish good looks, but as the night progressed, she'd found his goofy and self-deprecating personality to be his most endearing quality. Bobby had explained to her that he was a student at NYU getting his doctoral degree in climatology.

Like herself, Bobby Buchanan was an incredibly driven person, but what she hadn't known that night at the bar—or even two years later at their wedding—was that Bobby Buchanan would one day become the most influential climate scientist in the world.

A year after their wedding, Buchanan had quit her job at a prestigious law firm in New York City, and for the next eight years she had followed her husband all around the world. From scientific stations on Elephant Island in Antarctica, to sub-Saharan regions in Africa, Angela Buchanan had been at her husband's side as he conducted his experiments, collected his data, and published his papers about an ever-warming planet.

After nearly a decade of travel, and with Bobby making a name for himself in the scientific community, the Buchanans had finally decided to slow down their nomadic life when Angela had become pregnant with their twins.

They resettled back in Angela's hometown of Ann Arbor, and Bobby took a job at the University of Michigan while they raised their children; she opened her own firm, focusing on environmental law.

Over the next few years, Angela—driven by the passion of her husband, and their extensive travels around the world—focused her professional time and energy fighting against the powerful petrochemical and fossil fuel industries.

Even as her firm grew larger, and after she'd won a handful of high-profile cases against big corporations, she had grown exponentially frustrated by the government's lack of action in tackling climate change.

Angela Buchanan had seen the writing on the wall. She was married to the most famous climatologist in the world. Not only did she see the oceans rising, the winters shortening, and the wildfires decimating the earth's forests, but she also understood the raw data coming in from the scientific community—that unless something drastic was done, and soon, the world as we knew it would cease to exist.

It was around this time that Buchanan had hired Katherine Healey to join her small firm in Ann Arbor. A Michigan native herself, Healey had returned to her hometown to be closer to her ailing father.

Buchanan saw a younger version of herself in Healey, an optimistic, determined individual who ferociously went after everything she set her mind to.

Over the next year, Buchanan and Healey had grown incredibly close—so much so that Buchanan began to see Katherine as the younger sister she never had. As Healey got to know Bobby and Angela, as well as their children, and after she had gotten to see how discouraged the couple were that their government was not taking the necessary action on climate change—Healey had proposed a ludicrous idea.

She'd asked if Angela Buchanan would consider running for a Michigan Senate seat.

At first, Buchanan thought the idea was ridiculous. But as the weeks passed, and as she had become victim to Healey's constant badgering, she had eventually started to entertain the notion.

It wasn't until Bobby had jumped on board with his full support that Buchanan actually saw that it could be possible.

What she could never imagine at the time was that this crazy idea would actually take her all the way to the White House.

Releasing Healey's hands, President Buchanan asked, "Where are the children? I want to see them before the night begins."

Healey looked down at her watch. "They're probably still studying with Harry and Phyllis."

Moving out of the closet, Buchanan and Healey walked through the president's bedroom and out the door and into the Executive Residence's second-floor hallway, where they were met immediately by Mark Edwards, the Secret Service special agent in charge.

In his early fifties, Edwards was the number one agent in Buchanan's PPD, her Presidential Protective Detail, and the highest-ranking person in the Secret Service.

Agent Edwards was not only President Buchanan's body man, but he was also in charge of overseeing and implementing all three levels of the Presidential Bubble.

From what Buchanan understood, the Presidential Bubble was a name used by the Secret Service to describe the inner, middle, and outer levels of protection surrounding the president of the United States at all times.

The inner level of protection was the PPD.

The middle comprised all the law enforcement, government agencies, and military personnel that followed and monitored the president wherever she went.

And last, there was the outer level that consisted of the GeoFence, an invisible dome that covered the area around the president. Edwards had once explained to Buchanan that the GeoFence was crafted and operated by some of the country's smartest engineers. Engineers who designed a technological bubble that could not only jam enemy communications and transmissions but could also stop any "new age" threats against the president of the United States. According to Edwards, the Secret Service no longer necessarily feared a sniper. What they feared was a short-range missile, a UAV (commonly known as a drone), or a bad actor trying to detonate a remote bomb close to the president.

The GeoFence stopped all these threats.

Buchanan took in Edwards's appearance. "I'm liking the tuxedo, Mark."

Edwards was the ever-consummate professional, and his reaction remained deadpan. "Given the nature of the event tonight, ma'am, I instructed *The Show* that we needed to blend in. There will be lots of cameras out there tonight."

The Show was the nickname that the Secret Service had for the PPD.

Standing around Edwards, spaced out by eight feet, were four more Secret Service agents all wearing tuxedos. These four agents were members of the Shift, the Secret Service's most elite members who surrounded Buchanan in a square or diamond formation whenever she left the White House.

It was unusual to have this level of protection around her in the Executive Residence, but tonight was anything but usual.

Smiling at the four Shift agents, Buchanan looked at Edwards. "And where are Agents Tuck and Hewitt?"

Buchanan was alluding to Eunice Tuck, the Secret Service assistant special agent in charge, and Charlie Hewitt, the Secret Service Shift whip who controlled the movement of the four agents surrounding her.

Agent Tuck was the second-in-command in the Secret Service, and Hewitt the number three.

"Agent Tuck is just leaving the Blair House with your executive guests, ma'am," Edwards said.

"And I'm right here, Madam President," Agent Hewitt said, striding down the hall. "I was just double-checking on the children before we move downstairs."

In his late forties, Charlie Hewitt had a brilliant head of silver hair and a strong jawline. Like Edwards, and like all the Secret Service agents Buchanan had gotten to know over the last three and a half years, Hewitt was all business.

After securing her party's nomination to be the candidate running for president, Buchanan had been given a Secret Service detail, and for the first time in her life, all of her movements were noted, recorded, and in most cases, dictated by them.

That had grown exponentially worse when she had taken office.

Ironically, not only was Buchanan the most protected person in the world, but she was probably also one of the loneliest. With her husband now gone, and only her children and Katherine Healey to confide in,

Buchanan missed seeing her longtime friends. She missed going out to dinners and lunches. She missed the anonymity.

Three and a half years in, though, Buchanan had somewhat gotten used to an unmistakable truth—while she might be the most powerful person in the world, when it came to the terms of her mobility and free- dom to go where she wanted, the Secret Service made all the decisions, not her.

"And where *are* the children?" Buchanan asked, as Hewitt ap- proached.

"In the Lincoln Bedroom doing their homework."

Buchanan walked down the hallway, passed the Yellow Oval Room and the Treaty Room and then opened the door to the Lincoln Bed- room, which had been converted to a study area for her three kids.

Tommy and Emily, her thirteen-year-old twins, sat at a table, their headphones on, staring at the laptops before them. Sitting between them was Harold Knox, one of the full-time tutor-nannies working at the White House. Knox was married to the other tutor-nanny, Phyllis Winkle, who had Elise, the president's five-year-old in her lap, and was reading her Harry Potter.

Elise, who seemed more entertained at mashing the pink Play-Doh in her hands than paying attention to the book, suddenly looked up, lunged off her nanny's lap, and ran for her mother.

At any other time, Buchanan would have relished scooping up her baby girl and swinging her around until she squealed in delight, but this evening was the culmination of decades of hard work, vision, failure, tragedy, and now triumph.

Using her gown like a matador's cape, the president neatly spun out of her little girl's grasp. "You can't touch Mommy right now, my sweet. Not while she is wearing this dress, and not while you have those Play- Doh hands!"

Elise turned as Buchanan crouched down. "But you can give me some air kisses!"

Elise giggled and gave her mom a series of air kisses. Laughing in delight, Elise ran back to her nanny.

"And how are those essays coming along?" Buchanan asked her two twins, who hadn't even glanced up from their laptops.

Harold Knox said, "Once I took their phones away, they actually got to work. Shouldn't be more than an hour or two."

Not wanting to disturb the twins, Buchanan looked back over to her youngest and blew her another air kiss before stepping back out of the room and meeting Healey and her Secret Service detail in the hall.

"Agent Tuck has alerted me that the crown prince and the Saudi ambassador have just come through the South Portico, Madam President," Edwards said. "As requested, Tuck's taking them to the Oval first for the initial photo op, and then together you will greet everyone in the East Room."

President Buchanan took a deep breath as Healey began to jabber off some last-minute notes about the protocol for the upcoming state dinner, as well as reciting an updated arrivals list of various dignitaries who would later attend the big Rose Garden event at midnight.

Standing on top of the Grand Staircase, Healey finished her summary, then looked at Buchanan, and asked, "Are you ready, ma'am?"

Buchanan squeezed Healey's forearm, and returning her grin, she raised her chin in the air and said, "Let's go make history."

CHAPTER THREE

MOVING OUTSIDE ALONG the West Colonnade, President Buchanan walked in front of Katherine Healey and her security detail and waved at the gaggle of reporters and cameras sequestered in the Rose Garden before the newly constructed stage where tonight's grand finale would take place.

Her head high, she walked confidently as the media continued to record the culmination of her political life's efforts.

As she caught sight of the field reporters speaking into their microphones, she did not need to hear them to know that most were focused completely on the evening's state dinner and the midnight event that would showcase the "turning on" of the world's seven "clean-energy" thorium molten salt reactors.

Still walking down the colonnade, Buchanan became giddy with anticipation as she thought back to when her late husband had first told her about the experimental concept of using thorium to create uranium-233 by way of a fissile reaction in a nuclear power plant.

Bobby had been ecstatic when he'd heard about the concept. Using salts like lithium, fluorine, and chlorine to cool the thorium reactors, the fission and energy being created would have very little waste and would need very little thorium to be converted into uranium-233.

"The Chinese are using primitive forms of these reactors to fuel entire cities in remote areas," Bobby had said, dumbstruck. "I've talked with scientists and engineers who say that these kinds of *clean* reactors and others like them will be the future of energy production, along with advances of wind and solar technologies."

Still a freshman senator from Michigan, Buchanan had not entirely understood how the thorium molten salt reactors worked, but she had been a quick study, and then a vocal adherent of them when she came to understand their potential in curbing climate change.

And here I am, Bobby, she thought, walking toward the Oval, *to see our dream made real with the most unlikely of allies. Here I am—the universe works in strange and mysterious ways, doesn't it, my love?*

One of the Marine Corps sentries opened the French doors to the Oval, and as the reporters continued to shout questions, she turned and waved, calling out, "We will see you all soon!"

Pivoting and entering the most powerful office in the world, President Buchanan not only felt humbled, but damn proud of her meteoric rise and her accomplishments since entering politics.

Eight years ago, when she had run and then won her Senate seat, she had done so by making promises of going to Washington, DC, to enact legislation that would drastically and systematically tackle climate change.

And she had done just that.

Four years into her first term as a US senator, and with help from Bobby and Healey, she had introduced a nonbinding resolution to call upon the federal government to create what she called the *Green Initiative*.

The initiative was a bold and expansive proposition that called for the eradication of the United States' dependency on dirty energy. At first, the majority of the United States saw Buchanan's initiative as a joke.

But something odd happened over the course of that year. Maybe it was the record-setting global temperatures, the melting ice caps, and the short mild winters. Or maybe it was the wildfires that were growing increasingly common.

Whatever it was, the public's approval of Buchanan's Green Initiative started to gain traction—so much so that she'd announced that she would not seek reelection for her Senate seat but would instead declare her candidacy for president of the United States.

A year and a half later, and after a horrible tragedy, President Angela Buchanan had become the United States' first female president.

But in reality, that had only been the beginning. In the last three and a half years, Buchanan had thrown a giant wrench into the establishment, destabilizing and ripping down nearly a century of industry, and building it back from the ground up. But what had been so odd and remarkable about her crusade since she'd taken office was the support she'd found in the most unlikely of places, and in the most unlikely of personalities.

"Your Royal Highness," President Buchanan said, striding into the Oval, flashing her thousand-watt smile to the man who was leading Saudi Arabia into the future, "how wonderful to see you again."

The man she addressed was the Saudi crown prince, Raza bin Zaman. He was sporting a manicured black beard, wearing a ceremonial black and-gold-lined *bisht* with a matching *keffiyeh*, and holding a smartphone. Bin Zaman looked up and put his phone in his pocket, the grin on his face growing so wide that the edges of his mouth seemed to nearly touch his ears.

"The pleasure is all mine," the thirty-five-year-old de facto ruler said, shaking Buchanan's hand.

Releasing the young ruler's grip, Buchanan extended her hand to the man next to the crown prince, the Saudi ambassador to the United States, and the crown prince's younger brother, Prince Khalid bin Zaman.

Unlike his older brother, Khalid was not wearing a ceremonial *bisht* or even a traditional *thobe*. Instead, he was dressed in a tuxedo—following the Western dress code of the state dinner that would soon be taking place.

"Madam President," Khalid said, giving Buchanan a shake of the hand. "Thank you for having us."

"I should be the one thanking both of you!" Buchanan said.

"Nonsense," the crown prince replied. "You told me a year and a half ago that this night would come quickly if we worked hard together for a common goal, and here we are. If it wasn't for your enormous powers of flattery, leverage, and persuasion, the alliance we now share would have never paved the way for real systematic change and set the planet and all human industry on a new trajectory."

Buchanan laughed. "My *skills* aside, Your Highness, it took tremendous bravery and foresight on your part to be the first one to understand *what* my husband and I were trying to accomplish, and most importantly, *why*. I believe in giving credit where it is due, and I plan to do so this evening in front of the entire world, and then again next week in Davos for the signing of the Global Green Accord."

The crown prince nodded in appreciation.

Buchanan's attention then went to the gigantic woman standing over the crown prince's left shoulder. Like the other Secret Service agents in the PPD, Assistant Special Agent in Charge Eunice Tuck wore an immaculate tuxedo, her stoic face expressionless.

"And how is your Secret Service detail, Your Highness?" Buchanan asked the crown prince. "Have Agent Tuck and her men met your expectations?"

"Exceeded them, ma'am. My bodyguards have a lot to learn from your Secret Service. I look forward to their protection next week in Davos."

Buchanan gave Agent Tuck a satisfied nod. It had been decided months ago that President Buchanan would give the crown prince a Secret Service element led by Agent Tuck to accompany him and his bodyguards in Davos.

Tonight would be a dry run to make sure everything ran smoothly next week.

"The guests are arriving, Madam President," Healey said by her side. "Shall we bring in the photographers?"

"Please."

Edwards spoke into his wrist mike, and moments later, a group of presidential aides and staffers escorted a throng of photographers into the Oval.

Reenacting the handshake they'd done in private moments earlier, President Buchanan and the crown prince posed for the camera. After two minutes, Edwards escorted the cameramen out of the Oval, and then Healey ran over the instructions for the president's and the others' entrance to the East Room.

"Since this is her house, the president will enter the East Room reception first—"

"No," Buchanan said, firmly. "The crown prince and I will enter in unison. This is a night where we will do everything together, as equals, where our actions will be for the good of all."

The crown prince offered Buchanan his arm. "I like that, Madam President. For the good of all."

CHAPTER FOUR

ARM IN ARM, President Buchanan and the crown prince of Saudi Arabia moved down the Cross Hall heading toward the East Room. To their right, the United States Marine Band played "Hail to the Chief." To their left were their 120 guests lined up against the wall, clapping enthusiastically at their arrival.

As they stepped into the East Room, the United States Marine Band began their rendition of "The President's Own," followed by four ruffles and flourishes, finishing when Buchanan and the crown prince took their position at the eastern side of the room, to receive their guests.

Tonight wasn't just a night that would symbolize change, it was a night to celebrate the acts of cohesion and solidarity that had occurred in the last eighteen months.

A year and a half ago, right after President Buchanan's Green Initiative bill had passed in the House and Senate, and had been signed into law, she had vehemently called upon the world to come together and sign what she'd called the Global Green Accord. It was a sweeping pledge to turn the world's nations away from their dependence on fossil fuels, and to become carbon neutral in fifteen years' time.

President Buchanan, bolstered by her win of passing the Green Initiative at home, had pitched her idea for the Global Green Accord during last year's State of the Union address. She called upon the world to look at the science, and to move toward green energy options.

During her speech, she had then doubled down—stating that any developed nation that did not pledge to signing the accord would be dealt a 50 percent carbon tax if they wished to trade with the United States.

Knowing that President Buchanan was not one to bluff, the markets had hemorrhaged the morning after her speech.

In the two days that followed her State of the Union address, not one country came forward, nor showed any interest in her pitch.

Then something odd happened in the most unlikely of places.

Three days after Buchanan's speech, during the Saudi crown prince's Vision 2040 Summit in Riyadh, the crown prince, Raza bin Zaman, stood onstage in front of the world's most influential and powerful people and announced that Saudi Arabia would be the first country to step forward and pledge to sign the Global Green Accord.

The announcement went viral.

And two weeks later, the crown prince, honoring an invitation from President Buchanan, had showed up to the White House, and together, they made a speech calling for other nations to join.

Within a week, France, Germany, India, Switzerland, and the UK had all stood up alongside the United States and Saudi Arabia and pledged to the signing.

A week later, the European Union joined.

Within a month, all thirty-eight members of the Organization for Economic Co-operation and Development had pledged to sign the Global Green Accord.

Getting all the members of the OECD to come forward was a monumental win for Buchanan and the crown prince. As the weeks passed, and since the OECD was an official United Nations observer, their leadership had coordinated plans with UN leadership to help developing nations within the UN go green, and eventually become carbon neutral.

Buchanan and the crown prince had then developed a timeline for the signing of the Global Green Accord to take place on March 9, nearly a year later in Davos, Switzerland.

In an effort to bolster enthusiasm for the signing, Buchanan and the crown prince, along with the first five nations that had pledged to the accord, decided to each build a clean-energy thorium molten salt reactor that would power one of their cities. In an act of solidarity, these thorium molten salt reactors would be built and then simultaneously turned on at midnight EST, nine days before the signing ceremony in Davos.

And now we are just an hour and a half away from that very moment, Buchanan thought, watching as the long line of guests entered the East Room to greet the president and the Saudi crown prince.

The first five guests were the leaders of France, Germany, India, Switzerland, and the UK, plus their spouses. They had been selected to greet Buchanan and the crown prince first, because not only had they been the ones who had pledged first to the signing, but in an hour and a half, they would sit onstage next to the president and the crown prince and would watch, along with the world, as their respective thorium molten salt reactors were turned on in unison.

After the prime minister of the United Kingdom and his wife made their greetings, and continued to the refreshment table on the south side of the room, the vice president of the United States, Michael Dunn, and his wife, Eleanor, approached next in line.

"Michael, Ellie," Buchanan said. "You both look like you are enjoying yourselves."

If Buchanan learned one thing since entering politics, it was how to turn on the charm. Dunn and his wife were outspoken moderates in their party. The former Speaker of the House had been walloped by Buchanan in the primaries, but after Buchanan's win, the party decided that she'd need more of a centrist running mate to appease the masses. Though it was not a secret that Dunn disagreed with much of Buchanan's policy decisions, he was a party loyalist, through and through. So loyal was the Dunn family that Buchanan had used one of his family members as a pawn for a particularly sensitive upcoming political move.

After shaking hands with the crown prince, Dunn shook her hand.

"Madam President," Dunn said. "What an accomplishment tonight and next week are for this administration."

"Thank you, Michael," Buchanan replied, gazing over his shoulder at Dunn's daughter and her husband next in line. "And how is your son-in-law faring at his new job?"

"Why don't you ask him, Angela," Dunn said, before seeking solace at the bar.

After greeting the Second Lady, Buchanan shook hands with the

Second Daughter, Annie Dunn, and her husband, the newly appointed deputy director of the CIA, Garrett Moretti.

Moretti, who was at least ten years senior to Annie Dunn, was also one of the more fashionable individuals in Washington. "Garrett, so glad you could come. How is the new job treating you?"

"No complaints here, Madam President."

"And that thing we discussed?"

Moretti touched his eye with an index finger. "I'm always watching, Madam President."

"Good."

Next in line was Buchanan's secretary of defense, James Lake, and his wife, Lucille, followed by Secretary of State Allison Newman, and then President Buchanan's national security adviser, Peter Coolidge.

After greeting General Edward Toole, the chairman of the Joint Chiefs of Staff, the director of national intelligence, Johnathan Winslow, came up and greeted President Buchanan and the Saudi crown prince.

DNI Winslow congratulated the pair, then dropped his voice. "Ma'am, just a heads-up, I saw your *friend* arrive in the Cross Hall just after your appearance."

Knowing that there were obviously cameras documenting her every facial expression, Buchanan kept her grin wide and through gritted teeth said, "I thought she declined my invitation?"

"I guess not, ma'am," Winslow said, before moving on.

Buchanan swore under her breath, realizing that her *friend* must have gone through the chief usher to get back on the invitation list.

So consumed was she with this little snafu, Buchanan seemed to completely zone out when meeting the next dozen or so cabinet members and dignitaries who had stepped up to her and the crown prince in line. It wasn't until the smell of cigars reached her nostrils that she'd snapped to her senses and shook the massive hand of Declan Brandt, the longtime senator of West Virginia, and the chairman of the Senate Select Committee on Intelligence.

Though Brandt was technically on Buchanan's side of the aisle, he was a West Virginian, first and foremost, a man who'd made his fortune in the coal mining companies his family ran in his state. Due to his industry, he wasn't the biggest supporter of her Green Initiative, nor the Global Green Accord. Squeezing her hand harder than necessary, he said in his trademark gruff voice, "I thought Elizabeth wasn't attending this event."

"How far behind in line is she?"

"A dozen or so," Brandt replied, without trying to mask his disdain. "If you have me sitting at the same table as her tonight, Angela, I am leaving."

"I was not in charge of the seating arrangements, Declan."

Senator Brandt mumbled something indiscernible under his breath about needing to go to the bar as Buchanan looked at the line coming toward her and saw the vivid shock of curled silver hair, not ten individuals deep.

"Angela!" a booming voice said, and for a moment, she couldn't believe she hadn't seen one of her closest confidants, Texas senator Richard Lancaster. His arms spread wide in greeting.

Lancaster was nearly the same age and build as Declan Brandt, but unlike Brandt, Lancaster was one of her most ardent supporters.

"Oh, Richard!" Buchanan said. "Please, let me introduce you to—"

"Your Royal Highness," Lancaster said, extending a beefy hand in the crown prince's direction. "I'm a fan. A huge fan of yours."

"And I of yours, Senator," the crown prince replied.

"Have you two never met?" asked Buchanan.

"Can't say I have," Lancaster said. "But I have met your father, the king."

Senator Richard Lancaster had become one of Buchanan's closest and one of her most unlikely allies in the last year and a half. A millionaire many times over, Senator Lancaster came from a lucrative family of wildcatters, who'd made their fortune drilling oil from Texas shale.

Senator Lancaster had been the only politician from the other side of the aisle who had surprisingly voted in favor of Buchanan's Green Initiative. In an impassioned speech on the Senate floor, during the voting process, Lancaster renounced his background as an oil baron, pledged to break up his company, and vowed to focus on green energy.

Since that moment Lancaster had become a mentor for Buchanan while she'd navigated the trials and tribulations of trying to get the Global Green Accord signed.

Putting his hands on Buchanan's shoulders, Lancaster said, "I'm so damn proud, Madam President. So damn proud."

"This wouldn't have happened without you, Richard."

As Lancaster moved toward the rest of the guests who'd already showed their respects, Buchanan shook the hands of a few more dignitaries, politicians, and a celebrity or two before getting to the end of the line, where an older woman, with hawkish features and silver permed hair waited respectfully.

CIA director Elizabeth Hastings waited her turn before moving forward and bowing her head slightly toward Buchanan and the crown prince.

"Elizabeth," Buchanan said, the grin completely fading from her face, as she contemplated the old spymaster. "I thought you weren't going to make it?"

"My schedule opened up, Madam President," Hastings said, and she finally acknowledged the Saudi crown prince. "And I thought it would have been rude of me if I wasn't here to meet His Royal Highness and missed such a momentous occasion in our country's history."

It was no secret in Washington that a major tiff was occurring between President Buchanan and the director of the CIA. Buchanan and Hastings had conflicting views about the aggressiveness of America's foreign policies.

Buchanan had run on an antiwar, green energy agenda, and after she'd recently ended the twenty-year war on terror, she'd cut both America's military and the CIA's budget in half.

This created major animosity between Buchanan and Director Hastings.

Gazing into the yellow-tinged eyes of the old spymaster, the president became aware that the whole room was watching them to see how they would respond to each other.

Putting her million-dollar smile back on, Buchanan said, "I'm so glad you could make it, Elizabeth. Thank you for coming."

For the next twenty minutes, Buchanan and the crown prince mingled with their guests before everyone was told that dinner was finally served in the State Dining Room.

Leaving the East Room after their guests, Buchanan walked down the Cross Hall with the crown prince, who had taken his black smart-phone from his pocket and gazed down at it.

"Your Highness," Buchanan said, with a smile, pointing down to the phone. "Not here."

"I'm sorry, Madam President," Raza bin Zaman stated, with an embarrassed look. "Trying my best."

Buchanan patted the young man on the arm. It was widely known that the Saudi crown prince was afflicted by a mild case of obsessive-compulsive disorder, a disorder that he spoke about publicly and had since a child. His symptoms as an adult were slight, mostly manifesting in the need for the young ruler to check his phone every minute on the minute.

"You're doing great, Your Highness," Buchanan said, as they walked into the State Dining Room, where everyone applauded their entrance.

Moving to their table, Buchanan and the crown prince stood behind their chairs, and Buchanan reached down and picked up a flute of champagne.

"A toast," she said, raising the glass.

Looking out over the sea of excited faces as they raised their own glasses, Buchanan felt another familiar pang of sadness overtake her.

You should be here tonight, Bobby.

You should be here with me, to see what we've accomplished.

As she was thinking it, she caught sight of Director Hastings, standing at her own table, next to a very upset-looking Senator Declan Brandt, who was red in the face.

Averting her eyes to hide her own amusement, Buchanan spoke loudly, "In an hour's time, and after a year and a half of hard work, we in this room will watch along with the rest of the world as we welcome a new era of continued sustainability and progress. Let tonight be the spring-board for the signing of the Global Green Accord in nine days, in Davos."

Raising her flute up high, she listened as the whole room toasted one another, and as she finally sat down to eat her meal before she and the other six nations' leaders took the stage, she once again thought of how much she missed her husband.

CHAPTER FIVE

CUSTER BURST INTO his study, his fingers ripping the black bow tie from his neck that had been choking him the whole night, and made a beeline for the bar on the far wall.

Fingers dancing over the fifty-odd bottles of bourbon, he selected the Blanton's Black Label, grabbed a clean tumbler, poured himself three fingers' worth, and downed the entire glass.

As the bourbon slid down his throat and settled in his stomach, he let out a loud sigh of relief—the anger he'd been feeling all night abating, and another emotion manifesting itself in its place.

Excitement.

The White House state dinner had been so infuriating, the people, atmosphere, decorum, and fanfare so unbearable that Custer had gotten out of there as fast as possible.

He'd barely finished dinner, when he'd collected his jacket and met the limo under the east entrance veranda before the White House staff ushered everyone into the Rose Garden to watch President Buchanan and the other six world leaders sit onstage as all seven of the world's thorium molten salt reactors were turned on.

There was no way in hell I would ever do that, Custer thought, pouring himself another glass.

No, tonight Custer wanted to be alone so he could celebrate in the privacy of his own home.

After all, he'd been looking forward to this night for a year and a half.

All of the planning, scheming, and the careful manipulation would finally come to a head tonight and yield its first results.

At least that's what he'd been promised.

Wiggling out of his tuxedo jacket, he threw it on the floor, and then lit a fire in the hearth.

As the flames came to life, he grabbed his TV remote from the side table next to his wing-backed leather chair and turned on the flat-screen television hanging on the far wall.

Every news network in the world was showing the live broadcast of the event—focusing in on Angela Buchanan and the other six world leaders sitting together onstage, looking excited.

Custer snorted at the absurdity of the spectacle.

Moving through the television stations, he decided on a network that showed a live aerial shot of the thorium molten salt reactor located outside of Las Vegas.

The reason he'd picked this specific news channel was because it also displayed live coverage of the Rose Garden stage and was providing a close-up of President Angela Buchanan and the young Saudi crown prince, Raza bin Zaman, sitting next to her.

Custer stared in disgust at Buchanan, and then he nearly shivered with excitement for what was to come.

Five years ago, if someone were to tell Custer that he'd be witnessing a future president and the de facto ruler of Saudi Arabia sitting together with five other world leaders on a stage, he would have outright dismissed it.

Five years ago, if someone told Custer *why* the Saudi crown prince and a president of the United States were sitting together on a stage— and what state the country and the world were in—Custer would have thought he was listening to the rantings of a madman.

The thing was, though, the country and the world *had* gone mad. President Buchanan had seen to that.

Not only had Buchanan's political ascension been swift, but once she'd taken office three and a half years ago, she'd been like a bull in a china shop—smashing through and obliterating long-standing industries and institutions to get her damn Green Initiative signed into law.

Custer had been shocked when the young senator had become the presumptive candidate for her party. And that shock had turned to out-right distress when Buchanan clinched both the Electoral College and the popular vote—becoming the United States' first ever female president.

Not only had Buchanan won the presidential election, but her party had also miraculously secured a majority in both the House and in the Senate.

Custer would remember November 3, three and a half years ago, as one of the most horrendous nights of his life. He'd envisioned a world in which a mad president destroyed a century of industry. He'd envisioned the economy collapsing, joblessness, and a nation on the precipice of disaster.

Unfortunately, in his eyes, Custer had been correct, and then some.

Not only had Buchanan eliminated the filibuster to get the votes she needed to pass her Green Initiative, but she'd also granted statehood to Puerto Rico, and Washington, DC, whose new representatives had all won seats on her side of the aisle.

Custer had watched in terror during her State of the Union address the year before as, emboldened by the passing of the initiative, she'd called upon the world to come together and sign the Global Green Accord.

And now, to Custer's disgust, the result of what occurred after that State of the Union was now manifesting itself on his TV screen.

He checked his watch; it was 11:57 p.m., just three minutes until all the thorium molten salt reactors turned on simultaneously around the globe.

Custer drained his glass in jittery anticipation and realized he'd been so sidetracked that he'd forgotten to light one of his cigars.

Marching back toward the bar, he refilled his third glass, plucked a Gurkha cigar from his humidor, cut it, and then lit it, just in time to watch the countdown on the television screen hit the thirty-second mark.

Moving quickly to his chair, Custer took a seat, as the news anchor went quiet.

The screen cut into seven squares—each showing the live feeds of the seven reactors that were about to be turned on.

Custer leaned forward.

Five.

Four.
Three.
Two.
One.

Simultaneously, the seven thorium molten salt reactors in France, Saudi Arabia, Germany, India, the UK, Switzerland, and the United States all powered up. If Custer hadn't been so enamored by what was about to happen, he would have been disappointed at the lackluster display on the screen before him.

The news channel then cut to Times Square where people were dancing in the streets, then to images of the stage in the Rose Garden, where President Buchanan and the crown prince of Saudi Arabia were shaking hands with each other and the five other world leaders.

For minutes, Custer sat frozen, waiting, watching the images of celebration occur across the world.

Then it happened.

Sixteen minutes after the reactors were turned on, and while the network news channel was still showing reactions across the planet, a reporter cut in, and said that an anomaly was occurring to the reactor in Germany.

A minute later, more reports came in from India and the UK.

Unable to contain himself, Custer stood from his seat. The network cut back to the stage, where the earlier signs of jubilation had turned deadly serious. President Buchanan and the crown prince stood next to each other and, along with the crowd and the other world leaders, watched the jumbo screen that had been set up offstage in the Rose Garden. The screen cut back to the news anchor, who said, "We're getting reports of meltdown incidents in Germany, and India—"

Custer held his breath.

The anchor touched his earpiece. "We have just been notified that all seven thorium molten salt reactors are experiencing difficulties and have begun shutdown procedures—"

The anchor didn't finish his sentence. His hand flew back to his earpiece again. "I . . . I have just been informed that the reactor outside of Las Vegas has experienced a cataclysmic explosion."

Custer leapt into the air. "YES! YES!"

As the next five minutes flew by, video of all seven reactors showed different levels of explosions, meltdowns, and fires in their facilities.

Custer danced around his study. "Those sons of bitches did it!"

Cackling like a wild man, he realized he'd spilled the majority of his bourbon and hurried to his bar, filling himself a celebratory glass.

He stared at the television for another few minutes in delight, transfixed as chaos unfurled around the world.

Drunk on booze and exhilaration, Custer peeled his attention from the television and glanced over at the Edgar S. Paxson oil painting that hung on the wall behind his desk.

Moving over to the painting, he pushed it aside, revealing the door to a small reinforced steel safe built into the wall. Punching in his passcode, Custer wrenched the safe open. On the left side within the safe was a small black laptop, and the smartphone given to him by his benefactors. Both the laptop and the smartphone held the Orion encryption technology, the most secure telecommunications encryption system in the world.

As his hand grazed over the Orion devices, he moved aside one of his most prized possessions, an old silver Sony microcassette player. Inside the device was a tape that was worth more to Custer than anything in the world. Not only was the tape an insurance policy, but it was a tool that, if used correctly, could all but guarantee Custer's most lofty ambitions.

Moving his hand to the right side of the safe, he grabbed one of the ten prepaid burner phones and turned it on.

After the phone powered up, Custer then typed in a number with a +966 area code and texted:

Hurrah, boys. Hurrah!

Upon hitting send, Custer took the battery out, and then snapped the burner phone in half.

He knew he was supposed to maintain radio silence with his benefactors—but given the excitement of the night, and their success after all this time of planning, Custer couldn't contain himself.

With the meltdowns of the seven thorium molten salt reactors, Custer's operation in the United States was now a go.

Operation Little Bighorn could officially begin.

Grabbing the secure Orion phone, Custer locked the safe, snatched his bourbon, and then returned to his seat before the television.

He would keep the Orion phone on his person, just in case any of his lieutenants needed to reach out to him.

Reno, Benteen, Varnum, and McDougall will be much too busy tonight to contact me, Custer thought, taking a satisfied drag of his cigar.

One of the most amusing aspects of this whole plan was the fact that Custer had not only been able to name his operation after his favorite American battle, but that he had given himself a code name in reference to his favorite American general, George Armstrong Custer, who, along with his four officers, Reno, Benteen, Varnum, and McDougall had all made their legendary last stand at the Battle of the Little Bighorn.

And this is my last stand, Custer thought.

My last stand to save my country.

My last stand to save the United States.

As Custer continued to watch the devastation play out on the news, his mind wandered to the upcoming meeting with his beautiful handler and to the next phase of the operation.

In nine days, the world would change forever.

In nine days, Custer would rise like a phoenix from the ashes and cement his place in the annals of history as this nation's savior.

Raising his glass into the air, he said, "I will drink to that."

CHAPTER SIX

STANDING FROZEN ON the stage, her eyes focused on the jumbo screen across the Rose Garden—its muted images showing the destruction playing out all across the world—President Buchanan felt a large presence grab her around the waist and lift her into the air.

She could hear the yelling and confusion from the crowd and the shouts directed at her from the press corps—their cameras pointed directly at her, snapping shots of her fear and confusion.

Buchanan realized that the strong arms that had grabbed her belonged to the Secret Service special agent in charge, Mark Edwards, who was literally carrying her off the stage. The four members of the PPD, directed by Agent Charlie Hewitt, had cleared a path for them that led down the stairs, across twenty-five feet of lawn and then into the Oval.

Putting her down, Edwards then barked out orders as dozens of Secret Service agents burst into the room and secured it.

Buchanan turned a full three hundred sixty degrees and then caught sight of her chief of staff entering the room, looking just as confused and scared as she.

"What the hell is happening, Katherine?"

Healey stopped before the president. For what was probably the first time in her life, she was rendered speechless.

The Secret Service agents parted at the door that led to the Rose Garden, and Agent Tuck and her team, along with a group of Saudi security officers, were let inside, surrounding the crown prince and Prince Khalid.

"Your Highness, what the hell is going on?!"

Both the crown prince's and Khalid's faces were white.

"Ma'am," Edwards said, "for your safety, we are going to move you down to the Situation Room."

"For my safety?"

"There are a lot of people outside, ma'am," Edwards said. "And until we can fully secure the White House and understand the situation, we need you secure."

"They come with us," Buchanan said, pointing at Healey, Prince Khalid, and the crown prince. "That's an order, Mark."

"Fine," Edwards said, then motioned to Tuck. Seconds later, they were all escorted down into the Situation Room and into the large conference area.

Already, the Situation Room duty staff were running around, fielding calls. The numerous screens on the walls of the conference area were turned to the news, showing live video feeds of the seven reactors, each experiencing differing levels of meltdowns—but the one showing the worst destruction, the one billowing black smoke with half its side blown out, was the reactor in the desert just north of Las Vegas.

"The energy secretary is upstairs, get him down here," Buchanan said to no one in particular. "Then call in the National Security Council."

Buchanan made eye contact with Healey, who jolted into action, reaching down to one of the closed-circuit phones on the table.

"Madam President!"

Buchanan looked over and saw Raza bin Zaman walk out of a scrum of his aides and security, his phone in his hand.

"I can't get any service in the Situation Room, ma'am," the crown prince said. "Our reactor just outside of Tabuk is experiencing a full meltdown. I need to—"

"How could this be happening?!" Buchanan said more to herself than anyone.

As she stared at the crown prince, then at Prince Khalid and all their aides and security, and the destruction playing out on the screens all around them, she couldn't help but think that it was all over.

The accord signing in nine days.

Her and Bobby's dream of a new future.

Everything she had accomplished.

Gone.

She somehow verbalized these fears to the crown prince, but she hadn't heard herself say it, because a ringing in her ears had drowned everything else out.

"Madam President," the crown prince said, gazing at her concerned. "Madam President?"

Buchanan shook her head, and the world re-collected itself.

The crown prince was standing directly in front of her. "Don't worry about the accord signing. Tomorrow we will regroup, then we will re-assure the public—we can make a joint speech if we have to, okay?"

Buchanan felt herself nodding.

"Please," the crown prince said. "Can I head back to the Blair House? I have a lot to deal with back home—"

"Yes," Buchanan said. "Of course, of course."

She relayed the crown prince's pleas to Agent Tuck, who nodded and had a slew of agents escort the Saudis outside.

When the doors shut, Buchanan found herself alone with the screens depicting images of destruction.

She pulled out a chair and sat at the oval table as a tsunami of emotions started to pummel her, spin her out of control.

She put a hand on the table to steady herself, and for the hundredth time that night, she wondered why the hell Bobby wasn't there with her.

CHAPTER SEVEN

BRIAN RHOME PULLED the snowcat into the maintenance garage and killed the engine.

After his encounter with the wolf pack while he'd stood on top of Snake Pit Cliff, he'd trudged back to his cat and drove the machine to the top of Elk Park Ridge, where he had finally gotten ahold of his supervisor, Jimmy, on the radio, informing him that the snow was too deep and the visibility too poor to continue grooming on the western side of the mountain.

Jimmy had then ordered him to continue the rest of his shift on the lower, more gradual slopes near the base.

Rhome stepped out of the cat now parked in the garage, placed the keys on his boss's desk, and grabbed his belongings before punching out on his time card.

Walking to his old Dodge Ram in the workers' parking lot, he started the truck, then began wiping the snow from his windshield that had accumulated over the night.

Below, he could see the train of vehicles on Route 64 coming up off Highway 191 from Bozeman, inching their way toward the resort.

It was going to be an epic day of skiing.

Avalanche bombs reverberated in the clouds above him. The ski patrol on the summit of Lone Peak would have their work cut out for them this morning. Rhome estimated nearly twenty inches of powder had accumulated overnight.

Soon, the public parking lot would be at capacity and the resort workers would have to turn the remaining skiers and boarders away.

In the nearly four months that the resort had been open for winter, this was the first major storm of the season, a new reality that everyone in the world was slowly adjusting to as the climate continued to change.

After clearing the snow, Rhome entered his truck, and before he put the vehicle in drive, he reached down below his seat and felt the cold steel of the lockbox he'd welded to the floorboard.

This was something he did instinctually every time he entered his vehicle.

A habit he'd picked up from the stress and uncertainty of his old job.

The box was locked and untouched, just as he'd left it.

Putting the Dodge into four-wheel drive, he exited the workers' lot and began making his way down the plowed road toward Route 64 to his family's cabin.

As he drove, his mind floated to the events of the night before while he stood on the cliff.

He was ashamed of how close he'd gotten this time. Ashamed of how willing he was to just take one more step and end it all.

If it hadn't been for the wolves, would he have taken that final step?

As the mountain road twisted and turned, Rhome noticed that another vehicle was making its way down the road behind him.

He realized he'd caught sight of the vehicle a couple of minutes earlier as he pulled out of the workers' lot.

Rhome slowed his truck so he could see the front license plate of the black SUV with the tinted windows. It was a Montana plate, a Bozeman plate—most likely a rental vehicle from the airport.

These people just never give up, Rhome thought as he felt the familiar anger bubble up inside him, and he punched the accelerator.

He took the winding turns fast.

This is getting old. Why won't they just leave me alone?

Rhome kept the accelerator pinned as he blew by the cars still inching up toward the mountain, and he kept checking his rearview.

The black SUV had kept up with him for the first two turns but had fallen from view by the third.

Rhome pulled out a small key from his coat pocket, and then he reached between his legs and felt for the steel lockbox welded below his seat.

He'd practiced this move countless times and was able to get the key into the lock without fumbling. Turning the key, he opened the box with one hand and reached inside.

The cold, familiar grip of his Glock 19 found his hand and he pulled the weapon onto his lap, making sure, again, that the SUV hadn't kept up with him.

But it didn't matter, they knew where he lived.

They'd pounded on his door in the last couple of months many times before, and they'd keep doing it again, and again, until they got what they wanted.

Persistent bastards.

Haven't they gotten the hint that I just want to be left the fuck alone?

Seeing the Big Sky Meadow Village below, he slammed on the brakes before turning left onto the private road that led up to his cabin.

The road had already been plowed, but he could identify at least two sets of tire tracks entering and leaving at some point that morning.

Rhome slowed the truck and continued to study his rearview, trying to catch a glimpse of the black SUV following him.

But it never showed.

Am I just being paranoid?

Maybe the Third Option Foundation has given up on me?

Pressing down on the accelerator again, Rhome climbed up the snowy road, pulled into his driveway, and shut off the truck.

His family's four-bedroom log cabin, built sixty years before by his grandfather, sat before him. If it weren't for the dark memories that the place held, the cabin, with its pillows of snow forming on its roof, would look like something out of a Hallmark Christmas card.

Rhome sat in his truck and stared at the front door, his eyes settling on the bank's orange "Foreclosure" sticker that had been placed there a week before.

He could see a series of footprints, three sets of them, walking up onto his deck to his front door in the fresh snow.

The Third Option Foundation had been here all right.

Either late last night or early this morning.

When he'd first caught a glimpse of their presence three days before down at the local grocery store, Rhome had evaded them, collected his camping supplies, and spent the last three days sleeping in the wilderness, nearly two miles off the beaten path, only to leave in the evenings to head up to the resort for work.

These footprints weren't from the bankers; they'd come knocking during the day. Not at night.

Rhome wrestled with the thought of hiking back up to his campsite in the woods that very moment, when something hulking and dark slammed into his driver's-side window.

Rhome jumped in surprise and raised the Glock out of reflex.

The large paws and long, panting tongue of a massive Saint Bernard dog sent a blast of condensation onto the window.

Rhome quickly lowered the Glock and cinched it into the holster that always sat on his beltline, before opening the door.

The enormous Saint Bernard jumped up and down in excitement and then leapt onto Rhome, the dog's front paws resting on his shoulders.

"Dammit, Matilda, what did I tell you!" a shrill voice sounded from the front deck of the cabin next to Rhome's.

"It's okay, Mrs. J," Rhome said with a grin as he grasped Matilda's giant furry head and rubbed his face into the dog's big nose.

Mrs. Jorgensson let go of the shovel she'd been using to clear the snow from her front deck, placed both hands on her hips, and shook her head. "Two years old and nearly a hundred and fifty pounds and she still acts like a damn puppy. Could you imagine if she jumped on a child like that? I'd have to feed her to the wolves."

Rhome pushed Matilda into the snow and got down on his hands and knees. Matilda, sensing her friend's willingness to play, opened her jowls wide, and reared before launching herself back onto Rhome. They rolled around in the snow for nearly a minute until Rhome had her playfully pinned. "You're gonna have to do better than that, sweetie!" Rhome said, before letting the dog up and walking over to Mrs. Jorgensson.

Sporting a red flannel shirt, tan Carhartt pants, and knee-high rubber boots, Mrs. Jorgensson was somewhere between seventy and seventy-five years old, but Rhome had never dared ask her age. Mrs. Jorgensson was a lifelong Montanan and had the withered face of a woman who had spent her life outdoors. A widow of nearly twenty years, she had lived in the cabin next to Rhome's for as long as he'd been alive. From what he could remember, her late husband had built the place sometime in the late seventies and the Jorgenssons had been close friends of the Rhomes ever since.

Matilda playfully nibbled at Rhome's hands as he made his way to Mrs. Jorgensson's front porch.

"Get over here, young lady," she said, pointing an index finger to her boots. Matilda immediately snapped out of her playful state and joined her mom's side. She patted her head. "What am I going to do with you, huh?"

Mrs. Jorgensson then looked at Rhome standing before the deck. "And where have you been?"

"Camping during the day, working at night."

"Hmm," the old woman said. Then she pointed at the boot prints heading to Rhome's cabin. "They came by late last night, then again early this morning looking for you."

"The bankers?"

"No," Mrs. Jorgensson replied sternly. "Unless bankers these days look like big, bearded cage fighters. Me and Matilda scared them away with our shotgun. Told them you didn't want to be disturbed. Told them you were off in the mountains and to leave you alone."

"Thank you."

"Mm-hmm . . . But they did want me to give you this. Said to call them on the number on the back." Mrs. Jorgensson took out a dark blue business card and handed it to Rhome.

He looked down at the card and saw the familiar initials "TOF" emblazoned on the front.

Rhome pocketed the card, thanked the old woman, and moved toward his cabin.

"And where do you think you're going?"

Rhome turned around. "What do you mean?"

"I already got some of that elk backstrap that you gave me in the skillet. Get your ass inside. You think I'd let you eat alone? It's your birthday for God's sake."

CHAPTER EIGHT

JACK BRENNER LEANED against the stand-up desk now invading his workspace, rubbed at his tired, bloodshot eyes, and then continued to scrutinize the flat-screen TV mounted on the far wall of his office.

In his almost sixty years on earth, Brenner had only lived through one other event that had so relentlessly captured the world's attention like what was playing out on the TV before him and that was September 11, 2001.

The media was having a field day.

Every news channel in the world was replaying a continuous stream of footage from hours before when all seven of the world's thorium molten salt reactors had simultaneously turned on and, within a half hour, had experienced different levels of cataclysmic meltdowns.

India, the UK, Germany, Switzerland, France, Saudi Arabia, and the US reactors had each experienced different levels of meltdowns within minutes of each other while the whole world watched in horror.

Three Mile Island, Chernobyl, Fukushima, and now this . . .

Since the meltdowns had taken place in the late hours of February 29, the media had already dubbed the event the *Leap Day Disaster*, and naturally, accusations, conspiracies, and finger-pointing began to fly. Was this by accident? A manufacturing error? A lapse in oversight?

But the one theory that seemed to catch like wildfire was what every news network was now ramming down their audience's throats.

Was this a terrorist attack?

The fifty-nine-year-old director of the CIA's Special Activities Center, commonly known as the SAC, muted the TV and buried his head in his hands.

He, unfortunately, knew the truth.

A truth he so wished wasn't a reality.

Brenner eased his head out of his hands and blew out a long breath, a sense of confirmation and sadness sweeping over him. Confirmation because his deepest fear had manifested itself and sadness because he knew what lay ahead.

After a long and illustrious thirty-five-year career at the Central Intelligence Agency, Jack Brenner should have been spending his last month before retirement focusing solely on prepping his replacement and helping his wife, Mary, plan for the next phase in their lives.

Instead, he was bogged down by more stress than he could ever remember being under. A stress that he had to hide not only from his colleagues in Langley, but also from his wife and family.

It was killing him.

He should be helping Mary pack up their house in Virginia. He should be daydreaming about fishing off the dock of the dream home he and Mary had purchased two years before on Finley Point in Flathead Lake, Montana. Hell, he should be fantasizing about the mai tais he'd be sipping on the deck of the condo they'd purchased in Kauai for the winter months.

But again, sadly, that was a luxury he couldn't afford.

Not yet anyway.

Not with everything that was going on.

Brenner gazed back at the TV. The chyron under the news anchor was stating that President Buchanan and the crown prince of Saudi Arabia, Raza bin Zaman, would be giving a joint speech on the White House front lawn in an hour to discuss the reactor explosions and the status of the world's upcoming signing of the Global Green Accord.

A sitting US president and the crown prince of Saudi Arabia giving a joint speech defending the eradication of fossil fuels, Brenner thought. *How the world has changed.*

Brenner's personal iPhone chimed from his desk behind him. Tearing his attention away from the TV, he went to his phone and sat down in his cushy leather chair. Digging a pair of reading glasses from his suit pocket, Brenner put them on and looked at his iPhone's screen.

On it was a message from a number with a 406 area code. A message he was waiting for.

Brenner unlocked the phone.

No dice, Chief. He's completely avoiding us. Neighbor says he's working as a snowcat driver at the resort. Foreclosure slip on his front door.

Brenner cursed, put the iPhone facedown on his desk, and took off his glasses as a knock sounded from his office door.

"Come in."

A bald-headed, barrel-chested man, roughly Brenner's age, entered holding a stack of folders under one arm. The man nodded toward the muted TV. "You're still watching this shit?"

"How can I not be, Danny?"

The CIA's deputy director of operations, or DDO, Dan Miller, shut the door behind him and walked farther into Brenner's office before stopping short and staring at the stand-up desk against the wall. "What the hell is this?"

"That," Brenner said, "is a stand-up desk. Arrived this morning. Turns out my replacement doesn't see the value in sitting down."

"I'll never understand the younger generations," Miller grunted, slumping down in the chair opposite Brenner.

As the head of the Directorate of Operations, Dan Miller was one of the most senior officials in all of the CIA, and in a professional sense, Jack Brenner's boss. Behind closed doors, though, the two viewed each other as equals, lifelong friends whose bond had been forged by years of fighting side by side in one conflict zone or another.

Both Brenner and Miller were former Ground Branch CIA paramilitary operations officers, or PMOOs, knuckle draggers, who had risen the ranks to be SIS-4s and SIS-6s in a bureaucratic stronghold that usually scoffed at individuals with their particular backgrounds.

As the director of the Special Activities Center, Brenner was in charge of the Air, Maritime, and Ground Branches—the CIA's clandestine paramilitary force that was used to fight the United States' covert wars abroad.

The highly trained individuals under his command operated in the shadows of the most hazardous, denied areas in the world, by air, sea, and land.

While each branch contained highly capable men and women—one branch stood out among the rest in terms of danger, commitment, and specialization of those involved.

And that was the Ground Branch.

The few hundred individuals who made up this elite branch were plucked from one of the military's elite Tier One units and were trained in the arts ranging from spycraft and guerrilla warfare to assassination.

Miller stared at Brenner for a long time, before saying, "Christ, Jack. You look like shit."

"So do you, Danny."

For a few beats, both men kept each other's eyes locked firmly on the other.

Miller finally broke the silence. "Jack . . . I want to apologize for the other day. I shouldn't have spoken to you like that. I shouldn't have gone behind your back."

"You were right," Brenner said and pointed to the TV. "You were right all along."

"Yeah, unfortunately I was," Miller said, playing with the crease on his pants. "Still, I shouldn't have said those things. Sorry 'bout that."

Brenner nodded. "What are they saying upstairs?"

"About the meltdowns? They're just as confused as everyone else. At this point, they're getting more information from the news than anything. Right now it's been deemed a failure in oversight. The media is reporting the explosions were most likely from faulty graphite rods in the reactors."

"And the casualty count?"

"Not sure about the other countries, but our plant outside Las Vegas had over four hundred personnel on-site."

"Jesus," Brenner said. "They picking up any chatter?"

"No one is taking responsibility, if that's what you're asking."

After a moment, Brenner said, "So what can I do for you, Danny? You come down here just to apologize and say *I told you so?*"

"I . . . I came down for a couple reasons," Miller replied, his eyes dancing cautiously around the office.

"You're free to talk, I swept the place myself after I came in this morning. Still though—"

"Yeah, I know," Miller said, clearing his throat. "Coupla things. First off, the president has called for a National Security Council meeting after she gives her speech with the Saudi crown prince. Hastings has ordered us to sit seconds with her. Buchanan wants Hastings to brief her on the explosions."

"What's she going to say? I thought we don't know anything?"

Miller shrugged. "She's the director of the CIA, she's got to say something."

"And why do we have to sit seconds?"

"C'mon, Jack. She's on thin ice with the president as it is. My guess is she likes having us at her side—especially you. Shows competence."

Brenner cursed. "I'm turning sixty in less than a month. I'm nearly out the door; why not ask my replacement? Or why not drag in Deputy Director Moretti? He's number two, for Christ's sake—"

"Buchanan asked that Moretti be there as well."

Brenner arched an eyebrow. Everyone knew that a major falling-out was occurring between the president of the United States and the director of the CIA.

A falling-out that had been exacerbated when President Buchanan pulled America's troops out of Afghanistan the summer before and then slashed the military's and CIA's budgets in half.

Brenner had no idea how Hastings still had her job. From what he could deduce, it was Hastings's deeply entrenched Washington connections that helped her to keep her role as America's top spy.

Whatever string pulling Hastings had done to keep her employment over these last few months was beyond Brenner.

And quite honestly, he didn't care.

He hated politics.

The left. The right. The fighting, the infighting—it was all bullshit.

The only thing he cared about was doing his job, and keeping the American people safe.

But now, after Garrett Moretti had been appointed deputy director of the CIA, it looked like Elizabeth Hastings's days were numbered.

"Jack?" Miller said, watching as Brenner's gaze sat planted on his iPhone. "Jack, you okay?"

Brenner nodded, slowly.

Miller leaned forward and in a delicate voice said, "How did it go with the kid? Any luck?"

Brenner shook his head. "No, he's pulling the same shit he's been pulling for the last few months. Hasn't showed up to his cabin in three days. The Third Option Foundation guys said he's been working as a snowcat driver in Big Sky."

"A what?"

"A groomer. He's grooming ski trails at night for the resort."

Raised in Florida, Dan Miller was unaccustomed to the culture of anything cold weather.

Brenner continued, "And what about *your* guy?"

Miller's face turned deadly serious. "He almost got to him this morning, but he thinks he'll be able to establish contact within the hour."

Brenner snorted. "I can't see that going very well."

"Yeah, neither can I."

For a moment, neither of them said anything, their gazes going to a series of photographs mounted on the wall to the left of Brenner's desk. The picture they both locked eyes on showed an image of seven men dressed in green combat fatigues surrounded by a jungle landscape. All their faces were painted in streaks of black and green; their weapons were held loosely in their hands. Under the picture was a small plaque that read:

Special Activities Division
Ground Branch
ALPHA TEAM
1991

Brenner caught sight of his younger self standing next to the youthful behemoth Dan Miller in the jungle of Colombia. Then his eyes bore into the figure standing on the other side of Miller, and he felt that familiar pang of misery overcome him.

"He's a lot like his father, your godson," Miller said.

"That's what I'm afraid of, Danny."

"Back then, did you ever think we'd become desk jockeys?"

Brenner shook his head. "Not in a million years. I thought I'd be dead, or doing paramilitary work well into my sixties."

"Times change, Jack."

"Yes, they do."

"I miss those days."

"I miss our guys more."

Miller turned his attention from the photograph back to Brenner, and his face fell.

"I miss them, too. Only three of us left now. Me, you, and Willy," Miller said, then whispered, "Speaking of Willy, did you talk to him yet?"

"No," Brenner said. "I thought we could do that together."

"If it means anything, I had to force his hand; he didn't want to go behind your back—"

"I know that, Danny. I don't hold it against him," Brenner said. "And what about Benedicht Imdorf, did you speak to him?"

"I did," Miller said. "I briefed him as much as I could."

"And?"

"He's officially in charge of all the security and advance work in Davos. If all else fails, he'll be waiting for our call."

If all else fails, Brenner thought, shaking his head.

"Jack," Miller said, "I think it's time. You need to go to Montana. He'll listen to you. Kircher's got the jet waiting, and a car rented for you and Huey to get to Big Sky."

Brenner tried to hold back the emotion building behind his eyes. "I tried to help him, Danny. I really did."

"I know you did. You and TOF—"

"And now I'm about to do this shit to him—trap him into this whole mess." Brenner shook his head.

"Jack—he's the only one. We don't have any other choice."

"I know that now, Danny," Brenner said, pointing again at the TV. "I know that now."

For the last four days, Jack Brenner had been so unbelievably angry at Dan Miller. So pissed off at the secret operation his old friend had planned and orchestrated behind his back in relation to his godson that Brenner had snapped a few nights ago and stormed out on Miller.

But the events of last night had changed everything.

Now the threat was real.

"If Huey and I go to Big Sky tonight, what do I tell Hastings?"

"I already spoke with her. She knows he's been avoiding TOF. As far as she's concerned, you're doing your godfatherly duties. And we'll let her keep thinking that."

Brenner nodded, staring down at his iPhone. The thing was, Jack Brenner *had* made the decision to see his godson from the moment he watched the thorium molten salt reactors explode the night before. Those explosions validated a terrible reality, a reality Brenner had hoped in his heart of hearts somehow wouldn't be true.

Now, after all the arguments, Jack Brenner had no choice but to concede to Dan Miller's plan of putting in effect an operation he'd so desperately wished could have been avoided.

"Like I dubbed it the other day," Miller said. "It's our Hail Mary operation."

"Yes," Brenner said. "Unfortunately, it is."

———

Jack Brenner sat in the back seat of the agency SUV as it crossed the Arlington Memorial Bridge into Washington, DC, and couldn't help but look at his iPhone.

The trip from Langley to DC was taking over an hour. The police presence and security in the nation's capital had the place in gridlock.

Brenner heard Miller swear about the traffic in the seat next to him, but he didn't pay his friend any mind.

Flicking through his contact list on his iPhone, Brenner came to the contact labeled: LEGACY. And clicked on it.

Scrolling through the text messages he'd sent his godson in the last six months, Brenner counted all twelve of his texts that had gone unread and unanswered.

The SUV eventually swung past Pennsylvania Avenue and came to a halt at the security checkpoint at the west entrance of the White House. Secret Service cleared them thirty seconds later, and Brenner finally shut his phone and put it back in his pocket.

"Hastings is already here," Miller said, pointing to a woman in her late fifties, standing in the grass just outside the west entrance veranda, surrounded by aides and security.

Brenner stared at the hawklike figure of Elizabeth Hastings, the director of the CIA, and then his attention shifted to the crowd of press and cameras over her left shoulder on the White House front lawn. He could make out President Buchanan standing at a lectern next to a large bearded man with a long, hooked nose. The thirty-five-year-old crown prince of Saudi Arabia wore the same black-and-gold-lined *bisht* with a matching *keffiyeh* that he'd worn onstage the night before.

"The green duo," Miller grunted, also gazing at the scene taking place some hundred yards away. "Changing the world for better or worse."

"Two peas in a pod," Brenner said, and he couldn't help but smile at the speech that Buchanan and the crown prince were giving, the speech that was meant to quell the public's nerves, and push the Global Green Accord signing forward, despite the disaster the night before.

Maybe Jack Brenner was just secretly a nihilist. But for some reason he actually enjoyed that President Buchanan was such a disrupter.

Though Brenner had never made his political views known, he loved that Buchanan was doing something drastic to combat climate change.

Yes, maybe her Green Initiative was flawed, and the aggressiveness in the way she'd forced America's allies to sign the Global Green Accord a bit too audacious—but Brenner had to admit—the way that Buchanan had set fire to the Washington establishment and the fossil fuel industry was refreshing to see.

As Miller marched over to Director Hastings, Brenner found himself lagging behind, still staring at the speech, when something vibrated in the depths of his pants pocket. Turning away from the crowd of intelligence officials pooled under the west entrance veranda, Brenner fished out the secure burner phone and opened it. A text message showed on the screen:

Chief, we've just gotten confirmation that contact will be made within the hour. Did Danny tell you that Kircher and Huey have the jet ready? Do you want to go?

Brenner bit the inside of his cheek and typed:

I'll go. But I need to be back by tomorrow morning.

Without waiting for a reply, Brenner shoved the secure burner back into his pocket. For someone of his stature in the agency, it was unprecedented to be using a burner phone. But these were unprecedented times.

Walking toward the west entrance, Brenner ran over everything he'd need to do to get ready for his short trip. He'd have to call Mary and explain that he wouldn't be coming home again that night.

But for once, he wouldn't have to lie to her as to why. She knew how seriously Brenner took his role as the boy's godfather.

He'd head to the airport after the meeting and be in Bozeman by tonight. With any luck he could be back in DC by tomorrow.

Until then, he'd have to endure another—hopefully his last—long afternoon in the White House's Situation Room.

CHAPTER NINE

THE ELK BACKSTRAP, eggs, and avocado seasoned with Lawry's salt tasted amazing.

Rhome sat at Mrs. Jorgensson's modest kitchen table and finished the meal on his plate and then reached a hand down to pet Matilda, who had spent the last five minutes with her massive head on his lap, her wet nose inches from Rhome's plate, whining.

"They say having a dog keeps you young. But this little girl," Mrs. Jorgensson said, turning from the stove and sitting down across from Rhome and pointing a fork at Matilda, "has given me more gray hair than I ever imagined possible. Since the first day I got her she's been a whiner. Have I ever showed you the video I have of her as a puppy whining while she eats?"

Rhome scratched the Saint Bernard behind her floppy ears. He'd seen the video at least ten times.

"She's a good girl."

"She's a menace!" Mrs. Jorgensson said, affectionately. "Now go lie down, Matilda."

The dog grunted, sulking as she lumbered to her bed before the stone fireplace.

"You had enough to eat?"

"Yes, ma'am, thank you."

"It's not every day someone turns thirty."

"Twenty-nine."

"Ah, that's right," Mrs. Jorgensson said, cutting a piece of elk and putting it in her mouth. "What do you have planned for the day? Maybe finally cut that hair of yours and get a shave?"

Rhome put a hand through his bushy hair and beard and ignored the second question. "I've got to get some groceries in town and then do some work around the cabin. Hot water heater has been acting up again."

Rhome waited until Mrs. Jorgensson finished her meal, then he cleared their plates and cleaned the kitchen for her. Thanking her for the meal again, he patted Matilda on the head and walked to the door.

"Brian, wait," Mrs. Jorgensson said, standing up. "I know it's not my place, but I feel like I need to at least say something."

Rhome knew what was coming and stopped his retreat.

"Now, don't think I don't know that the bank is trying to take the cabin away from you. I've been at my wits' end thinking about it since your mother's death. If there is any way I can help out financially—"

"It's not yours to worry about, Mrs. J—"

"I understand. But I just can't bear to see them taking away Maria and David Rhome's home like that . . . I know you are struggling to pay your utilities. Wasn't there anything put aside in the trust?"

Rhome felt himself deflate. "The trust money was spent on the experimental treatments once the insurance kicked her off. She used the cabin as collateral."

"Damn thieves."

"I'm trying to figure something out."

"Secluding yourself in that snowcat all winter won't do you much help, Brian. Can't someone in your old line of work find you a high-paying job overseas? I've seen it on the news that contractors are working all over the Middle East—"

"I don't do that anymore, Mrs. J," Rhome said, putting his hand on the door handle.

"What happened to you, Brian? What made you come back?"

"My mother was sick."

"No, that ain't it. Even before she died, right when you got back—you were different."

Rhome opened the door slightly, looking down at his fingers on the brass door handle.

"Thank you again for breakfast, Mrs. J."

And left.

———

Trudging up the snowy front steps of his family's cabin, Rhome stopped at the deck, his face inches from the bright orange Foreclosure sticker on the door.

He tried wedging his fingernails under the sticker but the adhesive was too strong. When he realized he'd have to buy a putty knife to get the thing off, he made a mental note to pick one up at the hardware store before getting groceries.

Giving up, he stepped inside his cabin.

Turning on the lights, he took in the musky scent and the old furniture.

The plaid couch and two armchairs in front of the fireplace were unused. The old .375 rifle on the mantel sat with a coat of dust over it, and even the European mount of his grandfather's seven-point bull elk above the fireplace was collecting spiderwebs.

Rhome threw some kindling and wood into the fireplace and struck a match. Once the fire was sufficiently burning, he walked over to the sink and decided he needed to do some dishes.

He turned on the faucet, and it immediately started hissing out air.

"Shit." Rhome turned the faucet off and then on again.

No water.

Rhome went over to the gas stove in the kitchen and tried to ignite a burner, but the pilot light just clicked.

Utility company turned off gas and water.

The electricity would be next.

Sitting down at the kitchen table, he went over Mrs. Jorgensson's words in his head.

He was days away from losing the last thing he had left of his family. The home he'd grown up in, the home he was raised in.

All those memories, gone.

His hand went into his pocket, and he took out the business card Mrs. Jorgensson had given him.

The stout blue card with the three letters, TOF, stared back at him.

He flipped it over and noted the handwritten scrawl of the 406 phone number written on the back. He'd suspected the last group had been somewhat local, some retired Ground Branch guys up in Whitefish or Kalispell who'd made the drive south.

Rhome tossed the card onto the table in disgust.

He'd do everything in his power to try to keep the cabin, but he'd never go back to his old way of life.

Never.

Knowing he had the next night off from work, he didn't feel so bad staying up all day when he should be sleeping.

Errands in town shouldn't take more than an hour.

He'd sleep after that.

CHAPTER TEN

Big Sky, Montana
March 1, 11:00 a.m.

RHOME SPOTTED THE black SUV again as he left Ace Hardware and walked to his truck. The SUV was parked in the northwest corner of the lot, its engine idling.

He watched the vehicle out of the corner of his eye and could barely see the silhouette of the driver behind the windshield. Trying to act like he hadn't noticed the vehicle, Rhome got into his truck, made sure he had easy access to his Glock now in his holster, and drove across the street to the Roxy's grocery store.

The SUV didn't follow.

It didn't need to. It had a perfect line of sight.

Rhome walked inside, spent ten minutes buying his groceries, then exited the store. The SUV hadn't moved.

Putting his groceries in the seat next to him, Rhome got behind the wheel and turned onto Route 64, but instead of heading back to his cabin, he took a right and drove out of town.

The SUV followed.

"Enough of this," Rhome said.

Speeding down the icy road, he formed a plan. He took the chicane turns hard and fast, the SUV hot on his tail. For ten minutes they drove like this, Rhome testing his pursuers. Whoever was behind the wheel was getting the hang of driving in extreme winter conditions.

Let's see how good they are off the plowed roads.

Rhome cut left onto an old access road and hit the accelerator. The snowy road caused his truck to fishtail, then realign. In his rearview, he saw the SUV make the same correction as it followed.

Rhome knew there was a large twist in the road coming up; he'd just have to get far enough ahead to execute his plan perfectly.

He gunned it harder. He could hear his groceries fall out of their plastic bags next to him. Hitting the turn fast, Rhome watched the SUV fall out of view.

Completing the apex of the turn, he slammed on the brakes, threw the truck in park, and was out of the vehicle in less than a second. He cut right, stepping out of the road, his Glock up.

He could hear the motor of the SUV as it raced around the corner, then the squeal of brakes as the driver tried not to run into Rhome's parked truck.

Rhome had the Glock locked on the driver's-side window.

"Cut the engine and step out of the car!"

Inside, he could see the driver raise his hands, then slowly reach for the keys. Rhome thrust his Glock forward, just in case the figure reached for a weapon.

The SUV's engine cut, and Rhome took two steps backward and to the left so he could cover the front windshield, just in case anyone in the SUV tried something stupid.

"Get out of the vehicle!" Rhome shouted.

The door behind the driver's seat opened.

A pair of fine Italian leather dress shoes poked out first and landed in the deep powder. The man wearing the shoes wore an expensive suit with a crimson tie and held his hands out before him. Rhome noted his silver slicked-back hair and the perfectly manicured salt-and-pepper beard.

The man, who looked to be in his midforties, grinned at Rhome with bleached white teeth.

"Now the driver," Rhome demanded.

The driver's-side door opened and a tall, muscular man dressed in a black suit emerged from the SUV. Rhome clocked the bulge under his right lapel and noticed his left eye sported a black-and-blue shiner.

"Drop your weapon in the snow."

The driver looked back at his boss and the man nodded.

"This wasn't the introduction I had planned, Mr. Rhome," the man in the finely tailored suit said, in a crisp Swiss accent.

"I said drop your weapon," Rhome repeated to the driver.

"Do as he says, Sergei."

The driver, Sergei, shrugged, and his left hand went into his suit jacket. Rhome kept the Glock directly on Sergei's chest as he took out a SIG Sauer P226 semiautomatic pistol. Holding it gingerly in his fingers, he placed it in the snow.

"Now take three steps back," Rhome said. "And turn around, fingers interlocked behind your head."

He sounded like a cop apprehending a suspect, but it was a tried-and-true method.

The two men did as they were told and Rhome quickly checked the SUV for any more occupants. When he was satisfied there were none, he patted down each man, then told them to turn back around.

"Did TOF send you to find me?"

"Excuse me?" the man in the finely tailored suit asked. "Who?"

Rhome studied their faces, then lowered his Glock. "Who are you?"

"My name is Luca Steiner, Mr. Rhome. And this is Sergei, my associate." Steiner went for the interior breast pocket of his suit and then froze as Rhome raised his pistol again. "I'm going for my business card, Mr. Rhome. Is that okay?"

"Slowly."

Steiner's manicured fingers took out a white business card. "I am a lawyer, tasked with finding you."

"The agency sent you?"

"The agency?" Steiner replied. "You mean the CIA? No, Mr. Rhome."

Steiner held the card out and Rhome grabbed it.

"Like I said, Mr. Rhome, I am a lawyer. My firm in Geneva—"

"Geneva?" Rhome said, looking at the card with the fine gold lettering that read:

Steiner & Associates

"My firm in Geneva represents an elite clientele. One of our clients is particularly interested in someone of your skill set. I have to say, Mr.

Rhome, you keep a peculiar schedule; we've been here for nearly three days trying to track you down. The phone number we have listed for you seems to be shut off—"

"I don't carry a phone."

"Wise, for someone who doesn't want to be found."

"How *did* you find me?"

"Well, I wouldn't be very good at my job if I wasn't able to."

"What do you want?"

Steiner looked around at the snowy wilderness. "Well, at this moment I'd like to go someplace warm where we could have a conversation. I think it'd be worth your while. My client wants to offer you a job. A job that would pay much better than a ski groomer could possibly ever make."

Rhome snapped his Glock back into his holster.

"I'm not interested. I don't know who you think I am or how you found me. I just want to be left alone." Rhome walked back to his truck.

"Two hundred and twenty-three thousand dollars," Steiner said.

Rhome froze in his tracks and turned. "Excuse me?"

Steiner now held a check in his hand and waved it before him. "That's how much you owe the bank to keep your family's cabin? Two hundred and twenty-three thousand?"

Rhome gaped at the man.

"My client has given me permission to give you this check today, as well as a retainer, if you decide to sit down with me and take the job."

"Piss off," Rhome said and opened his truck door.

"Should you change your mind, Mr. Rhome. I'm staying at the Miller Château at the Yellowstone Club until tomorrow morning. A private dinner for us will be served at eleven o'clock tonight. I've given your name to the security guards at the entrance to the club."

Rhome, still holding on to his door handle, took one last look at the men and then climbed in and drove away without so much as a word.

Checking his rearview as he drove, he could see the Swiss lawyer still waving the check in the air, his million-dollar smile burning a hole into Rhome's mind.

CHAPTER ELEVEN

NEARLY TEN HOURS after his run-in with Luca Steiner and his associate on the access road, Rhome got down on his hands and knees and pulled out the three Pelican cases that sat collecting dust under his bed.

He plopped the cases onto his mattress and ran his fingers over them.

It had been over six months since any of them had been opened.

Rhome laid his hand over the smallest case, thinking of the objects that rested inside, and fought back a tidal wave of sadness.

"Not right now, Mack," he whispered. "Not right now."

Deferring his attention away from the smallest case, he grabbed the middle case, no larger than a briefcase, and, using a key he grabbed from under the floorboard, he opened it.

Inside, resting on the black foam interior, was a nondescript gray laptop and a silver, ten-year-old flip phone, its battery out.

Rhome let the flip phone be and grabbed the laptop, making his way back into the kitchen.

He set the laptop down and stared at it for a moment, the card Luca Steiner had given to him in his hand.

After his encounter with Steiner and his associate, Rhome had continued driving up the access road for nearly an hour until he'd reached a locked Forest Service gate.

Rhome had sat in his truck long after the sun had set, mulling over the conversation that had occurred down the road earlier in the day.

How had the lawyer found him all the way in Montana?

The cabin had never been listed in the Rhome family name; the CIA had seen to that ever since his grandfather had entered the agency back in the sixties. That lawyer—whoever he was—must be working for someone who had access to sealed records.

Had the Third Option Foundation floated his name and address around?

No, they would never stoop that low.

Or would they?

After running through every viable scenario as to why the lawyer was poking his nose around Big Sky, Rhome's mind then went to the check Steiner had waved in front of him.

How the hell does he know about the debt? How the hell does he know the exact number I owe the bank?

Holding the white-and-gold varnished business card Steiner had given him, Rhome decided he needed to do some sleuthing of his own.

Sitting at the kitchen table, he opened the laptop and powered it on.

Having no internet at the cabin, he logged onto Mrs. Jorgensson's Wi-Fi and then spent the next five minutes diverting his IP address through two highly encrypted government VPNs.

Once he was certain his connection was secure, Rhome googled: "Steiner & Associates."

The first hit came to a financial law firm in Geneva, Switzerland.

Clicking on the link, Rhome spent the next couple minutes reading through the firm's web page.

The site was spartan and vague—very Swiss. From what Rhome could gather, Steiner & Associates specialized in legally moving money into the Swiss banking apparatus.

With nothing really to glean from the site, Rhome opened a new tab and googled: "Luca Steiner."

The first hit was a translated page from a Swiss newspaper from five years ago, detailing the opening of Steiner & Associates.

Rhome read over the article.

Luca Steiner was from a family of successful bankers and lawyers from Geneva that went back generations who specialized in representing an "elite clientele" from all over the world. The article noted that Luca, specifically, specialized in representing oil and gas tycoons from Russia, Asia, and the Middle East.

Rhome clicked out of the article and spent the next thirty minutes opening the other links that Google had brought up.

As expected, they offered little information about the mysterious Swiss lawyer.

Rhome shut the laptop and sat at the kitchen table mulling things over again.

The blue TOF business card sat next to Steiner's white-and-gold varnished card, the utilitarianness of the TOF card a vast juxtaposition to that of the Swiss lawyer's.

Rhome sat there for what felt like an eternity and was only snapped out of his trance by the sound of an electric *click*, and the complete loss of power in the cabin.

Rhome swore and stood in the blackout.

The utility company had finally shut off his electricity.

Using his hands to feel for the kitchen counter, he opened a drawer and grabbed a match and an old kerosene lamp he kept next to the microwave.

He lit the lamp and stood in the kitchen.

It was only a matter of time before the people at the bank came over with the sheriff to have him evicted.

Both Mrs. Jorgensson's and Steiner's words floated in his head.

Can't pay the bills being a snowcat driver.

Deep down, Rhome knew that they were both right. He knew that wallowing in his depression and seclusion would only lead him to the inevitable.

But wasn't that what he wanted? Wasn't that the point?

He couldn't live this life knowing what he'd done.

Running it over in his head, he understood he was at a make-or-break point. He was going to lose the cabin. Lose the memories of his late father and mother. Lose the memories of his estranged older sister and their childhood.

Was his stubbornness worth it?

The way Rhome rationalized it—he could end it all the next night on Snake Pit Cliff. But that didn't mean he couldn't hear Steiner's pitch beforehand.

He checked his watch; it was 10:14 p.m., more than enough time to get to the Yellowstone Club before 11:00 p.m.

Grabbing his jacket, he walked to his truck, placed his Glock in the lockbox under his seat, and drove away.

CHAPTER TWELVE

THE YELLOWSTONE CLUB was a private ski resort nestled on the northeast side of Big Sky that catered to the rich and famous who paid top dollar for privacy, discretion, and world-class skiing.

Rhome had visited the club a handful of times in his early teenage years when he'd been invited by friends whose parents were members.

To the normal residents of the Big Sky community, the Yellowstone Club was always mentioned in a jeering, if not disdainful way. It was where sports stars, billionaires, and famous actors went to feel like they were tapping into the *wild* experience of Montana.

Well, a wild, *five-star* Montana experience.

Rhome had never shared the feelings of the Big Sky residents. To him, the Yellowstone Club offered work to the locals and caused a booming business in realty and construction. Not to mention all the ski instructors who made top dollar teaching an ultrarich clientele.

Driving up to the club's security entrance, Rhome gave the armed guards his name and waited as they checked their database. Thirty seconds later, he was given a pass to put on his windshield and directions to the Miller Château.

Driving into the club, even in the darkness and lightly falling snow, Rhome could make out the outlines of hundreds of mansions dotting the hills around the private resort.

Mansions that were probably lived in for less than two weeks a year.

Continuing to drive until he found the Miller Château, Rhome pulled under the mansion's stone entryway and was met by Sergei, Mr. Steiner's associate, who beckoned him inside. "Mr. Steiner is expecting you in the dining room. Please follow me."

Rhome caught the man's thick Russian accent and followed.

Stepping into the mansion, Rhome took in the ten-foot paintings lining the walls between massive mounts of moose, elk, and deer.

Following Sergei up a staircase and into an ornate dining room, Rhome heard a voice say, "Mr. Rhome, I was beginning to think you were going to blow me off."

Luca Steiner stood from his seat at the end of a long table that occupied a spread of candles, gold cutlery, and appetizers fit for a king.

"Can we get you anything to drink? Wine or—"

"Whiskey. If you've got it."

"Does scotch work?"

Rhome nodded.

Steiner snapped his fingers. Two waiters materialized into the room.

"Get our guest the fifty-year-old Macallan single malt. Bring the bottle and a glass for me too."

The waiters nodded and disappeared.

"Please, Mr. Rhome. Take a seat." Steiner motioned to a chair to his right.

Rhome walked around Sergei and sat beside Steiner.

"Help yourself to the appetizers; dinner will be brought out shortly. I hope you like moose."

Rhome realized that he hadn't eaten since breakfast. He looked over the impressive spread, grabbed two deviled eggs, and popped them into his mouth.

Then the waiters returned with the fifty-year-old Macallan and two tumblers and placed them before the men.

"This is the best scotch in the world, in my opinion, Mr. Rhome. Please, serve yourself."

Rhome reached for the bottle and poured two fingers of the amber liquid. He passed the bottle to Steiner, who did the same and took a sip. Rhome followed his host's lead.

The scotch was some of the smoothest he'd ever had.

"You like it?"

"It's incredible."

"I'm glad to hear it," Steiner said and leaned back in his chair. "I want to apologize for chasing you down this morning and afternoon. It was our last shot at getting your attention before we leave tomorrow. I'm sure you're curious why I invited you here?"

Rhome's face remained placid.

"Well then, I'll cut right to the chase," Steiner said, rubbing his palms together. "Someone in your old line of work put your name in the basket for a sensitive job opportunity. My client has entrusted me to vet the potential job applicants and then reach out to those who passed my vetting process. You, Mr. Rhome, ended up on top of my list."

"What kind of job?"

"Ah, well, I can't get into the nitty-gritty until you have signed on, but I can tell you it is an advisement role in a field that you are particularly familiar with, considering your previous line of work."

"Advisement role?" Rhome said. "Who's your client, Swiss intelligence?"

"No." Steiner laughed.

"Then who?"

"I can't divulge that information until you have agreed to our terms and conditions. Should you agree to work with us, a private jet will take you to your destination." Reaching into the breast pocket of his red velvet smoking jacket, Steiner took out the check that he waved in front of Rhome earlier in the day. "And this check is yours, plus a retainer, which I have permission to write tonight."

Rhome shook his head. "Why would I take a job without knowing who I'm working for, or what I'm supposed to be doing? I'm sorry, but you are wasting my time, Mr. Steiner."

Rhome scooted his chair back and stood.

Steiner sighed, then reached back into his pocket, pulled out a black-and-white photograph and placed it on the table.

Rhome looked down at the picture and froze.

Steiner smirked.

The picture showed a high-definition image of a bearded man with a significant scar on his forehead.

"When was that picture taken?" Rhome said, in disbelief.

"Two months ago. By the Israeli intelligence service. The man in this picture is someone you know?"

"Bullshit. Qasim al-Raymi is dead."

"He's not."

Rhome sat down and grabbed the picture, studying every millimeter of it. The photo was time-stamped: January 3.

"Impossible," Rhome said, an unbelievable rage building inside him. "Qasim al-Raymi is dead; the drone strike hit the compound—"

"Yet, here he is, Mr. Rhome," Steiner said, taking a proud sip of his scotch. "This photo was taken outside a mosque in Istanbul in early January of this year. My client knows your history with this man. It is most likely why someone at your old job put your name in the basket. As it turns out, my client is just as interested in al-Raymi as you are."

Rhome, with shaking hands, snatched his scotch and drained it, then grabbed the bottle and refilled his glass.

Steiner, amused at Rhome's response, continued: "I am aware of what happened to you in northwestern Pakistan, Mr. Rhome. I know all about the ambush Qasim al-Raymi orchestrated against your team."

His hands still shaking, Rhome barely heard Steiner. He scarcely noticed the man take out a checkbook and cut another check and slide it over to where the photograph sat.

"My client wants you to finish the job you started in Pakistan, Mr. Rhome. And he's offered to pay you exceptionally well for it."

Rhome's eyes floated to the new check for one hundred and fifty thousand dollars.

"This is your retainer. And should you succeed in killing Qasim al-Raymi, my client is offering to triple that."

Rhome stood up so fast his chair toppled over. His head was spinning. "This . . . this won't bring my men back."

"No. Mr. Rhome, it won't, but it will give you some closure."

Rhome took a step back and nearly ran into Sergei, before he collected himself and made for the door.

"Mr. Rhome," Steiner called back at him. "You forgot something."

Rhome turned.

Steiner held up the photograph, and the two checks.

"I don't want anything to do with that," Rhome said. "That's not me anymore, that's not my life."

"And what is your life, Mr. Rhome? Driving a snowcat? Standing on top of that cliff every night, wondering if you can jump?"

Rhome took a step back.

Steiner walked toward him with the photograph and checks.

"You are a man who has nothing to live for. You are on the cusp of losing everything. My client is giving you a lifeline. A job."

Steiner forced the papers into Rhome's hands. "You have until midnight, on March third, to call the number I've written on the back of that photograph to give me your decision. If you decide to take the job, a private jet will pick you up in Bozeman to take you to your destination. Good night, Mr. Rhome."

CHAPTER THIRTEEN

RHOME DROVE LIKE a bat out of hell through the Yellowstone Club gate, not stopping to return his guest pass at the security checkpoint.

His mind was reeling. His body driving for him.

Qasim al-Raymi was alive!

Alive this whole fucking time.

Rhome thought back to Pakistan six months before. The explosions, the gunfire, the screams.

Turning into the Big Sky Meadow Village, he hooked a left up Route 64 and made for his cabin, Steiner's words cutting through him like a serrated knife.

In the last six months, the only thing Rhome found solace in was the fact that Qasim al-Raymi hadn't survived the fateful raid. The al-Qaeda fanatic, whose allegiances spread all over the Middle East, was one of the most brutal and cunning jihadists in the world—responsible for killing thousands of American servicemen and -women during the war on terror.

But what had brought al-Raymi infamy were the cruel and unusual methods by which he fought his enemies. He'd climbed the ranks in al-Qaeda because of his prowess in orchestrating and implementing suicide bombings. He was one of the first jihadists to put suicide vests on not only women and children but also the mentally disabled—sending them to detonate their vests in crowds of innocent civilians.

Rhome balled his fist and slammed it hard against his steering wheel, a primal yell erupting from deep within.

It had all been for nothing. The whole raid, his men.

Consumed by his thoughts, Rhome didn't notice the fresh tire tracks on his long driveway, nor did he immediately register the red Suburban parked in front of his cabin.

As he came to his senses and threw his truck into park, he saw that his cabin's front door was slightly ajar, and a faint light shone from his kitchen window.

In an instant, he had the key out of his pocket and down by the lockbox. Two seconds later his Glock was in his hand.

Rhome exploded out of his truck and was at his doorway three seconds later. Gun up, he moved inside and cleared his living room, then faced the kitchen where the kerosene lamp cast a warm glow from the kitchen table, exposing the figures of two men. One was tall and lanky; the other, the size of a house.

"Hello, Brian."

Rhome lowered his weapon when he recognized the voice.

"Chief?"

Jack Brenner leaned into the light. His sharp features and thinning hair were the same as Rhome remembered, but the dark bags under his eyes was something new.

"Hello, Lobo," said the mammoth of a man sitting next to Brenner.

Rhome stepped forward and recognized his old colleague, Huston "Huey" Oliver. The man was six foot five and weighed over two hundred and sixty pounds. His big red beard and wild hair made him look like a wildling from *Game of Thrones*.

Rhome glanced down at the table before Brenner and Huey, and in the light thrown from the kerosene lamp, he saw the blue TOF card, Steiner's card, and then the orange Foreclosure sticker.

"I found the putty knife in your grocery bag and took the liberty of getting this thing off your door. When the hell did your power go out?" Brenner said.

Rhome stuffed his Glock back into its holster. "Today. Water and gas, too."

Brenner grunted, then grabbed the kerosene lamp and made his way to the framed photographs on the kitchen wall, leaving Huey at the table. Rhome's gaze followed the light. For nearly a minute, he watched as Brenner studied the photographs of Rhome's family.

There was a family picture of Christmas in 1998 that his mother had always been fond of. A picture of Rhome and his older sister, Annabelle, fishing in Lava Lake with their father.

Brenner stopped at a picture of Rhome at thirteen years old wearing a red ski racing spandex suit, his arm around a taller, good-looking boy, who wore a blue spandex suit. Brenner pointed at the picture. "Isn't that—"

"Yeah, that's him."

"I knew he was from here; I just didn't know you two are friends."

"*Were* friends. I haven't spoken to him in nearly a decade."

Brenner, who continued to gaze at the photograph, said, "Most decorated American winter Olympian of all time." Brenner faced his godson. "Isn't he dating that Brazilian supermodel? Mary likes to keep up with the tabloids."

"I wouldn't know, Chief."

"'Course you wouldn't," Brenner said, sitting back down next to Huey.

Rhome stayed planted at the foot of the kitchen. "TOF boys have been poking their heads around here. Your work?"

Brenner crossed his legs. "It's the reason the Third Option Foundation was created, Brian. Exactly for cases like you."

"I don't need any sanity checks, Jack. I passed all the agency's psych evals before I walked away. You know that."

"Those evaluations are bullshit, Brian. A bureaucratic necessity. I know just as well as you that Ground Branch guys will tell the psychologists whatever they need to hear to either get out of the game, or go back to their men. I was the same damn way, and so was every other guy I ran with."

"So what are you here for? A last resort?"

"Sit down, Lobo," Huey said.

"Shut up, Huey."

Brenner sighed again, his gaze going to the orange Foreclosure sticker, to the TOF card, and then to Steiner's. He grabbed Steiner's card.

"So they reached out. When?"

Rhome studied his godfather's tired features, then a realization hit him. "You were the one who put my name in the basket?"

"Of course."

Rhome stepped into the kitchen, then sat down across from the men. "Why?"

"Because we're worried about you. Because I'm your damn godfather, and other than your sister, I'm the only family you've got left. Both Mary and I have the responsibility—"

"You don't have any responsibility, Jack. Don't give me that bullshit. You told that Swiss lawyer where to find me? How to track me down? I suppose you used agency resources to tell Steiner about my financial situation?"

"No, Brian. Considering the Swiss lawyer's clientele—I'm sure he pooled his resources to get to know everything about you and your current situation."

"Who's his client?"

Brenner studied his godson for a moment, then looked at Huey, who said, "Do you watch the news, Brian?"

"Not in six months."

"I figured as much."

"Why?"

"You know of the Global Green Accord? The thorium molten salt reactors that were being built?" Huey said.

"I've heard of them."

"Well, if you'd have been paying attention to the news," Huey said, "you would have seen that the reactors malfunctioned last night."

This got Rhome's attention. "What are you talking about?"

Huey explained how all seven of the world's reactors had experienced different levels of meltdowns the night before.

"Was it terrorist related?"

Brenner hesitated. "We don't know."

Rhome was silent for a moment, then asked, "What does this have to do with me?"

"Absolutely nothing."

Bullshit, Rhome thought. His godfather, being a career spook, always had ulterior motives to his actions. Always.

"Washington is in chaos, Brian. The whole world is. Seven nations have a mini Chernobyl event on their hands, and now, nearly every nation that has pledged to sign the accord is balking."

Brenner looked down at the Foreclosure slip on the table. "Brian, I know what you are going through. I've been there, and so has Huey; what happened in Pakistan was terrible, but it wasn't your fault."

"I was responsible for my men, I was the PMOO on the ground."

"You and Mack were the two PMOOs on the ground, you both made the decision based on bad intelligence."

"Intelligence given to us by the agency," Rhome snarled. "I was the one who convinced Mack and everyone else that we had to act. He didn't trust the information given to us. He didn't want to enter that compound. I made him. And now his three daughters don't have a father and Kelsey doesn't have a husband."

"They're your goddaughters if I remember correctly?"

Rhome winced and glared at Brenner. "And what is the agency doing to help them, Jack?"

"You know their policy, Brian. They don't have the responsibility to help the families of the fallen."

"So we swear our loyalty and allegiance to the CIA, and the CIA just kicks their gold star families to the curb?" Rhome said. "Got it."

"I don't agree with it, Brian, but you knew what you signed up for, and so did the others who entered Special Activities," Brenner said. "And that's why we started the Third Option Foundation, to help those families—"

"And what's TOF doing for Kelsey and the girls?"

"They're doing what they can, but I'm sure Mack would have wanted you in their lives. When was the last time you spoke with Kelsey?"

Rhome didn't answer; instead he said, "My decision widowed six wives, took away nine children's fathers. How the fuck can I live with that? How the fuck can you two understand what I'm going through?"

For a long beat, Brenner said nothing, then he muttered, "Saudi Arabia."

"What?"

"The Swiss lawyer. His clients are the House of Saud. The crown prince specifically."

"You pimped me out to the Saudis?"

"I got you a job, Brian. You've worked with the Saudis before. The Saudi kingdom is changing. Saudi/US relations have never been stronger."

Rhome took out the papers Steiner had given him and slapped them on the table. Throwing the two checks aside, he unfolded the picture he'd been given and opened it, shoving it forcefully in front of Brenner and Huey.

"Qasim al-Raymi's alive. That's why you put my name in the basket? So I'd get back in the game? You're a real piece of shit, Jack. You know that?"

Brenner took the picture from the table and examined it. "Yes, al-Raymi is alive and back in Yemen. He's just been named the emir of Al-Qaeda Arabian Peninsula and has promised bloody jihad against the West, and its allies, specifically Saudi Arabia and its crown prince. You would know that if you watched the news."

"He's running AQAP?"

Brenner nodded.

"Do we know his location in Yemen?"

"No, but we know where he will be the night of March seventh."

"How?"

"The Saudis intercepted intelligence that Qasim al-Raymi will be attending the wedding of his brother, Ali Yahya Mahdi al-Raymi, on the seventh of March at the Ar Risan Palace in central-western Yemen. The agency has validated that intelligence."

"So why the hell am I being pimped out? Why not send in an active PM team? Why doesn't the crown prince use a drone strike?"

Brenner stood. "Because Raza bin Zaman wants to do it himself. Part of his popularity in Saudi Arabia is his progressiveness; however, the more conservative citizens in the kingdom think he looks too weak to their enemies, Iran and al-Qaeda specifically. The crown prince wants to show them otherwise, so he's hiring contractors to fill advisory roles to kill Qasim al-Raymi and deal a death blow to al-Qaeda. I couldn't think of a better person to help with that campaign than you, Brian. You speak the language—"

"The Saudis are terrible soldiers."

"I'm well aware," Brenner said. "For the last three weeks, the Saudis have been training on a mock rendition of the Ar Risan Palace. Supposedly, the crown prince wasn't satisfied with the effectiveness of his elite special operations team—so he's reached out and offered big money to hire specialists from around the world to do some last-minute training and to even participate in the raid itself."

Rhome shook his head. "March seventh is a week away; it would take at least a month to train a Saudi ground unit."

"Brian, read between the lines. The crown prince wants the advisers to do the killing. The Saudis just want the credit," Brenner said and pointed to the two checks. "Hence the reason you're being paid so well."

"What's the catch, Jack?"

"No catch."

"Bullshit. I went through training at the Farm just like the two of you. I know a recruitment when I see one."

Brenner slammed a fist on the table. "When will you get it through your thick fucking skull? TOF has been sending guys out here for months to check on you. They've offered you money to get you back on your feet!"

"I don't want TOF's money. That should go to Kelsey Mackenzie. Whip's family—Smitty's, Hurst's, and Flynn's! That money belongs to the families of the dead, not me!"

"You're a stubborn bastard just like your old man. You don't want handouts, fine. Work for your money then; the Saudis pay damn well. Or you can just piss your life away driving some damn snowcat."

Rhome realized he was biting the inside of his cheek so hard it was beginning to bleed. He licked it with his tongue.

Brenner continued, "The chief of station in Riyadh is William McCallister, old Ground Branch guy. Used to run with me and your father."

"I've heard of him."

"He's running point for the agency. He'll meet you at the Saudi drone base to help oversee the logistics of the campaign."

"I'm not going back downrange, Jack."

"Then throw your life away, Brian. If I learned anything trying to help your father over the years—it's that you can't help someone who doesn't want to help themselves."

Brenner grabbed the photograph of Qasim al-Raymi and then reached into his jacket pocket, pulling out a black diplomatic US passport. Walking around the table, he dropped the photo and passport into Rhome's lap.

"Huey and I need to get back to Virginia. Send me a text when you've touched down in the kingdom. Oh, and Brian, cut your damn hair."

———

Jack Brenner drove out of Rhome's driveway and onto Route 64, heading back to Bozeman, Huey sitting shotgun.

"Do you think we got to him?" Huey said.

"I don't know. His head is all over the place."

"Lobo has always had a short fuse, but he'll come around."

Brenner looked over at the big Ground Branch operator, forgetting that the guys Rhome used to run with called him *Lobo*. The Spanish word for wolf. Though he'd never asked, Brenner thought it probably had to do with the snarling wolf tattoo on Rhome's left forearm, and the fact that his mother, Maria Rhome, had originally come from Peru and had taught the kid Spanish.

His secure burner phone vibrated in his pocket. Brenner wrestled it out and handed it to Huey.

"Read me that text."

Huey grabbed the phone. "Danny says our friends are waiting for us in the hardware store parking lot."

"Tell him we're ten minutes away."

As Huey texted Dan Miller, Brenner drove down into the Big Sky Meadow Village and cursed himself for what he'd just done at the cabin.

After everything his godson had gone through in his short life, all the pain, the tragedy, the manipulation, Brenner was now exploiting him yet again—cornering him, trapping him.

But I don't really have a fucking choice, do I?

After all, sending his godson back downrange hadn't been his idea in the first place. Brenner had spent the better part of the last week viciously arguing against it, but in the end—after he'd seen the thorium molten salt reactors explode, and the subsequent signals intelligence they'd gathered over the last seven weeks—he knew they had no other choice.

Lost in his thoughts, Brenner almost missed the road for the Ace Hardware parking lot and had to slam on the brakes to make the turn.

Pulling in, he saw the black Suburban parked in the south side of the lot.

Brenner parked his own SUV alongside the vehicle, and both he and Huey got out.

The back-left door to the SUV opened and Luca Steiner, wearing a ridiculous red velvet smoking jacket, stepped out along with his Russian associate.

"How's that eye healing?" Huey said, pointing at Sergei with a slight grin on his face.

Steiner and Sergei scowled.

"I've done everything you people have asked of me," Steiner said.

Brenner took out a manila envelope and handed it to Steiner. "And you're going to continue doing more."

"What is this?"

"Instructions for your next task."

"Next task? I didn't agree on a next task."

"Inside is an address for a safe house in Riyadh. After the al-Raymi campaign, you'll drive the kid to that address. My people will contact you with a date and a time."

"I'm not doing—"

Huey took a predatory step toward the men, and Brenner held him back with a hand, then said, "Mr. Steiner, we made it *very* clear to you what would happen if you didn't obey our rules. Rules we laid out for you explicitly. One click of a button and everything we have on you gets sent straight to Interpol. You do as we say, and that button never gets pushed. Am I making myself clear?"

"You fucking CIA—"

"Careful . . ." Huey said.

Steiner scoffed, then, holding the manila envelope, he opened the door to the SUV.

"We'll be in contact," Brenner said.

Neither man replied as they climbed back into their vehicle and shut the door.

Brenner watched the SUV drive out of the parking lot and out of sight.

"Get in the car, Huston," Brenner said.

He was repulsed by what he'd done back at the cabin. What he was sending his godson to do.

He'd made an oath on the day of his godson's christening, twenty-nine years ago, to protect and watch over the boy should anything happen to his parents.

Now, the boy's parents were gone, and he could potentially be sending the kid to his death.

He should have just told the boy why he was *really* going to Saudi Arabia. Maybe, out of a sense of duty, the kid would go.

No, he would never do that.

His godson was hurting. His sense of duty to his country was gone.

Dan Miller had been right; the boy would have to be manipulated to go. The plan, and its dangerous endgame, would have to be fed to him slowly, delicately. At the right time.

With everything stacked against them, Brian Rhome going to Saudi Arabia was their only chance to stop what was surely coming.

CHAPTER FOURTEEN

PRINCESS AMARA SAT in a chair at the foot of her children's beds and finished reading their bedtime story. Mimi, five, and Ahmed, eight, had fallen asleep, nestled tightly under their blankets.

Amara closed the book and placed it on a nightstand that sat between the children. Their little chests rose and fell under the covers with each breath, and Amara bent down and kissed both of them on their cheeks.

"Good night, my angels," she said softly and moved out of the room, turning off the light. Before she shut the door behind her, she peered back inside and felt the familiar wave of love and gratitude she felt every time she tucked her children into bed.

Amara loved her children more than anything in the world. She lived for them, lived to protect them, to give them the happiest and most enjoyable life possible.

As she shut the door, she said a short prayer to Allah, asking him to bless them in their slumber.

Walking down the long, ornate hallway of her Riyadh palace, she passed Farid, her head of security, and gave him a warm grin.

"Are the children asleep, Princess?"

"Sound asleep."

Farid touched his earpiece, alerting the rest of his security team that it was time for nightly rotations. Then taking his earpiece out and turning it off, he whispered, "Will you need your study prepared for tonight, Princess?"

Amara looked up and down the long hallway, making sure no other security or palace staff were in earshot. "Yes, thank you, Farid. Would you mind setting up the computer?"

Farid bowed and walked off in the other direction.

Watching him go, Amara felt a sudden jolt of excitement and fear course through her body. It was the same feeling she got every night when she ventured into her office to access the secret, secure laptop Farid set up for her.

At forty-three years old, Princess Amara was one of the most famous women, if not *the* most famous woman, in all of Saudi Arabia. Her father, Prince Bandar, was the brother of the current king of Saudi Arabia, King Zaman. And her grandfather was Ibn Saud, the founder of the kingdom—which made Princess Amara a powerful force within the royal family.

It was no secret that Amara was a hard-line progressive—a modern-day feminist who was an outspoken advocate for women's rights in the kingdom.

Having grown up mostly in the United States, while her father had been the Saudi ambassador to Washington, Amara sometimes considered herself more American than Saudi. Georgetown educated, she had seen what life was like for women in the West. They had voices, they were free to say and do whatever they pleased. They could vote, start their own businesses, and even run for public office. It was not lost on Amara that her country had a long ways to go to bridge the social and cultural divide between men and women. That was why Amara had recently dedicated her life to bridging that gap. She wanted to create a reality in the kingdom where her daughter had every opportunity as her son. She wanted to show Mimi and every other little girl not only in the Middle East but across the world that women could do everything that men could do.

Amara smiled to herself as she walked down the long hallway toward her favorite lounge in the palace. In four days, she would be taking both of her children to the United States for the first time in their lives to watch their mother give the welcome speech at the first annual Middle Eastern Women's Rights Summit in Washington, DC, on International Women's Day on March 8.

Amara could barely contain her excitement.

But, stepping into her lounge, that excitement suddenly faded. The television was on, showing images from Al Arabiya, the kingdom's national news channel. Amara slumped down on the couch opposite the TV, which replayed images of the exploding thorium molten salt reactor outside of Tabuk.

As the Al Arabiya news anchor continued to talk, the images on the screen cut to a video of her younger cousin, the crown prince of Saudi Arabia, speaking next to the United States' president, Angela Buchanan, on the White House front lawn, two days before. The anchor went on to say that the crown prince had arrived back in Saudi Arabia following the speech with the president.

As always, Princess Amara felt a sourness in her stomach when she saw her cousin, the crown prince, Raza bin Zaman. She, unlike most, knew that he wasn't all that he seemed.

To many citizens in Saudi Arabia, and in most of the West, her cousin was a celebrity. A shining light for a new, progressive future. His public relations team in the royal court was top-notch, his ideas for Saudi Arabia full of glitz, glamour, and unlimited potential.

In the two years since King Zaman had appointed his son to the role of crown prince, Saudi Arabia had changed significantly.

With the king's health deteriorating due to a series of strokes he'd suffered over the last couple years, Raza bin Zaman had been given unprecedented authority in his role as crown prince.

Within weeks of being appointed the de facto ruler of the kingdom, Raza had disbanded the Wahhabi religious police and stripped most of the control from the kingdom's religious clerics. He pledged to his people that the kingdom would change under his rule, that his dream for Saudi Arabia was to turn it into the "America of the Middle East."

As Raza rose in prominence since his appointment, Princess Amara had seen an opportunity and capitalized on it.

Going to the Royal Palace to see her younger cousin, Amara had told him that while the disintegration of the religious police and the dismantling of the clerics was a step in the right direction, still more needed to be done to show the new generation of Saudis that Raza bin Zaman was truly a voice for change and here to stay.

It had been Princess Amara who'd convinced her cousin to lift the driving ban on women as well as abolish the guardianship laws. She'd pleaded with him to give the kingdom movie theaters and create venues for concerts that both men and women could enjoy.

Two weeks after their talk, Raza announced on Twitter that the restrictions on women had been lifted, movie theaters were to open, and concert venues would start to be built. Immediately, rumors began to swirl that it was Princess Amara who had convinced her cousin of doling out such change.

It was a win-win for Amara. A step in the right direction for both herself, and the kingdom.

But it also wasn't lost on the crown prince that his older cousin's popularity somewhat outshined his own. And it was probably why, in February of last year, the crown prince had done something that had truly shocked the world.

Just a year into his reign, the crown prince announced that Saudi Arabia would become the first country to step forward and join the United States in their pledge to sign the Global Green Accord.

It was the biggest announcement in the history of the kingdom.

During his declaration, the young monarch told the crowd that he would be ending the kingdom's dependence on oil, instead focusing on the investment of green energy technologies.

The world was changing, and nearly overnight, Princess Amara's cousin had become one of the most recognizable faces in the world.

But even a year after the crown prince's announcement, and after all the radical change taking place in the kingdom, Amara could see trouble brewing at home.

While most in the kingdom, especially its youngest citizens, applauded the crown prince's robust reforms, some questioned his leadership. As the months passed, some of his most vocal opponents—especially online, began to slowly disappear.

While these occurrences seemed like isolated incidents at first, that had changed seven weeks before, when a cadre of royal court officers began rounding up and arresting government officials, journalists, and even members of the Saudi royal family, holding them involuntarily at the Riyadh Ritz-Carlton.

Family members who had sucked at the tit of the royal family's vast amount of wealth, and even those government officials and journalists who had spoken out publicly against the crown prince, had been detained, their bank accounts frozen, their assets seized, and their freedoms stripped.

As the rumors began to circulate online in the days following, the crown prince and his closest allies had lit up the Twitter-sphere and accused those government officials, journalists, and members in the royal family of vast corruption.

The crown prince's right-hand man, Saud Rahmani, had launched a McCarthy-like purge all over social media using an army of royal court propagandists known as "flies" to create bots on Twitter to attack the crown prince's detractors and keep track of their activity online.

As news continued to circulate on social media about the happenings in the Ritz, Princess Amara began to worry. Would the Royal Guard come knocking on her door? Would she be rounded up like many of her family members and charged with corruption?

But in the seven weeks since the roundups started, the knock had never come.

Amara had always been extremely conservative with her money, shying away from a life of decadence that many in her family had gotten used to.

No.

She feared the knock due to something else.

Something much more sinister.

It was nearly four months ago that Amara had stumbled upon something in relation to her cousin that flipped her world upside down.

A rumor she'd heard that, if true, would blow up Raza's reputation and certainly sour and complicate Saudi Arabia's signing of the Global Green Accord.

"Princess," Farid said, entering the lounge, his voice low and cautious, "the computer is set up and ready for use in your study."

Amara turned to her old friend, who had protected her since she was a small child.

"Thank you, Farid. I shouldn't be more than an hour."

"I will stand guard outside your door as usual, Princess."

Amara walked toward her head of security and squeezed his arm. "What would I do without you, Farid?"

"You would be just fine, Princess."

Unlike most of the men in her life, Farid Hafeez had always been a pillar of security, a loyal, trusted father figure Amara had so desperately craved.

Her late father, Allah bless his soul, was a kind man at heart, but had never taken an interest in his daughter like he had his sons.

But Farid had always been there for her.

Amara let go of Farid's arm and together they walked down to her study.

Closing the door behind her, she moved toward the desk that held the secure laptop.

Amara sat down and gazed at the dark screen.

Tonight was an important night.

A night she had long awaited.

A night she was going to obtain *proof* of her cousin's secret.

Next to the laptop was a snow globe with a miniature rendition of Manhattan in it, the Empire State Building sitting in the middle. Farid had gifted the snow globe to Amara when she was a child. A secret compartment sat within the snow globe, no bigger than a matchbox, and was known only to Farid and Amara. It was a way for them to exchange handwritten messages to each other. A way for a young Amara to vent to someone when she was little—usually about her father, when he gave more attention to her brothers than her.

Now, the snow globe was used for something else.

Amara snatched up the globe, unfastened the secret latch on the bottom, and slid it open.

Out fell a small USB.

She turned on the laptop and laid the USB on her desk. As the computer came to life, Amara spent the next thirty seconds turning on her VPN and logging onto the TOR network that would give her access to the dark web. These precautions allowed her to hide her computer's IP address, which could expose her identity and physical location.

Having completed a dual degree at Georgetown in both political and computer science, Amara was still nervous using this clandestine, and illegal, technology inside the kingdom. Especially in this day and age, when Saud Rahmani and his "flies" within the royal court were using "cloak and dagger" software to catch dissenters of the state.

After accessing the TOR network, Amara went through the necessary firewalls to enter the dark web forum set up by a number of "Saudi revolutionaries"—as they liked to call themselves—until she opened and accessed a private chat portal with the person she'd spent the better part of four months conversing with.

Though Amara had never met this person in real life, nor did they know each other's true identities, he had confirmed for her that he was a "fly," working for Saud Rahmani in the royal court, who had grown disillusioned with the crown prince and his methods of ruling the kingdom.

This fly—using the alias *Qutrub*—had developed a friendship with Amara over the last few months and had confided in her secrets that could get him killed. Not only was Qutrub participating in the Saudi revolutionary forum speaking ill of the crown prince, but he was also selling secrets to the Americans at the Central Intelligence Agency.

As their correspondence and friendship continued to grow, Qutrub had recently shared with Amara a rumor—a rumor he'd heard at work, a rumor Amara had pushed for him to confirm, and then pass the evidence off to her tonight.

Staring at the empty chat portal and using her alias, *Scheherazade*, Amara typed:

:**//Scheherazade:** Brother, are you there?

A minute later, Qutrub replied:

:**//Qutrub:** I'm here, sister.
:**//Scheherazade:** Tell me, brother, were you successful?
:**//Qutrub:** Unfortunately I was, sister.
:**//Scheherazade:** What is that supposed to mean?
:**//Qutrub:** I got what you've asked of me, sister. I got into Saud
    Rahmani's personal work computer in his office and did a
    keyword search for the rumor I'd heard—and it is true. Every

word of it. The crown prince and his inner circle are planning
an operation to silence the Saudi dissident living in America
before he can publish a slanderous article prior to the signing
of the accord.

://Scheherazade: But that is good, right? We can warn the
dissident before the crown prince's men can get to him!

://Qutrub: It is good, yes! But when I did the keyword search for the
dissident, it led me to an unencrypted file called RIG.

://Scheherazade: RIG?

://Qutrub: Yes! I made the mistake of reading the file, confirming
the rumor, but I fear I also stumbled upon something much
worse . . .

://Scheherazade: What did you find, brother?

://Qutrub: The dissident is going to publish proof about something
called Dark Sun.

://Scheherazade: Dark Sun?

://Qutrub: I did another keyword search for Dark Sun—and it took
me to a password-protected encrypted file that I could not
open. I then panicked and copied both the RIG and the Dark
Sun files from Saud Rahmani's computer and smuggled them
out of the royal court offices on a flash drive.

Amara froze for a moment, not knowing how to respond, then she
typed:

://Scheherazade: Why did you do that?

://Qutrub: I told you, I panicked!

://Scheherazade: You need to give this information to your CIA
handlers, you need to tell them everything!

://Qutrub: I will. I have a meeting with them at the end of the week.
But I cannot share this burden alone, sister. If something
should happen to me, you'll need to warn the dissident—you'll
need to give this information to the Americans.

A file transfer notification suddenly arrived in Amara's chat portal,
asking if she wanted to download the files named *RIG* and *Dark Sun*.

Amara hesitantly accepted the files and watched as they downloaded and saved to her desktop.

Before she could type anything else, Qutrub logged out of the chat portal.

For a moment, she stared at her screen in disbelief, reading and re-reading the conversation she'd just had with the man.

Then, snapping to her senses, she logged out of the portal, exited the forum and the dark web, and was just about to open the folder labeled "RIG" on her desktop, when her iPhone began to vibrate.

Amara looked over at her iPhone's screen, recognized the number reserved only for those who worked in the Saudi royal court, and felt herself flush.

Her hand moving slowly to the phone, she answered the call.

"Yes?"

Heavy breathing sounded over the line, then the familiar voice of the crown prince's right-hand man, Saud Rahmani, spoke through the phone, "Princess, the crown prince is requesting your presence tonight."

Amara tried to keep her fear at bay.

Have they been monitoring my correspondence?

Are they onto me?

"It . . . it is very late," Amara said, trying to keep her voice calm.

"A motorcade will be at your palace in twenty minutes."

With that, Saud Rahmani hung up and Amara put the phone down. Staring ahead at the purple curtains hanging in her dark study, she could only think of her children. What would happen to them if she was taken? Would she survive the purges inside the Ritz-Carlton? She'd heard rumors of the interrogations, of the torture.

Staring at her computer screen, she grabbed the USB and jammed it into its port, then copied both the RIG and Dark Sun files on her desktop and dropped the copies onto the USB.

Making sure the download was complete, she then password protected the USB, ejected it from the computer, and placed it in the hidden compartment within the snow globe.

Shutting the laptop, she grabbed it and hurried to the door.

Poking her head into the hallway, she motioned for Farid to step inside.

Her head of security saw the troubled look on her face. "What is wrong, Princess?"

Amara told Farid about her conversation with Saud Rahmani. "He said a motorcade will be here in twenty minutes. I need you to do something for me, Farid." She handed him the laptop. "Hide this. Hide it so it cannot be found if someone were to search the palace, but hide it in a place you can access it quickly if need be."

"And what are you going to do, Princess?"

"What other choice do I have? I must do what the crown prince has ordered."

Stepping around her old friend, she made her way to her bedroom and spent the next ten minutes changing into a fashionable, yet tasteful *hijab* that would be acceptable when meeting a senior royal. As she finished putting on the last of her jewelry and makeup, she looked out the window to the front, wraparound driveway and saw a motorcade of black Range Rovers pull up to her palace gates.

As the gates opened and the eight black Range Rovers spilt onto her driveway and stopped at the front entrance, she couldn't help but feel complete dread. She had been so careful.

But it hadn't been enough.

She'd undoubtably been caught.

She'd gone behind the crown prince's back.

The transgression was treason.

Walking down to meet the motorcade, Princess Amara stepped out of the front doors and stopped amid her security, who stood guard before her palace. Farid stood on the bottom steps, closest to the motorcade.

The doors to the Range Rovers opened and two dozen Royal Guards stepped out, armed with AK-47s.

Then the passenger door opened in the Range Rover right in front of Farid, and a short, pudgy man wearing a white *thobe* and red-and-white-checkered *keffiyeh* stepped out. Saud Rahmani, her cousin's cyber warrior and infamous thug, smirked, showing off his yellow-stained teeth.

"Princess, it is an honor."

Amara kept her head high. "My men could have driven me to the royal *diwan*. There is no need for any of this."

Rahmani chuckled. "He is requesting to see you at his new palace, Your Highness, not at the royal court."

Amara took a breath through her nose and held it. This was most unexpected.

Holding the door to the Range Rover open, Saud Rahmani said, "Please, Princess, after you."

"My security will follow me there."

"Of course," Rahmani said, acting offended.

Princess Amara walked down the steps to the Range Rover, then gazed up at the window of her children's room.

Closing her eyes, she said a small prayer.

Allah, if anything should happen to me, please watch over my children.

CHAPTER FIFTEEN

PRINCESS AMARA KEPT her hands in her lap, kneading her knuckles to prevent them from shaking. Sitting in the back seat of the Range Rover, she kept her eyes locked out the window, and away from Saud Rahmani, who sat in the back seat next to her, his chubby fingers tapping on his iPhone. Amara had wanted to crack the window due to the stench of body odor emanating from the plump man to her left, but found it locked.

They drove southwest down the Makkah Al Mukarramah highway bisecting the city of Riyadh, and she could see the towering sand-white building of the Ritz-Carlton in the distance. As they drove toward the now-infamous hotel, Amara felt her lungs constrict.

Is that where we are going?

What will they do to me there?

As the motorcade got closer and closer to the exit for the Ritz, Amara felt like she was going to vomit.

Amara closed her eyes and said a quick, silent prayer to Allah. When she opened them, she realized they'd passed the exit, the Ritz now behind them.

Saud Rahmani must have noticed Amara's unease and let out a chuckle as he looked up from his iPhone and pointed a thumb back at the Ritz. "Don't worry, Princess. It's not going to be that kind of night."

Amara couldn't help but be disgusted by the man next to her, who had quickly returned his attention to his iPhone. She'd heard from reliable sources that Saud Rahmani was one of the few within the crown prince's inner circle who personally watched the "interrogations" of her family members detained in the Ritz.

If the crown prince isn't going to imprison me, why send for me at such an hour?

For the next twenty minutes, Amara agonized over what the crown prince could possibly want from her.

Have they discovered my correspondence with Qutrub?

Will they interrogate me in the crown prince's palace, or will they take me elsewhere?

Eventually, the motorcade made it to the crown prince's newly built palace and parked outside the front entrance as a Royal Guardsman opened the door for her.

Immediately upon stepping outside, she saw her own security team pull up behind the motorcade. She spotted Farid as he exited his vehicle and flashed her a concerned look.

"Your security can leave their weapons and cell phones with the Royal Guard," a voice said, from the main entrance doors.

Amara turned to see Turki Shahidi, her younger cousin's brutish enforcer. Broad shouldered, and standing at six foot four inches, Shahidi was an infamous former security officer, rumored for being the one who physically tortured her family members in the Ritz while Saud Rahmani would watch.

Turki Shahidi's reputation in the kingdom was that of a sociopathic thug who had somehow found his way into the crown prince's inner circle. While Saud Rahmani was known for his brains and cunning, Turki Shahidi was known for his muscle.

Farid walked up beside Amara. "What do you want us to do, Princess?"

Amara looked into the black, dead eyes of Turki Shahidi. "Do as he says."

After giving up their weapons and phones to the Royal Guard, both Amara and her security detail were escorted inside.

The decadence of the newly built palace took her breath away. Gold-encrusted pillars sat interspersed along the long velvet-draped hall as far as the eye could see. In the middle of the hallway was an elongated pool with countless solid-gold fountains spewing out water.

"Come with us, Princess," Shahidi said. "Your security will stay here."

Amara reluctantly followed Rahmani and Shahidi down the opulent hall, before turning down another corridor and stopping before an elevator. Amara followed the two men inside, trying to keep her attention focused on the marble tile as the elevator rose.

When the lift stopped, the two men escorted her through another corridor and then to a gold-plated door where a group of men waited.

As Amara and her two escorts approached, the tallest man in the group turned.

Khalid bin Zaman, the crown prince's younger brother and Saudi ambassador to the United States, frowned when he spotted Amara.

"What is *she* doing here?" Khalid asked.

Before Amara could answer, the gold-plated door behind Khalid opened and out stepped one of the most beautiful women Amara had ever laid eyes on.

She was immaculately dressed in a stunning pantsuit and a beige *hijab*, and her almond-shaped eyes danced over the crowd outside of the door.

Amara had never seen this woman in person but had glimpsed pictures of her on social media. Tara Devino, the American-Emirati fashion model turned businesswoman, glowered at Saud Rahmani and Turki Shahidi, before her attention settled on Amara, and a brilliant smile crept onto her face.

Completely ignoring Khalid and his men, Devino walked up to Amara, and bowing slightly, said, "Your Royal Highness, it's an honor."

Amara didn't have time to respond to the woman, because Shahidi grabbed her by the elbow and ushered her toward the gold-plated door. As Amara looked back at Devino, wondering why the former fashion model was in the royal palace, Shahidi opened the gold door and pushed Amara inside.

The lounge was decorated in red velvet curtains and carpeting. It was surprisingly small and comfortable, unlike the vaulted open space of the rest of the palace.

Two couches sat facing each other in the middle of the room, a gold-varnished table between them.

Amara's attention went to one of the two figures sitting on the couches.

Before she could say anything, Khalid entered the lounge, pushing his way past Saud Rahmani and Turki Shahidi, and in a loud, annoyed voice, he said, "Brother, why the hell was I made to wait outside?!"

The larger of the two men sitting on the couch stood up. His big, hooked nose flared wide in agitation. "Because I had business to attend to, Khalid."

"We have been waiting for nearly thirty minutes. What were you discussing with that woman that could be so important?"

The crown prince of Saudi Arabia, Raza bin Zaman, ignored his little brother and stepped around him.

"Your Royal Highness," Amara said, bowing deeply.

"Ah, my dear cousin," Raza said.

The crown prince wore a white *thobe* and a red-and-white-checkered *shemagh* headdress and extended his right hand toward Amara. She bent over slightly and kissed the back of his palm, aware it was shaking.

He's taking too much Adderall, Amara thought, thinking back to all the times she'd seen her little cousin pop the prescription pills.

Taking his phone from his pocket, Raza glanced at it, before turning to his younger brother. "Please, let's all sit down. We have much to discuss."

Khalid grumbled something under his breath and sat down next to a man who scooted forward on the couch, a friendly expression on his face.

Major General Ahmad Azimi took in Amara. "Princess, it is great to see you. How are Mimi and Ahmed?"

Azimi, a known confidant and close adviser to the king, was also the director of the Al Mukhabarat Al A'amah, or more commonly known as the General Intelligence Presidency—Saudi Arabia's intelligence agency.

Having been a close friend of her father's, General Azimi had always taken a great interest in Amara and her children. "It is great to see you as well, General. The children are wonderful, thank you for asking."

Amara's attention then went from Azimi to Raza, who plopped his hefty figure next to Amara, as Shahidi and Rahmani took positions standing behind Khalid and Azimi, their eyes boring into her.

Amara's stomach soured the moment she'd entered the lounge, ever aware that she was sitting among the most powerful and dangerous individuals in the kingdom.

"How . . . how is your father?" Amara asked the crown prince.

Raza pulled out his phone and looked at it again, shrugging. "The king has good days and bad. He is staying on my yacht right now in the Red Sea."

"Tell him I think of him often. That I pray for his recovery."

"I will," Raza said, and then he clapped his hands together, looking from Amara to Khalid. "Now, you're both probably wondering why I've called you here?"

"Yes," Khalid said. "I would very much like to know why I was ordered to take an impromptu twelve-hour flight from DC."

The crown prince stood up and ignored his younger brother. "Due to the events of the last couple of days, I have decided to shake things up. I've decided that the kingdom needs a fresh face for our friends in the West. Someone who can represent Saudi interests in the United States."

Amara glanced over at Khalid, who looked just as confused as she.

"What are you saying?" Khalid asked.

"Effective immediately, Khalid will relinquish his role as ambassador to the United States and be appointed deputy defense minister, here in the kingdom." Raza looked at Amara. "You, cousin, will take his spot in Washington."

Amara's jaw went slack.

Khalid leapt from his seat. "Tell me this is a joke!"

"It is no joke," Raza said, his eyes never leaving Amara's.

"She's not qualified!" Khalid cried. "She knows nothing of diplomacy. She's—"

"A woman?" Raza asked, finally turning to his brother.

Khalid snapped his mouth shut.

Raza turned back to his cousin. "You will be the first woman in the history of the kingdom to hold such a coveted role. In these trying times, I need you to make sure US and Saudi relations hold firm. I need someone in Washington who knows the American culture. Someone to represent our undying pledge to sign the Global Green Accord. But most importantly, I need someone to keep the American president reassured in these troubling times."

Amara nodded her head, but her mind was spinning.

Why would my cousin choose me?

Surely, this was a political move—her cousin wouldn't be doing this unless he had bigger things at play. Raza was a lot of things, but a fool was not one of them. He was a chess master; he could be warm and affectionate, but menacing and ruthless when he needed to be. But most importantly, he was always fifty moves ahead of everyone else. Amara thought back to how she remembered Raza as a child. Back then, his obsessive-compulsive disorder—his repetitive movements and his ritualistic behavior—had consumed his life.

Having worked with the best doctors and therapists in the world, Raza had learned how to live with his condition, but still, his hypervigilance persisted in the way he micromanaged those around him. As far as Amara could tell, the only compulsive behavior she could spot in her brilliant younger cousin was the way he impulsively and continuously checked his phone.

Knowing that she couldn't possibly say no, Amara said, "It would be an honor, Your Highness."

"Great," Raza said. "I will announce it on Twitter within the hour. And, don't thank me, Amara, thank the king. It was his idea."

"I will send him a letter."

"Good," Raza said. "Your work begins now."

"This is madness!" Khalid snarled. "I will not put up with this. I've lived in the United States as long as our cousin. I've been trained by their damn air force, for crying out loud. I'm a seasoned diplomat!"

Raza rounded on his brother. "Sit down, Khalid!"

Khalid stood defiantly for a second, then sat.

When he did, Raza said, "Do you think I have not thought extensively about this? Do you think there is no reason for my actions?"

Khalid remained silent.

Raza continued, "Certain things have come to light. Things I will need you, in your new position in the Defense Ministry, to oversee." Scooting forward in his seat, Raza then said, "As both of you are probably aware, the al-Qaeda terrorist Qasim al-Raymi is alive."

Amara nodded, remembering the headlines in the news from a few months back.

"We have vetted intelligence that he is back in Yemen and has been named emir of Al-Qaeda Arabian Peninsula."

Amara of course knew all about Qasim al-Raymi and his brutal history of spilling blood all over the Middle East.

"Al-Raymi wishes to refuel al-Qaeda's fight against our kingdom and me specifically. He is back in Yemen and recruiting at a great pace. Luckily for us, Major General Azimi and the Al Mukhabarat Al A'amah have discovered he will be attending his brother's wedding four nights from now."

Raza went on to brief Amara and Khalid that a Saudi-led campaign was currently training and preparing for the assassination of Qasim al-Raymi at a secret drone base in southern Saudi Arabia.

"The CIA has helped us vet the best of our kingdom's soldiers. Along with some Western advisers, it will be Saudi soldiers who will ultimately kill the terrorist," Raza said, then gazed at his brother. "Khalid, I want you and Major General Azimi to personally oversee the success of the campaign. Is that clear?"

Khalid frowned. "You have spent billions buying drones from the United States to kill our enemies. Why not use them to kill Qasim al-Raymi? Why are you sending in Saudi soldiers?"

"Because I wish to make a statement, brother. I wish to show our enemies across the Persian Gulf that our kingdom is strong and capable. The Iranians will do anything to destroy us. We know al-Raymi is being funded by the Iranians. I want to send a message before the signing of the accord." Raza motioned to Amara. "You are to leave for Washington immediately. I want you to thank President Buchanan and her CIA for helping assist in the selection process for the campaign."

Amara nodded, wondering why she would have to leave so fast. Wasn't the crown prince just with the president of the United States two days ago? And what of the Middle Eastern Women's Rights Summit in Washington she'd been planning to attend for over a year? Would her new appointment as ambassador prevent her attendance?

Before she could voice her concern, Raza's face turned serious. "It is imperative that the Americans know we are grateful for their help in the Qasim al-Raymi campaign because what I am going to disclose to you next is going to upset them quite a bit."

Raza motioned to Azimi and the old major general reached down between his feet and brought up a silver external hard drive and handed it to the crown prince. "I am sorry to say that the royal court and the Al Mukhabarat Al A'amah have unearthed something terrible."

Raza held the external hard drive in the air for Amara to see.

"What is that?"

"This," Raza said, "contains an intelligence report you must hand deliver to the president of the United States and her National Security Council. Our intelligence officers have found proof of what actually caused the thorium molten salt reactors to explode."

Amara's eyes grew wide.

The crown prince inserted the external hard drive into a laptop sitting on the table, then mirrored the laptop's screen to a TV monitor on the wall.

For the next thirty minutes, he detailed the contents of the intelligence report to Amara.

When he was finished, he brought up a video file and played a six-minute clip.

When the video ended, Amara sat there paralyzed. Finally she said, "You . . . you want *me* to deliver this to the Americans?"

"Are you up for it?"

Amara gave a reluctant nod, then said, "Excuse my bluntness, Your Highness. But you were at the White House two days ago, why didn't you inform the Americans of this then?"

Raza's eyes narrowed. "We weren't able to confirm the intelligence until I had left the United States. General Azimi and his men finished the report hours ago."

Khalid spoke up. "Brother. If the contents of that report are true, it could mean—"

"It could mean war," Turki Shahidi said, finishing Khalid's sentence for him.

"Do you understand now why I brought you back to the kingdom, Khalid?" Raza said. "Do you understand why I need your military expertise here?"

Khalid gave a reluctant nod.

Azimi took the external hard drive from the laptop, then grabbed a black diplomatic pouch that had been leaning against the table and put the hard drive inside, zipping it shut.

"Amara," Raza said, sensing his cousin's unease. "Our enemies will do everything they can to stop the Global Green Accord from being signed. They will do everything they can to sow discontent. The world is changing, our kingdom will be at the forefront of that change. Make sure the president understands. In offering this to the Americans, we are showing our good faith, and our trust in them. In return, it is critical they show trust in us. Do you understand?"

"I . . . I do."

"Good, your plane leaves for Washington in an hour. Saud Rahmani will escort you to the royal airstrip. Your belongings will be sent to you later."

"I'm . . . I'm leaving now? What of my children?"

"They will join you in America at a later time. Your next week in Washington will be busy, you won't have time for such distractions."

Grabbing the black diplomatic pouch containing the external hard drive, Saud Rahmani escorted Amara out of the room and back to the motorcade.

As her security was given back their weapons and cell phones, Saud Rahmani climbed into the back of the Range Rover next to her.

"Not what you were expecting, Princess?"

No, Amara thought, *not what I was expecting at all.*

———

Gazing out of the Range Rover's window as she was driven to the royal airstrip, Amara took in the mass of blinking lights that was Riyadh at night and thought over everything her cousin had detailed for her in the lounge. The contents of the intelligence report was not only alarming but incredibly disturbing.

Thinking back to nearly two hours before when she had tucked her children into bed, the princess could hardly believe how quickly and seriously her life had just changed.

Then her thoughts seized on the secret conversation she'd had with Qutrub.

That conversation seemed to pale in comparison to what she'd just learned in the lounge.

The intelligence report sitting between herself and Saud Rahmani overshadowed everything Qutrub had brought to her attention.

"It's official," Saud Rahmani said, looking up from his iPhone and turning the screen toward Amara. "The crown prince has just announced *you* as the new Saudi ambassador to the United States. Come morning, you will be one of the most famous women in the world, Princess."

Amara didn't reply and gazed back out of the window, not wanting to communicate with the slimy man next to her.

Saud Rahmani continued to speak. "After we drop you off at the royal airstrip, I will have my men go to your palace and collect your belongings. They will be on the next diplomatic flight out. Is there anything in particular you would like me to pack for you?"

The way Rahmani said the last part, with a sly, all-knowing smile, made Amara quake with fear.

Does he know of my secret communications?

Does he know what I've done?

Not letting Amara return to her palace to collect her things spoke volumes. She knew it was not safe keeping the secure laptop and the USB in the kingdom.

"My head of security will tell you what to pack for me," Amara said, looking out the window as the motorcade drove into the royal airstrip and stopped alongside the tarmac, where one of Raza's custom 747s sat waiting.

A member of the Royal Guard opened her door and she stepped out into the hot night.

Holding the black diplomatic pouch, she saw that her security detail had followed the motorcade to the royal airstrip and saw Farid climb out of his vehicle.

"Princess, you need to get going," Saud Rahmani said.

"One moment," Amara said and walked toward Farid.

When she got to him, she wrapped her arms around him and whispered sharp and pointedly into his ear. When she finished, her misty eyes bored into his. "Can you do that for me?"

Farid, his eyes hooded, nodded. "Of course, Princess."

"And if anything happens to me, Farid, please protect my children."

"With my life."

Turning from Farid, Amara scooped up the black diplomatic pouch, moved past Saud Rahmani, and wiped a tear that was falling down her face.

As she boarded the 747, she couldn't help but think that she was just a pawn on a chessboard, a sacrificial lamb headed for slaughter.

But what else could she do?

She had no choice but to keep moving forward.

CHAPTER SIXTEEN

STANDING ON THE edge of Snake Pit Cliff, Rhome shut his eyes and felt the cold, biting wind assault what little skin was exposed on his face.

It had been almost forty-six hours since Huey and Rhome's godfather, Jack Brenner, had challenged him in his cabin, and Rhome had spent the interim wrestling with his options.

He'd made a vow to himself that he'd never return to the world of his old job. But that was before the realities of home had settled in.

Jack Brenner had been right. Mrs. Jorgensson had been right. He couldn't spend the rest of his life secluding himself for low pay in a snowcat, not when the only thing he had left of his family was hanging in the balance.

If he stayed, he'd be homeless. All those memories from his childhood, gone.

There were other options, of course. He'd heard of an oil boom in the Bakken, in North Dakota. He knew it would pay decently, but he also understood that wallowing in his self-pity would only get him so far. At the end of the day, he'd find himself staring over a precipice again, or gazing at the wrong end of his Glock.

After getting up from the kitchen table earlier the morning before, Rhome had packed his backpack with five large rocks and put on his snowshoes. Exiting his cabin, he took off uphill in a sprint.

It was a workout he'd done as a ski racer in his teenage years to get himself in shape for the upcoming season. After he'd shattered his leg in a skiing accident and decided that he was going to join the marines at eighteen years old, he'd used the same workout style to get ready for basic training.

Reaching a mountaintop in the Spanish Peaks two hours later, he stood on the summit, overlooking Big Sky proper. He had made a decision.

He'd go to Snake Pit Cliff the next night when he was back on shift and settle everything then.

Now, standing above the cliff, the half-moon casting a faint glow on his surroundings, Rhome looked up at the stars and closed his eyes.

This would be his test.

One step forward and it would all be over, one step back and he'd trudge to his snowcat, finish his shift, tell his boss he was done, and call Luca Steiner.

As Rhome stood on the edge, he could hear the Wapiti Lake wolf pack howling in the valley below, and he thought of the twists and turns his life had taken to get him to this very moment.

He'd joined the US Marines because that's what his father had expected of him. He'd entered Recon to show his father that he was as tough. And then he became a Marine Raider to show his father that he was tougher.

After his father had drunk himself to death, Rhome had been operating overseas with the marines when Jack Brenner had approached him with an offer to join his father's old clandestine line of work.

Rhome had accepted.

After nearly two years of training, he'd graduated from the agency's programs and at twenty-seven years of age, Brian Rhome had become the youngest Ground Branch paramilitary operations officer the CIA had ever employed. A legacy, following in the footsteps of his father and grandfather.

And look where that got me.

Standing on the edge of a fucking cliff.

Rhome had the picture of Qasim al-Raymi that Steiner had given him in his jacket pocket.

The only solace he'd found in his life in the last six months after the events in Pakistan was that the al-Qaeda terrorist was dead.

Now that was all out the window.

Rhome's mind floated back to that fateful night in the Federally Administered Tribal Areas of northwest Pakistan.

For nearly a year, Rhome and Mack had led their team through the most treacherous regions of the FATA searching for one man.

Qasim al-Raymi.

For nearly a year, they'd embedded with local tribes and militia to find and assassinate the al-Qaeda fanatic. They'd gotten close many times, but the infamous jihadist had always slipped away.

It wasn't until last September, just weeks after the US pulled out of Afghanistan, that CIA command passed Rhome and Mack a piece of intelligence stating that Qasim al-Raymi was supposedly staying the night in a remote compound, a valley over from Rhome's team's location.

Rhome and Mack were given the orders to move their team to a rocky mountainside above the compound and get a positive ID on al-Raymi, so a possible drone strike could be carried out. When Rhome's team slipped into position just after midnight, they'd used their night-vision capabilities to scan the compound below.

Within an hour, they'd gotten a positive ID on the terrorist.

What they hadn't accounted for, though, were the politics happening back stateside.

With the war on terror freshly over, the Washington pencil pushers were hesitant to carry out a drone strike in the region.

As the hours passed, and with Washington continuing to shuffle its feet, Rhome realized that come morning, Qasim al-Raymi would slip through their fingers once again.

As a CIA paramilitary operations officer, Rhome had been taught to think on his feet and make split-second decisions.

Qasim al-Raymi was on the United States' terrorist watch list. His killing was not only approved, but sanctioned and legal.

When word came back to Rhome and Mack that the drone strike would not occur, Rhome asked CIA command if his team could personally carry out an assault on the compound.

The CIA gave them the green light.

Mack, though, had been hesitant.

There were only six members in their team, and dozens of al-Qaeda terrorists in the compound below. Even with the Reaper drone flying above them, surveilling the compound and the mountainside, Mack was worried that they hadn't gotten a detailed pattern-of-life analysis of all the combatants in the area.

But Rhome had been insistent, and he finally convinced Mack and the rest of his team to make the assault.

What Rhome and everyone else didn't know was that they were walking straight into an ambush.

The moment Rhome and his men blew the compound's gates, the whole region came alive. With dozens of cave systems on that mountainside, soon hundreds of al-Qaeda fighters descended on the compound.

Only later would Rhome discover that the intelligence fed to the CIA was fake.

Qasim al-Raymi knew a CIA paramilitary unit was in the area, and knowing that the United States would be reluctant to use their drones, the jihadist had lured them in and sprung a trap.

Pinned down from all sides, Rhome's team made their last stand in a small building on the southern perimeter of the compound's walls.

After watching each of his teammates get hit and go down, Rhome had called in an emergency drone strike to light up the mountainside, and the building within the compound Qasim al-Raymi was last seen going into.

Following the bombardment, Rhome found himself alone among his dead teammates and the al-Qaeda fighters—the compound and the mountainside completely obliterated.

Following his evacuation via an army special forces unit, it was determined with high probability that all hostiles in the area had been eliminated, Qasim al-Raymi, included.

But that was obviously not true.

Somehow, Qasim al-Raymi escaped.

Still staring down over the edge of the cliff, Rhome could see the faint outlines of the jagged rocks below, which would certainly end his life—end the torment and guilt he was living with.

He thought of the families his men had left behind. Their wives and children. The children who would never grow to see their fathers at their birthdays, their graduations, or their weddings. The fathers who would never be able to hold their wives, children, or their grandchildren.

Qasim al-Raymi was alive and well, probably devising another sadistic attack on innocents.

Rhome felt his chest tighten, then he let out a sob that turned into a yell.

The wolves, way down the valley below, answered his cries.

Soon, Rhome found himself on his knees.

"No," he said, shaking his head. "Not like this."

He owed it to his fallen men.

Not like this.

Not when Qasim al-Raymi still walked the earth.

Putting a fist in the snow to steady himself, he stood.

Rhome pulled out the black-and-white photograph of Qasim al-Raymi, gazed at it in the moonlight, and made his final decision.

He'd cash the Saudi's checks.

He'd pay back the bank to keep the cabin.

Then he'd do everything in his power to avenge his brothers.

He would kill Qasim al-Raymi.

CHAPTER SEVENTEEN

"CHRIST, JACK, WOULD you stop that? It's driving me insane," CIA director Elizabeth Hastings said from across the table, her yellow-tinged eyes boring a hole into Jack Brenner.

"What?" Brenner said, distracted, still tapping his pen against the table in the White House's Roosevelt Room.

"The damn pen!" Hastings said, snatching it from Brenner's hand.

Brenner snapped back to reality.

"You look like hell," Hastings said. "Please tell me you got some sleep yesterday."

After Brenner and Huey returned to DC from Montana the morning before, Brenner had come in early to Langley and taken a long nap on his couch in his office, only to be awoken by Elizabeth Hastings, who saw his delirious state and sent him home.

"Slept like a baby most of the day," Brenner lied. "And like the dead last night."

The truth was, Brenner hadn't gone home, and he hadn't slept a wink since being roused in his office by the director of the CIA.

Hastings's lips pursed, but she didn't push the subject further. Instead, she said, "And the sanity check with your godson, how'd that go?"

"I don't know, Elizabeth. He's pretty messed up. Doesn't want anything to do with us or TOF."

"Well, his old man was the same damn way," Hastings replied. "But he's lucky to have you looking out for him."

Brenner felt a pang of guilt and glanced up at Dan Miller, who sat at the table opposite him.

If only you knew what Danny and I were about to put him through, Elizabeth, Brenner thought.

Brenner didn't like operating behind Hastings's back. Though he'd been a spy for the majority of his life, he didn't enjoy the lying and sneaking around that he and Dan Miller had been forced to do in the last seven weeks. But here they were, the deputy director of Operations and the director of the Special Activities Center—covertly going behind their boss's back.

Brenner checked his watch. It was just after 10:30 a.m., and he was growing restless. Upon arriving at Langley that morning, he'd found a note from Dan Miller on his desk, informing him that they were being summoned by Director Hastings to sit seconds again for an emergency meeting in the Situation Room.

So far, they'd been waiting for President Buchanan and her National Security Council for over three hours, and Hastings was starting to fume.

Brenner glanced up at the muted TV in the Roosevelt Room that was turned to a network news channel.

"Did they give you any indication as to the subject of this meeting, Elizabeth?" Miller asked.

"The office of the DNI said the Saudis requested the meeting, so it probably has something to do with her," Hastings said, pointing to the TV, which showed a video clip of the Saudi princess, Princess Amara, exiting a private 747 holding a black diplomatic pouch that morning and walking to an awaiting motorcade. The chyron under the clip, read:

**Princess Amara named Saudi ambassador to the
United States arrives in Washington, DC, in a historic
moment for the kingdom and its crown prince . . .**

"But an emergency meeting . . . what's the emergency?" Miller asked.

"To the *green witch*, everything is an emergency," Hastings said.

Just as Hastings was about to go on a lengthy diatribe about the sitting president, she was interrupted when the door to the Roosevelt Room opened, and Mark Edwards, the Secret Service special agent in charge, poked his head in.

"Elizabeth, Jack, Danny, the president is ready to see you all in the Situation Room."

"About damn time, Mark," Hastings said, standing.

Following Edwards out of the room, Brenner and Miller shook the man's hand, and as they followed him down the stairs that led underneath the West Wing, Hastings asked Edwards, "So, the green witch has made you her errand boy, now? Isn't that a little beneath you? Where is Agent Tuck?"

Brenner saw Edwards crack a small grin as he opened the door to the John F. Kennedy Conference Room, better known as the Situation Room.

"Buchanan has Tuck on ambassador duty," Edwards said. "I'd heard how long you've all been sequestered upstairs, so I thought I could at least extend you the courtesy of looking at my ugly mug before you enter the lion's den."

Hastings gave off a small snort, then for the second time in four days, Brenner, Miller, and Hastings deposited their cell phones into the lead drawers built into the walls by the entrance—Brenner making sure to slip in his burner phone without catching the wandering eyes of Edwards and Hastings.

After securing their devices, Edwards leaned in to the trio and dropped his voice. "POTUS has been up all night, and she's in a foul mood. So please, Elizabeth, tread softly in there."

"I don't know how you do it, Mark," Hastings muttered.

"Neither do I, Elizabeth," Edwards muttered, then moved toward the Secret Service agents manning the door to the main conference room. "All right, Agent Hewitt, let them in."

Brenner looked up at the Secret Service Shift whip, Charlie Hewitt, who opened the door and ushered them inside.

Brenner entered the room last and noted the cast of characters.

President Buchanan was sitting at the head of the table. To her left was Secretary of State Allison Newman. To her right was the vice president, Michael Dunn.

Next to Dunn sat the director of national intelligence, Johnathan Winslow, and the secretary of defense, James Lake. Next to Lake was National Security Adviser Peter Coolidge and the chairman of the Joint Chiefs of Staff, General Edward Toole.

"Sorry, we're late," a voice said as Brenner took a seat next to Miller behind Hastings, as she sat across the table from DNI Winslow, the president to her right.

Brenner's attention went to the conference room door as Garrett Moretti, the new deputy director of the CIA, strode in.

Moretti's two-thousand-dollar suit, bleached white teeth, and perfectly combed brown hair made him look like a living, walking caricature.

"Garrett," the president said, standing and greeting the new deputy director of the CIA. "Thank you for escorting our guest to the White House."

"It was an honor, ma'am," Moretti said. "Madam President, let me introduce Princess Amara, the new Saudi ambassador to the United States."

Brenner then saw three women enter the room. One was the White House chief of staff, Katherine Healey. The other was the Secret Service's assistant special agent in charge, Eunice Tuck, who escorted a short, attractive woman wearing a gray pantsuit and a dark blue *hijab* to her seat between DNI Winslow and SecDef Lake.

"Princess Amara, congratulations," Buchanan said. "Or shall I call you Madam Ambassador?"

Thanking Agent Tuck, Princess Amara set down a black diplomatic pouch on the table in front of her and said, "Whichever you prefer, Madam President."

Watching Tuck leave the room, and Garrett Moretti take a seat at the other end of the table, opposite Buchanan, Brenner noticed that the newly appointed Saudi ambassador to the United States had a slight American accent; then he remembered that her father had once held the same role in the eighties and nineties.

"So," Buchanan said, "the crown prince wanted me to call this emergency meeting for you, Princess. He said you are carrying information you'd like to share?"

"Yes, Madam President," Amara said. "Thank you for meeting me on such short notice." She took in the members of the room. "I understand this is not usually how things work in terms of intelligence sharing, but my cousin has insisted that I brief you all personally on this matter."

This is unorthodox, Brenner thought. Never in his career had he ever witnessed an ambassador of a foreign state, allies or not, brief the president of the United States along with select members of her National Security Council *in* the Situation Room.

Princess Amara put her hand on the black diplomatic pouch. "The crown prince would like to send his gratitude to you, Madam President, for giving us the resources necessary to help vet our special operation soldiers for the upcoming Qasim al-Raymi campaign in Yemen."

"Of course," President Buchanan said. "As long as the United States isn't directly dropping any more bombs or pulling triggers—we're happy to help. Tell the crown prince if he needs anything else, just ask."

Princess Amara opened the black diplomatic pouch, took out a silver external hard drive, and said, "Yesterday, after I was named Saudi ambassador to the United States, my cousin and his most trusted advisers briefed me on a series of events that unfolded in the last couple of days in our kingdom."

The princess cleared her throat. "Four nights ago, after the explosions of the thorium molten salt reactors, the crown prince ordered his officers in the royal court and in the Saudi intelligence agencies to launch an investigation into the explosions. It wasn't until after he had left the White House and was on his way back to the kingdom that he was alerted by the royal court to a crucial piece of intelligence that had just been unearthed."

Amara held up the silver external hard drive and asked if she could plug it into the Situation Room's computers and route the feed to the LCD screen on the wall.

President Buchanan gave her permission.

Amara continued to talk as she went to work plugging in the external hard drive. "As you are all probably aware, Saudi Arabia closely monitors the movements of known enemy agents around the world. We, like you, keep track of who comes into and goes out of our country and our neighboring regions to ensure the safety of our public. Four days ago, after the crown prince ordered his royal court to investigate the explosions, they unearthed something of great concern that occurred in India during September of last year."

Amara pointed to the LCD screen behind her, which now showed a series of time-stamped, black-and-white surveillance photographs, depicting two middle-aged men going through a border security checkpoint station.

"These images, Madam President," Amara said, "are from September twenty-second of last year, taken at the customs terminal in Wagah on the Pakistani, Indian border."

Brenner adjusted his glasses to better see the photographs of the two men as they were being processed through customs. Even though the photos were in black and white, the image quality was razor-sharp.

"These two individuals, carrying valid visas and Pakistani passports, traveled under the names of Makan Chagatai and Nizar Bhabra, two businessmen who ran a textile company in Faisalabad, Pakistan," Amara said.

Amara clicked a button on the laptop, and the scanned images of Chagatai's and Bhabra's passports appeared on the screen. Amara said, "Both men informed Indian customs agents that they were heading to the Indian city of Ludhiana on a two-day business trip and declared that they were staying in the Hyatt Regency Hotel."

The next photographs were in color and depicted both Chagatai and Bhabra checking into the Hyatt in the hotel's lobby.

"Both men stayed a total of two nights at the Hyatt, before heading back to Pakistan via the Wagah border," Amara said. "Four days ago, when the crown prince instructed the royal court to investigate the explosions, they began to run facial recognition software across the globe, in and around areas where various components of the thorium molten salt reactors had been manufactured, tested, or had been in transit to their final destinations. And our facial recognition technology got a result from September twenty-second of last year, when Mr. Chagatai and Mr. Bhabra crossed into India via the Wagah border on their way to Ludhiana."

"And why were these two men flagged by facial recognition?" President Buchanan asked.

"Because, Madam President, Mr. Chagatai and Mr. Bhabra are not Pakistani, and neither are they textile businessmen from Faisalabad. Mr. Chagatai is actually a man named Dr. Mahdi Farahani, an Iranian nuclear scientist, and Mr. Bhabra is a senior Iranian MOIS officer named Mahmoud Ghorbani."

The whole room stiffened as older images of Mahmoud Ghorbani and Mahdi Farahani filled the screen.

Amara continued, "The crown prince, upon hearing this new information, then instructed the Saudi intelligence agency to take over the investigation into why Ghorbani and Farahani were in Ludhiana for those two days in September, which led us to this."

The image on the screen changed and showed a satellite photograph of a warehouse in a congested urban area.

Amara said, "The reason we ran our facial recognition software on the Wagah border was because of its close proximity to Ludhiana, where an engineering company that produces the graphite rods for the thorium molten salt reactors is located. This facility in Ludhiana has strict oversight by both the Nuclear Suppliers Group and the International Atomic Energy Agency, which both oversee the control, production, and exportation of materials that could potentially aid in the manufacturing of a nuclear weapon."

President Buchanan pointed to the screen showing the dilapidated building. "And this is the facility that produces these rods?"

"No, Madam President," Amara said. "The facility that manufactures the graphite rods is incredibly secure. This building is an overnight storage facility that houses cargo that will be loaded onto the rail system heading into New Delhi. On the night of September twenty-third, the second day that Mahmoud Ghorbani and Mahdi Farahani were in Ludhiana, the shipment of the graphite rods spent the night in this facility before heading to New Delhi and then were flown to their various destinations all over the world."

Amara zoomed in on the storage facility. "As Saudi intelligence continued their investigation, they discovered surveillance photographs of Ghorbani and Farahani leaving the Hyatt Regency Hotel late the night of September twenty-third and returning early the next morning, before heading back to Pakistan. Consequently, Saudi intelligence officials discovered that not only were there no guards on duty at the storage facility that night, but the surveillance system had been completely dismantled."

"Holy shit," Secretary of State Newman said.

"Hold on," President Buchanan said. "Are you saying that an Iranian intelligence officer and a nuclear scientist broke into that storage facility and manipulated those graphite rods?"

"Not manipulated, ma'am," Amara said. "But exchanged them with faulty, lower-density rods."

The room again went silent.

"Do you have definitive proof that these Iranians entered that storage facility on September twenty-third?" Director Hastings asked.

"As a matter of fact, we do," Amara said, and then brought up a video of a beaten and bruised man sitting on a wooden chair in a concrete room. "On the night of March first, after Saudi intelligence was able to confirm that Ghorbani and Farahani were in Ludhiana during the night of September twenty-third when the graphite rods were in the storage facility, they began searching for the current whereabouts of each man. Since he is a MOIS officer, we knew it was a shot in the dark at finding Ghorbani, so we focused on Dr. Farahani and we got lucky."

Amara explained that the Saudis discovered that Dr. Farahani was in the middle of a two-week vacation in Paris with his wife when the thorium molten salt reactors exploded.

"The crown prince sent a team of Saudi officers to Paris two days ago, and they were able to apprehend Dr. Farahani and take him to the Saudi kingdom."

"The crown prince sent a rendition team to Paris?" asked National Security Adviser Coolidge. "Are the French aware of this?"

"No," said Amara. "That was kept quiet."

"Jesus," Coolidge said.

Amara turned her attention to President Buchanan, "Ma'am, for the remainder of March second and into the late afternoon of March third, Saudi officials interrogated Dr. Farahani, who eventually confessed that he and Mahmoud Ghorbani, at the behest of the Iranian Quds Force commander, General Soleimani, had entered the storage facility in Ludhiana, disrupted its surveillance system, then replaced all seven graphite rods with lower-density rods. Rods with a density that would pass every heat and stress test put upon them, but with a density that wouldn't be able to withstand the temperature and pressure of a fully running thorium fission reactor."

Princess Amara clicked play on the video, and Brenner and the rest of the individuals in the room watched as Dr. Farahani confessed to the whole series of events.

Six minutes later, when the video ended, the room sat in stunned silence.

Brenner, who had been tapping his pen against his leg for the duration of the video, froze, trying to absorb what he'd just seen.

Then President Buchanan broke the silence.

"How many people know about this?"

"The crown prince has kept it all incredibly quiet, Madam President," Amara said. "It's why he didn't notify the French about the rendition of Dr. Farahani in Paris. Only his most trusted advisers and a few senior officials within the royal court and Saudi intelligence are privy to this information. The crown prince wanted you briefed on this first, so your National Security Council would have time to vet the intelligence."

President Buchanan stood from her chair and pointed at the screen. "I want this information vetted immediately. And if it's validated, I want it concealed under lock and key until *after* the signing of the accord." The president shook her head in disbelief. "If one iota of this is true—"

"Then it's an act of war, ma'am," General Toole said.

Buchanan blinked at the general.

"Madam President," Hastings said, "I have to agree. If this is true, it means that the Iranian Quds Force commander, General Soleimani, is responsible for the meltdowns of the seven thorium molten salt reactors. He and the Iranian government are responsible for the four hundred and eleven American lives lost outside of Las Vegas, and the thousands of others who died around the world. This is a time to act, ma'am, not sweep it under the rug. We must be preemptive in our response, either covertly or militarily. I say we target Soleimani directly—"

Buchanan held up a hand to Hastings. "I am dealing with a cloud of nuclear radiation on its way to Las Vegas, I'm dealing with the potential collapse of the signing of the Global Green Accord next week in Davos. I don't have time for your warmongering rhetoric, Director!"

"Ma'am, for decades, General Soleimani has been responsible—"

"Enough, Elizabeth!" Buchanan half shouted. "What do you expect me to do? Start World War Three?!"

"Absolutely not, Madam President—"

Buchanan ignored Hastings and then pointed at the new deputy director of the CIA, sitting directly across from her at the table. "Garrett, I want you and your office at the agency to personally vet this intelligence report. Pass your findings directly to DNI Winslow."

Hastings shot up from her chair. "Madam President, the responsibility of vetting that report falls under my leadership, not my subordinate's!"

Buchanan rounded on Hastings. "Under your leadership the CIA caught none of this!"

Brenner closed his eyes, knowing that Hastings wouldn't be able to control what she was going to say next.

"Well, excuse me, Madam President," Hastings growled. "But maybe if you hadn't cut our budget in half, we would have been able to more thoroughly monitor General Soleimani and curb Iranian provocation in the Gulf States!"

Brenner opened his eyes and stared at Buchanan, who looked like she'd just been slapped. Slamming her fist onto the table, Buchanan shouted, "Let me remind you, Elizabeth, that I am the president of the United States. *Not* you. If I give Deputy Director Moretti the task of vetting this report, that is what is going to happen, is that clear?"

For a moment, Hastings and Buchanan just stared at each other like two gunslingers squaring off—then Hastings sat down in her seat.

A five-second silence fell over the room, then Vice President Dunn spoke up, "The nuclear scientist, Dr. Farahani, where is he now?"

All eyes turned to Amara, who cleared her throat, obviously somewhat flummoxed by the interaction that had just occurred between the president and the director of the CIA. "Doctor Farahani is dead. He died in Saudi custody yesterday after his confession."

"Christ," Brenner heard Dan Miller say under his breath.

"And Ghorbani?" asked SecDef Lake.

"We don't know," Amara said. "He hasn't been seen since reentering Pakistan on September twenty-fourth."

For a long beat, no one spoke, then Buchanan said in a somewhat calm voice, "Thank you for briefing us, Madam Ambassador. I will speak to the crown prince after the CIA has time to vet your report."

DNI Winslow reached over and pulled the external hard drive from the laptop, then put it back into the diplomatic pouch before sliding it over to Garrett Moretti, who acted like he'd just been handed the Holy Grail.

"Everyone is excused," President Buchanan said. "Except you, Elizabeth. You stay right here."

———

Jack Brenner and Dan Miller leaned against the wall in the hallway below the West Wing and watched as the CIA deputy director, Garrett Moretti, strode out of the Situation Room clutching the black diplomatic pouch before walking up the stairs that led to the West Executive exit.

Brenner, who waited until nearly everyone who was in the Situation Room had gone up the stairs, stared at Agent Tuck waiting with Princess Amara in the hallway and grabbed Dan Miller by the shoulder. "Danny, what the hell was that?"

Miller turned away from Tuck and Amara. "I don't know. But you need to get *up north* as fast as possible."

Brenner nodded, knowing what Miller meant by *up north*. "I'm going to need a copy of that Saudi intelligence report—we're going to have to go through it with a fine-tooth comb."

"I'll try to figure out a way to get a copy from Moretti's office and get it to you."

"You need to keep an eye on Elizabeth—"

As soon as Brenner said it, the double doors to the Situation Room burst open, and Director Hastings came barreling out.

Face beet red, she spotted Brenner and Miller and marched over to them.

Behind her, President Buchanan stepped into the hallway surrounded by Agent Edwards, Agent Hewitt, and the rest of the PPD before being escorted upstairs.

Noticing that Tuck and Princess Amara were still hanging behind, Hastings lowered her voice and hissed, "I have never been so blindsided in my entire life! She's been waiting for something like this to happen so she can finally have a reason to fire my ass."

"The CIA wasn't the only agency who missed this, Elizabeth," Brenner whispered. "It was the whole IC."

"No shit, Jack."

"What'd Buchanan say?" Miller asked.

"She chewed me out for even suggesting a retaliation against Iran. She said the only thing that matters is getting that accord signed. She told me she doesn't trust my leadership capabilities anymore—and if I don't step in line, she'll find a replacement," Hastings said in disgust. "I can't believe she gave Moretti the task of vetting that intelligence report. That's not going to fly. Not while I'm running the show."

Hastings turned abruptly on her heel, but Miller reached out and grabbed her arm.

"What are you planning on doing, Elizabeth?"

Hastings looked around, to make sure no one was listening. "What I should do is *leak* that fucking report. Maybe then, the rest of the world would put pressure on the *green witch* to grow a pair of balls and retaliate against General Soleimani and the fucking Iranians!"

"Jesus, Elizabeth," Miller said.

"No, Danny. I'm going to do whatever I need to do to keep my job. And I sure as shit won't allow Moretti to vet that report. Not while I'm director."

Hastings stormed off past Tuck and Amara, then up the stairs.

"Keep a close eye on her, Danny," Brenner repeated.

"Always," Miller replied. "I'll give you a ring after I get that report. I'll see you tonight."

Ten minutes later, after Brenner left the White House grounds, he climbed into a Mercedes sedan that sat in an underground parking garage, took out his burner phone from his jacket, and texted:

New development unfolding. Make sure everyone is awake. I'll be there in an hour.

Driving north out of the city, he merged onto the 190 highway and bore down on the Mercedes's accelerator.

Gunmetal clouds were roiling in by the time he crossed into Maryland, and a light snow had started to fall.

Brenner kept both hands on the wheel as he weaved in and out of traffic, thinking the whole time of what the Saudi intelligence report could mean for what lay ahead.

CHAPTER EIGHTEEN

IT HAD BEEN nearly seven hours since Garrett Moretti had left the White House Situation Room, and he still couldn't believe his luck.

Not only had the president of the United States asked him to personally escort the new Saudi ambassador from Andrews Air Force Base to the White House that very morning, but he had gotten a front row seat to one of the most important and earth-shattering intelligence briefings in decades.

Iranian Quds Force Commander General Soleimani and the Iranian government were behind the thorium molten salt reactor explosions, Moretti thought, standing before his office's floor-to-ceiling windows, looking out on Langley's grounds below, as the sun dipped under the horizon, a light snow falling from the clouds above.

His office offered a nice, western-facing view, but it was not the best view on the floor.

That was reserved for the office of the director of the Central Intelligence Agency, Elizabeth Hastings—whose seventh-floor suite across the hall faced east and provided a stunning panorama of the Potomac River.

But that view will soon be mine, Moretti thought, turning from the window and walking beyond his desk, to the leather couch on the far side of the room.

Lying on the couch, he propped his feet up on the cushions, a wide grin surfacing on his face.

At just forty-six years old, Garrett Moretti had achieved the impossible.

In only ten years, he had gone from a lowly staff lawyer in the office of the SSCI—the Senate Select Committee on Intelligence—and had meteorically risen to become the deputy director of the CIA, all because he had made one great life decision a decade before.

Marrying Annie Dunn.

He'd initially met Vice President Michael Dunn's eldest daughter on the first day of her summer internship at the SSCI. Back then, Michael Dunn had been the Speaker of the House—a senior congressman from Massachusetts who'd had his eyes set on a future White House run.

Even though Annie Dunn was nothing special in the brains or the looks department, Moretti knew that if he didn't make bold decisions in life, he'd be stuck in his dead-end job in the SSCI for the rest of his career.

Understanding that proximity in Washington equals power, Moretti began a whirlwind courtship with Miss Dunn—and sealed the deal two years later with an extravagant wedding on Martha's Vineyard.

That had been eight years and three kids ago.

And in that time, Moretti had stuck to his father-in-law's side like sap on tree bark.

Within weeks of marrying into the Dunn family, Garrett Moretti had been hired to be his father-in-law's chief of staff, while he'd been Speaker of the House.

Then, when the leadership within the House of Representatives changed after the next election cycle, and Michael Dunn lost his role as Speaker, his father-in-law came to him and asked if he would like to run his campaign for the next presidential election.

Ecstatic with the offer, Moretti dove headfirst into the role of campaign manager for his father-in-law.

And if it hadn't been for Angela and Bobby Buchanan's crazed grassroots campaign, Garrett Moretti was certain that his father-in-law would have been the party's presumptive presidential nominee.

But in the end, Moretti and Michael Dunn had settled for second best and took the offer to run as vice president alongside the Buchanan campaign.

It was probably for the best, Moretti thought, the grin still on his face as he lay on the couch.

Since Buchanan's election Moretti had taken the role of the vice president's chief of staff, and while it did seem like a stagnant, and even unimportant, job at times, he was glad it kept him and his father-in-law out of the spotlight.

President Buchanan and her Green Initiative had pitted the American people against one another in ways not seen in modern history. With the country split down party lines, and with the economy in tatters since the initiative was passed into law, Garrett Moretti had essentially watched from the sidelines as the country burned from both sides of the aisle.

And quite frankly, he couldn't give two shits.

He couldn't care less that the Senate had passed the Green Initiative into law, or about the signing of the upcoming Global Green Accord. And if he was being completely honest with himself, he didn't have an opinion about climate change in the first place.

Quite frankly, all Garrett Moretti cared about was power.

And as luck would have it, his power had been rising exponentially lately—mostly due to a meeting he'd been invited to four months before at the house of a very powerful individual.

He'd first run into the individual at a fundraising gala in DC, and after a few drinks, the man had offered to host Moretti at his estate in Fairfax County the next weekend.

Moretti had been flattered by the invitation and had spent the night getting drunk on expensive bourbon and buzzed on Dominican cigars in the politician's grand estate.

It wasn't until Moretti was sufficiently drunk that the man had entertained him with a surprising offer.

The man had said that he was acting under the orders of the president to find someone who could fill the position of deputy director of the CIA.

"President Buchanan is looking to get rid of Elizabeth Hastings," the man had said. "We just want a loyalist inside Langley until that time comes. Is this something that would interest you, Garrett?"

"To be the deputy director of the CIA?" Moretti had said. "Of course it would!"

The man had then confided in Moretti. "Wonderful, and between you and me, son, if you prove your loyalty to President Buchanan, I can't see why she wouldn't make *you* director of the CIA once Hastings gets the boot."

Moretti couldn't believe his luck. Shaking the man's hand, he said, "I'm all in, sir, just tell me what you need me to do."

His new mentor had then studied Moretti. "We want you to keep a watchful eye on Hastings, and maybe do a few favors for us, here and there. Once you are confirmed by the Senate and appointed deputy director, I will give you a phone so we can correspond in private. This phone is the most secure on the planet and will only be linked to me. You will never tell a soul about this phone. Not your wife, or your father-in-law, nor will you ever speak privately or publicly about any of this with the president, is that clear?"

"Crystal."

"Good," the man said. "Now, even though our communications from here on out will be through the best encryption software money can buy, I never want us to use our real names. From now on you will refer to me as *Custer*, and I will refer to you as *Varnum*."

Moretti had of course thought that using code names was a bit of overkill, but he had agreed anyway, saying, "So are you really working with the president?"

Custer winked at him, then in a nonanswer said, "You do some favors for Buchanan in Langley, and we'll make sure you're the next director of the CIA. Sound good, Varnum?"

"That sounds great, sir."

And it still sounded great, Moretti thought, from his position on the couch.

A month after that conversation, Garrett Moretti had resigned as his father-in-law's chief of staff and had been appointed deputy director of the CIA by a majority vote in the Senate.

The day after his confirmation, a package containing a nondescript black smartphone showed up in a box on his doorstep.

The phone had one contact in it: *Custer.*

Since the moment that phone arrived Moretti had kept it on his person, waiting for it to buzz.

But it never had.

Until earlier today.

When Moretti had gotten back to his office after the emergency meeting in the Situation Room, he and his staff were in the middle of vetting the Saudi intelligence report, when the secure phone had finally vibrated.

Excusing himself, Moretti had gone to his private bathroom and read the message from Custer twice over, memorizing it in its entirety, before it self-erased.

Custer had given him a task.

A task that he had twenty-four hours to complete.

Walking back into his office, Moretti and his staff then spent the rest of the afternoon finishing their vetting of the Saudi intelligence report. Just before they were going to send their results to the office of the DNI, Moretti had secretly made a copy of the report, stashed it on an external hard drive, and then concealed it in his jacket pocket.

As the original report and Moretti's findings from the vetting process were sent to the office of the DNI, Moretti had then personally called the White House and spoke to President Buchanan directly, updating her on his office's findings.

When Moretti finished the call, he twirled the small external hard drive in his fingers and wondered how he would fulfill the instructions Custer had detailed for him in his message.

A knock at his door roused him from his thoughts as one of his assistants poked her head in. "Sir, the director has requested your presence in her office."

Moretti, who had been caught up in his daydreams, sat up and checked his watch. "Really? Right now?"

"Yes, as soon as possible."

Moretti smiled to himself, again, not believing his luck.

The instructions on the phone gave him twenty-four hours to complete his task, but now he would get his opportunity to do it this evening.

Custer will be pleased.

Making sure the hard drive with the copy of the Saudi intelligence report was still in his suit pocket, Moretti strode out of his office, and down the hall, where he knocked on the door leading to the suite of the director of the Central Intelligence Agency.

"Madam Director, I didn't think you'd still be here this late," Moretti said, striding in.

Hastings, who always reminded Moretti of Margaret Thatcher, both in looks and demeanor, was sitting in her chair before her desk, her arms folded and a magnificent scowl creasing her face.

Not only did Hastings's office need redecorating—the furniture looked like it belonged on the set of *The Brady Bunch*—but it also sported one of the more lewd photographs Moretti had ever witnessed in a professional setting.

Encapsulated and enshrined ever so *inelegantly* in a gold frame on the wall behind Hastings's head was the iconic photograph of Johnny Cash flipping off a photographer during his infamous performance in San Quentin.

While the photograph was something of legend within the halls of Langley—and the quintessential metaphor for Hastings's career—Moretti saw it as a stain on the office.

And the first thing to go when I am named director, he thought.

"What can I do for you, Elizabeth?" Moretti said, sitting before Hastings.

Moretti, of course, knew why he was here.

He'd heard the office gossip since leaving the Situation Room that Elizabeth Hastings had been apoplectic about President Buchanan casting her aside and giving Moretti the task of vetting the Saudi intelligence report.

Hastings leaned forward in her chair. "Garrett, don't insult my intelligence; you know very well why I called you here."

Moretti faked a sigh. "You want the results of the vetting process my office ran on the Saudi intelligence report. My team finished it an hour ago; it's on its way to the office of the DNI via courier as we speak."

Hastings already knew this, of course.

"And what did your results conclude?" Hastings asked.

"Elizabeth, the president of the United States doesn't want me sharing information—"

"I heard you just spoke with the president?"

"I did," Moretti replied, a bit taken aback.

"And what did you two talk about?"

Moretti bit his lip, thinking back to the conversation he'd had with President Buchanan an hour before.

"I'm not at liberty to say."

"Really?"

"Yes, really," Moretti replied, growing more and more uncomfortable. *Focus*, he thought to himself. *You have a task to complete . . .*

"Hmm," Hastings said, leaning back in her chair, Johnny Cash's stout middle finger looking like a crown above her head. "What if I told you that I know the subject matter of your call."

"And . . . and how would you know that?"

Hastings opened her hands in amusement. "I've worked as a spy for thirty-five years, Garrett. That's thirty-five years more than you. I wouldn't be very good at my job if I didn't know what was going on in my own halls, now would I?"

Moretti, now actually uncomfortable, just shrugged.

Hastings steepled her fingers. "I heard that you briefed the president on your findings, and that she ordered you and your team to remain absolutely silent about the results of the Saudi intelligence report, is that right?"

"It is," Moretti said.

"Silent even from me, correct?"

"That is correct."

Hastings stood up slowly, resting her hands on her desk. "You see, Garrett, as the director of the CIA, I have a *very* big problem with that."

"Then that's something you are going to have to take up with the president," Moretti said, seeing his opening.

Hastings's hand slammed down so fast on the desk that Moretti jumped in surprise.

"This is my ship!" Hastings snarled. "I am the captain. Not you. Not the president. Me! Don't think for one second that I don't know why Buchanan placed you in this agency. I know you were sent here to watch me, to report to Buchanan the happenings within *my* halls."

Moretti, gaining his confidence back now, recalled Custer's message over the encrypted phone. Leaning forward, he dropped his voice to a whisper, "You know what, Elizabeth, I actually agree with you. I don't think the president has the right to withhold intelligence from the director of the CIA."

Hastings cocked her head.

Moretti continued, trying to sound as sincere as possible, "Frankly, I thought it was disrespectful to you and your office. President Buchanan had no right to go around your back and give this task to me."

Moretti shook his head, and reaching into his pocket, he pulled out the small hard drive and placed it on Hastings's desk. "I made a copy of the Saudi intelligence report to give to you, Elizabeth. And I want you to know that my team was able to confirm its validity. The Saudi's intelligence was sound. Without a shadow of a doubt, we can conclude that General Soleimani and the Iranian government were behind the meltdowns of the thorium molten salt reactors. It was a terrorist attack, Elizabeth."

Hasting's eyes shot to the hard drive, her mouth slightly agape.

When she didn't say anything, Moretti stood. "Elizabeth, as much as you hate me, you have to understand that I'm still on your side. I am an employee at the Central Intelligence Agency, and you are my boss."

Without waiting for a reply, Moretti exited his soon-to-be office, a slight skip to his step.

That went much better than I'd expected!

Walking back into his own office, Moretti shut and locked the door, then dug out the secure cell phone from his pocket and opened it.

Holding the phone in his hands, he created a new message to Custer, and typed:

Task complete—DCI Hastings is in possession of a copy of the Saudi intelligence report.

After sending the message, Moretti stuffed the phone into his pocket with his other cell phone, collected his things, and made for the door.

Moving through the hallway, he fantasized about his soon-to-be nomination as the director of the Central Intelligence Agency in the coming weeks.

What had Custer told him at the end of their meeting those months before?

Everything would change after the signing of the Global Green Accord.

CHAPTER NINETEEN

CUSTER TRUDGED THROUGH the two inches of snow that had fallen on his sprawling estate in the last few hours and noted how silent everything was.

The glow of his mansion behind him, which was one of the most expensive in his elite zip code, lit up the way toward the horse stables in the northwest corner of his grand property.

Bundled in a down jacket, Custer raised a hand to his lips and puffed on a Gurkha cigar.

Though it was still early in the night, Custer had reason to celebrate.

Operation Little Bighorn—while having hit a little bit of a speed bump earlier in the day—was smoothed out an hour and a half ago by Varnum, one of Custer's lieutenants.

Custer had been briefed almost immediately over the Orion phone of the events in the Situation Room by one of his other lieutenants who had also attended the emergency meeting that afternoon. The lieutenant, who went by the code name Benteen, had alerted Custer that President Buchanan had *not* given Elizabeth Hastings the Saudi intelligence report to vet. Instead, she had given that responsibility to Varnum.

For the plan to work, the Saudi intelligence report needed to touch Hastings's hands.

Having to frantically improvise, Custer had sent a message to Varnum via the Orion phone, with a task and a time limit.

Surprisingly enough, not only had Varnum completed the task, but he'd done it so much faster than Custer had ever anticipated.

Maybe he's not as dumb as I was led to believe, Custer thought, as he made his way to the entrance of his horse stables.

Opening the front door to the barn, he was hit by the unmistakable aroma of a well-kept, well-run horse racing operation.

Walking toward the three-year-old offspring of the latest Triple Crown winner, Custer stopped before the magnificent beast and put the back of his palm to the horse's snout, letting the animal smell his scent.

"How's my boy tonight?" Custer cooed.

The horse, named Bluest Light, rubbed his nose into his master's outstretched hand and blasted a warm exhale onto Custer's face. Custer grinned and thought of everything that had transpired in the last four days since he'd watched the thorium molten salt reactors melt down on the news. So far, other than the hiccup this morning, the plan was working perfectly, the chips falling into place more neatly than he'd ever imagined. Soon, the next phase would begin. A phase that Varnum had rescued from calamity, and a phase that Custer was about to initiate.

A shrill noise cut Custer off from his thoughts.

The Orion phone.

Custer's heart nearly skipped a beat—the only reason one of his lieutenants would be calling him this time of night was if something had gone horribly wrong.

Given to him by his benefactors, the Orion phone was the most secure phone in the world.

He was initially given the phone so he could speak to his benefactors directly, but he had since opted to communicate with them on secure, one-time-use burner phones, or directly through his handler.

Though Custer fully trusted the Orion encryption system when his calls took place domestically, he was wary of using it to speak with his benefactors halfway across the world.

Trying to keep his emotions in check, Custer took a step back from Bluest Light, pulled out the phone, and groaned when he saw the name on the screen.

"Hello?"

"You fucking sonofabitch!" screamed the voice on the other line. "You tricked me, implicated me in—"

"Calm down, Reno," Custer said.

"Don't you tell me to calm down—"

"No names!" Custer snapped. "Code names only, we've talked about this!"

Heavy, angry breathing sounded over the line. "Fine. *Custer*—you tricked me! You made me give you the travel routes that the graphite rods were taking out of India! Please tell me you didn't give that information to the Iranians!"

"Sir, I did no such thing," Custer said. "And quite frankly, I'm offended you even suggested that."

"Then why the hell did you make me give you that information?!"

"Our benefactors—given what they are promising you—wanted to make sure that you had more skin in the game. That you couldn't back out. That you will see this operation all the way through."

"But the fucking Iranians, General Soleimani?!" Reno yelled. "Thousands died in those explosions. Americans died! You told me that there would be no innocent casualties!"

"Sir," Custer said, growing more and more annoyed, "I have no idea what our benefactors have planned. That's the genius of this operation. The only thing we all share is a common interest in an end goal. We are compartmented from each other for a reason."

Reno cursed.

Already knowing the answer to the question he was about to ask, because of his conversation earlier in the day with his other lieutenant, Benteen, Custer said, "If you don't mind me asking, how did you find out about the Iranians?"

Reno detailed for Custer the events in the White House Situation Room earlier that morning.

"And how did President Buchanan take the news of the Saudi intelligence report?"

"Not well. She's blaming the CIA director—I'd be surprised if Hastings lasts till the end of the week. All Buchanan cares about is getting the accord signed and pleasing her boyfriend, the crown prince!"

Blaming the CIA director, Custer thought, grinning broadly. "And what did President Buchanan say about releasing this intelligence report?"

"She doesn't want it exposed until *after* the signing. Her main concern is making sure this doesn't stop the progress of the accord."

"So, girl wonder wants to keep this tight-lipped?"

"Yes. Could you imagine if the press got hold of this? Washington would burn! The West would be on a war footing with Iran. The signing of the accord would fracture—" Reno's voice stopped. "Wait! Is that part of the plan, leaking this to the press?"

"You let me take it from here. You covered your tracks. Trust me, and trust the plan."

"And what is the rest of the plan? Who else is working with us?"

"Even I don't know who else is involved," Custer lied. "And even if I did, I wouldn't tell you. The stakes are simply too high."

"I don't know if I can do this, Custer," Reno said. "I don't like being in the dark."

Custer sighed deeply, remembering the Sony microcassette player he'd taken from his safe and put in his pocket early that night, just in case Reno called him. Knowing the man would likely be in a tizzy after his meeting in the Situation Room, Custer lifted the device from his pocket, held it to the Orion phone, and pressed play.

Reno's voice from a year and a half before played for ten seconds until Custer stopped the tape.

"You asshole!" Reno yelled over the line.

Pocketing the microcassette player, Custer said, "Every time you get cold feet, I will replay that tape for you, reminding you of your complicity and your promise to me. From the beginning, I told you the rules, now you must abide by them."

Reno cursed again.

Custer said, "Now, you made sure you covered your tracks when you obtained the travel routes of the graphite rods?"

"Of course!"

"And you went through the necessary back channels?"

"Yes, yes! Just like you taught me."

"Good, then you have nothing to worry about. Your job going

forward is to remain stoic. To remain steadfast. I will contact you if I need you."

With that, Custer ended the call.

How annoying.

Checking his watch, he determined now was as good a time as ever for the next phase of Operation Little Bighorn to begin. After saying his goodbyes to Bluest Light, Custer marched back toward his mansion and into his study, where he poured himself a glass of bourbon and walked over to the wall safe built behind the Edgar S. Paxson painting above his desk. After moving the painting aside, and typing in the code, he opened the small reinforced steel door, placed the microcassette player back inside and then snatched the secure Orion laptop given to him by his benefactors.

Plopping the laptop down on his desk, Custer powered it on, and thought of the next steps he would need to take.

Being a man of his generation, Custer was the first to admit he wasn't the best with computers, but after a few lessons with his handler, Custer was confident in what he was about to do.

After all, framing someone wasn't the most difficult task in the world.

Logging into the Orion laptop, Custer opened a remote desktop application that granted him access to the personal computer of the individual he was about to frame.

Two weeks prior, Custer had physically accessed his victim's personal computer, set up a series of previously purchased VPNs and onion accounts that would hide his victim's identity, and then bought a specific VPN from Sweden. Next, he enabled the same remote desktop application that would allow his Orion laptop to access his victim's computer. He had also tinkered with the computer's settings, making sure it would not power off when closed or idle. This was crucial, as it would guarantee he would always have access to it.

After waiting a few moments for the remote desktop application to connect, Custer smiled when his victim's computer screen finally showed up on the Orion laptop.

He was in.

With half of the Orion laptop's screen displaying his victim's screen, and half of the screen displaying his own, Custer used his own screen to access a secure dummy email account set up by his benefactors. In the Drafts folder of this account sat an exact copy of the Saudi intelligence report.

Damn, my guys are good, Custer thought and downloaded it to the Orion laptop's desktop.

Then, accessing his victim's computer, he set up a fake Gmail account, and with the ability to share files between both laptops, via the remote desktop connection, Custer attached the Saudi intelligence report onto a composed email.

After spending five minutes copying and pasting the email addresses to the dozens of recipients, Custer triple-checked that he'd done everything correctly, then hit send.

Laughing to himself, he then closed out of the remote desktop connection and leaned back in his chair, satisfied.

Within seconds, the *BBC*, the *New York Times*, *Al-Jazeera*, and every other major news publication in the world had received the unredacted intelligence report that Saudi Arabia had given to the Americans.

Soon the world would know that General Soleimani and the Iranians had blown up the thorium molten salt reactors, and the West would be on the precipice of war with Iran.

But more importantly, after a day or so, when authorities had tracked his victim's IP through all the various onion accounts and other VPNs that the mysterious sender had used to purchase the Swedish VPN, a certain *very important* person would not only lose their job, but most likely go to prison.

Custer laughed out loud when he envisioned the expression on that particular person's face, when the leak would be traced back to the VPN, and then to the personal computer that he'd hacked into.

Draining his glass of bourbon in delight, Custer powered off the Orion computer and locked it back in the safe.

In a few days, he would be sitting down with his handler to receive his next instructions. Pouring himself another glass of bourbon at his bar, he took a celebratory sip and daydreamed about his upcoming meeting with his beautiful handler.

Sitting down on his favorite chair before the burning hearth, Custer checked his watch.

It was 8:37 p.m.

Turning on the television, he made a bet with himself.

By 11:00 p.m., the leaked Saudi intelligence report would be the biggest story in the world.

He'd wait until then to have his next glass of bourbon.

Then the fireworks would begin.

CHAPTER TWENTY

PRINCESS AMARA PRESSED her iPhone to her ear and gazed out of her room's window within the Saudi ambassador compound, taking in the thin layer of snow that had collected on the moonlit shores of the Potomac River.

After twenty more seconds of continuous ringing on the other line, Amara ended her call and cursed.

In the roughly sixteen hours since she'd been in the United States, she'd tried calling Farid and other members of her staff dozens of times, but none of the calls were going through.

Not even her WhatsApp was working.

What the hell is going on? Amara thought as she moved from the window and sat down on her bed, examining the phone. It was 10:30 at night, which meant it was 5:30 in the morning in Riyadh. Farid should be waking Ahmed and Mimi by now.

So why wasn't anybody answering?

That very morning, when she had arrived at the ambassador compound following her meeting at the White House, she had been greeted by a man named Wali Mattar, who introduced himself as her new chief of staff.

Mattar was a skinny, stooped man with large glasses, a thinning hairline, and a gray goatee, who didn't seem thrilled that he was working for the first ever *female* special envoy of the Saudi kingdom.

Upon her arrival to the United States, Amara had immediately tried to contact her children. At first, when the calls, texts, and WhatsApp messages wouldn't go through, she'd thought it was a simple problem with her SIM card. She voiced this concern to her new chief of staff, and Mattar had even purchased her a new one after her meeting in the White House, but still the phone wouldn't work.

In fact, it was acting quite weird.

The phone was incredibly hot to the touch, and the battery was draining at nearly three times its normal rate.

Strangely enough, Amara could still access the internet, which she used to send countless emails and private Twitter messages to both Farid, her family, and her staff in the kingdom.

So far, she hadn't received one reply.

Were the crown prince and his slimy sidekick Saud Rahmani doing this? Had they hacked into my phone?

Of course they had.

Trying to get her mind off her predicament, Amara opened Twitter and saw that she was the number one trending topic in the world.

"A new face for a progressive leap forward," one user tweeted.

"A true Saudi feminist leading the world into a new green era. Positivity for the signing of the Global Green Accord," another user noted.

But not all the attention was spotlighted on her. The crown prince was the second-most trending topic, followed by the Global Green Accord.

If giving Amara the ambassadorship role was all a publicity stunt set up by her cousin, it had definitely worked.

Raza bin Zaman was looking like a hero in a time of uncertainty.

Princess Amara knew that a few nations that had pledged to signing the accord were now showing signs of backing out after the thorium molten salt reactor explosions. But her cousin's unwavering support for the president of the United States seemed to quell some nerves.

France and the UK had, in the last few hours, made statements that they would continue to move forward with their pledge to sign the accord.

But would they really?

Amara exited out of Twitter and lay down on the bed, the earlier events in the Situation Room playing out in her mind.

She recounted everyone's shocked expressions when she'd detailed the contents of the Saudi intelligence report. Their faces had indeed been a reflection of her own face when she'd been briefed in the crown prince's royal palace in Riyadh the night before.

During the flight from Riyadh to DC, Amara must have gone over the intelligence report a dozen times, memorizing every last detail of it. Not to mention watching and rewatching the confession video of Dr. Mahdi Farahani.

Though she had zero experience in diplomacy, she did believe that she had done a decent job briefing the president and her National Security Council.

But something still bothered her.

While going through the Saudi intelligence report during her flight to Washington, Amara noticed something that she hadn't initially seen before.

In nearly all the surveillance photographs of Dr. Mahdi Farahani and Mahmoud Ghorbani at the Wagah border, and in the Hyatt Regency Hotel in Ludhiana—Ghorbani seemed to have been looking directly at the camera.

It was almost like he wanted to be seen.

What was also odd about the report was how *quickly* the Saudis discovered that Dr. Farahani and Ghorbani had traveled into India last September. Not to mention how fast and efficiently they were able to target and capture Dr. Farahani in Paris.

Maybe Amara had always just underestimated her younger cousin and his capabilities.

Amara was still lying on the bed as her thoughts drifted from the Situation Room and seized on Qutrub, the "fly" she'd corresponded with over the dark web and the information he'd given her that was still hopefully hidden on her USB within the snow globe in Riyadh.

Amara sat bolt upright.

She'd nearly forgotten about the correspondence with the fly over the dark web. Compared to everything that had occurred over the last thirty hours, Amara's and Qutrub's fight for justice seemed incredibly insignificant—overshadowed by the reality of the Iranian terrorist attacks.

Amara thought back to the two files that Qutrub had sent to her over the dark web. She'd cursed herself for not having opened the files when Qutrub had sent them to her. But she hadn't had the time; Saud Rahmani's phone call had seen to that.

Amara went back to her conversation with Qutrub, how he said that the RIG file he'd stolen from Saud Rahmani's computer confirmed the rumor he'd heard circulating around the royal court offices—the rumor of the Saudi dissident living in America, and how the crown prince wished to silence him before the signing of the Global Green Accord.

While insignificant compared to the news of the Iranian terrorist attacks—this was still someone's life that was at stake.

It was common knowledge that this dissident was living somewhere in Washington, DC.

Immediately, Amara's mind began to churn.

Somehow I need to warn this man—warn him so he can flee my cousin's wrath.

But how?

From the moment she'd stepped foot in the United States, her new chief of staff and his cadre of minders had loomed over her, dictating her schedule, shuffling her around from place to place, and now even confining her to her room.

With her phone surely compromised, how could she warn this Saudi dissident that his life was in danger?

Thinking back to what she had whispered in Farid's ear before she had gotten on the plane to the United States, she hoped her old friend would be able to get the snow globe containing the USB to her safely.

But I can't count on that, Amara thought.

Then suddenly, something came to her—a memory from a guest list she'd reviewed a couple of months before.

The Middle Eastern Women's Rights Summit!

The dissident journalist had been invited to the Middle Eastern Women's Rights Summit here in DC!

Amara jumped out of bed and hurried to the door.

Grasping the handle, she twisted and pulled.

But the door wouldn't budge.

They locked me in? Amara thought, her panic rising.

"Hey!" Amara shouted. "Hey, open up!"

Amara heard a dead bolt being thrown, and the door swung open.

Taking a step back, she took in the two burly men standing before her. Both wore black suits and were clearly members of the Saudi Royal Guard.

Amara tried to step around them, but one of the two men stepped in front of her and held up a hand. "Your chief of staff has insisted you stay in your room for the night, Princess."

"Excuse me?" Amara said. "I am the ambassador. This is *my* estate."

"This estate belongs to the crown prince of Saudi Arabia," the other man said. "You are merely an envoy. A guest."

Amara gaped at the men. "Then . . . then I wish to see Mr. Mattar."

"Your chief of staff has retired for the night. If you wish to give him a message, you can do so through us."

Amara stared at the two men for a few seconds, then holding her chin up high, said, "In four days, I am scheduled to be the keynote speaker at the Middle Eastern Women's Rights Summit here in DC. I still wish to attend the summit even in my new role as ambassador. Tell Mr. Mattar that I want to see the confirmed guest list by breakfast tomorrow morning."

The two men told her they would relay the message.

"Thank you," Amara said. "And I would like it if Mr. Mattar could also find me a new cell phone. Mine isn't working."

The two men nodded.

"And one more thing. Do not lock my bedroom door."

"We are under orders—"

"The door will remain unlocked. I am the ambassador, not a prisoner. Good night, gentlemen."

Amara shooed the men out and closed the door behind them.

Tears began building in her eyes. Walking over to the bed, she snatched her phone, marched into the bathroom, and gazed at herself in the mirror.

Streaks of mascara stained her cheeks and she let out a small sob.

What had she gotten herself into? What kind of danger had she put her children in? Why was she being locked in her room?

Amara turned on the faucet and cleaned her face with some cold water.

As she patted her face dry, she heard her phone vibrate on the bath-room counter. Hoping that she'd finally gotten a text message from Farid, she gazed down at the screen.

But it wasn't a text message.

It was a push notification from Al Arabiya, the Saudi national news site.

Swiping open the notification, Amara gawked at the headline dis-played on the screen.

For a moment she stood there paralyzed, then her lips moved as a single, exasperated word escaped her mouth.

"*No!*"

CHAPTER TWENTY-ONE

East Riyadh, Saudi Arabia
An Nahdah District
March 5, 5:30 a.m.

THE HARSH, OBNOXIOUS ringtone bleated loudly, rousting Abdulmalik Hassen from a fitful sleep.

Cursing, he fumbled for the phone on his nightstand and snatched it, gazing with tired eyes as he read the caller ID from the screen.

Suddenly he was fully awake.

Silencing the unpleasant ringtone, he felt his wife, Munira, stir in bed next to him.

Hassen climbed out of bed and hurried into the bathroom. Shutting the door behind him, he answered the phone, "Hello?"

"Abdulmalik," Saud Rahmani's raspy voice said, "are you awake?"

"I am," Hassen replied, staring at his gaunt, pale reflection in the mirror. His usual plump, rosy cheeks looked emaciated and devoid of color. His hair and beard, which had always been jet black, now showed lines of white and streaks of silver.

Hassen listened to his boss on the other end. "I need you to come to work early today, Abdulmalik. Something has come up and we need your expertise."

The forty-five-year-old Saudi royal court computer scientist felt a tinge of terror run down his spine. "Why, what is going on?"

It was not unusual for his boss to call him into work at odd hours of the night, but considering everything that Hassen had been up to, he had reason to be on edge.

"We are going to have a busy day today," Saud Rahmani replied. "The bots will need to be running at full capacity. I will tell you more when you get to the office. How fast can you get here?"

Hassen sighed deeply, relief cascading over his body. "I can be there in forty-five minutes."

"Hurry," Saud Rahmani said and then hung up.

Hassen set the phone down on the counter and continued to gaze at the mirror, not liking the reflection staring back at him.

After splashing water over his face, Hassen reached under the counter and felt around, making sure the flash drive that he'd hidden there two nights before was still duct-taped under the sink.

Satisfied, Hassen walked back into the bedroom he shared with his wife.

Unlike most married couples in the kingdom, Hassen and Munira slept in the same bed and had done so every night of their twenty-year marriage. Staring at his wife's sleeping figure, Hassen felt a pang of guilt course through his body, guilt for the risks he'd recently taken and the potential danger he'd put his family in.

After getting dressed, he walked over to the side of the bed and kissed Munira gently on the cheek.

She stirred, then murmured, "What time is it?"

"Early, my love," Hassen replied. "Keep sleeping. I've been called into the office."

Munira groaned and rolled over.

Hassen then walked quietly to Rafi's room, poking his head inside to make sure his five-year-old son was still asleep.

Pleased to see the little boy tucked in his bed, Hassen continued into the living area and stuffed his laptop into his briefcase, before exiting his apartment and taking the stairs down to his car waiting in the ground-level parking garage.

Hassen had nearly gotten to his car when he felt his phone vibrate in his pocket. Shifting his briefcase to his other hand, he fished out the phone. A push notification from Al Arabiya showed on his screen.

Climbing into his car, he stared down at the Al Arabiya headline, and froze.

Iran Behind Thorium Molten Salt Reactor Explosions

Whistleblower leaks Saudi intelligence report with evidence that Iran switched out a component of thorium molten salt reactors under the directive of the Iranian Quds Force commander, General Soleimani.

Hassen skimmed the article in disbelief. As it turned out, the Saudis had captured an Iranian nuclear scientist, who confessed that he and an Iranian intelligence officer had swapped out a component found in each of the seven reactors.

According to the article, the crown prince had given the intelligence report to the president of the United States the day before.

This must be why Saud Rahmani called me into work, Hassen thought, pulling his car onto the street.

One fortunate thing about being called into work so early was that Hassen wouldn't have to worry about traffic on his way to the office in the royal court buildings in Al Safarat, Riyadh's Diplomatic Quarter.

He was just about to take a right onto a main drag that would lead him into the city, when he suddenly slammed on his brakes. A white-and-green garbage truck had pulled out of an alley and stopped in the middle of the road—blocking Hassen's path.

Hassen stopped directly behind the garbage truck and was about to roll down his window and curse at the driver, when he heard the squeal of tires.

Hassen looked left to right wildly as two black Mercedes sedans screeched to a halt on either side of his vehicle. Confused, he whipped his head around to see a third sedan parked right on his bumper.

He was boxed in.

Before Hassen could react, a woman in a burka exited the black sedan to his right, entered his car, and shoved a pistol in his face.

"You are Abdulmalik Hassen, the computer scientist working in the royal court under Saud Rahmani, are you not?" the woman in the burka asked, except the voice coming from under the veil was not that of a woman, but of a man, with a deep, commanding voice.

Hassen gaped at the gun.

"Answer me!" the man yelled, pressing the pistol into Hassen's forehead.

"Yes!" Hassen sputtered. "I am Abdulmalik Hassen!"

This was it, Hassen thought. *I've been found out, and now I'm going to be assassinated in the street.*

"Saud Rahmani told you to come into work early today, did he not?"

"How . . . how did you—"

"He has figured out what you've done, Abdulmalik. He called you in early today to have you arrested. He knows you stole information from his computer and gave it to a person over the dark web forum. He knows you gave the information to Scheherazade. You will be killed for what you've done . . . Qutrub."

"Please—"

"Shut up!" the man in the burka shouted, moving the pistol more forcefully into Hassen's forehead. The man wore blue latex surgical gloves, and Hassen watched as his index finger applied pressure to the trigger.

"Please," Hassen begged, tears now streaming down his face. "I have a family!"

"I know you do. And if you go into work today, your child will soon be fatherless, your wife a widow. Instead you are going to do something for me."

Hassen let out another tear-soaked whimper.

The man in the burka continued, "You stole some files from Saud Rahmani's computer two nights ago and smuggled them out on a flash drive, did you not?"

"Yes," Hassen croaked. "I . . . I did."

"Do you still have the flash drive containing the files?"

Hassen thought back to the flash drive duct-taped under his sink. "Yes."

"Good," the man said. "Now, listen to me carefully. You are going to turn around and head back to your home. You are then going to make a duplicate of the flash drive, and then you are going to get your wife and child out of the city before Saud Rahmani and his men can get to them."

"Saud Rahmani would never hurt my family."

"Oh, yes, he would, Abdulmalik. He will do anything to get those files back."

Hassen's deepest fear had finally manifested itself.

Why had I taken such a risk?

Why did I put my family in danger?

"I was only trying to get information for Scheherazade—I was only trying to confirm a rumor for her!"

The man slapped Hassen hard across the face. "Listen to me!" he snarled. "You are going to go home and make a duplicate of that flash drive. Once you get your family to safety, you are going to give one of the flash drives to your CIA handler as soon as possible."

"How did you—"

The man struck Hassen again. "The other flash drive you will keep with you as an insurance policy, should Saud Rahmani find your family. You will use the flash drive as a bargaining tool should he get to Munira and Rafi."

Hassen was too scared to be disturbed by how much this man knew about his predicament and personal life.

Reaching under his burka with his free hand, the man came out with a black *agal*. "Today, when you meet your handler, you will also give him this."

The *agal* was a black circlet of rope used to hold a Muslim man's headdress in place.

The man dropped the *agal* on Hassen's lap.

Confused, Hassen's mind started to churn, but before he could speak, the man in the burka pointed to Hassen's phone sitting between his legs. "You of all people should know that Saud Rahmani can track your every movement with your phone and computer. Get rid of them immediately. Tell your wife to ditch all her electronic devices too. Do you understand me?"

"Yes . . . yes!"

Hassen felt the barrel of the pistol slide down his forehead, over his nose, and into his mouth.

"Fail to give the flash drive and the *agal* to the CIA by the end of the day or utter a word of this to anyone other than your handler and I'll find you and your family and hurt them in ways Saud Rahmani and his thugs could never imagine."

With that, the pistol was yanked out of Hassen's mouth, and the man in the burka was out of his car and back into the sedan to Hassen's right. A moment later, the garbage truck and the three black Mercedes boxing him in sped off.

Hassen sat in his car for what felt like an eternity, his body trembling so violently he was unable to grip his steering wheel.

Eventually, the shaking subsided, and he looked around, wondering if he was still being watched.

In that moment, Hassen perceived the reality of his situation.

It would take a half hour to get to the internet café in the heart of Riyadh to issue the contact with his handler.

But he wouldn't be doing that. Not at first.

First, he would rush home and get Munira and Rafi out of the city.

Stepping out onto the street, he walked over to the closest vehicle parked on the curb, put his phone under the lip of the vehicle's bumper, and climbed back into his car.

Hopefully, the owner of the vehicle now containing his phone would head to work later that morning and send Saud Rahmani and his thugs on a wild goose chase.

Hassen threw his car into gear and gunned it back to his apartment.

He would destroy his laptop and throw its remains out the window as he drove home.

If all went well, he could get his family out of the city within an hour.

In two hours he could hopefully establish contact with his handler.

Hopefully.

CHAPTER TWENTY-TWO

IT HAD BEEN nearly five hours since the Saudi intelligence report had leaked to the world's press showing evidence that Iran was behind the thorium molten salt reactor explosions and the CIA's Riyadh chief of station, William J. McCallister, thought his damn stomach ulcer might explode.

Thumbing an antacid from its tinfoil wrap in his pocket, he threw the tablet into his mouth and stepped off the elevator onto the third floor of the United States Embassy, marching toward the first security checkpoint that allowed him entry into the CIA's Riyadh Station.

It had been a hell of a morning and McCallister couldn't see it getting any better. Every news organization in the world was running the story of the leaked Saudi intelligence report. In the last two and a half hours, McCallister had personally taken two meetings with the American ambassador to Saudi Arabia.

During one of McCallister's many calls with Langley, he'd been informed that the British Royal Navy would start escorting commercial ships in the Persian Gulf just in case the Iranians upped their provocation.

It was a complete clusterfuck.

And the Iranians weren't making things any better.

Within an hour of the release of the leaked report, both the ayatollah and the president of Iran made statements condemning such "slanderous lies against us," then upped their rhetoric, saying, "Iran will do everything in its power to crush the Great Satan and its allies if they continue to propagate such falsehoods."

That rhetoric had then escalated, when the IRGC Quds Force commander, General Soleimani, had posted a speech to social media, saying, "The Great Satan and their delusional 'little girl' president can blame me all they want for their technological failings. In no way did I order Dr. Farahani and Mahmoud Ghorbani to manipulate the graphite rods. This is all a setup of the highest order, and when the Global Green Accord fails, the world will be looking at Iran for help to power their cars, their boats, and their planes."

So, yeah. Chief of Station McCallister was having a morning.

Clearing the second and third security matrixes, McCallister stepped into the CIA station's bullpen and made a beeline for his office in the northwest corner of the giant room. It was utter bedlam. Phones rang off their hooks as his officers and staff ran around shouting and fielding calls.

In his office, McCallister drew the blinds, sat down, and gazed at the dozens of cables that his special assistant had put on his desk in the last twenty minutes he'd been upstairs speaking with the American ambassador.

Going through the cables, McCallister realized most of it was Langley bureaucratic bullshit that required more of his time than attention— paperwork mostly, and a couple of meetings he had to sit in over the CIA's secure video teleconferencing system, or SVTC.

When he got to the bottom of the stack, he stopped at one that was sent to him nearly nine hours before by the director of the Special Activities Center, Jack Brenner.

McCallister frowned, realizing that he must have missed the cable when he'd gotten to the office that morning.

Willy, give me a shout on the SVTC when you get to your office.
—Jack

"Shit," McCallister said. This cable had been sent to him *before* the news broke about the leaked Saudi intelligence report. He'd told his special assistant that any cable coming in from DDO Dan Miller or the director of the SAC, Jack Brenner, should be flagged as top priority.

McCallister stroked his walrus mustache and huffed in frustration.

He had a lot on his mind even before this bombshell report had been leaked to the press.

Just over a week ago, Dan Miller had sent him a random, restricted handling cable, kind of like the one he'd just received, and told him to hop on the SVTC.

In the hour-long secure conference with his old friend, Miller had read him in on the most earth-shattering, outrageous, and preposterous briefing of his entire career.

At first, McCallister had outright denied what Miller was telling him.

Then he'd grown angry when Miller showed him the evidence.

That anger had driven him to come up with excuses as to why the evidence couldn't be true. When those excuses couldn't hold their own against the intelligence Miller provided, McCallister got upset.

Really. Fucking. Upset.

After Miller gave McCallister a few minutes to calm down, he explained to him that he and Jack Brenner were running an off-site, off-the-books program, to try and stop what was coming.

McCallister had then asked Miller how he could help.

Miller had already known that nearly a month before, COS McCallister had been invited to the Saudi royal court, where he had met personally with the crown prince. Raza bin Zaman had told McCallister that he had obtained intelligence that the terrorist Qasim al-Raymi had returned to his native country of Yemen and had been named emir of Al-Qaeda Arabian Peninsula.

McCallister knew of Qasim al-Raymi's return to Yemen, but he had been surprised by what the crown prince had asked of him next.

Raza bin Zaman told the CIA station chief that he had intelligence that Qasim al-Raymi would be attending the wedding of his brother, Ali Yahya Mahdi al-Raymi, on March 7, just days before the signing of the Global Green Accord. The crown prince stated that he wanted to create a squadron of elite Saudi soldiers to neutralize the new al-Qaeda emir, and that he wanted help from the CIA to vet a list of potential candidates.

McCallister had told the crown prince that he would speak to his chain of command and get back to him. The chief of station relayed the crown prince's proposal up the necessary channels and had received word that the Saudi intelligence was sound and that McCallister had the green light to assist the Saudis in vetting their special operations soldiers for the campaign.

Over the course of that next week, McCallister had spearheaded a team in-station to vet over twelve hundred Saudi special operations soldiers.

The task had been monumental.

In the end, McCallister and his team had focused on the soldiers with Bedouin backgrounds. Men who had grown up rough. Who could listen and improvise. But who were also smart, and physically fit. Out of twelve hundred candidates, McCallister had given the Saudis a list of twenty-two men he believed fit the profile of taking on such a delicate operation.

From what McCallister knew, those twenty-two Saudi SF soldiers had been sent down three weeks ago to a secret drone base in southern Saudi Arabia to train for the upcoming Qasim al-Raymi campaign. He'd been told that the Saudis had built a real-life rendition of the Ar Risan Palace in Yemen—where al-Raymi's brother was to be married.

Still annoyed that he'd missed Brenner's cable by nearly nine hours, McCallister double-checked that the blinds in his office were completely shut, before turning on the SVTC through his laptop and dialing Jack Brenner.

The director of the Special Activities Center answered within ten seconds, his tired features filling the screen.

"Jack, I'm sorry, it's been crazy over here—I just saw your cable."

McCallister could see people walking behind Brenner in a small, concrete room. He knew the off-site location where Brenner and Miller's secret program was being conducted was somewhere in Maryland.

"It's fine, Willy," Brenner said, then explained that he and Dan Miller had been in the Situation Room the day before when the new Saudi ambassador had briefed the president and her National Security Council on the Saudi intelligence report. They had been trying to get ahold of McCallister to tell him what had occurred in the Situation Room.

"Any idea who leaked it?" asked McCallister.

"The only people who had access to it were Garrett Moretti's office and the office of the DNI."

Brenner massaged his forehead, and McCallister could see the stress on the man's face. "Jack, when you and Danny were in the Situation Room, what was your first reaction to the report—knowing what we know?"

"Our first reaction was that we questioned its legitimacy," Brenner said. "Then we tried getting our hands on it, so we could go through it with a fine-tooth comb."

"Now that the report leaked, have you been able to go through it?"

"We have."

"And?"

"At face value, it looks legitimate."

For a moment, the two men sat in silence. Then, changing the subject, Brenner asked, "What time are you heading down to the drone base?"

"My plane is leaving Riyadh in two hours."

"And were there any problems of getting you into the Fusion Center during the operation?"

"Danny set everything up," McCallister said. "Are you going to be able to watch from your location?"

"We're working on that," Brenner said. "Did you get those contingencies set up for Brian?"

During their last conversation, Brenner had informed McCallister that Brian Rhome had taken the advisement job and was on his way to Saudi Arabia.

"I've got a SEAL team on standby if anything goes wrong, and I'll give Brian a secure phone when I meet him later today."

McCallister could see how anxious and nervous Brenner was about sending his godson on such a dangerous operation. And quite frankly, McCallister couldn't blame him.

"All right, thank you, Willy. I'll be in contact."

After logging out of the SVTC, McCallister shut his laptop, his mind poring over everything that was happening. And everything that was about to happen.

Turning around in his swivel chair, he examined the framed photograph on the wall behind him. It featured seven men dressed in green combat fatigues in a dense jungle. A silver plaque below the framed photograph displayed a carved inscription that read:

Special Activities Division
Ground Branch
ALPHA TEAM
1991

McCallister beamed at the memory of the picture.

Colombia, at that time, had been like the Wild West. Looking at his younger self, he also took in the faces of a young Jack Brenner and Dan Miller, his senior officers. Miller and Brenner had been McCallister's team leaders back in the day, when they'd operated in denied areas like Serbia, Colombia, Peru, and Nicaragua.

As he continued to gaze at the picture, his eyes settled on the man standing next to Miller, and a familiar sadness swept over him.

David Rhome had always been a complex individual, a man who had succumbed to his demons.

A sharp knock sounded at McCallister's door. He walked across his office and opened it.

Nora Ryder stood in the entryway. Her short blond hair was tied up in a ponytail.

"What can I do for you, Nora?"

Concern lined the thirty-two-year-old operations officer's face. "We need to talk."

McCallister let Ryder into his office, then shut the door.

"It's Apache," Ryder said.

Apache was the code name of one of Nora Ryder's assets. She had flipped the man just over a year ago. Apache was a computer engineer in the Saudi royal court and was also one of Saud Rahmani's infamous flies.

"What happened?"

"He just requested an emergency meeting."

"He's blown?"

"I don't know."

"What did he say?"

"He signaled me for an emergency meet. What do you want me to do?"

"Didn't you have a scheduled meeting with him in a couple of days?"

"Yes, that's why I'm concerned."

McCallister leaned against his desk. Nora Ryder had targeted Apache due to his financial struggles and his close proximity to Saud Rahmani. Recruiting Apache hadn't been difficult. The man's gambling addiction had put him into a crippling hole of debt he was unlikely to get out of. Over the course of a few meetups with Ryder, McCallister's young operations officer had offered to pay the man's debts in exchange for passing information to the Americans. Specifically, Apache was feeding the CIA bits of intelligence on the lengths the royal court would go to keep track of Saudi dissidents who had fled to the West.

"Okay, fine. Meet with him. Use one of our safe houses. Take Dennis O'Hare and his team."

"No, I don't want to spook Apache. Let me go in alone and see what he wants."

McCallister stared at the young operations officer and couldn't help but think of how much she reminded him of his own daughter, Amanda—whip-smart, intense—a go-getter in every sense of the word. Ryder had been in-station for nearly two years, and in that time, she'd recruited four high-value assets from various Saudi ministries.

"Chief?" Ryder asked.

"Fine. Go alone, but I want you taking precautions."

"Copy that," Ryder said, understanding what her boss meant by *precautions*.

"I'm jumping on a plane soon to head down to the southern border, I'll be back this evening, keep me in the loop if anything comes up."

Ryder nodded and left McCallister's office.

Reaching into his pocket, he thumbed another antacid from its foil roll and plopped it into his mouth.

It was going to be a long day.

CHAPTER TWENTY-THREE

RHOME STARED DOWN at the endless sea of sand in every direction and felt the Gulfstream G700's landing gears activate.

Sitting in the leather chair within the jet's luxurious cabin, he glanced over at the flat-screen next to the bar and buckled himself in for landing.

The flat-screen was turned to the news, showing constant replays of the meltdowns of the seven thorium molten salt reactors. The continuous chyron under the images read:

> **Leaked Saudi Intelligence Report Provides Evidence That**
> **Iran Behind Thorium Molten Salt Reactor Explosions**

. It had been seventeen hours since Rhome had left the Bozeman airport, and nearly thirty-two hours since he had retreated from Snake Pit Cliff and called Luca Steiner, confirming that he'd take the job.

Much had happened since then.

After driving his snowcat back to the garages without finishing his shift, Rhome drove straight to his cabin.

The first thing he did when he got there was grab a mirror from his shed and take it back to his bathroom. Under the kerosene lamp's light, he'd proceeded to shave his head and trim his beard to an acceptable length.

Satisfied, Rhome had then taken the kerosene lamp into his bedroom, got down on his hands and knees, and stared at the three Pelican cases sitting under his bed.

The biggest case contained his primary weapon from his old line of work—a well-oiled HK 416D assault rifle.

During his call earlier with Steiner, the Swiss lawyer had told him that the Saudis would be providing Rhome with everything he would need for the al-Raymi campaign—so the weapon would be staying home.

He then grabbed the two other cases and rested them on the mattress.

One of the cases contained his secure laptop and the secure flip phone.

Opening the case, he put the flip phone's battery in, and then texted Jack Brenner that he had accepted the Saudis' job and was heading to the kingdom that evening.

Rhome then took the battery back out, placed the phone back next to the laptop, shut the case, and then shoved it back under the bed.

Standing, he stared down at the remaining Pelican case on the mattress. It hadn't been opened since he'd quit his job and flew back to Montana six months before.

He willed his fingers to unclamp the latches.

Inside sat three items.

The first was a photograph of six smiling bearded men in desert combat fatigues, their weapons pointed skyward. He stared down at the faces of his old team—he saw himself, Smitty, Flynn, Whip, and Hurst. Then his eyes settled on the big man who rested his beefy arm on Rhome's shoulder, and Rhome couldn't stop the sob that escaped his throat.

The bear of a man was Michael "Mack" Mackenzie, the other PMOO in Rhome's team, his mentor, and his best friend.

Holding the photograph in his hand, Rhome then grabbed the second item, a small vial of Mack's ashes, and gazed down at the third item in the case.

Curved Damascus steel and iron stared back at him—dried blood crusted both the hilt and blade. Rhome put down the vial and the photograph, then ran his fingers over the eight-inch axe, stopping over the carved skull and crossbones insignia on the hilt. Under the skull and bones was the inscription that read *Mack*.

Memories of that fateful night in Pakistan came roaring back. Mack's words reverberating in his head as he'd handed Rhome the combat axe before dying in his arms.

Qasim al-Raymi had killed his team.

Killed Mack.

Smitty.

Flynn.

Whip.

And Hurst.

Rhome considered all three items, then decided they'd all accompany him to Yemen.

Grabbing his Glock from its holster, Rhome placed it in the empty Pelican case, then returned it to its spot under the bed near the other two.

Standing, he took a towel from his bathroom, wrapped the axe, and put it into the rucksack he'd be taking with him to the Middle East.

The photograph and vial would stay in his pocket.

After spending the rest of the night packing and cleaning his place, Rhome marched over to Mrs. Jorgensson's cabin at 8:30 a.m., knocked on her door, and asked her if she would like to accompany him into town.

They'd taken Rhome's truck, Matilda panting and slobbering in the back seat, while Rhome drove to the office of his family's old lawyer.

In the attorney's office, Rhome had handed over the two checks written out to him by Steiner & Associates.

Rhome had then detailed that he was handing over power of attorney to Mrs. Jorgensson of the Rhome family trust and estate while he was gone.

He had told the lawyer, "The first check pays off what I owe the bank. I want the second check put into the same account that held my family's trust. If something should happen to me, split up the money and send it to these addresses." Rhome handed over a slip of paper with five addresses on it. After dealing with the lawyer, they'd then driven to the bank and spent an hour finalizing everything.

By that time, it was noon and Rhome drove Matilda and Mrs. Jorgensson home.

Mrs. Jorgensson hadn't said a word since the bank and slammed the passenger door as she exited the vehicle and walked Matilda back to her cabin.

With Steiner's private jet set to arrive in Bozeman at 5:00 p.m., Rhome spent the rest of the afternoon packing, before grabbing his ruck and marching over to Mrs. Jorgensson's.

He found her smoking a cigarette on her front porch, reading a paperback and petting Matilda, who jumped up excitedly as Rhome crested the deck. "I wanted to give you the cabin's keys. If I don't come back, you'll need a way to get inside."

Mrs. Jorgensson took a long drag of her cigarette. "And why wouldn't you come back, Brian?"

"I took a job overseas—like you suggested."

"Mm-hmm," Mrs. Jorgensson said. "You know, I'm not comfortable being executor of the Rhome family trust. Not when Annabelle is alive."

"My sister wants nothing to do with me or the trust," Rhome said. "She's got her own life and family in New York City. She's asked me to respect her privacy."

Rhome's older sister had never approved of their father's line of work. She, like everyone else in the family, saw what it did to him, what it turned him into—a distant, angry, alcoholic patriarch.

When Rhome decided to enter the marines, and then transition into the agency, Annabelle swore him and the rest of their family out of her life forever.

After a moment, Mrs. Jorgensson opened her palm. "Fine, give them to me."

Rhome handed the keys over to the woman, then gave Matilda a big hug before walking to his truck.

As he reached the door, Mrs. Jorgensson shouted, "What time is your flight?"

"Five."

"Well, the least I can do is drive you. It's been a damn long time since I've seen Boz-Angeles. I guess they have a Whole Foods now."

Two hours later, Rhome boarded a Gulfstream G700.

The two pilots, who spoke with thick Arabic accents, told him to make himself comfortable and that their flight to Saudi Arabia shouldn't be more than seventeen hours long.

Now, after sleeping the majority of the flight, Rhome continued to

look out of the window at the vast, endless desert as the plane made its
final descent.

Five minutes later, the G700 touched down, and then taxied before
coming to a stop.

Rhome picked up his ruck, thanked the pilots, and stepped off the
plane and into the oppressive desert heat.

In front of him was a small military base, comprising two barracks
and a windowless, single-story building, its roof dominated by satellite
dishes and high-reaching antennas.

A good quarter mile behind the base was a massive wooden structure,
most likely the rendition of the palace where al-Raymi's brother was
going to be married.

One thing that struck Rhome was that the base was teeming with
Saudi Royal Guard soldiers.

Unsure where to go, Rhome looked to his left and saw two clamshell
hangars a hundred yards away. These hangars, he knew, were usually
used to house Predator or Reaper drones.

In front of the hangars were three C-130s, a collection of Gulfstream
jets, and a Boeing 747.

"Mr. Rhome?"

Rhome turned his attention to an approaching Royal Guardsman.

"You are the last to arrive," the man said in Arabic. "This way, please."

Ruck over his shoulder, Rhome followed the man toward the door of
the small concrete building.

As Rhome walked, he glanced to his right and noticed a beaten-down
white Toyota van parked next to the barracks.

Among the hundreds of Saudi soldiers milling around, not only did
the decrepit van stick out like a sore thumb, but so did the five men
who sat in the shade before it. Each man wore a headdress, an oversized
cotton shirt, and baggy pants and had a sheathed *jambiya*—a ceremonial dagger—fastened to their belts. Having operated extensively in this
region over the last few years, Rhome wondered what a group of indig-
enous Yemeni tribesmen was doing at a Saudi drone base.

An electronic buzz sounded as his escort opened the door to the
concrete building and led Rhome inside and then down a flight of metal
grated stairs.

After descending three floors, the man opened a door, and together they marched down a short hallway, before stopping at another door, guarded by two more Saudi Royal Guards.

"You will have to leave your bag here, sir," one of the guards said.

Rhome handed his ruck to the man, who then ushered Rhome inside.

The nine people sitting around a rectangular table in the cramped room turned as he entered.

"Good, you're here," the man closest to him said in an American accent.

The man stood and ran his fingers through his walrus mustache. "I'm—"

"William McCallister," Rhome finished for him. "I know who you are."

McCallister gave Rhome a grin, then motioned to the empty chair to his left. "Take a seat Brian, we are just about to begin."

CHAPTER TWENTY-FOUR

RHOME PULLED OUT a chair next to William McCallister and sat down before the CIA station chief passed a series of folders to the men at the table.

Taking everyone in, Rhome immediately recognized the person sitting at the head of the table as Prince Khalid bin Zaman, the crown prince's younger brother.

He'd seen the young prince's face on the news during his flight from Montana. The news had said that Khalid had recently been stripped of his role as Saudi Arabia's ambassador to the United States and had been appointed the kingdom's deputy minister of defense.

Khalid stared down at the table, looking withdrawn and distant.

The only other person that Rhome recognized in the room was Major General Ahmad Azimi.

Azimi had been in charge of the Saudi coalition in Yemen while Rhome and his team had operated in the country two years before. From what Rhome had heard over the grapevine, Azimi now headed the kingdom's intelligence agency.

The whole room was looking at Khalid to start the meeting, but the young prince didn't seem to have noticed.

"Your Highness, would you like to begin?" Azimi said.

"Huh?" Khalid said, looking up. "No, General, you can do the briefing."

Azimi nodded, then opened the folder on the table in front of him and indicated for everyone else to do the same.

"Gentlemen," Azimi said in accented English. "First, I would like to thank you all for taking this job on such short notice. And I apologize that some of you have not been briefed as to the nature of why you are here."

Rhome continued to glance around the room and took in the two men in Saudi military garb sitting next to Khalid. From the insignias on their uniforms, it looked like one of them was a brigadier general and the other a brigadier colonel in the RSLF—the Royal Saudi Land Force—basically the Saudis' version of their army.

But Azimi wasn't looking at these two men when he spoke; instead he directed his attention to Rhome and the four men sitting across from him.

Sun-weathered, tattooed, bearded, and with hardened physiques, three of the four men were obvious Westerners—seasoned Special Forces types.

If Rhome were to guess, he'd pin them as British or Australian.

But the fourth man was different.

Unlike the other three, he was skinny, built like an endurance athlete. His hair and manicured beard were jet black. The skin on his face was taut, like it had been pulled back over his sharp nose and cheekbones.

The man caught his gaze—and Rhome nearly winced as he recognized something in his dark eyes.

He'd seen eyes like that before.

They were battle hardened.

Eyes of a hunter—a killer—a man who needed to be watched.

"In front of each of you," Azimi said, "are the details of the campaign you have signed onto. You may open these documents now."

Rhome gazed down at the folder in front of him. He opened the first page, and saw the same black-and-white photograph of Qasim al-Raymi that Luca Steiner had showed him in the Miller Château a few nights before.

"Two months ago," Azimi said, "Qasim al-Raymi returned to his home country of Yemen and has since been named the emir of Al-Qaeda

Arabian Peninsula. Since his arrival in his homeland, al-Raymi has pledged a renewed vigor of jihad against the West and its allies, especially Saudi Arabia and our crown prince. We view his return to Yemen and his promise of bloody jihad as a direct threat to our kingdom's well-being, and we have done everything in our power to track him down."

Azimi pointed a remote at the large TV behind Khalid. The screen powered on, showing an aerial photograph of a mountain range. "Through thousands of communications we have intercepted from known al-Qaeda members in the last month, we can confirm with a high degree of certainty that Qasim al-Raymi will be attending his brother's wedding at the Ar Risan Palace northeast of the Yemeni town of Bayhan in two nights' time."

Azimi clicked the remote, and the screen displayed a zoomed-in aerial image of a palace sitting at the base of two mountains.

"Four weeks ago, the crown prince ordered that a Saudi Special Operations Force be built with the help of the CIA to kill or capture Qasim al-Raymi," Azimi said, acknowledging McCallister. "Under the command of Brigadier General al-Hassad, and Brigadier Colonel al-Malki, a rendition of the Ar Risan Palace has been built here at this drone base, and for the last three weeks, a group of twenty-two Saudi Special Operations soldiers have been training on the rendition for the raid that will take place on the night of March seventh." Azimi paused. "You, gentlemen, have been hired to oversee the final stages of the preparation as well as participate in the raid itself."

For a moment, no one said anything, then the largest of the four advisers sitting across from Rhome spoke up.

"Hold on," the man said, in a thick Australian accent. "Are you telling me that we have two days to train your men to kill Qasim al-Raymi? Are you nuts?"

"Not train, Mr. Rish," Azimi said. "Our men are already trained. The crown prince has hired each of you to guarantee the success of the raid."

If Rhome hadn't already known the details of the campaign beforehand, he would have been just as taken aback as the man Azimi called Mr. Rish.

"Each of you has already been paid handsomely for blindly accepting this job," Azimi said. "And if the mission is a success, if you are able to kill Qasim al-Raymi, the crown prince will pay each of you half a million dollars—plus the opportunity to work for us in the future."

"Doesn't sound so bad when he says it like that, huh, Rishy?" the blond-haired, blue-eyed operator sitting next to Rish said, also with an Aussie accent.

"Brigadier General al-Hassad," Azimi said, pointing to the older RSLF officer sitting next to Prince Khalid. "Would you like to brief the advisers on how your Special Operations Force plans on carrying out the raid?"

Al-Hassad stood from his chair, grabbed the remote from Azimi, and said, "Yahya Mahdi al-Raymi's wedding is expected to begin at 8:00 p.m., on the night of March seventh. The signals intelligence we have intercepted from Qasim al-Raymi's lieutenants indicate that al-Raymi is to arrive fifteen minutes before the wedding is to begin. We estimate that he will bring between thirty and forty bodyguards. We also estimate that no less than sixty military-aged males will be in attendance, meaning there is potential of ninety to one hundred armed men at the wedding."

Al-Hassad changed the image on the screen, widening it out to show the mountainous landscape of the region in which the Ar Risan Palace sat. "Tomorrow morning, one of you will go with Mr. Shurrab and a group of Saudi-paid Yemeni tribesmen and enter Yemen to provide us a pattern-of-life analysis at the palace before the raid."

The brigadier general pointed to the man with the taut face and dark eyes. "Mr. Shurrab is an experienced sniper in the Emirati army and has extensive experience operating in Yemen. Whoever chooses to accompany Mr. Shurrab will also act as a spotter during the raid as he provides cover fire for the assault team. Would anybody like to volunteer now for this job?"

Rhome immediately raised his hand.

"Very well, Mr. Rhome," al-Hassad said.

Rhome had no intention of joining the Saudi assault force on their raid of the palace. Being in a sniper perch with Shurrab before and during the raid would "free him up," giving him mobility should an opportunity arise to engage al-Raymi.

Al-Hassad then went on to explain that three C-130s were going to land thirty miles north of the Ar Risan Palace in the middle of the desert twenty minutes before the wedding. Inside one of the C-130s would be fifteen Saudi assaulters, including three of the Western advisers, as well as seven enablers—ranging from dog handlers, JTAC operators, and radiomen—twenty-five operators in total.

The two other C-130s would carry the necessary fuel, Saudi security forces, and vehicles needed for the mission and its support.

"We will use three armored trucks to transport the assaulters from the C-130s in the desert to the palace walls to begin our assault," al-Hassad said.

"That's not a good idea, General."

Al-Hassad looked at Rhome, and for the first time since he'd been in the room, Prince Khalid's face perked up.

"And why is that not a good idea, Mr. Rhome?" asked Prince Khalid.

"Speaking from experience," Rhome said, "armored trucks will be too bulky and slow. You are going to want speed and precision. I would suggest using at least eight Toyota Hiluxes; they're fast and tough as shit. You've got twenty-five assaulters participating in the raid; that means you can put three guys per vehicle; the empty seats can be used for Mr. Shurrab and myself, or for contingencies, should we need to carry back any prisoners or any wounded."

General al-Hassad's face turned red. "Toyota Hiluxes are not bullet-proof. My men have trained in those armored vehicles for the last three weeks—"

Rhome opened his hands. "I was hired to give my two cents, General."

"We'll consider it, thank you, Mr. Rhome," Azimi said.

Over the next hour, it became pretty clear that the Saudis did not want the advisers to advise; they wanted specialists on the ground pulling triggers so the Saudis could take all the credit.

After explaining that a Reaper drone would be providing live aerial footage of the assault, and that COS McCallister would be in the Fusion Center in the Al-Qirawan Military Base in Riyadh for the duration of the raid, General Azimi had then told the group that there was an armory below the barracks next door that held any weapon or equipment imaginable for the campaign.

At the end of the briefing, Brigadier General al-Hassad took everyone outside and to a caravan of jeeps that drove them up to the rendition of the Ar Risan Palace, where they watched the Saudi operators run a mock assault.

When the assault finished, one of the Western advisers came up to Rhome and introduced himself as Billy Baker, then asked, "You former SEAL or Delta?"

"Marine," Rhome replied.

"Former Special Air Service," Baker said, pointing at himself. Then the SAS man indicated the two Aussie advisers behind him. "These two are Matt Rish and Seth Proctor, former Australian special forces."

Each man shook Rhome's hand, and Rishy lowered his voice. "We're going to have our work cut out for us, here, mates. There was some shit muzzle discipline going on."

"Well, we got two days to fix that, Rishy," Baker said.

"And then a fat paycheck," replied Proctor.

As the group talked, Rhome's attention went to Azimi and Khalid, who were speaking to COS McCallister and the brigadier general and the brigadier colonel near the palace rendition.

Off to the side, smoking a cigarette was the skinny man with the dark eyes, who the brigadier general called Mr. Shurrab.

"Any of you know that guy's deal?" Rhome asked.

Baker and the Aussies gazed at the man, then Baker said, "His name's Kazem Shurrab, guess he is a crack sniper—I doubt he's actually Emirati army—probably SIA."

Rhome knew that SIA stood for Signals Intelligence Agency—the Emirates' version of the CIA.

A few minutes later, the group piled back into the caravan and drove back down to the base. Al-Hassad and al-Malki had Rhome and Shurrab meet with the five Yemeni tribesmen and then spent the afternoon going over the route they would take the next morning into Yemen.

After their meeting, Rhome felt a hand on his shoulder. "Brian, can I speak with you for a minute?"

COS McCallister motioned for Rhome to follow him behind the barracks. When they were out of view and earshot of anyone, McCallister pulled a flip phone from his pocket.

"I spoke with Jack earlier today; he wanted me to give you this."

Rhome grabbed the phone.

McCallister dropped his voice. "If for any reason you need an emergency extraction—I've set up an assisted recovery for you. This phone is completely secure and links straight to me. Give me a ring, and I'll get a team to pull you out."

Rhome thanked the man, and then McCallister held his gaze a long time. "Brian, Jack told me what al-Raymi did to your men in Pakistan. I'm truly sorry."

Rhome nodded.

McCallister said, "I have to get back to Riyadh. Don't hesitate to call me if you need anything."

Rhome watched as McCallister walked toward the jets parked in front of the clamshell hangars.

Pocketing the flip phone, he marched to the armory, so he could get his gear ready. Later he would go to the shooting range and dial everything in.

In just over twelve hours, he would join Kazem Shurrab, and the five Yemenis and together they would head south into Yemen. Into a raging proxy war between Saudi Arabia and Iran. A hornet's nest of rival factions, of terrorist organizations—all fighting for control.

He would need to be on his game.

CHAPTER TWENTY-FIVE

CIA OPERATIONS OFFICER Nora Ryder stepped into the black *abaya,* then placed the *niqab* over her head, making sure she could see properly out of the narrow slit over her green eyes; then she stared at her reflection in the mirror. The women's bathroom in the CIA's Riyadh Station within the United States Embassy gave her the privacy she desired when donning the fundamentalist Muslim attire, but it did little to settle her nerves.

Operating under the veil of the *niqab* in the streets of Riyadh had always been a moral hurdle for Ryder. Though the laws were relaxing under the rule of the reformist Saudi crown prince, the Minnesota native despised the fact that it was mostly compulsory for women in this part of the world to wear some sort of headdress or veil in public. Whether it was the fundamentalist burka, or the *niqab*—or even the more liberal *chador*, or *hijab*, Ryder believed forcing women to cover themselves in public was demeaning and degrading. On the other hand, it was a blessing, given her role as a spy.

It allowed the thirty-two-year-old American camouflage in a culture that forced women to exist unseen and unheard.

Making sure the well-concealed slit tailored into the right side of the *abaya* was fitted over a spot where her pistol sat in its holster on her beltline, Ryder left the bathroom, then went down the stairs and into the underground garage to the idling SUV that would take her into the city.

"We're still a go?" Ryder asked the male CIA officer behind the wheel.

"Just got the green light."

They drove from the underground garage, past the two armed security checkpoints out of the US Embassy compound, and onto the dark streets of Riyadh.

It had been thirteen hours since Ryder received the emergency message her asset in the royal court had sent her. The CIA safe house she had designated for the meeting had gone through surveillance for the last eight hours and had been deemed clear.

Ryder tried to relax as the driver began his hour-long SDR, or surveillance detection route. They had a team of four vehicles out on the streets trailing, overlapping, and spotting Ryder's SUV for any signs of "coverage" or traces of a tail.

As they drove their circuitous pattern through the city, Ryder tried to figure out why her asset, code name Apache, would call for an emergency meeting with his handler, especially when they were scheduled to meet later in the week.

"We're almost there," the driver said.

Ryder peered through the windshield, seeing the lighted Al Nakheel shopping mall in the distance. The SUV drove into the vast parking lot under the mall and dropped Ryder off at an elevator. Taking the elevator up to the crowded shopping center, Ryder spent the next thirty minutes walking through the various shops and food courts running her own SDR.

When she was satisfied she had no tail, she made her way back into the underground garage and walked to a silver Range Rover sitting in a predetermined parking spot left there by the agency.

Taking a set of keys from within her *abaya*, she climbed inside and drove away. It had barely been a year since Saudi Arabia's Council of Ministers approved a royal decree put forth by the crown prince to loosen the *Wilayah*, or guardianship laws on women. Before the decree, women by law needed the permission or accompaniment of a close male relative in matters of work, leisure, finances, law, and health. Now, women in the kingdom were allowed unprecedented mobility—especially since the crown prince had also just recently lifted the women's restriction on driving—something Nora Ryder was taking full advantage of tonight.

The usual five-minute drive to the safe house took her twenty-five minutes as she performed one last SDR and was satisfied, yet again, that she had no tail.

She parked the Range Rover two streets over from her destination and walked to the residential building and up to the third floor.

Unlocking the door to apartment 301, she turned on the lights and moved over to the window to peer through the blinds at the street below.

Sensing no threat, she took off her *niqab*, made sure her pistol was hidden under the *abaya*, then sat down on the couch in the living room, and waited.

The knock came twelve minutes later. A series of patterned raps on the door, indicating it was Apache and that he hadn't been followed.

Ryder opened the door cautiously.

Apache blew into the apartment.

"Please," he said, in accented English, moving by Ryder, "I can't stay long."

"Abdulmalik, what's going on?" Ryder said, shutting and locking the door.

Abdulmalik Hassen went straight to the blinds, cracked them, and peered out to the street below. Then he faced Ryder. "I'm in trouble!"

"What do you mean?"

"They know about us—they know *everything!*"

"Who— What are you talking about?" Ryder asked, alarmed.

"Someone entered my car while I was leaving my apartment on the way to work this morning. It was a man, dressed in a burka. He held me at gunpoint. He knew I was spying for the CIA!"

Ryder's hand went instinctually to her Glock as she hurried to the window. "You were followed?"

"No!" said Hassen. "At least I don't think so."

Ryder cracked the blinds. "What did this man want from you?"

Hassen took a black *agal* and a small object from his *thobe* and handed it to Ryder. "He wanted me to give you these. He said if I didn't give them to you, he'd kill my family!"

Ryder stared down at the *agal*, wondering why someone would want to give a Muslim man's fashion accessory to the CIA. Her attention then went to the small object in her other hand.

It was the size of a matchbox and was wrapped in a piece of paper held together tightly by a rubber band. "And what is this?"

"It's a flash drive, containing the files I stole from Saud Rahmani's computer."

"You stole files from Saud Rahmani's computer . . . why?"

Hassen started pacing frantically.

Ryder grabbed him by the arm. "Abdulmalik, breathe."

The man took a series of staccato breaths.

"Okay," Ryder said. "Now tell me what is going on."

"You know that Saudi revolutionary forum I told you about? The one that Saud Rahmani told me to investigate?"

"Yes," Ryder said, remembering a few months back, when Hassen had told her that he'd been instructed by his boss to find a dark web forum of individuals speaking ill of the crown prince.

"Well, I found the forum. And . . . and then I started participating in it."

Ryder let go of the man's arm.

Hassen continued, "I met someone on the forum, a woman who calls herself Scheherazade. We developed a friendship. After a couple of months, I informed her that I was a fly working under Saud Rahmani in the royal court. We spoke openly over the forum and one day I told her of a rumor I'd heard at work, about a Saudi dissident living in America. Over the last couple of weeks, she convinced me to obtain the evidence of that rumor. So a few nights ago, I snuck into Saud Rahmani's office and stole some files from his work computer. I don't know what I was thinking! I found the evidence to confirm the rumor, but I also took another file—something called Dark Sun!"

"Abdulmalik, slow down!" Ryder said, trying to take it all in.

Her asset wasn't listening. "Saud Rahmani called me into work earlier today. That's when the man in the burka stopped me on the street and got into my car. He said Saud Rahmani knew everything—that I was a CIA informant, that I stole the files. He said I was going to be arrested and killed if I showed up to work."

Hassen then explained what the man in the burka had told him to do. How he'd given Hassen the *agal*, how he told him to hand over the files on the flash drive to his handler.

"That's it," Ryder said. "You're blown. We're taking you in, giving you protection."

"No!" said Hassen. "Not without my family. I need to get to them and go into hiding."

"We can protect your family—"

Suddenly, a revving engine and the squeal of tires sounded from outside.

Hassen blew by Ryder and went to the window, cracking the shades.

Letting out a small cry, he backed away from the window like it was on fire, and then ran for the door.

"Wait!" Ryder hissed, chasing after him.

"No!" Hassen replied, still heading for the door. "I've sent my family out of the city. I need to get to them!"

Opening the apartment door, Hassen spun around and pointed to the flash drive wrapped in paper in Ryder's hand. "I wrote the password to the flash drive on that paper. I will contact you when I get to my family!"

Before Ryder could grab her asset, he sprinted down the hallway.

For a moment, Ryder stood there, stunned. Then snapping back to her senses, she pocketed the flash drive and the *agal* and hurried to the window.

The street below lay quiet and deserted.

Ryder threw on her *niqab* and then took out her pistol.

If what Hassen had told her was true, she needed to get back to the embassy as fast as possible.

Ryder exited the safe house with her pistol in her hand, her head on a swivel, and her senses primed to any kind of threat.

CHAPTER TWENTY-SIX

Riyadh, Saudi Arabia
Shumaisi District
March 6, 1:30 a.m.

ABDULMALIK HASSEN GOT out of his taxi three blocks from his destination and gazed up and down the dark street, looking for any signs of a tail. Confident there was none, he started fast-walking to his brother's apartment building.

His brother—a well-to-do businessman who was rarely in town—had given Hassen a key to his apartment a year before. Due to the apartment's close proximity to his royal court office in Al Safarat, Riyadh's Diplomatic Quarter, Hassen was allowed to crash there when Saud Rahmani made him work late nights and when he didn't want to drive the forty-five minutes to his home in An Nahdah.

Wiping at the sweat that poured down his face, Hassen hurried down the sidewalk, his mind racing over the events of the last day.

After his run-in with the man in the burka that morning, Hassen had dumped his laptop and sped home. He'd run into his own apartment, woken up his wife and son, packed some bare essentials, then hurried them down to his car.

"Abdulmalik, what is going on?!" Munira had shouted, as Hassen strapped Rafi into the back seat, and stuffed their suitcases into the trunk.

"My love, give me your phone," Hassen had said, wrestling the phone from her grip. "Take the car and drive to Sajir."

"To Sajir?!" Munira asked, startled, wondering why she had to travel to the small village in the middle of the desert. "Are we in trouble? You're not gambling again, are you Abdulmalik?!"

"No, no!" Hassen replied. "Please, Munira. Something is going on at work and I need you and Rafi out of the city."

"What are you saying? Are we in danger? Why can't I take my phone?!"

"I will explain everything tomorrow when I meet you in Sajir."

"And why can't you come with us? Tell me what is going on, Abdulmalik?!"

At this point, Hassen had shoved a wad of Saudi riyals into Munira's hands. Opening the car door, he kissed her on the cheek, said goodbye to Rafi, who was crying in the back seat, and saw them off.

As their car disappeared down the street, Hassen ran back upstairs to their apartment with Munira's phone and left it on the bedside table.

Hassen then ripped the flash drive he'd duct-taped from under the bathroom sink; hurrying to the kitchen table, he grabbed Munira's laptop, powered it on, then stuck the flash drive into the computer. He copied the flash drive's contents, dragging them onto the laptop's desktop, then went about finding a second flash drive he knew he had somewhere in a drawer in his kitchen.

Eventually finding a second flash drive, and with the files he'd stolen from Saud Rahmani still on Munira's desktop, Hassen ejected the original flash drive, stuck in the second, and transferred the files onto it.

Ejecting the second flash drive, Hassen made sure there was no evidence of a file transfer on Munira's computer, then slapped her laptop shut.

Holding the original flash drive and the duplicate, both containing the stolen files, Hassen stood in his kitchen, trembling.

When he finally left his apartment, he took a cab to an internet café in the heart of Riyadh.

In the café, he logged onto an Instagram account and searched for a popular page dedicated to cats; scrolling until he found the particular picture he'd need to alert his handler, he liked the image.

An hour later, a coded message with an address and a time from a dummy account arrived in his direct messages.

The meeting set for later that night, Hassen had decided to pay cash for a room in a crappy hotel and not draw attention to himself before he could pass the *agal* and one of the two flash drives to his handler.

Now, after his meeting with Ryder, Hassen turned onto his brother's street, dipped into the alley, and used his key to enter through the building's back entrance. He huffed it up the five flights of stairs to his brother's apartment.

Since leaving his handler he decided that he was not going to meet his family in Sajir until the next day.

Opening the fifth-floor stairwell door, Hassen walked down the dimly lit hallway until he got to his brother's apartment.

Moving aside the duplicate flash drive in the pocket of his *thobe*, Hassen dug out his keys and opened the door.

Overheated and parched, he strode into the apartment, flicked on the hallway lights, and walked toward the kitchen. His mind was so consumed with quenching his thirst that he hadn't noticed the figure sitting on his brother's couch in the shadows of the living room.

It wasn't until he turned into the kitchen and had the barrel of a suppressed pistol shoved into his face that he realized he was not alone.

Hassen let out a sharp yell as a tall bearded man wearing all black took a step toward him.

Backpedaling away from the raised weapon, Hassen tripped over his *thobe* and landed on his ass in the hallway.

"Abdulmalik," a familiar voice said from the living room. "So glad you could join us."

Hassen's attention shot to his right as Saud Rahmani's squat figure rose from the couch.

The man dressed in black kept his pistol trained on Hassen, and Hassen let out a small cry as he recognized the man as Turki Shahidi, the crown prince's ruthless enforcer.

Shahidi bent down and dragged Hassen into the living room, before tossing him onto the couch.

Rahmani stood on the other side of the coffee table, his yellow teeth exposed in a Cheshire grin. Shahidi stood to his left, his pistol aimed at Hassen.

"I missed you at work today, Abdulmalik," Rahmani said.

"I . . . I wasn't feeling well," Hassen stammered. "Must have caught a cold from my son."

"Ah, yes," Rahmani said. "Little Rafi, how is he doing?"

"He— He's fine."

"That's very good to hear," Rahmani said, before walking over to the kitchen. Hassen watched over the bar top that separated the kitchen from the living room as his boss opened the freezer and took out a clear glass bottle and returned to the living room.

"That's . . . that's not mine!" Hassen said, eyeing the bottle of vodka that his brother kept hidden.

"Don't worry, Abu Rafi. I know it's not yours."

Hassen winced at the way Rahmani addressed him. *Abu Rafi* meant *father of Rafi*. It was supposed to be an affectionate way for men in his culture to greet each other, but Hassen knew that Rahmani was using it in a sinister way to remind him of his son.

Rahmani unscrewed the lid and took a large gulp, then held the bottle out for Hassen.

Hassen shook his head.

It was well known at work that Rahmani was an alcoholic and a drug user.

Though it was *haram*, or forbidden to indulge in the kingdom, many knew that Rahmani had an Adderall prescription and there were rumors that he even supplied the amphetamines to the crown prince and his inner circle.

"Take a sip, Abu Rafi," Rahmani said.

Hassen reluctantly grabbed the bottle from his boss's hand, and took a small sip, gagging as the firewater seared his throat and settled into his stomach.

Both Rahmani and Shahidi laughed, and then Rahmani snatched the bottle back and took another sip, before saying, "So, Abu Rafi. Why weren't you *really* at work today?"

"I told you I was sick—"

The speed and ferocity with which the butt of Shahidi's pistol collided with the bridge of Hassen's nose was mind-boggling.

His nose spurting like a fire hose, Hassen pitched forward onto the coffee table and shrieked.

"What a mess!" Rahmani said. "Let me get you something for that."

Rahmani left the room and came back a moment later with a towel from the bathroom and threw it to Hassen. "Every time you lie to us, Abu Rafi, the beatings are going to get worse. Most of your brother's neighbors are gone—so nobody is going to hear you scream. Now, I'm going to ask you again, why didn't you come to work today?"

Hassen, wheezing underneath the bloodied towel, said, "I . . . I was told not to!"

"Really?" Rahmani said, taking another swig of vodka. "And *who* told you not to go to work today?"

"I don't—"

Shahidi moved forward, but Hassen screamed, "It was a man wearing a burka!"

Hassen explained how his vehicle had been boxed in on his way to Al Safarat that morning. How a large man with a deep, commanding voice wearing the fundamentalist veil had entered his vehicle, aimed a pistol at his head, and told him he'd be arrested if he went to work.

When he finished, he saw Shahidi and Rahmani exchange a concerned look.

"This man," Shahidi said, his voice also a deep rumble. "Was his voice deeper than mine?"

"Yes."

Shahidi looked at Rahmani, who said, "What else did this man say?"

"He said I would be killed, that you would kill me if I went to work . . ."

Rahmani feigned confusion. "And why do you think I would do that, Abu Rafi?"

"I . . . I don't know."

Rahmani shook his head. "Wrong answer."

For the second time that night, Shahidi moved at blinding speed. He jumped on the couch and pinned Hassen down. Handing the suppressed pistol to Rahmani, he reached in his pocket and procured a pair of pliers.

Screaming in protest, Hassen squirmed under the big man, his arms flailing. Shahidi pinned down Hassen's left arm using his right knee, and then grabbing Hassen's right hand, he found his index finger and, using the pliers, ripped his nail clean off.

"Actual fingers and toes will be next!" yelled Rahmani over Hassen's wails.

Shahidi got off him and grabbed his pistol from Rahmani.

Hassen clutched his right index finger and sobbed.

"Now," Rahmani said. "I'll make this a little easier on you. Last night we discovered that you snuck into my office three days ago. We know about the files you copied from my computer, and the flash drive you smuggled out of the royal court building. We know all about your correspondence over the dark web forum with Scheherazade . . . we know who you are . . . Qutrub."

A small croak escaped Hassen's mouth. The ruse was up.

Creeping closer to Hassen, Rahmani whispered, "Now, I am only going to ask this of you once, Abu Rafi. What did the man in the burka ask you to do with the flash drive you smuggled out of the Royal Court?"

Hassen's mind spun.

How did he know the man in the burka told me to do something with the flash drive?

"He . . . he told me to give it to my CIA handler!"

Rahmani, seemingly pleased with this answer, said, "And did you? Did you give the flash drive to your handler?"

Hassen shook his head as convincingly as he could.

This was the part where he needed to lie—now fully understanding why the man in the burka had told him to make a duplicate—it could save his life, save Munira's and Rafi's.

"No," Hassen sputtered. "I made contact with my handler, but they couldn't meet until tomorrow."

Rahmani studied Hassen's bloody, tear-soaked face. "And where is the flash drive now?"

"I . . . I have it!"

Fumbling with his *thobe*, Hassen dug out the duplicate flash drive, handing it to Rahmani.

The man brought the flash drive over to the kitchen counter, where a laptop Hassen had never seen before sat.

Inserting the flash drive into the laptop, Rahmani said, "There is a password. What is it?"

Hassen gave him the twelve-digit password, and for the next few minutes, Rahmani quietly went through the contents of the flash drive.

Obviously satisfied, the man shut the laptop, pocketed the flash drive, and walked back over to Hassen.

"So," Rahmani said. "We can sit here for the rest of the night, and you can tell us why you betrayed the kingdom. Or I can tell you *how* we caught your little friend Scheherazade. But that would be a waste of our time. What I really want to know is if you read the files you stole from me."

Hassen shook his head. "Only the information in the RIG file concerning the Saudi dissident!"

"The dissident journalist in America?"

"Yes. The information Scheherazade wanted confirmed."

"And the other file? Did you read about Dark Sun?"

"No! The Dark Sun file was encrypted."

"Then why did you steal it in the first place?" Rahmani asked.

Hassen gulped. "While I was on your computer, I saw in the RIG file that the Saudi dissident was going to publish something about Dark Sun before the signing of the accord. I saw that the crown prince ordered him to be silenced. I was just curious—"

"So you stole it."

"I panicked! I never meant to take it. I don't know why I did it," Hassen said, more tears spilling down his bloody face.

"I believe you," Rahmani said, squatting down in front of Hassen. "But you still read the RIG file. You know what we have planned for the dissident. You know about the existence of Dark Sun."

"Please—I don't know anything. I won't speak about it to anyone—"

"Abu Rafi, I can't take that risk."

"I swear!" Hassen pleaded. "You must believe me. I'll . . . I'll give you the identity of my handler. She's young. Green eyes. Blond hair. She goes by the name of Sloan!"

"Sloan?"

"Yes!"

"Thank you for that information, Abdulmalik," Rahmani said, with a sincere voice. "We will look into your handler. Is there anything else you would like to say before we finish up here?"

"What?!" Hassen said, his eyes darting from Rahmani to Shahidi's weapon that was still trained on his head. "No—please, you must spare my life, I won't say anything—"

But Abdulmalik Hassen never finished his sentence, because two rapidly occurring plumes of light ejected from Shahidi's suppressed pistol, sending Hassen to the afterlife.

CHAPTER TWENTY-SEVEN

CHIEF OF STATION William McCallister stared down at his laptop sitting on his desk, the flash drive Nora Ryder had just handed to him inserted into the laptop's port.

In his hands was the small piece of paper that had been wrapped around the flash drive with a rubber band.

His attention going from the laptop to the note, McCallister noted Ryder, who paced before his desk.

"The flash drive has a twelve-character alphanumeric password," McCallister said, holding up the piece of paper. "This paper only has six readable characters on it; the last six digits are smudged and indiscernible."

Ryder grabbed the paper. "Shit, Apache had it in his *thobe*, his sweat must have bled into the ink."

Ryder had called McCallister an hour before on a secure emergency line, waking him in his home. Her voice had been frantic, telling him that he needed to meet her immediately at the station.

He'd arrived forty minutes later and found his operations officer waiting in front of his office.

Once inside, she'd told him everything that had transpired earlier in the night with Apache, then handed him the black *agal* and the flash drive.

"The files on the flash drive, did Apache tell you what they contained?" McCallister asked, concerned by what he'd heard.

"He said one of the files held evidence of a rumor about a Saudi dissident living in America, but I don't know what that means and he never elaborated."

McCallister felt himself stiffen, and he immediately thought of Jack Brenner and Dan Miller and the operation they were running stateside. "And the other file?"

"Something called Dark Sun."

"Dark Sun?"

"Again, Apache didn't elaborate," Ryder said. "He said that the man in the burka had told him to give the flash drive and the *agal* to me."

What the hell is going on? McCallister thought, his attention shifting to the *agal* sitting on his desk.

Picking it up, he scrutinized the black rope. "Why would the man in the burka want to give you an *agal*?"

"I have no idea."

Studying the *agal*, McCallister twisted it in his hands, and then suddenly he heard a faint cracking noise from within. "Nora, get me some latex gloves and a pair of scissors."

Ryder darted out of the room and returned with the items thirty seconds later. McCallister donned the gloves, then used the scissors to carefully cut at the fabric.

As the black nylon peeled away, McCallister glimpsed something white embedded within the rope.

Cutting down the length of the *agal*, he realized that the cracking noise was from a piece of paper that had been rolled up and sewed inside.

Digging the paper out, McCallister unrolled it, and recoiled when he saw that it was a typed-up letter addressed to him.

"What does it say?" Ryder said, walking around the desk.

McCallister had just read the first few lines, then shouted, "Nora, stop! Stand over there!"

Unsettled by his outburst, Ryder froze, then took a few steps back.

McCallister looked back down at the letter and continued to read.

When he finished, he stared blankly at the paper.

"Chief?" Ryder said. "What does it say?"

A growing sense of panic and urgency started to bubble in McCallister's stomach, and he thought, *Jack and Danny need to be alerted about this immediately!*

"Chief?" Ryder repeated, trying to grab the letter from his grasp, but McCallister was too quick for her. He folded the letter and stuffed it into his pocket.

"Nora, I need you to step out."

Ryder looked at him, stunned.

"Now!"

When Ryder finally backed out of the room, McCallister drew the shades to his office's windows, then went back to his desk, where he pulled out his secure laptop and powered on the SVTC.

Checking his watch, he saw that it was close to 7 p.m. in Maryland. *Jack and Danny should be there by now.*

Dialing Brenner on the SVTC, McCallister waited nearly thirty painstaking seconds before Jack Brenner's face appeared on the screen.

"Jack, something big just happened, get everyone in on this call."

McCallister watched Brenner say something to someone off-screen, and within ten seconds, Dan Miller and six other faces appeared behind Brenner.

McCallister then took out the letter and explained everything that Ryder had just detailed for him in his office. Holding up the letter, he said, "You're going to want to record what I'm about to read to you."

McCallister waited until Brenner started recording the SVTC, then read the letter aloud.

Stunned silence filled the screen when he finished, then Miller said, "Have you accessed the flash drive yet?"

"No," McCallister said, then explained that the last six characters of the twelve-digit alphanumeric passcode Apache had written out had been smudged. "I'm going to do everything in my power to find Apache so we can get the remaining six digits."

"You said he skipped town, though, right?" Brenner asked. "You have no idea where he could be?"

"No idea."

"Then let's *not* focus on him," Brenner said. "We have computers that can crack that passcode here. Give us the first six digits, then we need that flash drive brought to us immediately."

McCallister read off the six digits on the smudged paper, then said, "I can get the flash drive out on a diplomatic flight today. We'll put the letter and the flash drive in the pouch and have a diplomatic courier bring it to DC—"

"No," Miller said. "We can't take that risk."

"What do you mean?"

"Your officer's asset is blown. He's gone underground. If what this letter says is true, I don't want a paper trail of any diplomatic pouches leaving the Saudi kingdom to the United States. We get this flash drive out of the kingdom by other means."

McCallister said, "Danny, it's against international law to open or even x-ray another country's diplomatic pouch, the Saudis would never—"

"It's not the Saudis I'm worried about," Miller said.

McCallister blinked, then finally understood what his boss was saying.

"We need to be overly cautious with the flash drive. If you're okay with it, let's have your officer bring the letter and the flash drive directly to us. She can bring it straight here and join our team."

"You want her to join you in Maryland?"

"She's been running an asset in the royal court who's been handing her information on Saud Rahmani and the Saudi dissidents living abroad. I couldn't think of a better person to bring in. You okay with that?"

McCallister really didn't know what to think. Nora Ryder was an exemplary officer without so much as a blemish on her record. Sending her to join Brenner and Miller's program could be a death sentence for her career.

Nodding slowly, he eventually said, "Fine."

"Thank you," Brenner replied. "No need to tell Langley where she's going, I'll take care of it. Do you think you could get her and the flash drive and letter into Bahrain today?"

"Into Bahrain?" McCallister said, thinking. "Yeah, I can do that."

Brenner then turned around and said to Miller, "Get ahold of Huey and Kircher. See how fast they can get to Bahrain."

Miller left the screen.

Brenner then told McCallister that he'd get back to him ASAP with details on the jet, when McCallister interrupted.

"Jack, wait a minute, what about the *other* thing that was written in the letter?"

"Which part?"

"About Director Hastings—if what the letter says is true, she needs to be informed immediately."

Brenner nodded. "You're probably right. We might have to read her in tonight."

Finally, McCallister thought. In his opinion, it was long overdue for Jack and Danny's secret program to be shared with the director of the CIA.

"Okay, Willy," Brenner said. "We've got to go, you just work on getting your officer and that flash drive and letter safely out of the country."

With that, the screen went black.

For a moment, he stared down at the letter and the flash drive in contemplation.

Then, snapping back to his senses, he opened his office door and waved Ryder inside.

Before the young operations officer could say anything, McCallister said, "Pack your things, Nora. We're getting you out of the kingdom. Now."

CHAPTER TWENTY-EIGHT

PRESIDENT BUCHANAN LEANED over the Resolute desk and buried her head in her hands. Not only was this the worst week of her presidency, but it was shaping up to be one of the worst of her life.

The stress of the job was becoming overwhelming, but it was the loneliness and isolation that were killing her.

Raising her head, she stroked the greenstone pendant hanging from her necklace and stared at the empty Oval Office.

Late last night, when the Saudi intelligence report had leaked, Buchanan had lost her temper worse than she'd ever lost it before.

Calling all her cabinet members and senior staff into the Oval, she'd demanded that they do everything in their power to find the leaker.

When she'd been briefed yesterday in the Situation Room on the Saudi intelligence report, she'd made the decision to keep it under wraps until next week—not wanting the world's attention to be focused on Iran while she was trying to get the Global Green Accord signed.

But that plan, of course, had now failed miserably.

After spending the entire night doing damage control, she'd made the mistake of checking Twitter and watching network news while she ate breakfast that morning.

Twitter had been a dumpster fire of people calling for her head.

But while Twitter was bad, the network news stations were even worse.

Pundits on both sides of the political spectrum were calling for Congress to draw up articles of impeachment against her. The media had discovered that Buchanan had planned on not informing the public of Iran's involvement in the reactor meltdowns. Doubting her leadership, some of the talking heads had even questioned the safety of the world leaders in Davos, while others had called for the accord signing to be canceled outright.

While everyone had differing opinions on Buchanan's actions, one opinion from both sides of the aisle seemed to catch like wildfire—and that was that the United States must retaliate against Iran, and specifically against the Iranian Quds Force commander, General Soleimani.

Buchanan shook her head and stared blankly at the Oval.

What do they expect me to do?

Start a damn war?

No, Buchanan thought. *The best way to punish the Iranian government is to get the Global Green Accord signed and leave Iran and their oil reserves dated and useless.*

Still stroking the greenstone pendant, she thought back on Bobby and that fateful day just six weeks before the election.

They'd been onstage together at a rally in Des Moines, Iowa, trying to bolster enthusiasm for her campaign, which was struggling to keep pace with her opponent's, when disaster struck.

Halfway through her speech, she'd been cut off when Bobby had stumbled to the ground next to her, clutching his chest.

He died from the heart attack five minutes later in the back of an ambulance.

In the days that followed Bobby's death, the media had focused on Angela Buchanan's reaction to the crisis that had unfolded on that stage. They lauded her for remaining calm under pressure, and for the stoicism she possessed when she'd ordered her Secret Service detail and the paramedics to take her husband to the hospital.

The American public must have thought the same thing, because nearly two days after Bobby's death, Angela Buchanan's poll numbers shot past her opponent's.

She had been on the verge of backing out of the race altogether, but it had been Katherine Healey and Buchanan's children who had pressed her to continue on in her late husband's memory.

Six weeks later, on the night of November 3, Angela Buchanan had won the election in a landslide. The country had not only sympathized with her situation, but had latched on to the strength she'd displayed in dealing with Bobby's death.

But now, nearly twenty-four hours after the Saudi intelligence report had leaked, that strength was being questioned.

Checking her watch, she saw it was just after 7:15 p.m.

A meeting was to start any minute now with DNI Winslow and the director of the FBI, James Burke, who were supposedly briefing her on a recent development in the search for the leaker.

DNI Winslow had organized the meeting, and having borne the brunt of Buchanan's wrath the night before, he was trying to do everything in his power to appease the president, given the fact that the Saudi intelligence report had been in his office's possession when the leak occurred.

A knock came from the right side of the Oval.

Chief of Staff Healey poked her head inside.

"Madam President, are you ready for them?"

Buchanan waved her in, then stood.

Healey walked in first, followed by DNI Winslow and FBI director James Burke, who had been instructed to head the investigation into the leak.

As the three strolled in, Buchanan was surprised to see three *other* individuals enter behind them—one of them was CIA deputy director Garrett Moretti, the other two were—

"Senator Brandt? Senator Lancaster? What are you two doing here?"

Senator Declan Brandt was the chairman of the Senate Select Committee on Intelligence and Senator Lancaster the minority acting chair.

Buchanan had heard that earlier in the day both Deputy Director Moretti and DNI Winslow had been called before the SSCI to give unofficial testimony about their handling of the Saudi intelligence report.

"Madam President," Senator Lancaster said, in his jovial voice, offering Buchanan a hand. "How are you doing?"

For the first time that day, President Buchanan felt herself relax.

Lancaster was not only a friend, but he had been the first and only politician from the other party who had voted in *support* of the Green Initiative.

"I've had better, Richard," Buchanan said, shaking Lancaster's hand.

"I can't even imagine, Angela."

Buchanan was just about to ask Lancaster again what he was doing in the Oval, when she heard the clinking of crystal from the other side of the room.

Senator Declan Brandt was pouring himself a glass of bourbon from the small bar to the right of the Resolute desk.

Buchanan frowned at the West Virginian senator.

Holding the bourbon, Brandt walked over to Buchanan and handed her the glass.

"Pardon my manners, Madam President, but you're going to thank me for pouring you this drink later."

Buchanan took the glass. "Does someone want to tell me what's going on?"

"Why don't we all take a seat, Madam President," Lancaster said.

Buchanan took her seat before the fireplace as the group settled into the two couches before her, and for the first time, she noticed that FBI director Burke was holding a file under his arm.

Brandt spoke up first. "Ma'am, I insisted that Senator Lancaster and myself attend this meeting because of the events that unfolded earlier today in the SSCI testimonies with Deputy Director Moretti and DNI Winslow. But before we get to that, I think it's wise that Director Burke brief you on what the FBI unearthed this evening."

Burke opened the file. "Madam President, my agents have tracked the Saudi intelligence report leak that was sent to all the major news networks last night back to a specific VPN, a virtual private network, that is located in Sweden. This VPN was used to hide the leaker's computer IP address. Earlier today, the bureau tried to obtain a warrant to figure out who purchased the VPN, and uncover the IP address of the computer that made the leak, but unfortunately, Swedish officials wouldn't budge. So we had to get creative." Burke shifted uncomfortably in his seat. "With help from the NSA, we used some of our more classified technology to figure out who purchased the Swedish VPN. The purchase was made by someone using various onion accounts, and other VPNs that we traced from South Africa, Taiwan, and India—"

"Please, Director Burke," Buchanan said, "spare me the specifics and get to the point."

Burke cleared his throat. "Ma'am, what I'm trying to say is that the person who made the leak went through an incredible amount of hoops not to get caught. But we believe we found them."

Buchanan sat more upright. "You know who leaked the report?"

"Yes, ma'am."

"And?"

Burke shot a furtive glance around the room. "The leak came from a computer in a private residence in Fairfax County, Virginia. The computer is registered to Elizabeth Hastings, the director of the CIA."

Buchanan's mouth fell open. "Are . . . are you serious?!"

"Unfortunately, ma'am," DNI Winslow said.

Nearly losing the grip on her glass of bourbon, Buchanan asked, "How the hell did Director Hastings get ahold of the report in the first place?!"

Senator Brandt glanced over to CIA deputy director Moretti.

"I gave her a copy, Madam President," Moretti said, his voice weak. "I gave her a copy of the report after my office was done vetting it."

"You what?!" Buchanan said. "Why the hell would you do that?!"

"To maintain civility at Langley," Moretti said. "Elizabeth runs the place with an iron fist. You appointed me to keep an eye on her, to give you the insider account of what she's up to in those halls. I can't do that job if she's constantly railroading me at every turn. I gave her a copy of the report to mend the animosity between us, but I never imagined she'd end up doing something like this!"

Buchanan, glad that Brandt had given her the bourbon, took a sip.

"Ma'am," Moretti continued, "I just want you to know that I take full responsibility for my actions."

Buchanan lowered her glass, her anger building. But strangely enough, the anger wasn't directed at Moretti, it was focused squarely on Director Hastings.

"Ma'am," Brandt said, "when Deputy Director Moretti gave us his account today, the SSCI immediately told him to share this information with DNI Winslow, who in turn gave it to Director Burke at the FBI, who, as it turned out, had just zeroed in on Hastings's computer."

President Buchanan noted the huge smirk on Declan Brandt's face.

It was common knowledge to every person sitting in this room that Senator Brandt hated Elizabeth Hastings with a passion.

Brandt and Hastings had married each other young when Hastings was still in college at Harvard, and Brandt had just graduated from law school and was running for Congress. Their marriage had lasted for twenty years before it went nuclear.

It was rumored that Hastings had caught her husband in a web of infidelity stretching back decades and had eviscerated him in divorce court.

"Ma'am," Brandt said, "I know the leaked report is disastrous for your accord signing, but you need to view this as a win."

"And how's that?" asked Buchanan.

Brandt pointed to Moretti. "You can finally fire Elizabeth no questions asked. Hell, I'd suggest you sic the attorney general on her. Make sure she sees the inside of a prison cell for the rest of her miserable life. In the meantime, appoint Garrett here as acting director of the CIA. That's always been the plan, has it not?"

Senator Brandt was right, Buchanan thought. This was the nail in the coffin for Elizabeth.

"Oh, come on, Declan," Lancaster said, sitting next to Moretti. "The purchase of that VPN and the leak might have come from Elizabeth's computer, but that doesn't mean she hit send."

Brandt laughed. "Richard, please. You can't seriously stick up for her?"

"Why not?" Lancaster said. "You're a trained lawyer, Declan. Do you think you could convince a jury that it was one hundred percent Elizabeth who leaked the report?"

"It came from her home computer, Richard. Garrett handed her a copy of the Saudi intelligence report just hours before the leak. How obvious could this be?"

Director Burke interrupted. "Madam President, I agree the evidence against Director Hastings looks pretty damning. I have spoken to the attorney general, and he agrees, given your blessing of course, that a warrant be drafted, and Director Hastings's house in Fairfax County be searched immediately."

"Of course," Buchanan said. "And I agree, this is grounds for Elizabeth's removal and for an investigation to be opened at the attorney general's office—"

"Ma'am," Lancaster said, "I think we should think about the optics of this first."

"Meaning?"

"Madam President, this week has been a nightmare for you. With everything going on, I think it might be wise to *not* open a public investigation into Elizabeth until *after* the accord is signed. The last thing the world needs to see right now is more turmoil in Washington. If it gets out that the director of the CIA leaked the report, how would that look? It would look like you didn't have command of your ship. I suggest you remove Elizabeth quietly and open the investigation after the signing."

Buchanan nodded, respecting her friend's opinion and seeing the logic to it. She also knew that, unlike Brandt, Richard Lancaster was incredibly close to Elizabeth Hastings.

They'd grown up together in Texas and saw each other as siblings.

"I'll think about that, Richard," Buchanan finally said, then looked at Burke. "James, go ahead and get that warrant to search Elizabeth's house. I'll make a statement and inform the public that Hastings has resigned from her job as director of the CIA, and that Mr. Moretti will be taking the reins as acting director."

Moretti nodded in appreciation at Brandt.

Standing, Buchanan excused everyone from the Oval.

A minute after they left, she stood in the middle of the room by herself, the details of the conversation she'd just had spinning around in her brain.

For the last three and a half years, Elizabeth Hastings had been a thorn in her side, a warmonger, who'd spoken out publicly against her policies.

In a fair world, she would give Hastings the opportunity to save face and let her hand in a letter of resignation.

But this wasn't a fair world.

Hastings had crossed a line.

Taking her phone out of her pocket, Buchanan began to compose a tweet.

She decided that she wouldn't give the public the reason for Hastings's expulsion. The wolves in the media would eventually figure that out for themselves.

Two minutes later, Buchanan finished writing her tweet and blasted it out to the world.

Pocketing her phone, she gazed out of the windows behind her desk and took in the rain pummeling the White House grounds outside.

Four more days, Bobby.

Four more days, and then all of the madness of this past week will be worth it.

CHAPTER TWENTY-NINE

JACK BRENNER AND Dan Miller hurried out of the Maryland ranch house and toward Brenner's Mercedes, which sat in the driveway in the pouring rain, McCallister's words from the SVTC reverberating in his ears.

After McCallister had read the letter to them, both Brenner and Miller made the decision that it was time for Elizabeth Hastings to be read in on the secret program they'd been keeping from her over the last seven weeks.

Jumping into the car, Brenner was just about to pull out of the driveway, when Miller peered down at his phone, and said, "Oh fuck."

"What?"

Miller looked like he'd just seen a ghost.

"She did it," Miller said. "Buchanan just fired Elizabeth on Twitter."

Brenner stared at his friend.

Miller said, "If what the letter said was true—the authorities are going to be on her ass."

McCallister's words still ringing in Brenner's head, he threw the Mercedes in reverse, and barreled down the long gravel driveway.

"Then we need to get there before they do," Brenner said. "Now we know she's not involved. We might have time to read her in."

———

Elizabeth Hastings hadn't felt this good all week.

Lying in the lavender-scented bath, she reached over and grabbed her glass of Bordeaux and took a sip.

After the week I had, I deserve this, she thought, a feeling of vindication coursing through her veins.

From the moment the Saudi intelligence report leaked twenty-four hours ago, President Buchanan's crosshairs had been taken off her and placed firmly on Garrett Moretti and DNI Winslow.

Like everyone else, Hastings had been disturbed by the news of the leak.

Absolute incompetence, Hastings thought, taking another sip of her wine.

Both DNI Winslow and Moretti clearly didn't have control of their staff—and had obviously been sloppy with who they let handle the report.

She, like all the other members of the National Security Council, had been called into the White House last night—and had borne witness as an irate President Buchanan chewed out Winslow and Moretti for the leak.

It was amusing to see those two imbeciles squirm under the president's wrath, but Hastings had been surprised when she started to feel bad for Moretti.

He might be a moron, but his actions last evening when he had given her a copy of the report had softened her bitterness toward the man.

Maybe he's finally learning, Hastings thought and was just about to take another sip of wine when a loud knock sounded on her bathroom door.

"I told you, I am not to be disturbed!"

She had left all her phones in her bedroom and had told her security not to disturb her unless the house was burning down.

"Ma'am," her head of security said, through the door, "someone is downstairs wishing to see you."

"Who?"

The agent replied, but Hastings couldn't hear what he'd said.

Cursing, she got out of the tub and threw on a bathrobe.

Who the hell would they let into my house this time of night? she thought, opening the door, crossing through her bedroom and then marching out into the hallway and down the stairs. She could hear men's voices coming from her living room.

Hitting the first floor, she saw her four security agents and Richard Lancaster speaking to each other in urgent voices.

"Richard, what are you doing here?"

Richard Lancaster's face was pale white.

"Lizzie!" he said, walking toward her. "I've been trying to get ahold of you for the last hour. I came straight from the White House!"

"I was taking a bath. What do you mean you just came from the White House?" Hastings said, noticing the distress on her friend's face. "Richard, what's wrong?"

"You don't know?" Lancaster said, grabbing ahold of her hands. "Lizzie, the president fired you forty minutes ago on Twitter."

"What the hell are you talking about, Richard?"

Lancaster gave her hands a light squeeze. "Lizzie, listen to me. I know you already have some damn good lawyers, but let me call some of my own to help. They can meet you down at the Hoover Building."

"The Hoover Building—"

But Hastings never finished her sentence, because flashes of blue and red lights streamed through her living room windows.

"Please, Lizzie," Lancaster said. "You've got to listen to me; we'll get this all cleared up—"

But Hastings wasn't listening, because her front door had suddenly burst open, and a dozen FBI agents swarmed into her house, one of them holding up a warrant for everyone to see.

———

Fairfax County, Virginia
March 5, 8:41 p.m.

Brenner blew by the security booth at the entrance to Hastings's property, and then slammed on the brakes.

Parked in front of her home were a dozen FBI vehicles, their lights flashing.

"Oh shit," Miller said. "That was quick. Should we get out of here?"

Flexing his fingers on the steering wheel, Brenner said, "No, let's see what we can find out, first. If the feds ask us why we're here, we'll say we came to comfort her once we heard the news."

Climbing out of the Mercedes, Brenner and Miller hurried through the pouring rain toward Hastings's front deck and were met by a group of FBI agents asking them for credentials.

"We're here to see the director," Miller said, pointing toward the front door.

As he said it, the door swung open and two FBI agents escorted a large man wearing a black trench coat out of the house and onto the porch.

The man was in the middle of a heated argument, when he suddenly locked eyes with Brenner.

"Jack!"

"Senator," Brenner said. "What's going on?"

Senator Richard Lancaster pushed aside the two FBI agents and waved Brenner and Miller forward. "Let these men get up out of the rain."

The FBI agents blocking them moved aside, and Senator Lancaster grabbed Brenner by the arm and escorted him and Miller over to the far side of the deck, out of earshot.

Before Lancaster said anything, Brenner glanced through the window and into Hastings's living room. Elizabeth was sitting on her couch in a purple bathrobe, her face beet red as she yelled at a group of FBI agents huddled around her.

Lancaster said, "Buchanan just fired Lizzie."

"We know," Miller said. "We saw the tweet."

Lancaster shook his head in disgust.

"Why's the FBI here?" Miller asked.

"FBI tracked the Saudi intelligence report leak back to Lizzie's home computer."

Brenner exchanged a look with Miller, then said, "How's that possible?"

Lancaster said, "Garrett Moretti testified before the SSCI this afternoon that he gave Lizzie a copy of the report yesterday before the leak. The FBI then traced the leak back to Lizzie's home computer."

Lancaster then detailed the events in the White House from an hour before.

"FBI's going to take her in for questioning," Lancaster said. "I'm going to have some of my lawyers meet with her counsel at the Hoover Building."

Brenner's mind was churning. "Moretti testified that he gave Elizabeth a copy of the intelligence report yesterday?"

"Yes, and now he's been named acting director," Lancaster replied. "I tried to tell the president to keep this quiet until after the signing of the accord, but she obviously didn't listen. It's only a matter of time before a neighbor sees this damn circus and calls the press."

Brenner's attention flickered back to the window. A herd of agents were coming down the staircase with all of Hastings's electronics in clear evidence bags.

"I'm going to follow them to the Hoover Building and see if I can do some damage control," Lancaster said. "You gentlemen want to tag along?"

"No," Brenner said. "I think it's best we get going. You have my phone number?"

Lancaster nodded.

"Give me a ring when they let her out of questioning."

"Will do," Lancaster said.

Brenner and Miller headed back to the Mercedes and climbed inside.

"What now, Jack?"

"I don't know, Danny, I don't fucking know."

"The letter told us explicitly that this would happen."

"I know it did."

"If they were right about this, that means we need to get that flash drive into our possession ASAP."

"What's Huey and Kircher's ETA in Bahrain?"

"Fueling up and heading there within the hour," Miller replied.

"Good," Brenner said, and he was about to throw the Mercedes in reverse when he heard two identical chimes from both his and Miller's Langley-issued work phones.

Both men looked at each other, frozen.

Then simultaneously, they both fished their phones from their pockets and gazed down at their screens.

An email from the office of the acting director of the CIA stared back at Brenner.

As his eyes robotically read through the email, he realized he could hear his heart pounding in his ears.

It grew louder, and louder.

Glancing over at Miller, he saw that his old friend had received the same email, telling them that effective immediately, both men—after nearly seventy years of collective service to their country—had just been fired from their positions in the Central Intelligence Agency.

CHAPTER THIRTY

A SHARP KNOCK at the door roused Princess Amara from a dreamless sleep.

She sat up in bed and fumbled for her iPhone to check the time.

The phone was hot to the touch, and as Amara stared down at the screen she saw that it was just after nine in the morning.

How long have I been out? she thought to herself. She tried to remember going to sleep the night before, but her mind felt sluggish.

Confused, she turned on the bedside lamp and tried to recall anything from the day before.

She could remember eating her meals—both breakfast and dinner had been served in her room by her two Saudi Royal Guard minders. Dinner had occurred sometime around 7:30 p.m., because it was around that time that she'd seen the tweet from President Buchanan firing the director of the CIA, Elizabeth Hastings.

And as her memory started coming back to her, she recalled that she'd eaten lunch yesterday with her chief of staff, Wali Mattar, in the dining room downstairs.

During the lunch, Mr. Mattar had handed her the guest list of the Middle Eastern Women's Rights Summit she'd requested to see the day before.

She recollected scanning through the list of dignitaries, celebrities, politicians, and Middle Eastern royalty and then trying to hide her en-

thusiasm when she saw the name of the particular individual she wished
to meet.

"Due to everything that has happened in the last day," Mr. Mattar
had said, alluding to the leaked Saudi intelligence report, "the royal
court is debating whether or not it is appropriate for you to attend the
summit."

"Appropriate?" Amara had said. "I'm giving the welcome speech!"

"The royal court wants you focused on your job."

"My job?!" Amara replied, growing angry. "I have been locked inside
my room since I've left the White House!"

"Take a deep breath, Princess," Mr. Mattar had said. "The royal court
will send its decision by tomorrow morning."

Amara wondered why there were so many gaps in her memory—
when another sharp knock sounded from her bedroom door.

"Just a second!" she said, crawling out of bed, throwing on her *hijab*
and opening the door.

Mr. Mattar and her two minders stood in the hallway, a large stack
of luggage sitting before them.

"Madam Ambassador," Mr. Mattar said, "your personal belongings
have arrived. May we bring them in for you?"

"Yes, yes, please!"

As they deposited her belongings before her bed, Mr. Mattar then
handed her an envelope with a House of Saud insignia on the front.

"Madam Ambassador, the royal court has made the decision to *deny*
your attendance at the Middle Eastern Women's Rights Summit. Due
to the timing of the event, they believe you should be focusing on your
role as ambassador and not engaging in such frivolities."

Amara tore open the letter and read it, then crumpled it up and
threw it on the floor.

"Absolutely not. Tell the royal court that I will absolutely *not* cancel
my attendance at the summit!"

"The royal court—"

"I don't care what the royal court says. The crown prince gave me the
ambassadorship title to represent our undying support for the accord. To
show the world that the kingdom is changing. That women now have a
voice! Silencing me and not allowing me to attend the summit—"

"This comes straight from the crown prince, Princess."

"Then I wish to speak to the crown prince at once!"

"Unfortunately, that is not possible."

"Then why the hell am I here? Why was I flown to the United States just to be locked in a room? Why can't I call anyone? Why can't I speak to my children?!"

"Your children are fine, Princess," Mattar said. "The crown prince told me they will be flown to the United States after the signing."

"I want to speak to them. Get me a phone that works."

"You are being hysterical, Princess," Mr. Mattar said. "Unpack your belongings, then we can bring up breakfast for you."

"I don't want breakfast," Amara said. "I want to speak to my children."

"Maybe tomorrow."

"You said that yesterday, and the day before," Amara growled. "Why am I being treated like a prisoner?!"

Mr. Mattar laughed. "You must still be jet-lagged, Princess. How are you a prisoner? You have this beautiful room in this beautiful compound. You are the Saudi ambassador to the United States!"

Amara took a step toward Mr. Mattar.

Instantly, her two minders moved in between them.

"Madam Ambassador," Mr. Mattar said, "why don't you take the day to rest? We can talk more tomorrow once you've calmed down."

Amara was just about to protest, but Mr. Mattar and the two minders turned on their heels and exited the room, locking the door behind them.

Frustration, fear, and anger boiled over inside of her.

Then she whirled around to face the luggage at the foot of her bed, the conversation she'd had on the royal airstrip with her chief of security, Farid, surfacing in her memory.

She began opening the bags, one by one, tearing through the mounds of clothes, searching—

She found what she'd been looking for in the bottom of the fifth bag, wrapped in a purple *abaya*.

Almost certain that Mr. Mattar had bugged her room and probably even had hidden cameras watching her, Amara kept the object hidden within the *abaya* and then marched to the bathroom.

Locking the door behind her, Amara turned on the shower.

Standing in front of the mirror, she pulled the item from the *abaya* and gazed at it.

The snow globe showing a miniature rendition of Manhattan stared back at her.

Amara flipped the snow globe over, wedged a fingernail under the snow globe's base, and pried open the latch concealing the hidden compartment within.

Amara smiled in relief as a small folded note and her silver USB clattered to the tile floor.

Bending down, Amara scooped up the USB and the note.

Farid did it!

He'd successfully gotten the USB out of the kingdom.

She placed both the snow globe and the USB on the bathroom counter and unfolded the note.

Recognizing Farid's handwriting, she began to read.

My Dearest Princess,

I pray to Allah that this letter gets to you safely. Unfortunately, I have some terrible news. After you left the kingdom, Saud Rahmani and his men ransacked your palace.

They never told me what they were looking for, but it's obvious they were searching for the USB and the laptop.

Forgive me, Princess, but they found the laptop before I could destroy it.

They arrested me, and all your staff and security personnel and brought us to a facility, where Saud Rahmani and his men questioned us throughout the night.

Princess, they kept asking me questions about some files that were stolen from the royal court.

They said they found a copy of those files on your computer.

They wanted to make sure that you didn't make any copies.

I of course told them nothing! Nothing about the USB!

They must have believed me, because they sent me back to your palace and ordered me to pack your belongings.

Since my release this morning I have tried calling and emailing you. But have gotten no reply, that is why I am writing you this letter.

Princess, there is no easy way to say this . . . When I was released and brought back to your palace this morning, I found that the children were missing.

I confronted Saud Rahmani, and he told me they were now under the care of the royal court.

Princess, I do not know what to do next. I have failed to do what you've asked of me. I have failed to protect the children. The royal court has stripped me of my passport. From what I've been told, I will soon be taken to a detention center.

Please, Princess. Whatever trouble you have gotten into with those files, whatever you did to anger the royal court—please find a way to make amends.

May Allah protect you and the children.

Yours,
—Farid

Amara felt the note slip from her grasp. The room began to swim. She felt dizzy, unbalanced.

Her knees buckled, and the tile floor came rushing up at her.

On impact, she let out an anguished cry, the tears flowing red hot from her eyes.

Her children—Mimi—Ahmed . . .

Her children were gone, taken from her, because of *her* actions.

She never should have participated in the dark web forum. She never should have asked Qutrub to confirm the rumor for her. She knew the risks involved—but she'd done it anyway.

And now she was paying for it.

The crown prince hadn't locked her in the Ritz-Carlton for what she'd done.

No.

He'd named her ambassador and sent her halfway across the world.

This was her punishment.

But to what extent?

Why send her here?

Lying down on the cold tile floor, Princess Amara envisioned the frightened faces of her children crying for their mother.

Ahmed.

Mimi.

Alone.

Scared.

Amara sobbed for what felt like an eternity, then an unfamiliar feeling manifested itself in her chest.

Rage.

Red hot. Boiling. Searing. Electric *rage*.

Lifting herself on all fours, a plan formed in her mind.

She would not be a victim of her cousin and his sadistic thugs.

Standing, she picked up Farid's letter from the floor and then wiped the condensation that had built on the bathroom mirror and stared at her reflection, envisioning what she was going to do next.

Everything depended on her attending the Middle Eastern Women's Rights Summit.

There was a person who would be there.

A person she needed to save.

But also the person who could possibly save her.

Save her children.

It was time to act.

Amara flushed Farid's letter down the toilet and snatched her iPhone from the counter.

Saud Rahmani and his hackers might be able to block her private correspondences, but she highly doubted they could prevent her from sending out a public message on an open source social media platform.

Amara opened Twitter on her iPhone.

She was still logged in!

For two minutes, Amara's fingers danced over the screen, then she examined her handiwork.

Satisfied, she hit: *Tweet.*

The blue loading bar on the top of her screen shot to the right, and then stopped.

"Come on . . ." she said, urging the app to work.

A second passed.

Two.

Amara held her breath. Then the app chirped back at her.

Tweet sent!

Amara sighed in relief.

With any luck, her tweet would go viral.

The crown prince and his royal court would be backed into a corner.

Shutting off the shower, Amara put the USB back inside the snow globe and exited the bathroom. Holding her chin up high, she placed the snow globe on her bedside table.

A minute later, thunderous footsteps came from the hallway.

She heard keys jingling and the dead bolt being thrown as the double doors blew open and Wali Mattar burst into her room, followed by her two minders.

"What have you done?!" Mattar yelled.

"What do you mean?"

Mattar held up his own iPhone.

"Oh, my tweet? I was just trying to bolster some enthusiasm for the summit on March eighth."

"The royal court forbade it!" screamed Mattar.

"Really?" Amara asked. "That's not what my tweet says."

"TAKE HER PHONE!" Mattar bellowed.

Her minders wrestled the iPhone from Amara's grip.

She eventually let them take it and couldn't help but smile as they stormed out of the room.

The damage was done.

She had upwards of fifteen million Twitter followers.

Her announcement of attending the summit could not be rescinded.

The crown prince had no choice.

She had forced his hand.

Still gazing at the double doors, Amara said, "Your move, little cousin."

CHAPTER THIRTY-ONE

CUSTER HAD BEEN looking forward to this day for weeks.

Driving his silver Audi RS7 off his property, he turned onto I-66 heading east toward Arlington and gunned the 4.0 liter V8 engine. The car rumbled onto the interstate, going zero to sixty in 3.5 seconds.

It was the perfect time of day to take all 591 horses out for a run into the beltway.

In thirty minutes, he'd be meeting face-to-face with his handler, and Custer couldn't be more excited. Having taken out all the Audi's GPS devices when he'd purchased the vehicle a month before, and having left all his personal and expendable burner phones back in the safe in his study, Custer traveled into the capital technologically incognito.

Well, not exactly.

He did have with him the Orion phone that linked him directly to his lieutenants and specifically to Reno, the most important individual involved in the plan, and a person he was getting more and more irritated with.

In the last few days, his Orion phone had been squawking every three to four hours, and Reno was growing more and more anxious and upset each time he called. It was all Custer could do to keep the man reassured and calm—to trust the plan.

But still Custer worried.

Reno could be a huge pain in the ass.

Custer decided that he would need to brief his handler on the incessant calls. She would know how to deal with it.

Custer crossed the Potomac River via the Theodore Roosevelt Bridge and found parking on E Street and Twentieth NW and then began walking the few blocks south toward his destination.

Out of every aspect of the plan—all the acting, the masquerading, and the manipulating, nothing gave Custer more delight than the moments he got to spend face-to-face with his handler.

It was the best part of this whole situation.

After Custer had insisted that he and his benefactors not speak over the Orion cell phone, he had demanded that the only way he would communicate would be through a handler, or through a one-time-use burner phone.

It had gone this way for a year and a half without so much as a hitch.

The first time he'd met his handler was at a bar in the Paris Ritz-Carlton, during a vacation over a year ago.

He had been drinking in a booth by himself when the most beautiful woman he'd ever seen entered the bar, ordered a drink, and then made eye contact with Custer. To his great surprise she made her way toward him and took a seat at his booth.

Custer had been rendered speechless.

The woman, who wore a red cocktail dress, put her purse and her dirty martini on the table and crossed her legs. "You must be Custer. Our mutual friends have sent me to set up communications with you."

From the moment his beautiful handler opened her mouth, Custer had been utterly smitten.

During their subsequent meetings since that initial contact, Custer had used the encounters to unabashedly flirt with the woman.

But his handler had remained coy—telling him that their relationship would have to remain strictly platonic. That had not stopped Custer. After all, he was a man who was used to getting what he wanted.

Crossing Constitution Avenue into the National Mall, Custer straightened his black wool cap and fished out a fresh Gurkha cigar from his coat pocket. Clipping the cigar, and lighting it, he sat down at a bench before the Lincoln Memorial Reflection Pool.

Puffing on the Gurkha, he felt the familiar tingling sensation in his loins whenever he was about to meet with his handler. He rehearsed in his mind what he was going to say to her. He would certainly have to be charming, witty, and confident. He would make her laugh, and then maybe, just maybe he would have a shot this time of getting her in the sack.

Returning to reality, Custer checked his watch, and looked up and down the mall, wondering why she picked this stereotypical place to meet.

Like an asset meeting his handler in some bad eighties spy movie, he thought, gazing at the nearly empty mall.

Two minutes later, Custer heard footsteps coming up behind him, then he recognized the voice that sounded like warm honey.

"My darling, smoking all those cigars will kill you one day."

Custer took in Tara Devino, the former American-Emirati fashion model turned businesswoman. She wore a black knee-length coat, a white knitted hat, a matching scarf and gloves.

Custer stood, taking in the woman's brown, almond-shaped eyes, her high cheekbones, pouty lips, and tanned skin.

"You look as radiant as always, my dear," he said, extending a hand.

She put her gloved hand in his, and he helped her sit on the bench next to him.

Taking another puff of his Gurkha, he smiled at her, and she shot him an annoyed look.

"What?"

"I truly don't like the smell of smoke," Devino replied.

"Oh, right."

Custer dropped the cigar and extinguished the tube of Dominican tobacco with his boot. Then turning to Devino, he said, "My dear, why did you want to meet out here in the freezing cold? I could have gotten us a table at the bar in the St. Regis."

"The bar at the St. Regis? My darling, who meets at a bar at ten in the morning?"

"Well, if not the bar, we could have checked into a room, ordered room service."

Devino rolled her eyes. "Not today, my darling."

Custer loved it when she called him, *my darling*. Though she was young enough to be his granddaughter, Custer couldn't contain himself when he was around her. She was like a drug.

Devino said, "Our friends want to know if you've experienced any hiccups on your end of the operation?"

Custer frowned as his mind jumped to the individual who'd been calling him incessantly over the Orion phone in the last few days.

"Reno has been calling me nearly nonstop. He's been getting cold feet."

"Hmm," Devino replied, deep in thought. "You might want to play him the recording you have of him again. Remind him of his complicity."

"I've played the tape for him three times in the last two days."

"And?"

"He's still being a pain in the ass."

"That could be problematic," Devino said.

"If he keeps pestering me, I'll head over to his house and knock some sense into him."

Devino crossed her legs. "And other than Reno, how are the others faring?"

The *others* Devino was alluding to were Custer's other lieutenants.

"So far so good," Custer said. "The schematics Benteen obtained for us have been invaluable. Did the component McDougall sent our benefactors arrive on time?"

"It did," Devino said. "It is being sent to Switzerland as we speak."

"Wonderful," Custer said. "McDougall has been a hell of a soldier, a true believer. Anyone willing to put themselves in harm's way is a hero in my book."

Devino nodded. "Our benefactors are pleased at the way you were able to get the Saudi intelligence report into the hands of the director of the CIA."

"It was nothing," Custer said. "As it turns out, Varnum proved himself useful."

"They also would like to congratulate you on getting into the director's personal computer. I know how confusing all that technology can be."

Custer laughed. "It was easy as pie, my dear. After all, I did have a good teacher."

Devino blushed slightly, then her demeanor turned serious. "And Director Hastings—has the FBI officially arrested her?"

"An arrest most likely won't be done until after the accord; she's being put under house arrest in the meantime," Custer replied. "But as far as we're concerned, Hastings is finished—Varnum cleared house over at Langley last night. And at my direction, he'll be appointing sympathizers to our cause in the coming week."

"Very good," Devino said.

"Is everything all right on your end? You seem distracted."

Devino sighed again and took her secure Orion smartphone from her pocket. "I have been in the United States for a few days keeping an eye on a Saudi dissident—a dissident who wishes to publish something that could potentially ruin the operation."

Custer stiffened. "Operation Little Bighorn?"

"No, Dark Sun."

Custer knew that his benefactors called the international aspect of the plan Dark Sun, while he'd been the one who'd insisted that the domestic facet of the scheme be dubbed Operation Little Bighorn. As far as Custer was concerned, both operations at home and abroad had to succeed for the final goal to be accomplished.

"Is it serious? Do you need my help?"

"It is serious, but our benefactors have already come up with a way to silence the dissident before he can publish his article."

"And this dissident, you said he's living in the United States?"

"Yes."

"Well, I can help. I know people."

Devino waved her gloved hand. "This dissident is extremely prominent—he will need to be handled by a professional."

Custer stared at the beautiful young woman as she rotated her Orion phone in her hands, still looking worried. "Then what's bothering you? You seem upset."

"I don't suppose you use Twitter?"

"Oh, god no."

"It is Princess Amara," Devino said. "She is being difficult to handle. Mr. Mattar has had his hands full in the last few days, and then she did this an hour ago."

Devino swiped open her Orion smartphone, opened Twitter, and handed it to Custer.

He looked down and read:

Princess Amara

@Amara_ArabianPrincess

The royal court has just notified me that it would be insensitive, and too hard on me, a woman, to go to the event I have been planning on attending for the last year. These men in the royal court insisted that given my new role as Saudi ambassador, I would have too much on my plate to stand up for women's rights. They are wrong. I do not have too much on my plate. I'm not too tired, nor am I too busy. I have just spoken to His Royal Highness the Crown Prince and he stands with me 100%. So join me on the morning of March 8 at the LINE Hotel for the first annual Middle Eastern Women's Rights Summit in Washington, DC, on #InternationalWomensDay.

Custer finished reading the tweet, then asked, "What's the problem?"

"The problem is that our benefactors wanted the princess out of the limelight until the accord signing. We have been trying to keep her hidden and docile, but she's been lashing out."

"Has Mr. Mattar been drugging her food, like I suggested?"

"He has."

"Then tell him to up the dose. Hell, I don't see a problem with her attending her little summit. What harm could be done there?"

"What if she tells someone how she is being treated?"

"Just keep a close eye on her, then get her out of there after her speech. All she needs is to get on a jet the morning of March ninth and then on that stage in Davos."

Devino nodded slowly.

Custer smiled, trying to change the mood. "So, why are we meeting like this? Is it just because you've missed me?"

"No, my darling. I have come with your next instructions. Now that Varnum is in place, we can move forward."

"Well, I'm all ears."

For the next ten minutes, Custer listened as his handler detailed the next step of the plan.

When Devino finished, Custer gazed at her dumbstruck. "Are you serious?"

"Deadly serious. The target package will be in your in-box in the Orion computer. You are to meet with President Buchanan as soon as possible and convince her that she needs to act on this right away."

"I don't see how the president would ever agree to this," Custer said.

Devino rubbed a gloved hand down Custer's face. "You are the most charming and convincing man I have ever known. People listen to you when you speak. The president will do what you tell her to do. Just be your usual, persuasive self."

Leaning forward, she kissed him on the cheek, and whispered into his ear, "Convince the president, and I will make sure you are *well compensated* the next time we meet."

Custer felt the tingling sensation in his loins run up his back, and he nearly verbalized his delight.

Biting her lip, Devino stood. "Signal me after your meeting with the president so I can tell our benefactors how it went."

With that, she walked away.

Custer, his chest aflutter, his mind dancing over the possibilities of what she had meant by *well compensated*, reached into his coat, took out his flask of "emergency bourbon" and took a nip to settle both his nerves and his excitement over his handler's proposition.

Taking one more swig of the flask, Custer stood.

He would need to head back to his estate and figure out a plan.

Walking back to his car—he realized he would need all hands on deck, all the help of his lieutenants, to convince the president of his benefactors' wishes.

And if he succeeded—if he could pull this off—he *might* just get a shot at spending a night with Tara Devino.

Crossing Constitution Avenue, toward his parked Audi, he chuckled and thought to himself, *Well, if that isn't motivation, I don't know what is.*

CHAPTER THIRTY-TWO

BRIAN RHOME'S RIGHT hand gripped his suppressed Glock loaded with the subsonic ammo under his loose-fitting robe, the business end of the weapon pointed directly at the tribal militia guard talking to the driver at the security checkpoint just north of the Yemeni city of Shabwah.

His face neutral in the back seat of the Toyota van, Rhome wore the attire of a Yemeni tribesman—a loose turban, an oversized cotton shirt, baggy pants, and a large belt containing a sheathed *jambiya*, or ceremonial dagger—all under a sprawling camel hair robe used to conceal the suppressed Glock that he was currently pointing at the militia guard's head.

Altogether, there were seven men in the van—the Emirati sniper Kazem Shurrab, Rhome, and the five Yemeni tribesmen who had been paid by the Saudis to smuggle Rhome and Shurrab into the country.

Each man had an AK-47 either between his legs or by his side.

Kazem Shurrab shifted in the back seat next to Rhome as he listened to their driver explain to the tribal militiaman that all the men in the van were cousins trying to see their sick uncle in the Yemeni city of Ataq.

It had been the same story they'd used all day since they'd left the drone base in southern Saudi Arabia.

Passing through the Yemeni border had been easy, but as they drove farther and farther south into the various tribal regions and al-Qaeda-controlled territories, they had been met with continuous roadblocks and checkpoints.

Weapon still trained on the militia guard, Rhome watched as the driver handed over the necessary documents and identification, his peripheral vision tracking the other militiamen circling the van.

"You usually travel with five," the guard said, then pointed to Rhome and Shurrab in the back seat. "Who are these other two?"

Rhome's finger tightened around the trigger.

"I already told you," said the driver. "They're our cousins. Look at their documentation. Our uncle is dying. They wanted to pay their respects to him one last time."

The driver handed the guard a wad of money.

The guard pocketed the bribe and waved them through.

Rhome exhaled a sigh of relief, and the van drove into the Yemeni town of Shabwah.

If the guards had searched the van, they would have found two black neoprene bags sitting under Shurrab and Rhome's seat containing some less than savory items they'd taken with them from the Saudi armory.

And if they had looked under the vehicle's chassis, they would have found the parts of a disassembled sniper rifle.

As they drove into the town of Shabwah, Rhome checked his watch; it was nearly 6:15 p.m.

"We will stop over here to refuel and wait until it is completely dark," the driver said and pulled behind an abandoned building on the southern side of town.

Rhome got out of the van and stretched his legs as the Yemenis took a gas canister secured to the roof of the van and began refilling. With the sun setting to the west, Rhome could hear the *Isha*—the sunset call to prayer—sounding from a nearby mosque to their north.

There had been much discussion back at the drone base about this next leg of the trip. If they were to continue south on the N19 highway toward Ataq, and then west on the N17 toward the Ar Risan Palace, there would be an incredibly high risk of running into problems with the locals.

Not only was driving at night in Yemen a bad idea, but driving the length of the N17 from Ataq to Ar Risan would be virtual suicide. The area was a hyena's den of al-Qaeda, ISIS, and Houthi rebels.

It had been the Yemeni tribesmen who'd had the idea of waiting in Shabwah for the sun to set, refueling, and then driving the eighty miles across barren desert to their target area in the mountains just south of the Ar Risan Palace.

Thirty minutes later, with the sun fully set, everyone jumped back into the van.

Digging into his neoprene bag under his seat, Rhome dug out a pair of NODs, night-vision goggles, he'd grabbed from the armory and instructed the driver to cut the van's headlights and use the goggles to see as they drove into the desert.

For the next four hours, Rhome used the GPS he'd taken from his bag to guide the van on its journey through the desert, and when they were a few hundred yards away from the N17 highway, Rhome told the Yemeni driver to keep the van's headlights off, as they crossed slowly over the highway and drove up a small canyon into the mountains, until they were directly south of the Ar Risan Palace.

"Stop here," Rhome said, then instructed everyone to get out of the van.

With only a steep mountain separating them from the palace, Rhome and Shurrab spent the next couple minutes getting the disassembled sniper rifle from the bottom of the van's chassis and putting it together.

Having gone over this part of the operation last night at the drone base, the Yemeni tribesmen began taking the van's left rear tire off its axle and pulling the van's spark plug.

The plan was to make it look like they were stranded with a broken-down vehicle.

Rhome checked his watch again; it was nearly 10:30 p.m.—right on schedule.

Armed with his suppressed pistol and an AK, plus the contents in his neoprene go bag, Rhome, backed up by Shurrab, told the Yemenis that they were not allowed to leave until 7:30 p.m. the next day. The reasoning behind this was simple. If the operation was canceled or if the assault team could not get to the palace, Rhome and Shurrab would need to exfil via the Yemeni tribesmen. With the assault scheduled to take place at 8:15 p.m., the Yemenis would have ample time to get out of the area before bullets began to fly.

After triple-checking that the Yemenis were all squared away—both Rhome and Shurrab put on their NODs and began the steep climb up the mountain.

Making it to the backside of the summit thirty minutes later, Shurrab stopped and whispered, "We will set up our gear here before sliding into position."

Shurrab lay down the sniper rifle, then dropped his own go bag at his feet.

Rhome did the same.

Then they both stripped out of their Yemeni garb and took out the gear they'd need for the rest of the op.

Rhome slid on his black tactical getup, which included a Kevlar vest and ceramic plates. All together he had six AK magazines, with twenty-eight rounds in each. Three of the mags he'd secured to his chest, one sat in his AK, and two more were clipped to either side of his CamelBak.

His suppressed Glock was secured to his holster on his waistline.

In total, he had three magazines for the Glock and had already attached a Crimson Trace infrared laser to the base of the pistol's muzzle. This IR laser could only be seen through the infrared of the NODs.

Next, he slipped off his baggy pants and sandals, and put on a pair of breathable cargo pants, and lightweight shoes, before stuffing the Yemeni garb into the bottom of his bag and moving the rest of the items he might need for the operation to the top.

Last, Rhome took out Mack's combat axe and secured it to the front of his chest rig.

"Are you ready?" Shurrab asked.

Rhome nodded, and Shurrab handed him a 60x spotting scope and a bag of camouflage netting they'd use to conceal themselves once they got to their vantage point.

"I'll go first," Shurrab said.

Rhome followed Shurrab as they both got on their stomachs and crawled slowly around to the other side of the mountain.

Shurrab stopped on a small ledge and pointed downward.

Below, nearly three hundred meters away, sat the mud and brick Ar Risan Palace.

Shurrab told Rhome not to move as he grabbed the bag of netting from Rhome. Five minutes later, Shurrab had the netting staked down over them like a low-hanging tent.

Rhome placed his bag by his side and took out the comms relay, before placing the 60x spotting scope in front of him next to Shurrab's sniper rifle.

Putting on his earpiece and throat mike, Rhome turned on the comms that overlaid through the Saudi Reaper drone flying above them at fifty thousand feet. The Reaper would then relay the comms to the drone base and finally to the Fusion Center in Riyadh, where COS McCallister would later be overseeing the operation.

Rhome spoke into the mike, "Wolf in den."

CHAPTER THIRTY-THREE

CLUTCHING A LARGE purse and small carry-on suitcase, Nora Ryder stepped out of the concierge's Range Rover that had taken her from the Bahrain International Airport's private aviation terminal to her awaiting jet.

The Gulfstream G550 sat in front of a hangar, its aircraft door open and staircase down.

Thanking the concierge, Ryder made a beeline straight for the jet. She couldn't help but feel frustrated and confused at everything that had transpired since she'd met Apache the night before.

Immediately after COS McCallister had read the letter he'd ripped from the *agal*, he had ordered her to run a nearly six-hour surveillance detection route through Riyadh to a predetermined safe house until he could figure out a way to get her out of the country.

She had repeatedly pleaded with her boss to tell her what was going on, to tell her what the letter had said, but McCallister—more frantic and upset than she'd ever seen him—wouldn't disclose anything.

After she'd run her SDR and waited another six hours by herself at the safe house, a man had knocked on the door and showed himself inside.

"Your boss sent me to get you," the man had said in Arabic.

In his hands was a large purse, and a small carry-on suitcase—as well as a shopping bag, which contained hair dye, brown contact lenses, an *abaya*, and a *niqab*.

Not giving Ryder his name, the man told her to go to the bathroom; she was to dye her hair and put on the contact lenses and clothing he'd brought for her.

"Where are we going?" Ryder asked.

"Bahrain International Airport," the man replied and told her to hurry.

A half hour later, Ryder—her hair now matching her brown contact lenses—put on the *abaya* and *niqab* and was then escorted to the man's vehicle to begin their drive to the small island Kingdom of Bahrain.

As they got closer to the Customs and Immigrations in Al Khobar, the man had dug out a Bahrainian passport and a visa from his pocket and handed it to her.

"Study the documents in case you are questioned," the man said and then explained that they were traveling as a husband and wife who were coming back to Bahrain from a five-day trip to Riyadh.

Looking at the visa and passport, Ryder saw the necessary stamps that corroborated the man's story, and when she got to her photograph on the passport, she couldn't believe it when she saw an image of her face surrounded by the fundamentalist veil—the flap of her *niqab* up, exposing her fake brown eyes, and a wisp of brown hair.

How had McCallister doctored this image of her and constructed this passport in just twelve hours?

Driving up to the customs area that sat before the seventeen-mile King Fahd Causeway that would take them over the sea to the Kingdom of Bahrain, the man posing as her husband had handed over the documents, and Ryder was surprised when they were waved through without any hassle.

As they cleared customs and drove onto the King Fahd Causeway, the man had then reached under the steering column and popped out a maroon Canadian passport and handed it to Ryder.

"You will be leaving Bahrain as a Canadian citizen," the man said, instructing her to take off her *niqab*, and her *abaya*. "Keep the contact lenses on; the Western clothing you are wearing underneath will be fine to travel in."

As they drove northeast through the capital city of Manama, and then to Muharraq Island, where the Bahrain International Airport sat on the northern shoreline, the man pulled the vehicle up to the private terminal, handed Ryder the purse and small suitcase, and said, "You're flying private so you won't need a ticket. Use your Canadian passport at the counter and you will be taken to your jet."

With that, the man drove off without another word.

With the bags, and the passport in her hands, she checked in at the front desk, went through security and was then escorted by a concierge to a Range Rover that drove her to an awaiting jet.

"You Nora Ryder?" a voice asked, after the concierge drove away.

Looking up, she saw the backlit silhouette of a gigantic figure standing atop the jet's staircase.

Exhausted from not sleeping in nearly thirty-six hours, and incredibly irritated that she was being herded around with zero justifiable explanation, she nodded.

The man spoke over his shoulder, "Hey, Kirch. Wake up, she's here."

Cresting the staircase, the man stepped aside and Ryder marched into the cabin, then examined the two men in the plane.

The enormous man who had been waiting for her at the top of the stairs wore a ball cap, khaki cargo pants, and a green shirt that fit tightly over a muscular chest. His arms were covered in tattoos, and he sported an unruly orange beard.

The second man was the antithesis of the first—he was tall, and wiry, with a dark complexion and jet-black hair.

After shutting the cabin door, both men grabbed the purse and the carry-on from Ryder and plopped them down on a leather seat next to them. The enormous man said, "We've been waiting here all day, what the hell took you so long?"

As the men began tearing through the contents of the purse and the suitcase, Ryder clenched her fists at her side. "Will someone please tell me what the hell is going on?!"

Ignoring her, the big man took an old Dell laptop out of the purse, and popped out its bottom compartment, and Ryder saw the silver flash drive Apache had given her fall into his hand.

The skinnier man had the black *agal* out and was ripping at the fabric that had been seemingly sewn back together until he had dug out the letter.

Both men studied the letter for a moment, before the orange-bearded man handed both items to the skinnier man, who marched back to the cockpit.

"I'm Huey," the huge man said. Fishing a cell phone from his pocket, and putting it to his ear, he flicked his head over his shoulder. "And that's Kircher—he'll be flying us outta here tonight."

Ryder felt the jet's engines rumble to life, and simultaneously, she heard Huey say into the phone, "Chief, Nora Ryder is on the plane with us. The letter and flash drive are in our possession. Heading to Frederick now."

Huey listened to whoever was speaking on the other line, then gazed up at Ryder and said, "Copy that."

Hanging up, he looked at Ryder, who asked, "Frederick? As in Maryland?"

"As in Maryland," Huey repeated.

"Why the hell are we going to Maryland?"

"I'm not at liberty to say. People way smarter than me will be in charge of that."

Pointing to a couch in the back of the plane, Huey said, "That thing turns into a bed. Drinks and snacks are in the cupboard over there. McCallister said you probably haven't slept in a while—so make sure to get some shut-eye, because you ain't gonna get much after we land."

Huey then walked into the cockpit, locking the door behind him.

Her fists still clenched at her side, Ryder shook in anger.

What the fuck have I gotten myself into?

What the hell is happening?

Five minutes later, the Gulfstream barreled down the runway before lifting off into the night sky.

Letting her exhaustion take over, she removed the brown contact lenses and heeded Huey's words by curling up on the couch.

She was asleep before they reached thirty thousand feet.

CHAPTER THIRTY-FOUR

Valais, Switzerland
Somewhere in the Pennine Alps
March 7, 7:00 a.m.

THE ENGINEER MOVED at a steady pace through the deep snow, following the tracks left from his snowshoes nearly thirty-six hours before.

He was breathing hard as the sun began its ascent over the treacherous landscape to his east—an orange globe of light creeping its way over a white, glacial tapestry.

For the first time in nearly five months, the engineer could feel the seasons finally beginning to change, the days becoming longer, the volume of snow collecting on the glaciers starting to decline.

It would be an early spring after such a mild winter.

The straps of his heavy backpack cutting through his shoulders, the engineer stopped, planted his ski poles in the snow, and took in the beautiful scenery—the scenery that reminded him so much of his childhood home in the Alborz Mountains in northern Iran.

The nearly seven-mile climb down to the Swiss mountain village of Arolla the night before had been difficult. The engineer's muscles had withered in the last five months that he and his two brothers had been cooped up in the desolate alpine hut on the north side of the frozen Lac de Mauvoisin.

The alpine hut, resting in the valley north of the lake, had been stocked full of supplies for the winter, with enough food, firewood, and even an encrypted satellite internet connection to keep the engineer and his two brothers sustained during the winter. After all, their job wasn't only to lie low, but to prepare themselves for the mission thrust upon them by Allah.

Since their rescue from the Yemeni prison last September the engineer and his eight other Quds Force brothers had been split into groups of three, then given new identities and instructions to get to their predetermined destinations to prepare for the upcoming mission.

But most importantly, they had been given a phone—a black smartphone that would be used to receive directives from Colonel Ghorbani and General Soleimani for their task ahead.

The engineer had been grouped with the bomb maker, and the pilot—and their methods for getting into Europe had been to enter via cargo ship from Tunisia.

Docking in Italy, they crossed into Switzerland a few weeks later, and then into the Alps where they were ordered to spend the winter in the desolate alpine hut.

For the last five months, as the three men worked and planned, they sat by the black smartphone—keeping it charged, awaiting their next orders.

Those orders finally came two days before, by text, stating that the engineer would need to take a seven-mile trek to the Swiss alpine town of Arolla that night to receive a package for the next phase of the mission.

Knowing he had been selected to make the trip because of his experience as a climber in his youth, the engineer had collected his gear, checked the weather forecast on his laptop, and then tested the snowpack for avalanche danger before beginning his trek down to Arolla that very night.

As per the black smartphone's instructions, he had checked into a climbing hostel upon his arrival the morning he arrived in Arolla and asked the receptionist if he'd received a package under his Kazakhstani alias.

The receptionist had taken in the engineer's gaunt, bearded face—checked his fake Kazakhstani passport and then handed over a parcel the size of a small briefcase.

The engineer had then spent the day in the room he rented at the hostel, examining the component he'd pulled from the parcel, making sure everything was in order.

It wasn't until the sun was beginning to set that the black smartphone vibrated again, giving him his next instructions.

The engineer had gazed down at the text, committing it to memory, before it self-deleted.

Then, shoving the component into his backpack, he got some sleep and waited until midnight before sneaking out of the town and starting his seven-mile trek back to the hut.

Snowshoes punching over the snow, the engineer squinted in the early morning light, before rounding a bend and spotting the mountain hut two hundred meters away.

Ten minutes later, he unfastened his snowshoes and heaved open the heavy wooden door and stepped inside.

His brothers were waiting for him at the small table, eating breakfast, their prayer mats rolled up on the wall behind them next to the fire.

"Were you successful?" the bomb maker asked.

"I was. I also received more instructions. We are to leave tomorrow. Transportation is waiting for us in the town of Liddes. From there we head to Davos."

"Davos?" asked the pilot.

"Yes, brother—is everything ready?"

"We have been ready for months," the bomb maker said, glancing at his forty-pound spherical-shaped creation on the table at the far side of the hut.

"And have you decided which vehicle you wish to use?" the engineer asked the pilot.

"I have," the pilot said, pointing to the eight-propeller drone that was the size of a large desk.

Taking the component from his backpack, the engineer held it up for his brothers to see.

The bomb maker moved forward and examined it before pointing to the drone. "Will you be able to solder it to this model?"

The engineer walked over to the half-dozen drones stacked against the wall that they'd been testing in the last few months and studied the one that the pilot had selected. "It should take me the rest of the day, but it shouldn't be a problem. We will leave tonight—pack everything you need and prepare to destroy all evidence that suggests we were ever here."

"Do you know our target?" asked the bomb maker, who stepped back and ran his hand over his creation of C-4 and ball bearings.

The engineer glanced at the young man. "Not yet. That information will be provided to us once we get to Davos."

This, of course, was a lie.

In his room at the hostel, the engineer had hooked up the component to his laptop and studied the software inside. Not only did it contain technology that had the ability to infiltrate the most secure cyber bubble in existence, but it also held the most sophisticated facial recognition system money could buy.

His curiosity having gotten the better of him, the engineer had accessed the facial recognition system and discovered the identity of their target.

It was in that moment—gazing at one of the most recognizable faces in the world—that the engineer finally understood what General Soleimani and Colonel Ghorbani had planned for his team.

The component still in his hand, the engineer walked over to the table and thought of his six *other* brothers who had been rescued from Yemen.

Where are they?

What is their role in the mission?

And who is their target?

Leaning over the drone on the floor, and placing the component next to it, the engineer then looked over at the pilot and the bomb maker and said, "Now, leave me to my work."

CHAPTER THIRTY-FIVE

RYDER JOLTED AWAKE as she felt the Gulfstream touch down.

Rubbing at her eyes, she sat up from the couch as the jet slowed, and then realized that she must have slept for the whole trip from Bahrain.

Lifting the window cover to her right, she peered out into the half darkness and saw the illuminated lights of a small airport outside.

The cockpit door opened and Huey stepped into the cabin. "You were out like a light."

"What time is it?"

"Just after eight in the morning."

Huey handed her a bottle of water as the plane moved slowly down the tarmac before coming to a stop in a brightly lit hangar.

After powering off the jet, Kircher, the pilot, opened the cabin door for them and put down the stairway.

Ryder went to grab the suitcase and purse she'd taken with her from Bahrain, when Huey said, "Leave those here. We've got clothes and everything you need where we are going."

"And where are we going?" Ryder asked, following Huey down the stairs to a waiting SUV.

Ignoring her, Huey climbed in the driver's seat.

Ryder got in next to him.

Starting the vehicle, Huey was about to throw the SUV into drive, when Kircher tapped on the window.

Huey rolled it down.

Kircher said, "Tell Mansur and Bennett the plane is ready, just need to refuel."

"I'll send them over once we get to Lodgepole," Huey said. "When will you be back?"

"Tomorrow morning at the latest."

After Kircher walked back to the plane, Huey drove out of the airport and onto a highway.

"Lodgepole?" Ryder said, looking over at the man, whose right hand gripped the steering wheel. In the slowly rising sun, Ryder could make out the tattooed images on his arm. There was a purple Cheshire cat sitting in a tree with a mischievous grin, and a depiction of Alice gazing through the looking glass. Within the image of the glass was an inscription that read:

Tertia Optio

When Huey didn't answer her question about Lodgepole, she pointed to his arm. "You're Ground Branch?"

Huey gave a slight nod.

During her CIA training at the Farm, in Camp Peary, Virginia— Ryder learned quickly that there were two types of CIA recruits going through the agency's operations officer training.

The first were the stereotypical Ivy Leaguers—individuals who were fresh out of school, clean-cut, and institutionalized. These recruits usually ended up as operations officers, or bureaucrats, in Langley.

The other type were the former special forces guys. Men in their late thirties and early forties—who had been plucked from some military Tier One unit and trained by the CIA to be PMOOs, or paramilitary operations officers, within the agency's Ground Branch, under the direction of the Special Activities Center.

Even though Ryder fell into the former category of recruit, she'd found herself more comfortable and at ease around the PM guys. Maybe it was because they'd reminded her of her older, hockey-loving brothers—or maybe it was just because they were *real*. They'd already seen things, experienced things—things that most of her Ivy League classmates couldn't even comprehend.

Huey took an unmarked exit that led to a dirt road and drove for twenty minutes through a dense forest.

Suddenly, Huey took an abrupt right and gunned it up a steep gravel road that opened up to rolling fields of fenced-in horse pastures.

In the distance, Ryder could make out a white ranch house with a big red barn behind it.

Huey booked it up the driveway and came to a stop behind a handful of cars that sat parked in front of the house.

"C'mon," he said, opening his door.

Ryder stepped out of the SUV and shivered in the cool morning air, following Huey as he climbed up the ranch house's stairs and onto the deck. Opening the front door, he ushered her inside.

The house was warm and smelled like freshly brewed coffee.

Huey led her through the living room, and into the kitchen, where he opened the pantry door, and stepped inside, motioning for her to follow.

Confused, Ryder moved into the pantry and watched as the Ground Branch operator put a hand on the far wall, between the shelving, and pushed outward.

Ryder nearly gasped as the pantry wall moved away from them, revealing itself as a hidden door exposing a dark, concrete staircase that descended toward a dim light, a few stories below.

"Shut the door behind you, and watch your step," Huey said and made his way down into the abyss.

Ryder stepped in after him and swung the door shut, then followed Huey down the freezing corridor, before getting to a landing, where a reinforced steel door containing an alphanumeric keypad and a three-spoke handle sat within a concrete wall.

Huey punched in an access code on the keypad, and then a loud buzz filled the air. Heaving the three-spoke handle and yanking the door open, Huey motioned Ryder inside.

The room was brightly lit and in the shape of a hexagon.

Stepping inside, she took note that three of the six walls contained large LCD screens. The other three were covered in whiteboards and cluttered corkboards.

In the center of the room was a collection of workstations.

Eight individuals sat in the room.

A tall, bespectacled, older man with a tired expression stood up when she entered.

Ryder recognized him immediately as the legendary director of the Special Activities Center, Jack Brenner. Then her eyes flitted over to the people sitting at their workstations, before her gaze settled on a middle-aged Asian American woman, and then to a man wearing a Boston Red Sox hat to the woman's right.

Ryder's jaw dropped in recognition.

She knew who these people were.

Everyone in the agency did.

"Th-this is . . . y-you are . . ." Ryder stammered. "You're the team that—"

"Found Osama bin Laden," an older, hefty man said.

Ryder took a step back when she recognized the man.

The CIA's deputy director of operations, Dan Miller, adjusted his tie, and joined Jack Brenner at his side.

Both men appeared stressed and exhausted.

Brenner walked forward. "Welcome to Lodgepole, Ms. Ryder."

CHAPTER THIRTY-SIX

"LODGEPOLE?" RYDER SAID. "What's Lodgepole?"

"Why don't we get you introduced to everyone," Brenner said. "Then we can read you in."

He introduced the Asian American woman and the man with the Boston Red Sox hat as Elaine Cho and Mike Adams. "Elaine works with me in the Special Activities Center," Brenner said. "And Mike is our NSA liaison, also working in the SAC."

Ryder tried to mask her admiration for the pair.

During her training at the Farm, her instructors had recounted in vivid detail how a husband and wife team within the former Special Activities Division had found Osama bin Laden's courier by intercepting his text messages and cell phone calls. Not only had Cho and Adams found the courier that led them to bin Laden's compound in Abbottabad, Pakistan—but they had been the ones who'd convinced the president of the United States to send in two squadrons of SEALs to take him out.

"And this is Amina Bennett, and Zahir Mansur," Brenner said, indicating the two individuals standing behind Cho and Adams.

Brenner explained that Bennett and Mansur, both in their early forties, were two of the agency's top Middle Eastern specialists, operations officers who were experts on all things Saudi Arabia. Bennett and Mansur each picked up a duffel bag and slung it over their shoulders, then Bennett said, "All right, Kircher said the jet's ready. We'll see everyone later. Good luck."

The two walked out of the room and Ryder was about to ask where they were going when Brenner pointed to the two men in their fifties, standing next to Dan Miller. "This is David Bell, and Mark Silva."

Bell, who was short and stocky, sported perfectly combed bleached blond hair and had cauliflower ears that were so bulbous the bottoms of them nearly touched the top of his suit collar.

Brenner explained that Bell was an FBI liaison working for the CIA.

Ryder knew that since 9/11, the CIA employed FBI agents to work within the halls of Langley—acting as a bridge to help facilitate the flow of information between the United States' foreign and domestic intelligence institutions.

Silva was the physical juxtaposition of Bell.

Tall, and lanky, with a face that made him look like an aged movie star, Silva worked in the CIA's Office of General Counsel.

"Mr. Silva," Brenner said, "is making sure our actions in this basement are legal."

Silva glared at Brenner.

"And you of course have met Huey," Brenner said, nodding to Huey, who dug out the letter and the flash drive from his cargo pants and handed both items to Adams.

Staring at the letter and the flash drive, Ryder heard DDO Miller say, "Why don't we all sit down and get her read in as fast as possible. We're going to have another long day."

Ryder peeled her attention away from Mike Adams as he plugged the flash drive into the computer on his desk and then walked to the long metal table that everyone was moving to.

Ryder sat between Cho and Huey, directly across from Miller and Brenner. Bringing over a steaming cup of coffee, and placing it before Ryder, Silva sat across from Bell.

"First off," Brenner said, gazing at Ryder. "Allow me to apologize for keeping you out of the loop these last couple days. It was for your own safety."

Ryder folded her arms, her eyes dancing around the hexagonal room. "So what the hell is this place? What the hell is Lodgepole?"

"This is an old CIA subterranean mission center," Brenner said. "A relic from the Cold War, and Lodgepole is the name of the program we're running down here. As you can see, it's not your standard compart-mented program—in fact, other than your boss, COS McCallister, and Mansur and Bennett, only one other person outside of this room knows of this program's existence. And if everything goes as planned, no more than a few ever will."

"None of the other higher-ups at Langley know about this?"

"Correct."

"Is that legal?"

Silva, the OGC lawyer, gave a loud snort. "You mean is it legal for employees of the CIA, former or present, to siphon money from offshore accounts with no State, Justice, or congressional oversight to create and participate in a program that has no links to Langley? No. It is absolutely not legal."

"Given the special circumstances we are operating under," Brenner said, glaring at Silva, "we decided to have Mr. Silva read in on Lodgepole to ensure our operational methods moving forward were lawful, and within the lines of the agency's jurisdiction. Even though the *legality* of Lodgepole's creation is still up for debate."

"Up for debate?" Silva said. "If this gets out, we'd be lucky to be locked up in Leavenworth, and not Guantanamo!"

"There are risks and costs to action. But they are far less than the long-range risks of comfortable inaction," Miller said.

"Here he goes again with his JFK quotes," Silva said.

"Fuck you, Mark," Miller said.

"Where does Langley think you all are?" Ryder asked Brenner.

"As far as Langley is concerned, the individuals in this room, includ-ing yourself, are working on various compartmented programs around the world. Programs that Danny and I fabricated using the authority of our old jobs."

"Your old jobs?"

"You haven't heard?"

"Heard what?"

Brenner sat back in his seat and looked upset.

Silva said, "They were fired two nights ago. Director Hastings, too."

Silva described President Buchanan firing Hastings by tweet, and then promoting Garrett Moretti to acting director.

"Why were you fired?" Ryder asked.

"We'll get to that in a moment," Brenner said, gazing over at Adams, who still sat at his workstation. "Mike, how's that flash drive looking?"

Adams came over and sat down next to his wife. "I've got the program running now, shouldn't take more than twenty-four hours to crack."

Ryder noticed that Adams had brought over the letter that McCallister had taken from the *agal* and placed it facedown on the table.

"Twenty-four hours?" Brenner said, checking his watch. "That should work."

Then, reaching below his seat, Brenner came up with a stuffed green folder and slid it over to Ryder.

The words typed on the folder, read:

LODGEPOLE
Compartmented Program/Restricted Handling
Limited Dissemination: Eyes Only

"What's this?" Ryder asked.

"The reason we're all down here," Brenner said. "Go ahead, open it."

Ryder opened the folder to the first page and stared down at what looked like a transcript of a text message conversation.

Not understanding what she was seeing, she turned to the next page, and then the next, before jumping ahead through the hundreds of pages. The whole folder seemed to have similar transcripts.

"I . . . I don't understand," Ryder said.

"What you are looking at is a collection of signals intelligence that we have gathered in the last seven weeks," Cho said.

"Signals intelligence of what?" Ryder asked.

"Text, WhatsApp, encrypted messages, and phone calls," Adams said. "Messages we've intercepted from Saud Rahmani's personal iPhone."

"And what do these messages say?"

"Put together," Bell said, "these messages are a compilation of incriminating evidence. Evidence that implies that for the last year and a half, the crown prince of Saudi Arabia and members of his inner circle have been engaging in a conspiracy. A conspiracy involving a group of

Americans who are intending to stop the signing of the Global Green Accord by assassinating the very person who created it."

Ryder felt her stomach drop, not sure she'd heard Bell correctly. "A conspiracy to assassinate the person who created it . . . you don't mean—"

"The president of the United States," Brenner finished for her. "Yes, the crown prince and members of his inner circle along with a group of unidentified Americans are planning to disrupt the signing of the Global Green Accord, by killing the president of the United States."

CHAPTER THIRTY-SEVEN

"THAT'S . . . THAT'S RIDICULOUS," Ryder said.

"Ridiculous, but true," Miller replied, pointing to the Lodgepole folder. "All the evidence is in there."

A thousand thoughts running through her mind, Ryder said, "But the crown prince was the one pushing for the accord. He was the first leader to pledge to the signing. Why would he want to disrupt it? Why would he want to kill the president?"

Everyone sitting around the table shifted uncomfortably, then Brenner said, "We don't really know."

Ryder blinked. "What do you mean you don't know?"

"We don't know the crown prince's motive," Cho said. "We don't know his end goal."

Ryder studied everyone's faces, then in disbelief, she looked back down at the Lodgepole folder and asked, "Why were you even looking at Saud Rahmani's iPhone in the first place?"

"Because of the Ritz roundups that began in January," Cho replied, motioning to Adams. "Mike and I were trying to pull signals intelligence from the crown prince's inner circle to find out more about the round-ups. The inner circle uses government-level encryption phones, called Orion phones, to communicate with one another. The Orion technology is developed by a public Israeli company called NSO Group. Orion is the most unbreakable encryption software on the planet. Its sophistication rivals the technology found in our ICBMs, and their phones are impossible to penetrate."

"But here's the thing," Adams said. "We found out that Saud Rahmani also uses an iPhone. An iPhone he personally downloaded the Orion technology onto. What Rahmani doesn't know, though, is that Orion isn't compatible with the iPhone."

"And it was his iPhone that we targeted and infiltrated," Cho said. "And stumbled upon this whole mess."

Ryder said, "You're saying you can see everything on Rahmani's iPhone?"

"Everything," Adams said. "Even the calls and texts he sends and receives to and from the other Orion phones held by the crown prince and his inner circle."

"We've intercepted all kinds of conversations, from the benign, and mundane, to the outright inconceivable," Cho said, grabbing the Lodgepole folder, and flipping to the first page. "This is the intercepted conversation that started it all. A conversation we found in Rahmani's phone that occurred over a year and a half ago."

"A year and a half?"

"Yes," Cho replied. "This conversation is between Rahmani and an individual who calls himself Custer."

"Custer?" Ryder said. "Like George Armstrong Custer, the American general who died at the Battle of the Little Bighorn?"

"We believe so," Cho said. "We think that Custer is an American elected official involved in the conspiracy."

Pointing at the page, Cho told Ryder to read the transcript.

CIA/NSA INTERCEPT SIGINT/RH/CP/LODGEPOLE

RAHMANI: *Are you finally giving us your answer? It's been a week.*

CUSTER: *Yes. I've had time to think since Riyadh. I agree with the plan, and I have spoken to the others. We are going to have to keep them compartmentalized, but I think they will be very helpful to us. I just want assurances.*

RAHMANI: *Assurances?*

CUSTER: *That you can give them what we've discussed and they will not be caught. I for one am willing to die or risk federal imprisonment for my involvement. But I want the others to have plausible deniability.*

RAHMANI: *Fine. We will provide everyone with an Orion phone. From here on out, we use that.*

CUSTER: *There's nothing the NSA can't beat.*

RAHMANI: *You understand you are speaking to me now over an open line; you must not be too worried.*

CUSTER: *I'm using a burner—just delete your messages once we are done speaking.*

RAHMANI: *From here on out, we will only use the Orion technology. It can't be cracked.*

CUSTER: *Bullshit. I'm not going to let this whole thing be foiled by some damn NSA analyst. I want a handler and code names used from now on. Information will only be passed in person. From now on, you refer to me as Custer.*

RAHMANI: *Custer?*

CUSTER: *Yes. Always Custer—never my real name. Got it?*

RAHMANI: *Whatever—but there is no need to communicate through a handler.*

CUSTER: *Listen to me, you fucking prick, this isn't some dog and pony show. I am a United States elected official conspiring to put Buchanan in the ground. My partners are some of the most important people in the country. I will not risk us getting caught because of some bullshit encryption technology. Our cause is too important.*

RAHMANI: *You think I don't know the stakes and who is involved? Tell your partners that Orion cannot be hacked. If you want to stop Buchanan's accord, you do things our way.*

CUSTER: *You can't pull this off without me. You and I will communicate through a handler and burners from here on out, or I walk.*

RAHMANI: *Fine. A handler will be provided and contact established soon. The Orion phones will be given to you for emergencies only, and to be used between you and your partners.*

Ryder sat back, stunned.

Cho said, "We found this conversation on January tenth, of this year. That same day, we continued to scour Rahmani's phone, and we found two other conversations with Custer. Both conversations were from Rahmani's iPhone to random burner numbers with Washington, DC, and Virginia area codes."

"If they were random burner numbers, how do you know he was speaking to Custer?"

"Because Rahmani used the name *Custer* in both conversations," Cho replied.

Ryder said, "Do we know Custer's identity?"

"We've narrowed it down to a list of suspects," Adams said. "Reread the first two lines of the transcript above."

Ryder scrutinized the top of the page.

> **RAHMANI:** *Are you finally giving us your answer? It's been a week.*
>
> **CUSTER:** *Yes. I've had time to think since Riyadh. I agree with the plan, and I have spoken to the others. We are going to have to keep them compartmentalized, but I think they will be very helpful to us. I just want assurances.*

"Custer was in Riyadh a week before this conversation?"

"We believe so," Adams said. "When we initially caught this, we looked for any official or unofficial events happening in Riyadh concerning United States elected officials, and we discovered that there was a bipartisan delegation of ten US senators, and ten members of Congress who were in Riyadh the week before this conversation took place."

"So Custer is one of those twenty?!" Ryder said.

"Most likely," Cho said. "It was at this point that we brought the information to Jack and Danny, who told us to quietly keep digging."

"And what we found was incredibly troubling," Adams said.

"What did you find?"

"Dozens of other conversations from Rahmani's iPhone to random burner phone numbers in the Washington, DC/Virginia area. But what was even more alarming were the hundreds of messages we'd intercepted from Rahmani to various other members in the Saudi crown prince's inner circle, specifically Turki Shahidi, that detailed much more serious allegations."

"What kind of allegations?"

"Put together," Brenner said, "they paint a picture of a massive conspiracy. A conspiracy between the Saudi crown prince, Turki Shahidi, Saud Rahmani, and others in the inner circle who are working with Custer and individuals high up in the American government."

Ryder frowned. "How high up?"

Brenner said, "From the messages we've intercepted, we believe Custer is working with individuals in the Secret Service, people in Buchanan's own administration and White House, and even individuals who run some of the eighteen American intelligence agencies. From what we've pulled from Rahmani's iPhone, we believe that these people plan on assassinating President Buchanan as soon as she takes the stage in Davos."

"This was said explicitly?!" Ryder exclaimed.

"Yes," Brenner said. "When this information was brought to us, Danny and I ordered that it stay as compartmented as possible, given who could be involved. So we created Lodgepole."

"It was my idea to take Lodgepole off-site," Cho said. "Danny gave me a budget, and we got creative in our relocation and funding—and we moved here seven weeks ago, to begin our hunt for Custer and his coconspirators."

"And what have you found?" Ryder asked.

"To be brutally honest?" Cho said. "Not much. We've dug into the lives of the US politicians who were at the bipartisan Riyadh delegation—and have come up with nothing that could either confirm or deny Custer's identity. Nor have we been able to find anything concrete against any other individual who might be involved, and believe me, we've been looking."

"You've found *nothing*?"

"We've found some things, but after delving into the lives of nearly every Secret Service agent who has direct contact with the president, to those individuals who run our intelligence agencies, and even Buchanan's own cabinet and staff, we've found nothing that can either confirm or deny any involvement in the conspiracy against her," Cho said. "But it wasn't until last week that we figured out that this plot is much more sprawling than we anticipated."

"Meaning?"

Cho turned a page in the Lodgepole folder. "Read this."
Ryder looked down and read:

CIA/NSA INTERCEPT SIGINT/RH/CP/LODGEPOLE
March 1
12:24 a.m.

TEXT MESSAGE:
Pinged off Fairfax County cell tower
703-555-4431 to RAHMANI: *Hurrah, boys. Hurrah!*

Ryder was confused.

Adams said, "That message was sent minutes after the thorium molten salt reactors melted down from a number with a Virginia area code to Rahmani's personal iPhone."

"Holy shit," Ryder said.

"Holy shit is right," DDO Miller replied.

"You don't think . . . that the *Saudis* blew up the thorium molten salt reactors, do you?"

"We're almost certain of it," Brenner said.

Ryder tried to take it all in. "So the leaked Saudi intelligence report—"

"Is a fake," Miller said. "Or so we believe."

Cho turned to another page and said, "This intercept occurred the day after Dr. Mahdi Farahani and Mahmoud Ghorbani supposedly switched out the graphite rods in India."

CIA/NSA INTERCEPT SIGINT/RH/CP/LODGEPOLE
SEPT 24

RAHMANI: *Custer—everything is in position. Your friend will*
reach out to you soon with your instructions. There is no
backing out now.
703-555-9875: *Good.*

After reading the message, Ryder frowned. "But aren't Farahani and Ghorbani Iranian?"

"That confused us at first, as well," Brenner said. "It wasn't until McCallister read that letter to us over the SVTC two nights ago that it all started to make sense."

Ryder looked over at the letter that was still facedown on the table before Adams. "What does the letter say?"

"Why don't you find out for yourself," Brenner said, reaching over and handing her the crumpled paper.

CHAPTER THIRTY-EIGHT

Riyadh, Saudi Arabia
Al-Qirawan Military Base
Fusion Center
March 7, 7:15 p.m.

ESCORTED BY A group of Saudi RSLF officers, the Riyadh CIA station chief, William McCallister, popped an antacid into his mouth and hurried down a long hallway in a secure underground facility within the Al-Qirawan Military Base just outside of Riyadh, wondering the entire time if Nora Ryder had made it to Maryland yet.

The last couple of days had been some of the most stressful of his life—so stressful, he'd marveled how his stomach ulcer hadn't ruptured.

Getting Ryder, the letter, and the flash drive out of the kingdom without anyone knowing was incredibly difficult—but it was the stakes involved in doing so that had almost sent McCallister over the edge.

The letter had not only validated a series of terrible accusations, but it offered a glimmer of hope. Hope that Miller and Brenner's Lodgepole program might actually be able to unravel and thwart the conspiracy against the president of the United States and the Global Green Accord.

Hell, if what the letter said was true—which McCallister believed it was—this entire scheme could be thwarted within hours.

But we can't count on that, McCallister thought. *We need to continue with Danny's Hail Mary operation as if nothing has changed.*

And that was why McCallister was here.

Because nothing really had changed, not yet anyway—not until

Lodgepole could get into that flash drive and access the information inside.

After receiving word that Ryder, the letter, and the flash drive had successfully made it onto the jet in Bahrain, McCallister had jumped on the SVTC and asked his old bosses if they should carry on with Danny's plan. Surprisingly, it had been Brenner who had vehemently argued for it to continue, and thus the reason why McCallister was in this underground facility and not at his office at the CIA station.

His RSLF escorts led him through a series of double doors and then into the Saudis' state-of-the-art Fusion Center.

The Fusion Center with its numerous workstations, computers, and gigantic screens that covered the majority of the room's walls existed as a hub of sorts, where various Saudi intelligence and military agencies could work together to detect, prevent, and respond to terrorist activity.

In this case it was going to be used to coordinate the raid on Qasim al-Raymi.

And because of the strings Dan Miller had pulled while he'd still been the CIA deputy director of operations, McCallister would be getting a front row seat.

"Mr. McCallister, so glad you could make it."

McCallister turned to see Major General Azimi coming toward him, flanked by RSLF brigadier general al-Hassad, as well as Brigadier Colonel al-Malki, both of whom he'd met at the Saudi drone base two days before.

McCallister greeted the three men and then said, "Isn't Prince Khalid supposed to be joining us here tonight?"

Azimi's eyes darkened. "Unfortunately, I don't seem to know where Prince Khalid is at the moment."

"Oh?"

Azimi said, "The crown prince told me that Prince Khalid is assisting on another matter for the royal court. I will be running this operation from here on out. Come, why don't we get you situated."

Azimi led McCallister over to a chair next to the Saudi operations manager at a workstation with a front row view of the largest screen in the Fusion Center—the screen that showed a live aerial feed from the Reaper drone looking down on the Ar Risan Palace.

McCallister sat down and took in the operations manager, who wore a large headset.

Azimi explained that the young man would be acting as the operational OVERLORD—the individual who would be relaying information to the advisers and operators on the ground.

McCallister's brain jumped to Brian Rhome, who had volunteered to enter Yemen the day before with that Emirati sniper to provide a pattern-of-life analysis on the palace before the raid was to start.

"Did the advance group successfully get into position?" McCallister asked.

"They did," Azimi said and handed him a folder. "Mr. Shurrab and Mr. Rhome were able to give us a pattern-of-life throughout the day—and other than some slight tweaks, the assault team will converge on the palace as planned."

McCallister nodded as he skimmed through the folder.

"Sir," the operations manager said to Azimi, "C-130s are taking off in ninety seconds."

"Good," Azimi said, then motioned to Brigadier General al-Hassad. "Tell everyone to man their stations."

McCallister gazed at the gigantic screen depicting the Reaper's live aerial feed in front of him.

Somewhere on the mountainside above the palace, Brian Rhome was about to take the first step in Dan Miller's secret plan to stop the conspiracy against the president of the United States and the Global Green Accord, should the flash drive not be cracked.

"C-130s are airborne," the operations manager said. "Touching down at LZ in twenty-one minutes."

McCallister took a deep breath, then exhaled slowly—hoping to God that Rhome could get through this in one piece, hoping to God that Lodgepole could crack that flash drive and get the information they needed so Rhome wouldn't have to fulfill the final, Hail Mary operation Dan Miller had thrust upon him.

CHAPTER THIRTY-NINE

RYDER GRABBED THE letter from Brenner.

"Go ahead," he said. "Read it out loud."

Ryder held the crinkled, typed-up letter and began to read:

To Riyadh CIA Station Chief William J. McCallister,

I apologize for how this letter has been passed to you, but considering my social standing in Saudi Arabia I am unable to deliver this information to your embassy in person.

Just understand that I am close to the crown prince and his inner circle.

Hours ago, I stumbled upon a terrible truth concerning a conspiracy currently taking place between members of the crown prince's inner circle and high-level officials within the United States government—a conspiracy the crown prince has named Dark Sun.

From what I have discovered, Dark Sun not only involves the crown prince and members of his inner circle, but US elected officials, heads of American government agencies, and even people working in the White House close to the president of the United States herself.

From what I can determine, Dark Sun's goal is simple: to stop the signing of the Global Green Accord.

Mr. McCallister, you have to understand that the crown prince never intended to sign the Accord.

He never intended for the kingdom to go green.

Dark Sun has been years in the making—and first reared its ugly head last week when all seven of the world's thorium molten salt reactors exploded.

Though I do not know all the details of Dark Sun, I've heard pieces of it.

First and foremost, and even though it has not happened yet at the time of my writing this, the Saudi intelligence report given to President Buchanan will be leaked, and the blame thrust upon the director of the Central Intelligence Agency.

Mr. McCallister, the Saudi intelligence report given to President Buchanan is a fake.

Nor did your CIA director leak it.

This is all part of Dark Sun.

You should also know that the Iranian MOIS officer Mahmoud Ghorbani and the Iranian nuclear scientist Mahdi Farahani did switch out the graphite rods in India on September 23, but they did not do so at the behest of the Iranian Quds Force commander, General Soleimani.

Mahmoud Ghorbani is in fact a Saudi sleeper agent who was inserted into Tehran as a teenager by the Saudis, with orders to enter and climb the ranks of Iran's foreign intelligence agency.

Ghorbani was activated last September by the crown prince to participate and carry out multiple facets of Dark Sun—one of which included convincing Dr. Mahdi Farahani to switch out the graphite rods. From my understanding, Farahani believed he was doing so under the orders of General Soleimani.

Mr. McCallister, this information came straight from the mouth of the crown prince's right-hand man, Saud Rahmani, who told me just a few hours ago that Abdulmalik Hassen, one of his propagandists working in the royal court, had stolen two files from his computer.

The first file contained the details of Dark Sun.

The second file includes information concerning a Saudi

dissident living in the United States. Though I do not know this dissident's name, Saud Rahmani did tell me that the dissident had obtained information regarding Dark Sun and was going to publish the findings right before the signing of the accord.

Mr. McCallister, the crown prince and his thugs are willing to go to great lengths to silence this dissident, as they are willing to go to great lengths to get back the two files that Abdulmalik Hassen stole from Saud Rahmani.

Not only will I forcefully instruct Abdulmalik Hassen to give you these files—but I implore you to get him and his family to safety before Saud Rahmani and Turki Shahidi get to him.

I do not know Dark Sun's end goal or the methods by which its members wish to stop the Global Green Accord—but do not underestimate the crown prince and his inner circle's delusions of grandeur. Nor their capacity for cruelty.

Just understand that if the crown prince and his coconspirators could be so bold as to blow up the thorium molten salt reactors, do not underestimate what they may be planning next.

I fear this is only the beginning.

May Allah bless your path.

"Oh my God," Ryder said.

Her mind flew back to her meeting with Apache two nights before in the safe house.

He had no idea what he'd gotten himself into, Ryder thought. *Absolutely no idea.*

She said, "Do we know who wrote this letter?"

"We don't," Cho said.

"Can we confirm its validity?"

"We can confirm its validity with a high degree of certainty."

"How so?"

"Because an hour or so after McCallister read us the letter over the SVTC, one of the accusations came true," Miller said.

Ryder looked at the big man. "That's why Hastings was fired? She was framed for leaking the Saudi intelligence report?"

"Yes," Miller said. "The FBI tracked the leak back to her home computer and Buchanan fired her. Elizabeth is currently under house arrest until next week when the attorney general's office will be instructed to open a formal investigation."

"Holy shit," Ryder said.

"Holy shit is right," Miller said.

The biggest screen on the far side of the wall suddenly flickered to life, catching Ryder's attention. It showed an aerial drone feed of a mountainous desert landscape. Realizing that everyone at the table was now watching the screen, Ryder was about to ask where the feed was coming from, when Cho pointed to the letter.

"We've also looked into the validity of the other claims, especially the one about Mahmoud Ghorbani being a Saudi sleeper agent."

"And?" Ryder asked, tearing her attention from the screen.

Cho said, "He was adopted from an orphanage in Shiraz at the age of sixteen by a wealthy family who lived in Tehran. Other than that, he looks like the typical Iranian boy scout."

"He was adopted?" Ryder said. "That means he could have been a Saudi sleeper agent inserted into Iran as a teen?"

"It's possible," Cho said. "But we have no proof yet to back that up."

Ryder read the letter again, then placed her finger over one of the sentences. "So this conspiracy—Dark Sun—we have the complete details of it on the flash drive I brought back?" Ryder looked at Mike Adams. "You said the flash drive will take less than twenty-four hours to crack; that means we'll blow this whole conspiracy wide open within twenty-four hours, right?"

"Possibly," Brenner said.

"What do you mean, possibly?"

Miller cleared his throat. "When McCallister read us that letter two nights ago, we first thought that we had this whole thing in the bag, that all we needed to do was get the flash drive here and then crack it with our decryption program. And you are correct, within twenty-four hours we may very well be able to open that flash drive and access every facet of Dark Sun, as well as obtain the names of all the Americans involved. All of this, all our time down here these last seven weeks would be worthwhile. Our mission accomplished."

"So what's the problem?" Ryder asked.

"The problem," Brenner said, "is what if we *can't* open the flash drive? What if Adams's decryption program doesn't work? Or what if it does work, and we do get inside it, only to find that the files are damaged or have their own encryption and we're unable to access them? That puts us back at square one."

"So you're all just assuming we won't be able to access the Dark Sun file?" Ryder asked. "Then why the hell did you all go through such lengths to get me here?"

"Given the delicate nature of what we are trying to thwart," Brenner said, "we must operate expecting the best, and preparing for the worst."

Growing irritated by their runaround answers, Ryder said, "And what have you done to prepare for the worst? From where I'm sitting, it looks like Lodgepole hasn't accomplished anything in the last seven weeks."

In Ryder's eyes, she felt like she had every reason to be upset. She'd been manipulated by her bosses, smuggled out of the KSA, and brought into a seemingly illegal CIA program, and for what?

The whole room looked at Dan Miller, who said, "If we are unable to crack the flash drive, or if we are unable to get inside the Dark Sun file—I have another operation in play. A Hail Mary pass, so to speak, which I believe could crack this whole thing wide open, catch the conspirators, save the president's life, and make sure the Global Green Accord gets signed."

"And what operation is that?"

Miller reached under his chair and took out a red folder. But instead of opening it, or passing it to Ryder, he placed his big hands over it. "Before I start, it's imperative that you understand that we in Lodgepole have to act as if every single person surrounding the president is involved in the conspiracy. Everyone in the White House—from the chefs in the kitchens, to Buchanan's aides and staff, to her cabinet members, and even the Secret Service agents in her personal protective detail—not to mention the hundreds of United States elected officials she comes into contact with every week *could* be involved."

Ryder raised an eyebrow.

Miller continued, "Knowing this, we have spent nearly every second down here trying to figure out a way to get this information to President

Buchanan without *anyone* finding out, which, considering the Presidential Bubble, is impossible. The Bubble is set up in such a way that every step President Buchanan takes is not only closely watched, but monitored and recorded. The Secret Service knows where she is every second of every day. Getting access to the president means that people close to her would know about it, and at this point, we can't, nor have we been able to, take that risk. The advantage that we have is that the Saudis and the unidentified American conspirators have no idea that Lodgepole is aware of the threat to the president's life. Right now, our main goals are to make sure President Buchanan is not assassinated, and that the Global Green Accord signing goes off without a hitch. To do that, we need to identify Custer and his coconspirators and figure out the methods by which all those involved in Dark Sun plan on assassinating President Buchanan and disrupting the accord two nights from now in Davos. Considering who these American coconspirators could be, we want to flush them out quietly, and deal with them ourselves. And should we not be able to access the flash drive, or the Dark Sun file, this is my plan for how we are going to accomplish that."

Miller slid the red folder to Ryder.

She read the words written on the front.

HAIL MARY

Miller said, "Almost two weeks ago, we intercepted a phone call conversation from Saud Rahmani's iPhone between him and Turki Shahidi. The subject of the conversation was about a group that the crown prince wanted Shahidi to form, and then lead. The crown prince had instructed Shahidi to find individuals with particular backgrounds and skill sets who could be financially loyal to the crown prince. Shahidi told Rahmani that once these individuals passed a test of skill, they would be offered a job opportunity to join the group the crown prince wishes to build."

"And what is this group supposed to do?" Ryder asked.

"They are going to be a rendition team," Miller said. "A kill team, a kidnapping team, a team of highly trained individuals loyal to the crown prince."

Ryder blanched. "And you know all this from a phone conversation between Rahmani and Shahidi?"

"We do," Miller said. "Before I keep going—the letter you just read spoke of the other file that is supposedly on the flash drive your asset Apache stole from Rahmani's computer."

"The file about the Saudi dissident living in America?"

Miller smiled. "When we intercepted the conversation between Rahmani and Shahidi, they spoke of the crown prince wanting to send that newly formed rendition team on its first two missions. The first mission is supposed to take place in the greater Washington, DC, area the night before the signing. Can you guess what that mission entails?"

Ryder looked down at the letter. "The dissident. They want to grab the Saudi dissident, so he won't be able to publish his article about Dark Sun before the signing of the Global Green Accord?"

"Exactly," Miller said. "This group led by Turki Shahidi, which the crown prince has dubbed RIG, or the Rapid Intervention Group, plans on silencing—*killing*—a Saudi dissident living in the greater Washington, DC, area before they fly straight to Switzerland for their second mission."

"And what is their second mission?" Ryder asked.

"We don't know, exactly," Miller said. "But I'm sure it has to do with the accord and Dark Sun."

Brenner asked Ryder, "When Apache handed you the letter and the flash drive, did he happen to tell you the name of the dissident?"

"No, but what does this Saudi dissident have to do with your Hail Mary plan?"

"This dissident has *everything* to do with my Hail Mary plan," Miller said. "The dissident's very existence in Washington, DC, tells us one truth—that Turki Shahidi, and the newly formed Rapid Intervention Group, are coming to the United States right before they head to Switzerland. And we are going to be ready for them."

"What do you plan to do?"

Miller pointed to the Hail Mary file and told her to read it.

For the next ten minutes, Ryder read the file front to back, then looked up. "You want to insert someone into the Rapid Intervention Group? You want them to—"

But Ryder couldn't get it out.

Instead she said, "If we know that Shahidi knows everything about Dark Sun, why can't we just grab him and interrogate him when he gets to DC? Why go through all this?"

"Because," Cho said, "if we've learned *anything* about the crown prince these last seven weeks, it's that he's in constant contact with his inner circle. It's widely known that he's not only a genius, but an obsessive-compulsive. A severe micromanager. The crown prince will be in constant contact with Shahidi via their encrypted Orion phones the whole time they are in DC. If Shahidi were to go missing, or didn't check in with the crown prince for an unplanned extended period of time, the crown prince would know something was up, giving him the opportunity to change plans for how the assassination was carried out. We don't want that to happen, and Dan Miller's operation accounts for this; that's why he's planned to do it this way."

Miller said, "Again, Lodgepole's goal is to prevent the assassination of President Buchanan, and to make sure that the Global Green Accord gets signed. We want to find Custer and his coconspirators and apprehend who is responsible, and we want to do it quietly. If we are unable to access that Dark Sun file, I believe my Hail Mary operation is our best bet at success."

Ryder, still unconvinced, said, "So you're sending someone in to assassinate a Saudi dissident, just so they can get on that jet with Shahidi to Switzerland? Who the hell would sign up for this?"

"No one signed up for it," Brenner said. "The individual we are sending in is an unwilling participant."

"What does that mean?"

"It means we manipulated him to go under false pretenses," Brenner replied, and Ryder could see the emotion on the old spymaster's face. "I . . . I manipulated him to go."

Miller said, "Soon, this unwilling participant will be engaging in a test for the crown prince to solidify his spot in the Rapid Intervention Group. A test that will evaluate his skill."

"And what's the test?"

"To kill the emir of Al-Qaeda Arabian Peninsula, Qasim al-Raymi."

Ryder blinked. "And if he succeeds, how can you guarantee he will be accepted into the Rapid Intervention Group? How can you guarantee that he will even take the job? Hell, how do you know he will even survive this test?"

"He *will* survive," Miller said. "And your boss, William McCallister, will make sure he takes the job."

"And if he doesn't?" Ryder asked. "If we can't crack the Dark Sun file and if your Hail Mary operation fails, what the hell are we supposed to do?"

"We do have a final contingency set in place," Brenner said. "But we'll get to that only if we need to."

Ryder crossed her arms, trying to take all of this new information in.

"So," she finally said. "Who the hell did you unwittingly send on this insane Hail Mary operation?"

Miller pointed to the large screen displaying the aerial drone feed. "Jack's godson, Brian Rhome."

CHAPTER FORTY

LYING PRONE UNDER the camouflage netting, Rhome was now fully awake. To his southwest over the mountain range, he could hear the *Isha* call to prayer reverberating through the ravines and canyons from the town of Bayhan some six miles away. With the sun now set, Rhome placed his NODs back over his eyes and looked down at the palace below where Qasim al-Raymi was about to arrive.

After he and Shurrab had scaled the mountain at midnight and slid beneath the camouflage netting, Rhome had gotten some much needed sleep while Shurrab kept watch.

Rhome had woken at 4:45 a.m. to the sounds of the *Fajr*—the morning call to prayer—from Bayhan and had offered to stay awake if Shurrab wanted to sleep.

The Emirati had refused and then informed Rhome that the Yemeni tribesmen who had driven them into the country had jumped back in their van an hour before and hightailed it back the way they came.

"They left us?" Rhome said, growing angry.

"Does that surprise you?" Shurrab had said. "The Saudis paid them up front. We will hitch a ride with the assault group after the raid."

The sun rose two hours later and cooked the side of the mountain. For much of the day, Rhome and Shurrab had kept in contact with Saudi command at the Fusion Center in Riyadh, giving them a pattern-of-life on the palace below.

As the day progressed, more and more vehicles had arrived for the wedding. Rhome and Shurrab had counted close to sixty people who had entered the palace walls by 5:00 p.m.

Out of those sixty, they'd noted close to thirty military-aged males. Twenty-three of them were armed.

The layout of the palace was simple. Initially built as a tribal fortress in the 1700s and refurbished in the 1900s, the palace was constructed of mud and brick. It was three stories high and protected by a twelve-foot perimeter wall with one entrance—a large, double-door wooden gate on the eastern side of the wall.

The initial plan was to have the Western advisers and the Saudi assault force enter the compound by blowing the front gate. But when Rhome and Shurrab had studied the palace from their vantage point, they saw that a wooden boardwalk had been constructed on the perimeter wall above the entrance. This allowed the armed al-Qaeda guards to have a tactical advantage over anyone who came in or out.

Rhome studied the guards posted above the entrance throughout the day and decided that the assault group should not breach the palace gate. Instead, he told them to place their charges forty yards to the north and blow directly through the wall. Since there was no boardwalk to the north, the assault group wouldn't have to worry about getting fired down upon.

Billy Baker, the adviser who would be leading the assault force into the palace, agreed.

The former SAS man coordinated the change of plans with the Fusion Center in Riyadh.

At 7:25 p.m., Rhome and Shurrab were told that the C-130s had just taken off from Sharorah and would soon be landing in the desert thirty miles north of their location.

Nearly twenty minutes later, the Reaper drone had identified a caravan of twelve trucks, five miles away, driving on the N17 east toward the palace.

The large caravan meant one thing.

Qasim al-Raymi.

Rhome could hear music coming from the palace. The festivities were beginning. So far, he and the sniper had counted only ten men patrolling the compound. Two armed guards stood outside the wall in front of the main gate, and two more stood on the boardwalk above it. Four more patrolled the grounds within the perimeter wall, and two guards stood on the roof overlooking the palace grounds.

"C-130s have just landed. Assault group's ETA to your position in thirty minutes," Rhome heard the Fusion Center's Saudi operations manager say over his earpiece. "Eagle's expected arrival in one minute."

Rhome turned his attention to the north, where he clocked a dozen trucks turning off the N17 highway onto the dirt road that wove south toward the palace.

His heart started to hammer in his chest.

"I'm counting twelve Toyota Hiluxes," Shurrab said, gazing through his sniper scope. "DShk 12.7 mm mounted machine guns welded to each truck bed."

"I see them," Rhome said, looking through the spotting scope.

The headlights of the caravan disappeared for a moment behind a rocky outcropping, then came back into view some five hundred yards away, before driving into the open and toward the palace's entrance.

The two armed guards standing before the gate opened it quickly, and the twelve Toyotas drove inside and parked before the east entrance of the palace.

Through the scope, Rhome watched three dozen men jump from the trucks and spread out.

"I believe I have a visual on al-Raymi," Shurrab said.

"Where?"

"Fourth vehicle from the back, man walking with a cane, surrounded by five armed tangos."

Rhome jerked the spotting scope and found the group of men Shurrab had just described. They surrounded a limping figure, who hobbled up the steps to the palace's front entrance.

A roaring noise started building in Rhome's head. The sight of Qasim al-Raymi, the man responsible for the deaths of Rhome's men in Pakistan, triggered something primal within him. He could suddenly taste the blood in his mouth again and hear the screams of his men.

By the time he looked back down at the palace, al-Raymi was already inside, and nearly a dozen of his guards had situated themselves near the gate and around the palace's grounds.

"I see twenty-three tangos outside of the palace," Shurrab said. "Counting the rest of al-Raymi's guards, I estimate there are upwards of sixty to seventy armed military-aged males within the perimeter walls."

"Copy," Rhome said.

Shurrab repeated the information over the Reaper comms relay, then said, "I see four tangos wearing NODs. The two tangos on the palace roof. One on the boardwalk, and another patrolling the palace entrance."

Shurrab updated the Fusion Center about the NODs. "Tell the assault force to maintain IR discipline until they breach the perimeter. I will take out the guards wearing the NODs and the guards at the gate first, so the assault force can get to the wall unseen."

The plan was for the assault force to park their vehicles up the road around the rocky embankment and then cover the one hundred yards to the perimeter wall on foot.

Rhome heard Billy Baker's voice confirm a "good copy" and told them they were eighteen minutes out.

Fourteen minutes later, Rhome turned his spotting scope to the direction the assault force would be coming. As he gazed through the scope, he made out the faint outlines of three massive vehicles charging through the desert from the horizon.

Confused, Rhome said, "How many vehicles coming in from the north?"

Shurrab moved his rifle. "Three."

"Fuck," Rhome said. "They didn't take the Hiluxes like I told them to. Those armored vehicles are going to be slow as shit if we need to haul ass out of here."

Shurrab ignored him.

"Two minutes," the operations manager said in his earpiece.

Rhome turned back to the palace and the guards manning the perimeter.

"One minute."

Rhome heard Shurrab flip the safety off his sniper rifle.

"Thirty seconds."

"Neutralizing guards on roof," Shurrab whispered. His suppressed sniper rifle cracked softly twice in rapid succession. "Guards down. Eliminating guards at front entrance."

Two more light cracks.

Rhome could now hear the loud engines of the three armored vehicles as they crossed over the N17 and down the curved road toward the palace.

"Eliminating guards on boardwalk."

Shurrab's rifle thunked again, two more guards fell.

"What about the pair with the NODs?" Rhome whispered.

"One is at the palace entrance and won't be able to see the assault group from his vantage point. I can't find the other."

"Shit," Rhome said.

He turned his attention back to the road, where he watched the three armored vehicles ease to a stop behind the rocky outcropping. Billy Baker, Matt Rish, and Seth Proctor spilled out of the vehicles, followed then by the twenty-two Saudi assaulters. Slowly, they skirted the outcropping and began their hundred-yard dash toward their breaching point at the perimeter wall.

When they were fifty yards from the wall, Rhome heard Shurrab swear. "I've got the tango with the NODs, he's coming up the boardwalk—"

Rhome, whose attention had moved away from the assault group toward the man coming up the boardwalk with the NODs, suddenly caught something out of the corner of his eye.

Two beams of green light had activated from two of the Saudi assaulters' weapons and sliced through the night air. The al-Qaeda guard wearing the NODs who had just crested the boardwalk had simultaneously spotted his two comrades that Shurrab had recently shot, as well as the green IR lasers cutting through the night air below.

Shurrab's rifle barked and caught the man in the face, but not before the guard had let out a cry of alarm.

Rhome keyed his line-of-sight frequency and shouted, "Turn off your fucking IRs!"

But it was too late.

Mayhem broke out below. The sixteen al-Qaeda guards still alive outside started taking defensive positions around the perimeter of the palace.

More than half of them rushed to the top of the boardwalk above the gate.

Caught fifty yards from the perimeter wall, the Saudi assault force was out in the open, exposed as plumes of light flared up from the palace and bullets began to rain down from above.

———

Trapped in the middle of no-man's-land, fifty yards from the perimeter wall, Billy Baker couldn't believe what was happening.

He and the Saudi assault force had rounded the rock outcropping and were silently moving toward the perimeter wall when two green IR lasers suddenly turned on and cut through the air behind them.

Before he could react, he heard a shout of alarm from the palace, then the crack of a suppressed round from above.

He heard Rhome's urgent voice over the line-of-sight frequency, but he couldn't register what he'd said, because all hell was breaking loose inside the palace.

Now, forty yards from the perimeter wall, automatic gunfire rained down on them.

Bullets zipping over the former SAS operator's head, he heard the unmistakable *thwack* of a 7.62 round colliding with a human body behind him.

"GET TO THE FUCKING WALL!" Baker shouted.

Through his NODs he could see bullets kicking up dirt around him like snakes striking from the sand.

Firing his suppressed AK as he ran, he made it to the perimeter wall first, and then turned to see both Seth Proctor and Matt Rish slide in beside him, followed by only three of the Saudi assaulters.

Back against the wall, he watched the rest of the assault group run toward the main gate and engage the enemy on the boardwalk.

"WHAT THE FUCK ARE YOU DOING?!" Baker screamed.

This was exactly what he'd briefed the Saudis earlier in the day *not* to do: they were supposed to breach the wall, *not the gate*.

Watching in disbelief, Baker saw a Saudi assaulter catch a bullet in the face, as the rest of the group made it to the gate, forming a stack behind the wooden double doors.

Baker, sensing movement on the boardwalk, stepped out, aimed his weapon, and neutralized the threat. He could see that the Saudi breacher had just finished priming the charge on the gate. Not wanting to stay in the open, Baker threw his back to the wall and waited for the gate to blow.

But it never came.

"What do we do!" Rishy yelled in his ear.

Baker leaned over and saw that the Saudis were still stacked at the gate.

"Fuck this," Baker said, and then he grabbed the explosives from Proctor's rig and stuck them to the wall.

Baker primed and double-primed the explosives, then yelled for the men around him to brace. As he was about to depress the detonator, he saw a flicker of movement on the wall above him.

Raising his head, he stared into the barrels of three AK-47s, and before he could raise his own weapon, the barrels erupted in an explosion of light.

———

Riyadh, Saudi Arabia
Al-Qirawan Military Base
Fusion Center
March 7, 8:11 p.m.

Hands planted on the table in front of him, COS McCallister bit into an antacid and gazed at the live drone feed from the screens in the Fusion Center. He couldn't believe what he was seeing.

Halfway to the palace wall, two Saudi assaulters had turned on their IR lasers.

Pandemonium broke out within seconds.

In the confusion, nearly two-thirds of the assault force had not followed the Western advisers as they sprinted to the predetermined breaching site.

Instead they did exactly what they were told *not* to do.

They ran toward the gate, made a stack against the wall, and proceeded to prime their charges on the wooden doors.

"What the hell are they doing?!" McCallister asked the Saudi operations manager to his left, who looked to be in a state of panic.

When he didn't get a reply, McCallister's attention went back to the drone feed, waiting for the Saudi assaulters to finally breach the gate.

But they never did.

He could hear Billy Baker yelling over the comms and then watched the former SAS operator stick his own explosives on the wall.

That's when McCallister saw them.

Three guards had used ladders to climb up the interior of the perimeter wall, directly above where Baker and his men had primed their own explosives.

Before McCallister could react, the terrorists fired down on the group, and Baker and his men were cut to pieces.

Seconds later, the charges on the wall detonated.

———

From his perch three hundred yards up the mountain, Rhome watched the scene play out before him, his gaze catching on the three guards who'd made their way above Baker and his men.

"Shurrab!" Rhome yelled.

But it was too late.

The three terrorists rained bullets down on Baker, Proctor, Rish, and the three Saudi assaulters with them.

As they fell, Baker's explosives detonated, sending their crumpled bodies six feet through the air and into the dirt.

The three guards on the wall were also blown backward from Baker's explosive.

Shurrab's sniper rifle continued to bark.

Then another explosion pierced the night. Rhome looked toward the gate, as the wooden doors finally blew inward, and the fifteen remaining Saudi assaulters charged into the palace grounds, through the parked vehicles and toward the palace's east entrance.

A guard climbed on the back of one of the Toyota Hiluxes and was about to man the DShk 12.7 mm, when Shurrab's rifle shook the ground beneath them, sending the man sprawling.

Rhome called out shots for Shurrab, who made quick work of the terrorists at the palace's windows.

By the time the Saudis went through the palace's front doors, twelve of them remained standing.

Rhome listened intently to the gunfire happening inside and to the Saudi operations manager as he spoke to the assaulters via the comms.

They met resistance on the first floor.

The gunfire below reached a crescendo. A minute later the shooting completely stopped.

Rhome heard the Saudi operations manager say, "Assault force down. I repeat, assault force down."

As if in a dream, Rhome stared at the palace below, littered with the bodies of dead al-Qaeda and Saudi soldiers. He could see the corpses of Billy Baker, Matt Rish, and Seth Proctor.

Rhome lay there frozen, then said to Shurrab, "How many more rounds do you have?"

"Forty."

"Good enough," Rhome said, and he rolled sideways out of the camouflaged netting, scooping up his AK and his neoprene go bag. "Let's roll."

"What are you doing?" Shurrab hissed.

"Anyone with a weapon in their hand, you put them in the ground. No military-aged male with a weapon leaves that palace. You understand?"

Rhome threw his go bag on his back, clutched his AK, and started sprinting down the mountain.

Qasim al-Raymi had escaped him once.

He wouldn't again.

———

McCallister stared at the screen displaying the live drone feed.

Never in his career had he ever witnessed such a clusterfuck of an operation. It was utter bedlam in the Fusion Center, Saudi technicians and officers all shouting at one another.

Through the cacophony, McCallister heard Rhome's voice over the speakers.

"Anyone with a weapon in their hand, you put them in the ground. No military-aged male with a weapon leaves that palace. You understand?"

On the drone feed, Rhome took off down the mountainside toward the palace.

Brian Rhome is going in alone.

McCallister walked calmly over to the young Saudi operations manager and ripped the headset from his head.

As the young man began to protest, the Riyadh station chief grabbed him by the scruff of his uniform, lifted him out of his chair, and shoved him out of the way.

Sitting down, McCallister put the headset over his ears, and spoke into the lip mike, "Brian, this is Willy. I can see you're a little busy right now, and there is obviously no way I'm going to talk you out of what you're planning to do. So let me at least guide you through it."

———

Rhome held the AK in front of him like a battering ram as he sprinted down the mountain, McCallister's voice ringing in his ears.

"Copy that!" Rhome said through his throat mike, not stopping his rapid descent.

McCallister said, "From the heat signatures we are getting from the Reaper, it looks like the majority of the wedding party is on the first floor in a big room on the northwest side of the palace. There are approximately forty other heat signatures on the northeast side of the palace interspersed along the first, second, and third floors. Most likely tangos. I suggest going through the hole in the perimeter wall, and come around the back—"

"Negative," Rhome said, a plan having already formed in his mind.

He hit flat ground thirty seconds later and ran like hell toward the blown-in wooden gate. Reaching it, he slowed his pace and crouched, easing his way inside, the AK up—scanning for threats.

Hopping from parked vehicle to parked vehicle, Rhome crouched behind the back wheel of a Toyota Hilux and could hear men shouting from inside the palace.

The staircase leading to the front entrance was less than thirty yards away. To the north and south of the entrance were two open-air windows.

McCallister said, "You've got eleven tangos in the room north of the entrance."

Rhome carefully poked his head around the truck and caught a glance at the window.

A volley of gunfire discharged from the opening.

Rhome keyed his throat mike. "Shurrab, keep them pinned down!"

"Copy," Shurrab said. And Rhome immediately heard the sonic crack of a bullet pass above him.

"Willy," Rhome said, resting his AK on the Hilux's wheel and ripping his go bag from his back. "Are the innocents in the wedding party still huddled on the northwest side?"

"Affirmative," McCallister said. "Haven't moved."

"Good," Rhome said, then took out one of two oval-shaped devices the size of a football from his go bag.

This football-shaped device that he had taken from the Saudi armory the day before was a thermobaric grenade, or T-bomb.

Unlike a frag grenade, a T-bomb created such a massive pressure blast, that it would annihilate and suck the air out of a closed-in space. The pressure of the T-bomb blast would essentially rip the oxygen out of everything that contained air— this included eardrums, lungs, stomachs, and intestines—without doing much structural damage to the palace.

Rhome put his go bag back on, grabbed his AK, then with his free hand, pulled the T-bomb's pin. Scooting out from the wheel well, he chucked it into the open window.

He had seven seconds.

Sprinting to the south-facing side of the palace, Rhome counted in his head.

At five seconds, he hit the deck, and covered his ears.

The T-bomb shook the ground like an earthquake.

Rhome jumped up, ran around the compound before stopping at the stairs leading up to the palace's west entrance.

"T-bomb took out all eleven tangos," McCallister said. "Got at least two dozen heat signatures heading your way down the main hall to the west-side entrance. Wedding party hasn't moved."

Rhome took off his go bag and fished out the second T-bomb, as well as two frag grenades. He clipped the grenades to his chest rig.

AK in his left hand, he palmed the T-bomb, ran up the west entrance stairs, and took a position left of the open doors. He could hear men shouting and footsteps thundering toward him. Rhome peeked into the hallway and saw twenty al-Qaeda soldiers running directly at him.

Rhome counted to five, pulled the pin, then hurled the device down the hallway, before jumping off the stairs, and making himself small on the dirt below.

The blast was monumental.

"That seemed to do the trick," McCallister said.

Rhome asked how many more tangos were outside of the wedding party hunkered down in the northwest corner of the palace.

"I'm picking up fourteen heat signatures still scattered about the palace," McCallister said. "Nine are in a group heading for the vehicles."

Al-Raymi and his bodyguards, Rhome thought.

"Shurrab—keep them pinned down inside, I'll come in behind them."

Slinging the AK over his shoulder, Rhome grabbed the suppressed Glock, and not knowing if any of the standing soldiers had NODs, he made sure his IR was off.

Climbing back up the steps and into the pitch-black hallway, Rhome crept forward and observed the damage of the second T-bomb. Bodies that looked like they'd been turned inside out littered the floor. Rhome stepped over them, hugging the east wall, the Glock up.

"Two signatures coming down the stairs twenty yards to your left," McCallister said.

Rhome stopped—catching sight of two beams of green infrared light slicing down the staircase in front of him.

Five seconds later, two men with long beards wearing NODs stepped down into the hallway, their AKs up.

Rhome sent two suppressed rounds into the back of their heads.

"Twelve to go," McCallister said. "Keep moving northeast. Shurrab has them pinned down in the east room near the main entrance—wait STOP!"

Rhome froze.

"Two signatures just jumped from the second-floor balcony. They're coming through the west entrance behind you."

Rhome pivoted on his heel. The entrance was now fifty yards behind him, too far of a distance to be confident with the Glock, so he stepped sideways into an open room and waited.

Hugging the wall next to the open door, he listened to the heavy footfalls heading toward him.

Thirty seconds later, he heard two men walk by.

Gun raised, Rhome quietly stepped out behind them and fired two shots, one in the back of each man's head.

"Move," McCallister said.

Rhome traversed the grand hallway heading east. He could hear the sounds of women and children crying from the ballroom to his left.

"Heat signature exiting next room to your right!"

Rhome stopped in time to see a young woman stumble into the hallway, not ten feet from him. Her hands were stretched out in front of her, her headdress tilted, as she tried to find her way in the pitch darkness. Then she turned and headed straight for Rhome.

Tears streaked her dust-covered face, her hair was askew—she must have been close to the blast of the T-bomb, but other than looking scared, she appeared unhurt.

Rhome kept his pistol dead on her chest and stepped back as she continued forward.

When she got to within three feet of him, he pivoted and made himself tight against the wall.

Rhome held his breath as she passed, making her way to the wails coming from the wedding party.

I'm wasting valuable time!

"Keep straight and take the next hallway to your right," McCallister said.

Rhome turned right down the hallway, stepping over the dead bodies of the Saudi assaulters and terrorists.

The east entrance was now directly in front of him, about thirty yards.

"Shurrab has nine heat signatures hunkered down in the room to the south of where you threw the first T-bomb," McCallister said.

Rhome slowed his pace and could now hear the crack of Shurrab's rifle followed by interspersed AK fire.

Twenty yards from the door, Rhome eased a fresh mag into his Glock.

"STOP!" McCallister said.

Rhome froze.

"Six of the heat signatures just . . . just disappeared."

Rhome, uncertain, took a knee.

"Repeat?"

"There's only three heat signatures left in the room, six just disappeared."

Rhome realized what was happening.

He stood with his Glock pointed down the hallway at the door, and with his left hand, he grabbed one of the two frag grenades hanging from his chest rig and moved forward quietly.

Back to the wall, the open door now four feet to his right, he could hear men speaking frantic Arabic inside. Rhome was about to release the pin on his frag, when a man suddenly materialized in the hallway, turned, and walked right into him.

Reflexively, Rhome sent a round up through the bearded man's chin and out the back of his head. The man crumpled forward like he'd been unplugged. In one fluid motion Rhome stepped around the falling man, ripped the pin from the frag, and threw it into the room, before diving for cover.

The frag detonated and sent a cloud of debris out of the open door. Rhome leapt to his feet, swung into the room, and delivered security rounds into the two bodies on the floor. As the smoke settled, he examined the bodies.

None were Qasim al-Raymi.

Rhome keyed his mike. "The other six tangos, what was their location in the room when they disappeared?"

"Near the south wall."

Rhome moved there, seeing a collection of prayer rugs that had been blown around the room from the frag grenade. Throwing them aside, he got down on his hands and knees, and ran his free hand over the tiles on the floor, until he felt cold air rushing up at him.

Wedging his fingernails under one of the tiles, he felt it lift. Peering underneath it, he checked for booby traps.

"Got a tunnel here. Going dark."

"Negative, Brian. Wait for Shurrab—"

Rhome wasn't listening.

He slid the tile across the floor and looked down at a wooden ladder descending into the darkness.

Grabbing a small piece of rubble, Rhome threw it into the hole and heard it clatter a second later.

Not too far.

He jumped into the hole.

Landing hard, Rhome raised his weapon, adjusted his NODs, and took in his surroundings.

He was in a narrow tunnel, maybe three feet wide and seven feet high. It curved to the right twenty yards ahead.

Rhome took off. The six men who had dropped into the tunnel had a good minute head start on him.

Rhome was certain that one of these six men was Qasim al-Raymi. He'd seen the AQAP emir walking with five bodyguards as he exited his vehicle and entered the palace nearly thirty minutes before.

Knowing al-Raymi used a cane, Rhome took the straightaways in a dead-out sprint, and the turns more slowly, checking for booby traps or signs of an ambush.

After two minutes, Rhome checked his speed around a sharp bend in the tunnel and heard urgent voices ahead.

He peeked around the corner.

Six men were walking away from him, fifteen yards away. Four of the men were helping the man with the cane. The fifth man was wearing NODs, holding an AK and backpedaling behind the group, watching their six.

Suddenly, the man cried out and raised his weapon.

Rhome got off two abrupt shots and ducked backward before AK fire consumed the tunnel.

No need for stealth anymore, Rhome holstered his Glock and un-slung the AK.

He considered throwing a frag grenade, but not knowing how strong the structural integrity of the tunnel was, he decided against it.

The AK fire stopped momentarily, Rhome crouched down low, changed the AK to full auto, then panned the weapon around the corner and mashed the trigger until his magazine was empty.

Slapping in a fresh mag, Rhome listened.

There was no gunfire.

No screams of pain.

Just the smell of dirt, cordite, and blood.

AK up, Rhome peeked around the curve.

Five dead men sprawled in a heap in the middle of the tunnel.

He moved forward and put a security round in each man.

A blinding light ahead exploded through Rhome's NODs. He winced and recoiled as a pistol started barking in front of him. He was lifted off the ground and slammed on his back.

Air blown from his lungs, his AK ripped from his grasp, Rhome went for his Glock. He took the weapon from its holster, pointed it down the tunnel, and emptied the magazine.

Rhome heard a body hitting the ground, the blinding light extinguished.

Wheezing for air, Rhome finally caught his breath and propped himself up on his elbow and took stock of his body.

Two bullets had slammed into his chest armor, but the ceramic plate on the right side of his chest had done its job.

But Rhome's task wasn't complete.

Easing to his feet, ignoring the sharp pain in his chest, he took Mack's combat axe from his rig and moved toward the sound of agonized groans.

Stepping over the five dead bodies, he walked to the man trying to crawl away from him.

He stepped over the large extinguished flashlight and picked it up.

Qasim al-Raymi was writhing in the dirt like a wounded animal, trying to claw away from the pursuing predator.

Rhome flicked up his NODs and turned on the flashlight.

He wanted al-Raymi to see this.

Reaching down, he flipped the injured terrorist on his back.

At least two of Rhome's rounds had found their mark. One had nearly blown the terrorist's right shoulder clear off. The other had pierced his abdomen.

Al-Raymi wouldn't survive another two minutes.

Rhome got down on his knees, straddling the wounded man. Then he moved the flashlight's beam up to his own face so that the terrorist could see him.

"FATA, Pakistan, September sixteenth," Rhome said in clear Arabic. "You lured my men into that mountainside compound and ambushed us, you slaughtered my friends like animals."

He turned the light from his face and then shone it directly into al-Raymi's eyes.

The fear on the man's face was so primal, so complete, so perfect.

"But you didn't get me."

Rhome raised Mack's axe and then sank it into the terrorist's neck.

Again.

And again.

Heaving from the exertion, Rhome got off the dead terrorist leader and stood—images of Mack, Smitty, Whip, Hurst, and Flynn racing through his head.

Rhome snapped out of his trance a few seconds later and secured the axe to his rig before turning off the flashlight, flipping his NODs on, and finding his Glock and AK.

In a daze, he stumbled back down the tunnel. As the adrenaline wore off, the area where al-Raymi's bullets had smashed into his chest plate began to scream at him.

Minutes later, he climbed out of the tunnel.

"Brian?!" he heard McCallister say.

"Al-Raymi's dead."

"Copy," McCallister said, sounding relieved. "Rendezvous with Shurrab outside fast. You've got big problems. The whole region has woken up. Someone must have sent out a call the Saudis' jammers weren't able to stop. It looks like all of Marib and Bayhan are converging on your location. The C-130s were about to get overrun and had to leave."

Stumbling out of the palace's east entrance, Rhome said, "Good copy."

"Head northeast into the desert, then give me a call on the phone I gave you at the drone base. Our guys will be waiting. See you on the other side."

Rhome heard the noise of a diesel engine. A Toyota Hilux stopped in front of him, Shurrab behind the wheel.

The Emirati reached over and opened the passenger door.

Rhome climbed inside and repeated what McCallister had told him.

Without replying, Shurrab spun the truck around and gunned it past the rocky outcropping and the Saudis' armored vehicles, over the N17 highway and northeast into the desert night.

CHAPTER FORTY-ONE

PRESIDENT ANGELA BUCHANAN stood at the foot of her bed holding her five-year-old daughter, Elise, as she stared in irritation at the television screen on the wall across from her.

The channel was turned to an early evening news program where talking heads argued over the president and her failure to respond to the attacks on the reactors a week before.

The streaming chyron at the bottom of the screen read:

> President Buchanan silent on Iran, as hundreds
> of thousands evacuate Las Vegas.

Buchanan scowled at the screen. All anyone in the media could talk about was her reluctance to retaliate against General Soleimani and the Iranian government and how infrequently she'd been sighted recently.

In fact, she'd given two public speeches since the night of the attacks, focusing her rhetoric on making sure the signing of the Global Green Accord would move forward.

With the ceremony two days away, Buchanan needed to keep her eye on the ball. All that mattered now was taking that stage in Davos.

As the talking heads continued to ramble, she changed the channel to a local news station.

Buchanan smiled when she took in the young female reporter standing in front of the LINE Hotel in northern DC. The journalist was in the middle of a segment about Princess Amara, the Saudi ambassador to the United States, who would be giving the welcoming speech at the Middle Eastern Women's Rights Summit tomorrow morning.

Buchanan's smile broadened as she thought about the tweet the Saudi princess sent out the day before, calling out the Saudi royal court for trying to block her attendance.

Buchanan admired Amara's courage for sticking up for herself. Though Amara's cousin, the Saudi crown prince, was a reformer and believed deeply in changing the social mores of his kingdom, Buchanan understood that Amara and Raza bin Zaman were challenging religious and social institutions that were thousands of years old, institutions that strongly defended their *patriarchal* traditions. As the first woman US president, Buchanan could more than empathize with Amara's plight.

She found Amara to be strong-willed and formidable. She stood up for what she believed in and didn't let others step on her.

Maybe I need to do the same, Buchanan thought as her mind went to the Iranians.

A knock at the door tore the president from her thoughts as Eunice Tuck, the Secret Service assistant special agent in charge, poked her head inside the bedroom.

Elise stirred awake. "Tucky!"

Tuck moved into the room, her usual rigid face softening. "What are you doing awake, young lady? Shouldn't you be taking your afternoon nap?"

"Someone wanted to be with their mom," Buchanan said, letting Elise down so she could run to Tuck.

Scooping Elise into her arms, Tuck said, "They're ready for you downstairs, ma'am."

"Thank you," Buchanan said, then glanced at her watch, confused. "Why are you on shift right now, Eunice?"

"Special Agent Edwards is going over some last-minute protocols for the accord ceremony. I'm taking his shift, then heading to Davos tonight to lead the crown prince's security advance work."

Buchanan was familiar with the twelve-hour rotating shifts between

Special Agent Edwards and Agent Tuck. Usually, Tuck worked nights while Edwards ran the show during the day.

Staring at Elise in Tuck's arms, Buchanan marveled at her little girl's infatuation with the big, intimidating Secret Service agent.

Buchanan put a hand on Tuck's arm. "Eunice, I know I haven't gotten the chance to thank you yet, but I just want you to know how much it means that you are running point on the crown prince's security. I know it's not in your job description, so thank you for your flexibility."

"Of course, ma'am," Tuck said.

As a favor to the crown prince, it had been Buchanan who had insisted on sharing her Secret Service agents with the Saudis during the accord ceremony. Buchanan wanted Raza bin Zaman at her side as much as possible in Davos and realized that it would be easier if they shared the same security.

"Tell everyone I'll be downstairs in a moment," Buchanan said, then pointed to Elise. "Would you mind taking this little rascal to the kitchen? Phyllis should be in there with the twins."

"Of course, ma'am," Tuck said, carrying Elise out of the room.

In the last week, Buchanan's schedule was more jam-packed than any other time in her presidency. Between the crisis management meetings concerning the Las Vegas evacuations, to the meetings revolving around the leaked Saudi intelligence report, and everything in between, Buchanan felt like she hadn't seen her children at all.

And now I have to sit through another National Security Council meeting, she thought, going to the mirror to check her makeup.

Her aides had alerted her to the meeting earlier that morning. A meeting she found out later had been requested by Senator Declan Brandt.

Declan, she thought, shaking her head.

Even though Senator Brandt was the majority chair of the SSCI, the Senate Select Committee on Intelligence, it was unheard of for someone with his job title to call national security meetings.

He'd already finagled his way into a meeting in the Oval once this week—a meeting he had no business attending.

Making a mental note that Brandt needed to be reined in, Buchanan walked out of her room and was met by Katherine Healey, her chief of staff, and the Secret Service Shift whip, Charlie Hewitt, along with the rest of her PPD in the hallway.

"Elise is all set," Tuck said, coming out of the kitchen door. "She's eating Cheerios with the twins."

Thanking Tuck, Buchanan walked with Healey down the Grand Staircase. "Remind me again, Katherine, what's the topic of this meeting?"

"Wasn't stated, ma'am," Healey said. "Brandt wanted it hush-hush."

Buchanan rolled her eyes as they took the staircase under the West Wing and then marched through the double doors and into the Situation Room.

As she and Healey moved into the large conference room, the eight individuals sitting around the table all stood, and Buchanan saw in annoyance that Senator Brandt had positioned himself at the head of the table opposite her seat. To Brandt's right was the vice president, Michael Dunn.

"You may sit," Buchanan said, getting to her chair.

To her left sat Senator Lancaster.

Leaning over, she whispered into Lancaster's ear, "What are you doing here, Richard?"

The Texas senator, and minority chair of the SSCI, whispered, "Declan's idea."

Buchanan zeroed in on Brandt across the table. "Excuse me, Senator Brandt, but why are you and Senator Lancaster sitting in my Situation Room during a National Security Council meeting?"

Brandt cleared his throat. "Madam President, I know this is unorthodox. But these are unorthodox times. Acting Director Moretti and DNI Winslow invited us to this meeting, at my request."

"Your request?"

"Yes, ma'am," Brandt said. "Early this morning some intelligence was brought to my attention and to the attention of the SSCI by way of Acting Director Moretti and DNI Winslow. Intelligence that I pushed them to bring to your immediate attention."

Brandt indicated DNI Winslow, who passed a folder over to the chairman of the Joint Chiefs of Staff, General Edward Toole, who passed it to her.

Opening the folder, Buchanan saw a document that was headlined:

Memorandum of Notification
Title 10 Authority

Under the header was a page of fine print and a space at the bottom for her signature.

Knowing exactly what she was looking at, Buchanan glared at the individuals in the room.

"Ma'am," DNI Winslow said, "this morning, the Central Intelligence Agency came across a rare opportunity in regard to the Iranian Quds Force commander, General Soleimani. After sharing this information with my office, it was brought before your National Security Council, and then before the SSCI, who in turn, at Senator Brandt's direction, briefed Vice President Dunn, who suggested having the Title 10 lawyers draft this Memorandum of Notification and bring it to you."

Buchanan shot daggers at her vice president, before Winslow slid *another* folder across the table and went on.

"In exactly thirty-five hours, Madam President, General Soleimani will land in a private jet with members of his security at Baghdad International Airport. He will be there to participate in a secret meeting with the new Taliban command. It is the first time in nearly six months that General Soleimani has traveled out of Iran, giving us a rare opportunity to seize upon, should you be willing."

Buchanan shot daggers at her DNI. "Seize upon?"

DNI Winslow glanced at General Toole, who said, "Yes, ma'am, seize upon."

"And what exactly do you want me to *seize upon*, gentlemen?"

Senator Brandt spoke up. "A targeted assassination, Madam President. A retaliation for the attacks General Soleimani orchestrated on the thorium reactors."

Buchanan clenched her jaw. Not only could she not stand that her NSC was briefing the SSCI and her vice president before her, but it was obvious that the eight individuals sitting at the table had coordinated this meeting with a single goal in mind.

"You can't be serious," Healey said.

"We are deadly serious," said Brandt.

"Targeted assassinations are not only illegal, Senator, but they are against everything this administration stands for," Healey said.

"Targeted assassinations are *not* illegal when they apply to legitimate military targets," Brandt said. "I know they probably didn't teach you this at Yale, Katherine, but the Authorization for the Use of Military Force clearly states that an individual must pose an imminent threat to this nation to be dubbed a legitimate target. Under Article 51 of the United Nations Charter, a nation has an inherent right under international law to act in self-defense—"

"Self-defense!" said Healey.

"Yes, self-defense," Brandt said, acting offended. "General Soleimani has killed thousands of Americans over the last few decades by use of his Quds Force and proxy operatives, and he murdered four hundred and eleven more just outside Las Vegas last week. He *is* a viable military target, and he must be dealt with swiftly so he won't strike us again!"

Healey leapt out of her seat before Buchanan caught her by the shoulder and pulled her back into her chair.

Gazing at the Memorandum of Notification before her, Buchanan's mind floated back to the talking heads on the news and the posts on Twitter she'd seen over the week. The media had been all over her. Her constituents had been all over her. And now, the members of her own cabinet, the individuals *she chose* to fill America's top national security positions were meeting in secret with the SSCI and her vice president and drawing up Memorandums of Notifications behind her back.

An unfamiliar feeling crept up her spine, a feeling of not being in control.

Still staring at the document before her, she realized she'd been having that same feeling all week. Deep down she knew that the voices screaming at her online and on the news were correct. She knew that her lack of action against the Iranians was a display of weakness on her part.

On America's part.

Buchanan said, "Is it the consensus of everyone in this room that I should sign this Memorandum of Notification? That I should sign off on the targeted killing of General Soleimani?"

Nearly everyone nodded their heads.

"Richard," Buchanan said to Senator Lancaster, "you don't seem convinced."

His arms crossed, Lancaster sighed deeply. "I don't know, Madam President. It would be a bold decision given how close we are to Davos."

"A bold, but necessary decision," Senator Brandt said. "We would be drawing a line in the sand. The elimination of General Soleimani would be a show of strength before the signing. You've been watching the news, Madam President. We all have. The American people are hurting. Our country and our allies have been brutally attacked, and they are calling upon you to respond!"

"And tell me, Declan," Healey said, her voice like serrated wire. "How would killing General Soleimani protect the American people? How would his death not escalate tensions with Iran?"

"I'm not telling the president to start World War III, Katherine," Brandt said. "I'm telling her to cut the head off the snake that murdered three thousand people at seven reactor sites seven nights ago. I'm reminding the president that she took an oath of office to protect and defend the American people. We've been attacked, and we will be attacked again. Madam President, your polling numbers have plummeted this week. Even your own party is calling on you to retaliate."

Buchanan looked back down at the Memorandum of Notification, her mind blocking out Healey, who continued to argue with Brandt.

As much as she hated to admit it, Brandt was correct. Her polling numbers had hemorrhaged. And with nearly eight months until the next presidential election, Buchanan truly worried about her chances getting a second term if she let the Iranians slide. *Cutting the head* off the snake, as Brandt had put it, was not the same as waging war with Iran. General Soleimani *had* killed innocent Americans on American soil.

"Everyone other than Vice President Dunn, Secretary of Defense Lake, and General Toole are excused," Buchanan said.

Brandt and Healey went dead silent.

"Ma'am," Healey said. "I—"

"Now, Katherine!"

As everyone stood, Buchanan put a hand on Senator Lancaster's arm. "You stay, Richard."

After the rest of the individuals left the room, Buchanan pointed a finger at Vice President Dunn. "Michael, the next time you go behind my back with members of *my* cabinet and pull a stunt like this Memorandum of Notification, you're finished, do you hear me?"

Dunn, who turned a shade of scarlet, said, "Angela . . . I was doing you a favor. We know how busy you've been—"

Buchanan raised a hand, silencing her vice president, then she looked over at General Toole. "If I authorize this use of military force against General Soleimani, how would it occur?"

Toole said, "We would use a collection of Hellfire R9X missiles that would be fired from Reaper drones. They would target Soleimani's caravan as it leaves the tarmac of Baghdad International. These missiles do not contain an explosive warhead, but instead carry a ring of six massive blades that expand and spin on impact. The Hellfire R9X missiles would all but ensure that there would be no unintended casualties."

Buchanan looked to Lancaster. "Richard, what do you think?"

Lancaster put his elbows on the table. "Angela, you know my stance when it comes to things like this. I was one of the few who voted against going to war after the Towers fell on September eleventh. You know my thoughts on the war on terror, but—"

"But?"

"Despite all Senator Brandt's bravado, I think he's right on this one. You would be targeting an individual, not a nation. A war criminal who should have been dealt with decades ago."

"You think I should go through with it?"

Lancaster paused for a good fifteen seconds, and then gave her an almost indiscernible nod of his head.

Buchanan found herself stroking the greenstone pendant hanging from her neck. She could almost hear Bobby's voice in her head, reminding her of the values they'd shared. The values they'd based her campaign on.

She'd ended the war on terror.

She'd cut military and intelligence spending in half.

America was no longer the world's police.

But you're not here, Bobby, she thought. *The Iranian government has gone too far.*

Picking up a pen on the table, Buchanan said, "Very well."

Signing on the dotted line at the bottom of the Memorandum of Notification, the president shut the folder and slid it over to Secretary of Defense Lake and then stood.

"You have my permission to carry out the targeted assassination of General Soleimani. We will reconvene here then to oversee the operation. Now if you excuse me, gentlemen, I have a lot on my plate this evening."

CHAPTER FORTY-TWO

RHOME WINCED AS he delicately prodded the right side of his chest where al-Raymi's bullets had slammed into his ceramic plate.

Glancing down at the coordinates McCallister had texted him on his cell phone, Rhome took the GPS from his lap, and said, "We're almost there. Keep the headlights off and drive slowly. They're going to treat us like a threat until they determine we aren't one."

Shurrab nodded from under his night-vision goggles and gunned the Toyota Hilux up a large sand dune.

"All right, slow down," Rhome said, as the truck came over the top.

Flipping his NODs over his eyes, he spotted a UH-60 Black Hawk sitting in the sand below, six figures forming a perimeter around it.

Sixty seconds later, Rhome and Shurrab came to a stop in front of the Black Hawk. Sticking their hands out of their windows, they opened their doors and stepped onto the sand. Moving away from the vehicle, Rhome and Shurrab kept their arms out in an Iron Cross position, as three of the six figures approached, their weapons trained on them.

"Ringo," the operator in front said.

"Star," Rhome replied, reciting the validation code McCallister had texted to him.

The lead operator lowered his weapon, and so did the five other men.

Dropping their arms, Rhome and Shurrab stepped forward.

"Heard it got a little dicey down in Ar Risan a couple of hours ago," the operator said, then pointed to Mack's bloodied combat axe sitting in Rhome's chest rig. "When we got the word to come get you, we wondered if you brought that thing."

Rhome's eyes settled on the man's own identical axe in his rig, and the patch on his shoulder, realizing that he was looking at members of Mack's old SEAL squadron.

"You're—"

"Your ride home," the man said, introducing himself as a senior chief petty officer.

The five other SEALs came up behind him.

One of the younger assaulters carried a small cooler. "Heard you gave that piece of shit al-Raymi a dirt nap. You thirsty?"

The young SEAL reached into the cooler, pulled out a PBR, and handed it to Rhome.

Shurrab waved his away.

"A couple of us used to run with Mack back in the day, before he got soft and went to Ground Branch," the assault leader said, with a grin.

Rhome laughed and held up the beer. "PBR? I thought you Dam Neck boys only drank White Claw?"

That got a bunch of middle fingers.

"You ever find yourself in Virginia Beach," the assault leader then said, "the beers are on us."

The man then jacked a thumb over his shoulder. "C'mon. Let's get you boys home. You can drink that on the helo."

Rhome and Shurrab climbed into the Black Hawk with the SEALs, and as the chopper lifted from the ground, Rhome cracked his beer and gazed down at the endless sea of sand, before the bird banked to the north and headed back to Saudi Arabia.

CHAPTER FORTY-THREE

NORA RYDER YAWNED and reached for a cup of coffee that had gone cold hours ago. Taking a sip, she grimaced at its sour taste and then continued going over the hundreds of intercepted signals intelligence that Lodgepole had pulled from Saud Rahmani's iPhone in the last seven weeks.

Since arriving at Lodgepole's off-site subterranean mission center the morning before, and after watching Brian Rhome successfully eliminate Qasim al-Raymi in Yemen, Ryder had spent nearly every waking second poring over the Lodgepole folder, and Dan Miller's Hail Mary folder, trying not only to familiarize herself with the content, but to find ways Lodgepole could thwart the conspiracy against the Global Green Accord and save President Buchanan without Brian Rhome having to go off on Dan Miller's half-cocked operation.

But the more she'd learned about Hail Mary, the more she'd realized it was their best shot, should Lodgepole be unable to crack the flash drive and read the Dark Sun file.

Setting the coffee down, she looked up at Elaine Cho and Mike Adams, who sat at their workstation where the decryption program was still attempting to crack the flash drive. Next to Cho and Adams sat Miller, Brenner, and Huey, who had just finished speaking to William McCallister over the SVTC.

Catching her gaze, Huey excused himself from Brenner and Miller and sat down opposite Ryder.

"Rhome made it back to Riyadh late last night," Huey said. "McCallister hasn't been able to reach him yet, but he's just heard through Luca Steiner that everything is moving forward on schedule." Huey pointed to the folders before her. "Find anything we might have missed?"

Ryder shook her head.

After reading and rereading the Hail Mary and Lodgepole folders the night before, she'd been surprised how intrusive the members of Lodgepole had been in examining the lives of the Americans suspected of being involved in the conspiracy. Not only had Lodgepole done a deep dive into every Secret Service agent working in close proximity to President Buchanan, but Ryder had been astonished to see who they initially pinned as a prime suspect.

"You all thought Director Hastings was involved?"

Huey nodded. "We did until we read that letter."

"Why?"

"Because of her strained relationship with Buchanan. They can't stand each other. When we first got down here, we were looking for suspects who had a motive to act against Buchanan. That's why Hastings was never read in."

"You actually thought Director Hastings was capable of treason?"

Huey shrugged. "Like Miller said, we can't really trust anyone."

"So why were Miller and Brenner so insistent on sending Rhome to Saudi Arabia? Why not just send you, or someone else in Ground Branch who was briefed on Lodgepole and Hail Mary?"

"I couldn't go; I'm technically still working for the agency. The Saudis were looking for outsiders. Plus, I'm injured."

Pulling down his shirt collar, Huey exposed a freshly healed wound on his left pectoral muscle.

"I caught a round in the chest a few months back in Syria. Bullet bounced off my chest plate and lodged itself in my heart. I was on medical leave when Brenner and Miller pulled me into this."

"Jesus."

"And for the record, Brenner was incredibly against sending in his godson," Huey said. "It was all Miller's idea. Given Rhome's history with al-Raymi, Miller knew Rhome would do everything in his power

to make sure al-Raymi never left the Ar Risan Palace alive. He knew
Rhome would be the best candidate they could put forward to pass
the crown prince's test and be offered a spot on the Rapid Intervention
Group."

"What's Rhome's history with al-Raymi?"

"Al-Raymi killed Rhome's team in Pakistan last September. Rhome
was the only survivor."

"Okay?" Ryder said, confused. "I still don't understand *why* Rhome
wasn't briefed on Lodgepole and Hail Mary *before* he headed to Saudi
Arabia. Why is he being kept in the dark until the last minute?"

"Because," Huey said, "Rhome would never have gone if we briefed
him beforehand. The kid doesn't want to have anything to do with the
agency."

For the next two minutes, Huey told Ryder everything that occurred
in Pakistan.

When he finished, Ryder felt sick.

"Look," Huey said. "Rhome is a complicated guy. I worked with him
for years; he's one of the best. Now that al-Raymi is dead, Rhome will
see things clearly, and McCallister will convince him to participate in
Hail Mary."

"How can you be so sure? What if McCallister can't convince him?
And if he does, what if it fails?" Ryder shook her head in frustration,
then said, "Yesterday, when I showed up here, Mansur and Bennett were
leaving to go somewhere; where were they going?"

Huey looked uncomfortable. "They went to Davos, to be boots on
the ground with *another* individual who's been read in."

Ryder cocked her head. "Who?"

"One of Brenner and Miller's old friends. A guy named Benedicht
Imdorf. He's the deputy director of the Swiss Federal Intelligence Service, and the person in charge of security in Davos."

"He knows all the details of Lodgepole and Hail Mary?"

"No," Huey said. "But he's aware of the threat to Buchanan's life.
He knows the Secret Service might be compromised, and that Miller
and Brenner are running an operation to stop that threat. Bennett and
Mansur were sent to join Imdorf to be Lodgepole's eyes in Davos. If Hail
Mary succeeds, Imdorf, Mansur, and Bennett will be notified, and they

will work to neutralize the threat against Buchanan. If Hail Mary fails, we will all meet them in Davos right before the ceremony."

"We're all going to Davos if Hail Mary fails?" Ryder asked.

"Yes."

"For what?"

"To help Jack and Danny carry out the final contingency."

"And what's that—"

"WE'RE IN!!"

Ryder whipped around and saw Mike Adams with his fist in the air. The man jumped up, excitedly. "We're into the flash drive!"

From all sides of the hexagonal room, Brenner, Miller, Silva, and Bell ran over and grouped behind Adams and Cho.

Ryder peered down at Adams's laptop screen as the analyst clicked on the flash drive's icon on his desktop and up popped two files, labeled.

Dark Sun   RIG

"Click Dark Sun first," Miller instructed.

Adams clicked on the folder and cursed. "It's encrypted."

Ryder stared at the open file on the screen showing pages of nonsensical characters.

"Can you break it?" Miller asked.

"No, it's encrypted with the Orion technology."

"Then try the RIG folder."

Adams closed the Dark Sun folder and clicked on RIG.

The file opened and Adams scrolled through dozens of pages of what looked like account numbers, wire transfers, business transactions, and plans for the Rapid Intervention Group.

"Anything on the dissident living in DC?" Miller asked.

"Hold on," Adams said, still scrolling.

Ryder knew from reading the Hail Mary folder that there were nineteen Saudi dissidents living in the greater Washington, DC, area, all of whom had fled the kingdom in the last couple years. Having tried to find the specific dissident that the crown prince had ordered silenced, Lodgepole infiltrated the phones and computers of all nineteen dissidents and searched them using the keyword *Dark Sun* or anything related to the crown prince, Saud Rahmani, or Turki Shahidi. Lodgepole got nothing about Dark Sun, or anything about an article that was going to be published before the accord.

"Wait, here's something," Adams said. "The Saudis purchased a Pegasus system a few years back. They're using a Pegasus system to track their dissidents living abroad."

"What's a Pegasus system?" Silva asked.

Cho said, "It's a cloak-and-dagger system developed by NSO Group, the same company that makes the Orion encryption. Pegasus takes advantage of zero-day exploits—software loopholes in computers and phones. It's like a Trojan horse that can access your devices through innocuous means, kind of like the technology we're using to infiltrate Rahmani's iPhone. Once in, whoever is using Pegasus can virtually control your device, like turn on your camera or mic, see your location, and read your text messages."

"Guys!" Adams said, gripping the side of his laptop screen. "Guys . . . I think I got him. I think I got the name of the dissident the Saudis are coming to kill!"

CHAPTER FORTY-FOUR

Washington, DC
The LINE Hotel
The Church Venue
March 8, 8:00 a.m.

PRINCESS AMARA KNEW she was being watched.

Leaning against the second-floor balcony of the LINE Hotel's Church Venue, Amara scanned the nearly eight hundred guests gathered below for the Middle Eastern Women's Rights Summit.

She was looking for someone. A man she needed to save. A man she prayed could save her life and the lives of her children.

Taking in the politicians, dignitaries, diplomats, celebrities, and journalists all huddled around the breakfast buffet tables, she caught sight of the queen consort of Jordan, but she had yet to spot the man she was looking for.

Shooting a glance behind her, she noticed her chief of staff, Wali Mattar, and her two minders staring at her from ten feet away.

God, she hated them.

In the two days that had passed since she had sent out her incendiary tweet, her minders had kept her phoneless and locked away in her room, where she had found herself half delirious and exhausted.

It was apparent to Amara now that she was being drugged.

Locking eyes with Wali Mattar, she cursed him under her breath, and then returned her attention to the crowd below.

Since leaving the Saudi ambassador compound an hour before, Mattar and his men had never left her side, listening in on every greeting and conversation since arriving at the summit.

"Eight minutes until your welcome speech, Princess," Mattar said in her ear. "Afterward, we will leave. Is that clear?"

"Very."

Mattar moved away, and Amara was just about to shift her gaze back across the room, when she spotted him.

Bald head, short stature, with a salt-and-pepper goatee and glasses, Jabril Khashiri, the Saudi dissident journalist, meandered through the crowd before stopping in front of the Jordanian queen consort.

Trying to contain her fear, and focusing exactly on what she needed to do, the princess headed for the staircase, blowing by Mr. Mattar and her minders.

"Princess?" Mattar cried, hurrying after her. "Where are you going?"

Amara moved her agile frame through the crowd on the balcony much faster than her bulky minders. Hitting the stairs, she fumbled with the concealed slit she'd sewn into her abaya the night before and took out the USB, clenching it in her left hand.

Behind her, she heard Mattar and his men pushing aside guests to keep up. On the main floor, Amara darted through the crowd until she came up behind the Jordanian queen consort and put a hand on the woman's shoulder.

Queen Amal embraced Amara, then they exchanged kisses on each other's cheeks. When they let go of each other, a commotion sounded from behind them.

"Princess Amara!" Mattar yelled from back in the crowd. "Wait!"

Using the disturbance as a distraction, the princess took a step toward Khashiri, brushed his right shoulder, and then pivoted 180 degrees toward her minders. As she did, she slipped the USB into Khashiri's right jacket pocket before coming face-to-face with her furious chief of staff.

Khashiri, Queen Amal, and the others in the crowd stared at Mr. Mattar and his men.

"Mr. Mattar," Amara said. "What on earth do you think you are doing?"

Trying to catch his breath, and realizing that nearly half of the room was now watching, Mattar sputtered, "Y-Your speech . . . they want you to begin now. Early."

Amara shook her head. "Please tell the organizers that I will start at the scheduled time. I wish to say hello to my friends first. Alone."

Glaring at Khashiri, Mattar said, "I am under orders to stay at your side—"

Amara raised her hand. "Take five steps back, Mr. Mattar."

Still aware that all eyes were on him, Mattar took three steps back, and stood there, scowling.

Amara turned toward the journalist.

"Mr. Khashiri, it is so wonderful to see you."

Khashiri glanced nervously at Mattar, then to Amara. "And you, Madam Ambassador. Congratulations on your appointment."

"Thank you."

"Are you settling into Washington life?"

"Well enough," she said, trying to naturally turn the conversation. "I do wish my children were with me."

Khashiri arched an eyebrow. "They are still in the kingdom?"

"Unfortunately. But they will be meeting me here after the signing of the Global Green Accord. Tell me, Mr. Khashiri, how is your son, Subhi, doing? He must be old enough to be in university now?"

"Yes. He began his studies at the University of Riyadh this year."

"I haven't seen him since he was a little boy," Amara said, engaging the man's eyes. "Did you know that Subhi shares a birthday with my son?"

"I didn't," Khashiri said. "September twenty-third?"

"Saudi National Day," Amara said. "I remember my father saying that Subhi was born on Saudi National Day, which must have been what? Eighteen years ago?"

"Nineteen, actually."

"Well, my son is only eight, and my daughter is only five. Did you know that her birthday is just two days before my son's on September twenty-first? My children, of course, demand two separate parties, which can be hectic."

The dissident journalist cocked his head at Amara, in reappraisal.

The string quartet stopped playing, and the master of ceremonies went to the dais and tapped on the microphone.

"Madam Ambassador," Mattar said. "It is time for your speech."

Never breaking eye contact with Khashiri, Amara said, "As parents, we will do anything for our children. Won't we, Mr. Khashiri?"

Confusion lined the man's face. "Yes . . . of course."

Amara said her goodbyes, then made her way to the stage, praying that Khashiri would find the USB in his jacket pocket and remember their strange conversation.

It could save his life.

And maybe even her own.

CHAPTER FORTY-FIVE

Jabril Khashiri's Apartment
Washington, DC
March 8, 9:00 a.m.

JABRIL KHASHIRI STEPPED out of the Uber that stopped in front of his apartment building.

Looking down at the Uber app on his phone, Khashiri gave the driver five stars, then closed out of the app, and swore as the palm of his hand felt like it was burning.

In the last month, his iPhone's battery was not only draining at an alarming rate, but the phone would sometimes get so hot he could barely hold it.

He had taken it to the Apple store the week before, but the techs couldn't find anything wrong.

As his Uber drove away, his mind went to Princess Amara's opening speech at the Middle Eastern Women's Rights Summit from an hour before.

Having initially planned on eating breakfast at the event, Khashiri had gotten spooked at seeing Amara's chief of staff, Wali Mattar. He was a known confidant of the crown prince, and Khashiri had zero intention of being around the man. So, after slipping out of the venue after Amara's speech, Khashiri called an Uber and went home.

Still standing before his building, Khashiri placed his iPhone in his jacket pocket and felt something metallic brush against his knuckles.

What the hell? he thought, lifting out a small, silver USB.

The dissident journalist stared at the object. It certainly wasn't his;

he kept his thumb drives on his key chain. And it certainly had not been in his pocket before he'd gotten to the summit. He was sure of that.

Confused, he went into his building, and entered his first-floor apartment. Turning on the lights, he walked through his living room filled with the cheap, rented furniture. He placed the USB on the kitchen table next to his laptop computer and a stack of photographs, then went to the fridge and grabbed a bottle of water.

Taking a sip, Khashiri stared at his kitchen table, which was now serving as his makeshift work desk, and sighed.

Look at what my life has become. Look how far I've fallen.

Jabril Khashiri had once been one of the most prominent journalists in the Arab world.

But that was over.

The tides had shifted in Saudi Arabia from the old to the new.

In the old world, Khashiri had always walked a fine line with the royal family. He had never been one to shy away from voicing his opinions. He'd built a career calling out injustices when he'd seen them. And given his esteemed reputation, he'd gotten away with his criticisms without much blowback. That changed when the Saudi crown prince assumed power.

Very quickly, Khashiri had seen his articles censored, his Twitter account attacked, and his reputation questioned.

An early supporter of the crown prince, Khashiri had seen much potential in the young ruler. But every time he wrote any criticisms of Raza bin Zaman, he'd found himself silenced.

It started out small—routine visits from the royal court, especially from Saud Rahmani, who told him not to publish anything critical of the crown prince. Not willing to censor himself, Khashiri was soon fired by every paper he worked for.

With no publication behind him, his Twitter account locked, and his passport confiscated, Khashiri became a silenced and miserable man. An intellectually castrated *persona non grata*.

Just when he thought things couldn't have gotten worse, he'd received a phone call in the middle of the night from an old friend in the royal court.

His friend's voice had been frantic.

He'd told Khashiri that Saud Rahmani, by royal decree of the crown prince, would begin arresting dissenters of the state. A list had been made, and Khashiri's name was on it.

Khashiri packed a suitcase and, using a fake passport, fled Saudi Arabia for the United States. In his hotel room in Washington, DC, two days later, he'd watched the news of the "Ritz Roundups" happening in Riyadh, horrified, but grateful that he'd escaped in the nick of time.

That was seven weeks ago, and since then Khashiri rented a small apartment in DC and had tried getting a job at an American newspaper.

But that, too, proved difficult.

No US media outlet wanted to hire a Saudi dissident speaking out against the crown prince, especially with the Global Green Accord coming up.

That was why, five weeks ago, Khashiri started his own blog criticizing the crown prince.

But the traffic on his blog had been dismal, and with his finances drying up, Khashiri was growing desperate, until he was hit with a stroke of good luck.

Three weeks before, an old source contacted him with a story that had the potential to shake up everything, a story that could nail the crown prince.

Khashiri jumped headfirst into the project. He had spent every waking hour interviewing, collecting evidence, and writing an article that he planned to post before the world leaders took the stage in Davos.

If all went well, his career as a dignified journalist could begin again.

Khashiri stared down at his laptop and the photographs of the gruesome images his source had sent him.

Walking over to the kitchen table, he surveyed the images of the dead Sudanese children and shook his head in sadness. Then his attention returned to the USB he found in his jacket pocket, and his mind went to the conversation he'd had that morning with Princess Amara.

Khashiri had always adored the princess.

He'd known her since her birth.

Having been friends with her late father, Khashiri had watched her grow into a striking, outspoken force for good in the kingdom.

She was one of the best communicators he'd ever known—her speech that morning at the summit a case in point—which was why he'd found the conversation he'd had with her to be so odd.

Why had the princess been so fascinated with his son's, Subhi's, birthday? Why was she so insistent about drawing the parallels between her own children's birthdays and Subhi's?

Khashiri sat down and inserted the USB into his laptop's port. Immediately, the USB showed up on his desktop with the name:

Scheherazade

Khashiri stared at the name, confused. Then, clicking on the USB's icon, a smaller window opened, asking him to enter a password.

"Huh," Khashiri said.

Then it struck him like a lightning bolt.

He remembered Princess Amara brushing up along him when her chief of staff, Wali Mattar, and his thugs had chased her.

Had the princess dropped the USB into my pocket?

Why would she do that?

Why would she give me a locked USB without giving me the password—

Immediately, it all started to make sense.

The odd conversation.

The birthdays.

Her children's birthdays.

Growing excited, he tried to remember what Amara had said.

Her son shared a birthday with Subhi—September 23—Saudi National Day.

But how old did she say he was? Eight? Nine?

And her daughter? She was five? Or was she four? Amara definitely said she was born two days before Saudi National Day, so—September 21?

Khashiri spent some time plugging in various numbers into the password bar corresponding to the dates of Amara's children's birthdays.

After a handful of attempts, his computer dinged, and he was inside the USB.

A window appeared, with two files inside:

Dark Sun   RIG

Khashiri clicked on the Dark Sun file first and found dozens of pages of coded, jumbled characters.

Exiting out of that file, he clicked the next one, labeled RIG.

The file opened to documents displaying bank accounts, routing numbers, addresses, maps, and directives.

Khashiri's eyes grew wider and wider as he scanned through the pages.

Two minutes later, he read something that caused him to jump out of his seat so fast, his kitchen chair clattered to the floor behind him.

Alarm bells rang in his head, bells that coincided with an emotion he hadn't felt since his friend had called him and told him to leave Saudi Arabia seven weeks before.

Panic.

Ripping the USB from the port, he tried to get control of his faculties.

"Calm down," he said. "You set up a contingency for something like this."

Hurrying into his living room, he grabbed his external hard drive and began backing up the research and article for his blog post.

As they started to copy, he snatched the USB, marched into his bedroom, grabbed a suitcase, and threw it on the bed.

He shoved three days' worth of clothes and a toiletry bag into the suitcase, then got on his knees and reached under the bed frame. His fingers closed around a ziplock bag he'd duct-taped to the inside of the bed's sideboard. Wrenching out the ziplock, Khashiri fumbled with the plastic until he just ripped the whole thing in half, its contents spilling out on the floor. A prepaid flip phone, a locker key, a counterfeit Canadian passport, and five thousand dollars in cash stared up at him.

He pocketed the cash, passport, and locker key, then slapped the lithium ion battery into the prepaid phone and powered it on.

Recalling a number he'd memorized, Khashiri sent off a coded text message, shut the phone, walked back to his kitchen table, and stared at his iPhone.

Now, he understood why it was so hot to the touch.

Now, he knew why its battery was constantly draining.

Holding the burner phone, Khashiri picked up his iPhone, then threw both items down the garbage disposal and turned it on. Satisfied that both phones were shredded into oblivion, he walked back over to his laptop.

The article he'd been working on and the research he needed were now successfully downloaded onto his external hard drive. He spent the next five minutes erasing everything on his laptop's hard drive. Taking a hammer from his utility closet, he smashed the laptop into hundreds of tiny pieces.

Khashiri grabbed the photographs, and along with the external hard drive, walked to his suitcase and stuffed everything inside.

Not bothering to shut off the lights, or lock his doors, he exited the building via the back entrance, hooked a right down the alley, and disappeared into the cool Washington, DC, morning.

CHAPTER FORTY-SIX

"WHAT ARE WE waiting for?" Ryder asked Huey, from the passenger seat of a white utility van.

The CIA Ground Branch operator behind the wheel continued to stare at Jabril Khashiri's apartment building.

Huey touched the earpiece that linked him to Dan Miller, Jack Brenner, Cho, and Adams back at Lodgepole, then looked at Ryder. "Bell and Silva are finishing their sweeps around the neighborhood; once they're in position on each side of the alley, you'll make your move."

It had been nearly two hours since Lodgepole had seen Jabril Khashiri's name in the RIG file on the flash drive, and twelve minutes since Huey had parked the van up the street from the Saudi dissident's apartment building.

After discovering Jabril Khashiri was the target of the crown prince's Rapid Intervention Group, the members of Lodgepole had argued over their next course of action.

Dan Miller's original Hail Mary operation had called for the Saudi dissident to be sacrificed at the hands of RIG. But now that Lodgepole knew the identity of the target, Ryder had vehemently opposed letting Khashiri die.

In the end, though, after coming up with no way to save the dissident without blowing Rhome's cover, Lodgepole voted to move forward, make contact with Khashiri, find out what he knew about Dark Sun, and then throw him to the wolves.

Ryder, still upset with the decision, heard Huey say, "Bell and Silva are in position. You still want to go in alone?"

Back at Lodgepole, Ryder had insisted that she be the one to make contact with Khashiri. He was less likely to spook if a smaller woman knocked on his door, rather than someone as big and intimidating as Huey.

"Yes," she said.

Huey handed her an earpiece and she put it in her ear.

"You got me?" she asked.

Bell, Silva, and the rest of Lodgepole replied that they could hear her.

"Good luck," Huey said. "Anything goes wrong, give me the code word, and I'll be at your side in ten seconds."

Ryder stepped out of the van and walked to Khashiri's apartment building.

Luckily, the apartment that the Saudi dissident was renting didn't have a door where she would need to be buzzed in; it was one of those old apartments that had its own entrance facing the street.

Ryder stopped before the door and knocked.

To her left was the living room window, a light cotton curtain obstructing her view.

"Knock again," Brenner said, through her earpiece.

Ryder knocked more forcefully this time.

Nothing.

"Okay," Brenner said. "David, Mark, come up through the back."

Ryder waited until Bell and Silva got to Khashiri's back entrance.

"Jack," Bell said, "the rear door is wide open."

"Shit. Okay, Nora, wait until Huey gets to you—"

But Ryder had already slipped her hand under her jacket and pulled out her pistol, her other hand testing Khashiri's door handle.

It was unlocked, and as she turned it, and pushed her way inside, she could hear Huey over the earpiece ordering her to wait.

Gun up, Ryder stepped into the apartment, cleared the hallway, and moved into the living room. As she did, she turned toward the kitchen and saw Bell and Silva come through the rear door. Backtracking, she

moved into the hallway, then cleared the single bedroom and bathroom.

Khashiri was gone.

Holstering her weapon, she stepped into the living room to find
Huey, red in the face.

"He's not here," Ryder said.

"What the hell, Nora," Huey said. "I told you to wait!"

Ignoring the man, Ryder moved into the kitchen and saw Bell and
Silva standing over a smashed-up laptop.

"No suitcase in the closet, and all his toiletries are gone," Huey said,
coming into the kitchen.

"He ran," Bell said, then pointed to the sink. "Look at this."

Ryder, Huey, and Silva joined him, and she took in the small electri-
cal fragments collected around the garbage disposal rim.

"What's this?"

Bell found a pair of tongs in a drawer and inserted them down the
disposal, pulling up the mangled remains of an iPhone and a small silver
flip phone.

"Adams," Huey said into his earpiece. "Check every database and
run facial recognition on every transportation hub in and around the
city—rental cars, Uber, Lyft, subway, trains, and flights."

"On it."

Standing in the kitchen, Ryder turned 360 degrees.

What the hell caused Khashiri to run?

What spooked him?

"I got something, and you're not going to believe this," Cho said, in
their earpieces.

Huey said, "Facial ID?"

"No. Better than that. We just intercepted another conversation from
Saud Rahmani's iPhone to Turki Shahidi."

"What did they say?"

"Rahmani told Shahidi that *their DC dissident signaled another Saudi
dissident in Canada, and that he is fleeing there, now.*"

"Khashiri is fleeing to Canada?" Silva said.

"Affirmative," replied Cho. "The crown prince wants both dissidents
taken care of when RIG arrives tomorrow night—"

Adams cut off Cho. "Got positive facial recognition on Khashiri! He boarded a bus at the Greyhound Station over an hour ago. He bought a ticket to Montreal."

"Montreal?" Huey said. "What Saudi dissident lives in Montreal?"

Ryder snapped her head up. "I know who he's going to see."

She described a piece of intelligence her asset Apache had slipped her months ago about Rahmani tracking a Saudi dissident in Montreal—a young YouTube vlogger who had fled Saudi Arabia the year before.

"We should stop that bus and grab Khashiri before he gets to the border; hell, *we* could stop him at the border," Huey said.

"No!" Ryder said, and a plan began to build in her mind. "I know exactly where Khashiri is going and who he is going to see. I think we can save two lives tonight without tipping off the Saudis."

"Okay?" Miller said.

Ryder said, "Beirut, 1985. Operation Veiled Cobra."

"The Mossad/CIA joint extraction?" Cho asked.

"Exactly," Ryder said.

"But that means—"

Ryder cut Cho off this time. "Elaine—where is Rhome right now?"

"On his way to see the crown prince as we speak. Shahidi and Rahmani said they are meeting with him too."

"Good," Ryder said. "Get ahold of McCallister, tell him that we have a change of plans. In the meantime, we need to call every morgue in the area, hell, call every morgue in the United States and Canada. If this is going to work, we need to move fast."

CHAPTER FORTY-SEVEN

RHOME STEPPED INTO the luxury helicopter and sat down opposite Major General Ahmad Azimi, nodding to the man.

Azimi, his face pale and distant, diverted his attention.

It had taken the SEAL team thirty minutes to fly Rhome and Shurrab to the Saudi drone base, where he and the Emirati had boarded a jet that took them to Riyadh.

Rhome initially thought they'd be taken to Al-Qirawan Military Base but instead they were flown to a private airstrip and met by a caravan of Saudi National Guardsmen driving black Range Rovers.

The Guardsmen put Rhome in one of the vehicles and Shurrab in another and then drove Rhome to a private hospital on the outskirts of the city.

Throughout the course of the night and into the day, Saudi doctors had run a litany of tests on Rhome's chest, subjecting him to x-rays and even an MRI.

Other than a hairline rib fracture and some heavy bruising, Rhome was fine.

After his tests, Luca Steiner had come into his room. Rhome told the Swiss lawyer he was ready to get the hell out of the kingdom, collect his pay, and go home.

"The crown prince wants to meet you first, and thank you personally for what you did in Yemen. I'll take you to your flight afterward."

Rhome knew that the crown prince wasn't just meeting him to thank him. In this part of the world it never worked like that. The crown prince was going to offer him a job.

After Steiner left, Rhome had slept into the afternoon, then he was taken to a helipad.

Buckling himself into his seat, Rhome felt the chopper take off and head south into the desert.

For twenty minutes, he gazed down at the sand dunes painted in orange as the sun sank to the west.

When the chopper descended and landed, Rhome saw a group of helicopters in front of several Bedouin-style tents.

"This way, please," a guardsman said, opening the chopper's door, and ushering Rhome and Azimi toward the entrance of the largest tent. As they got closer, a tall figure exited the tent and came their way.

Rhome recognized the man's gait.

Kazem Shurrab locked eyes with Rhome and nodded as he headed toward one of the other waiting choppers.

Nice to see you, too, Rhome thought.

He'd decided on the mountain above the Ar Risan Palace that Shurrab was a strange guy. It wasn't that he was a man of few words—Rhome was as well—but there was something off about the Emirati, an intensity behind his dark eyes, that made Rhome uneasy.

The guardsman escorted him and Azimi into the tent, and Rhome was taken aback at the scene before him.

A feast, literally fit for a king, was sitting on a large table. Roasted goat and lamb, mounds of multicolored rice, and juices sat among gold cutlery. The ground was covered with opulent rugs and plush lounge pillows.

"Mr. Shurrab informed me that you are a talented soldier," a deep voice said to Rhome's left.

The crown prince, Raza bin Zaman, walked into the tent, flanked by two other men.

One of them was short and squat, the other tall, lean, and strong.

"Your Royal Highness," Azimi said, bowing his head.

"General Azimi, Mr. Rhome, thank you for coming."

Not entirely sure how to greet the crown prince, Rhome said, "Thank you for having me, Your Highness."

"Are you hungry, Mr. Rhome?" Raza asked.

"Not particularly."

Raza looked down at the black phone in his hand before introducing the tall man behind him as Turki Shahidi, and the short pudgy man as Saud Rahmani.

"Your Highness," Azimi said. "I want to apologize for the failure of my men in the assault."

"The campaign was a success, General, thanks to Mr. Rhome here."

"Still—"

"You have nothing to apologize for. Qasim al-Raymi is dead."

Azimi bowed, then said, "Your Highness, I was wondering if I could have a word with Prince Khalid. Is he here?"

Raza's eyes darkened. "My brother is not here. He is on official royal court business."

Raza motioned to the flap in the tent behind him. "General, I will meet with you later. I wish to speak with Mr. Rhome alone."

The color in Azimi's face drained as the man bowed and hurried from the tent.

Raza looked at his phone, then said, "Come with us, Mr. Rhome. There is something I wish to show you."

Rhome followed Raza and the two other men out of the tent. They walked straight into the desert and crested a large sand dune.

With the sun having now set, Rhome could see two oddly shaped figures lying before a massive bonfire below.

"This way," Raza said, descending the dune, toward the fire.

When they got closer, the figures stirred and rose. Rhome nearly stopped walking when he realized the figures were cats. Big cats.

"My snow leopard and my black panther," Raza said. "The rarest in my collection."

Raza approached the black panther first, the flames of the fire dancing in the animal's eyes. Crouching down, he grabbed the animal by its big head, and the panther purred.

"Would you like to say hello?"

"I'm fine, here, thank you," Rhome said.

Raza and his two men laughed.

"You are a dog person, no?" Raza said, indicating the wolf tattoo on Rhome's arm. "Come, sit."

Raza gestured to a spot away from the cats for Rhome to sit. When he settled onto the cool sand, Raza said, "I wanted to thank you personally for what you did last night in Yemen. Our doctors said you broke a rib?"

"Just a hairline."

Raza nodded, and then he gently pushed the panther away. "I don't know if you are aware of this, Mr. Rhome. But you and I both have something in common."

"We do?"

Raza's voice dropped as he sat. "We have both suffered unbearably at the hands of Qasim al-Raymi."

Rhome's eyes narrowed.

Raza said, "I know what al-Raymi did to you and your men in Pakistan last September, Mr. Rhome. I heard the entire horrible story. He took your men from you. He took something from me as well, my older brother, Ibrahim."

Rhome stared at the moving shadows caused by the fire as they crossed Raza's face.

"Nine years ago, my brother's F-15 was shot down by a SCUD missile in eastern Yemen. A SCUD missile al-Raymi purchased from the Iranian Quds Force commander, General Soleimani. Ibrahim was eight years older than me, but he was my best friend. He used to bring me and Khalid to this very spot, to sit before a fire when we were young. He challenged us to see a world that was bigger than ourselves. He challenged us to dream of a better Saudi Arabia—a modern, progressive kingdom, not constricted by the clerics."

Raza stared directly at Rhome. "It should have been Ibrahim, not me, to ascend to the role of king. I am merely building the kingdom in his image, an image I am blessed to take."

Rhome wasn't sure how to respond.

"I miss Ibrahim, every second, of every day. I miss him probably as much as you miss your men. So, thank you, Mr. Rhome. Thank you for killing the man who has haunted my dreams for the last nine years." For a beat, Raza wiped at his eyes, then asked, "What is next for you, Mr. Rhome?"

"I guess I'll go home."

"And where is home?"

"Big Sky, Montana."

"Big Sky, Montana . . ." Raza said, thoughtfully. "Why is it called Big Sky . . . this Montana?"

"The Native Americans named it that. The landscape is so vast and sprawling, it makes everything, especially the sky, seem so big—it reminds us how small we really are."

Raza smiled. "I would like to visit this Big Sky, Montana, someday."

Another awkward silence followed, before the crown prince said, "Mr. Rhome, you are probably aware that I haven't brought you out here just to thank you for what you did in Yemen. I have brought you here to offer you a job."

Rhome tried to keep his face calm.

"You see, Mr. Rhome, from a young age, my brother Ibrahim made me study the history of our world's greatest leaders. I read about everyone, from Alexander the Great to Genghis Khan. I studied their triumphs and their lowest moments. As I read, I began to see patterns among those who conquered, and those who failed to conquer. I read about great men who had fallen from grace, and oppressed men who rose up from bondage to become great. Both kinds of leaders all had one thing in common. Do you know what that was?"

Rhome shook his head.

"They surrounded themselves with advisers who spoke their minds— specialists in their fields who were expected to challenge their leaders' decisions. I try to do the same, Mr. Rhome. My vision for Saudi Arabia is to transform it into the America of the Middle East, to bring a different kind of prosperity to our kingdom. I want to diversify our assets away from oil, and to strategically defend ourselves, which is why I brought you here. I know of your specialties—you are not just a soldier, but a strategist, an improvisor. I saw the drone feed of what you did last night in Yemen, and that is why I am interested in hiring you as one of my security advisers."

Rhome began to say something, but the crown prince raised his hand. "I will pay you two million dollars a year, plus a signing bonus of another two million dollars should you accept my deal and complete your first two assignments."

Rhome's poker face cracked, and the crown prince noticed.

"Four million dollars is generous, I know."

Rhome felt conflicted. Nowhere in his wildest dreams did he think he'd ever hear a number that large for a year's worth of work. He knew he'd been flown out here to be offered a job, but four million dollars? His whole adult life he'd been subjected to a meager government salary under a State Department cover. For years, he'd risked his life hunting terrorists in the most dangerous areas in the world. But he'd done so out of a sense of duty to his country.

Now, the leader of a foreign nation was asking him to be a mercenary, a soldier for hire, a man of action who'd sell his soul to the highest bidder.

Rhome didn't like that.

But four million dollars would change his life. It would change the lives of the families of his teammates who'd given the ultimate sacrifice.

"The first two assignments," Rhome said. "What would they entail?"

Raza stood up. "Mr. Rhome, there is a man in Montreal, Canada, who has done a great deal of harm to my kingdom. This man wishes to damage my reputation before the signing of the Global Green Accord." Raza pointed to Turki Shahidi. "Tonight, Mr. Shahidi and your friend Mr. Shurrab will travel to hunt down and eliminate this man, this journalist, who wishes to hurt me. I want you to help them. If you are successful, you will then leave straight from Montreal and head to Switzerland for your second assignment."

"And what is the second assignment?" Rhome asked.

"Tying up a loose end," Raza said. "You will be briefed on the specifics during the flight to Switzerland. What do you say, Mr. Rhome?"

Rhome felt a sickness boil in his stomach. "Why choose me?"

"What do you mean?"

"You have obviously done research into my past," Rhome said. "I was trained to kill men like Qasim al-Raymi, not innocents and civilians. What in my history suggests that I would want to kill a journalist? What suggests I would want to be a hired gun?"

"This journalist is an evil man," Raza said. "I can assure you that."

"I didn't say he wasn't," Rhome said, annoyed. "You want people with my skill set and qualifications. I could think of a dozen guys out there from my old line of work who need the money, so why me?"

"Mr. Rhome, I didn't mean to offend you—"

"I'm not offended," Rhome lied. "I just want the truth."

"The truth," Raza said, glancing over at Shahidi and Rahmani. "Very well. I will give you the sincere truth. I want you, Mr. Rhome, because I told Mr. Steiner to seek out specific individuals. Individuals not only with your skill set, but those who could be loyal. Individuals who have been disillusioned by their government. Mr. Steiner told me that you were an honest, noble man, but a man who was looking for a purpose."

"A purpose?"

"Yes," Raza said. "Mr. Steiner told me that your whole adult life, your purpose has been your loyalty to your country, the CIA, and your men. Your purpose was to eradicate terrorists for your government. A government who proved they weren't loyal back to you. A government who never recognized your sacrifices, nor helped the families of your fallen brothers."

Rhome stared at Raza but said nothing.

"I am trying to change the world, Mr. Rhome. I am trying to elimi-nate extremism and bring peace to the Middle East. I am striving to get the Global Green Accord signed while my enemies try everything to stop it. In order for my lofty goals to succeed, I need loyal, driven individuals around me. Individuals who won't shy away from doing unsavory things for the greater good. Your government left you and the families of your dead men out to dry. Unlike your government, I am loyal to those who are loyal to me. I chose you, Mr. Rhome, because I think we believe in the same ideals."

Rhome tried to hide the disgust on his face.

The crown prince wanted him to participate in the killing of a jour-nalist. Nowhere in Rhome's moral framework could he wrap his head around that.

Wanting to leave as fast as possible, Rhome asked, "When do you need my decision?"

Raza grinned. "The jet is leaving for Montreal at nine o'clock to-night. That gives you four hours to decide. One of my choppers will take you back to Riyadh and then you can think about my offer. If you decide to take it, Mr. Steiner will drive you to the royal airstrip. If you decline, we can get you a first-class ticket back home. Now, Mr. Rhome, if you would excuse me, I need to speak to my advisers. Do you think you can find your way back to your helicopter?"

"Yes," Rhome replied, and stood.

"I look forward to hearing from you," Raza said, taking out his phone again.

Rhome bowed his head.

"Oh, and Mr. Rhome, when you get to the tents, could you tell General Azimi to join me at the fire?"

"Sure."

Walking away, Rhome could feel the men's eyes on him as he was swallowed by the darkness.

CHAPTER FORTY-EIGHT

RHOME STARED OUT of the helicopter window at Riyadh's glistening lights, the crown prince's offer Jackhammering in his head.

Two million dollars to kill a journalist and tie up a loose end?

And another two million for a year's salary?

And for what, a sense of purpose?

A promise of loyalty?

Rhome scoffed at the thought.

In Rhome's eyes, Raza bin Zaman was no different from any other dictator running a corrupt government.

Yes, four million dollars could do a lot of good for the families of his fallen brothers.

But at what cost?

As the chopper began its descent into Riyadh, Rhome took out the photograph of his old team, and the vial containing Mack's ashes that had been on his person since he'd left Montana. As he stared down at the items, he decided that there was no way he'd take the blood money. No way he'd sell his soul to the crown prince.

No.

He would go back to Montana.

His task was complete—Qasim al-Raymi was dead; it was time to move on.

When the chopper touched down, Rhome climbed out to see Luca Steiner and Sergei waiting for him next to a black Range Rover.

Sergei opened the door to the vehicle and Rhome got into the back seat without saying anything.

Steiner sat shotgun and Sergei climbed behind the wheel. As the Range Rover left the airfield, Rhome closed his eyes.

"The crown prince has ordered us to take you to a hotel, Mr. Rhome," Steiner said. "Then he has instructed us to drive you to the royal airstrip or the King Khalid Airport based on your decision."

"I've decided to go home," Rhome said.

"Very well."

As Sergei drove the car through the city, Rhome let himself doze off. It was only when he felt the car stop that he opened his eyes.

They were in an alley behind an industrial building.

"What's going on?" Rhome said, then noticed a dark figure approach his window.

Before he had time to react, Steiner pointed a pistol at his chest. "Get out, Mr. Rhome. Someone wants to talk."

CHAPTER FORTY-NINE

RHOME'S ATTENTION WENT from Steiner's pistol to the door that swung open, exposing the dark figure.

"Hello, Brian."

Rhome blinked. "Willy?"

Riyadh CIA station chief William McCallister motioned for Rhome to step outside.

Looking back at Steiner's pistol, Rhome got out of the vehicle.

McCallister shut Rhome's door, then motioned for Steiner to roll down his window.

"You can pick him up in thirty minutes."

"That's too long," Steiner said. "They're going to wonder where we've been."

"Then make something up, Mr. Steiner. You're good at that."

Steiner cursed, then ordered Sergei to drive.

"What the hell is going on?" Rhome said, watching the Range Rover disappear around the corner.

"I'll explain everything inside."

McCallister opened the industrial building's grated door and held it open.

Rhome stepped by him and into a cavernous room.

Locking the door, McCallister led him across the wide open area to another door, which exposed a smaller room, lit by a single light bulb hanging from the ceiling above a card table and two empty chairs.

McCallister took a seat and indicated that Rhome do the same.

As Rhome sat, he noticed a steel briefcase next to McCallister's chair.

"I had planned on having this conversation with you earlier today before your meeting with the crown prince, but I had no way of getting to you."

"How did you know I met with the crown prince?" Rhome said. "And the lawyer, Steiner—he's working with you?"

"Unwillingly, but yes."

"And what the hell are we doing in here?"

"Brian, we don't have a lot of time, so I need you to stay calm and let me speak. I can't have you interrupting me, no matter how upset you get, all right?"

McCallister pulled a key from his pocket, retrieved the steel briefcase from the ground, and plopped it on the table before unlocking it.

McCallister pulled out two folders, one green and one red, and placed them before Rhome.

The green folder was labeled:

LODGEPOLE

The red:

HAIL MARY

McCallister glanced at his watch. "You have twenty minutes to read both folders. An operational summary is provided in each followed by the subsequent intelligence gathered. Start with Lodgepole."

Rhome stared at his father's old Ground Branch teammate for a long beat, taking in the grim, tired expression on his face, before he opened the Lodgepole folder and began to read.

As the minutes passed, Rhome finished the operational summary and scanned over the intercepted signals intelligence, until he found himself at the last page in a state of bewilderment.

"The Saudis . . . the . . . the crown prince and a group of Americans are planning to kill the president tomorrow night in Davos?"

"We believe so."

"How—" Rhome sputtered, but he didn't have time to finish his question, because McCallister opened the red Hail Mary folder and pushed it toward him.

"You have ten minutes to read this. And then you are going to listen to me *very* carefully."

Trying to rationalize what he'd just consumed, Rhome looked down at the Hail Mary folder and began to read.

As the minutes ticked by, his confusion turned to incredulity, and then to seething anger. When he finished, he couldn't contain his emotions.

"This was all a setup to get me here. Jack and Huey going to my cabin. Steiner hiring me to kill al-Raymi! You—" Rhome said, and stood. "You all manipulated me?! Whose idea was this? Jack's?"

"Sit down, Brian."

Rhome paced over to the far wall, running his hands over the stubble on his head.

"This wasn't Jack's idea, Brian. It was Dan Miller's."

"Oh, and that makes it better."

"Believe me, no one wanted it to come to this. Miller chose you because you were an ideal candidate for the crown prince, and one of the few men in the world capable of seeing this through," McCallister said. Then he explained the phony Saudi intelligence report, and how the Saudis were blaming the Iranians for the thorium reactor explosions.

"And all of this intelligence you've gathered is from Saud Rahmani's iPhone?" Rhome said. "Jack and Danny have no other intelligence backing this up?"

McCallister told Rhome about the man in the burka who'd slipped a letter to a CIA asset in Riyadh. "The letter corroborated the conspiracy. It foretold Director Hastings getting the blame. Someone close to the crown prince's inner circle knows all about this and reached out to us."

"Do you know who they are?"

"No."

"I'm not taking the crown prince's assignments, Willy. I'm not murdering a journalist and doing whatever else he wants me to do in Switzerland."

McCallister stood up. "So he didn't give you any specifics of your second assignment?"

"No, he said I'd be briefed on the flight there."

McCallister nodded, deep in thought, then pointed to the Hail Mary folder. "Taking these assignments would be saving the life of the president, Brian."

"I told you," Rhome said. "I'm not an agency pawn anymore. When I got off that mountain in Pakistan, I swore I was done—"

"But you came back for al-Raymi."

"To avenge my men. To right the wrong for what I did."

"And what did you do, Brian? Why do you blame yourself for that night in Pakistan?"

Rhome could hear the screams again. He could see the faces of Mack, Hurst, Smitty, Whip, and Flynn.

"Stop it!" Rhome said, putting his hands to his ears. "Just stop it!"

"No, Brian," McCallister said, grabbing Rhome by the shoulders. "I know what happened to you. I read your debriefing. Washington wouldn't launch that drone strike, so you got the green light to enter that compound based on bad intelligence."

"I convinced Mack and the others to enter that compound!" Rhome said. "I told Mack that it was our only shot at getting al-Raymi. He didn't want to do it. Neither did the others, they wanted more intel. They felt something was off, but I pressured them into it and I got them all killed!"

Rhome staggered back into the wall.

"After everyone was dead, and Mack died in my arms, I called in an emergency strike. I told the drone operators to light up the compound and the mountainside. And . . . and . . . I specifically gave them my coordinates."

"What do you mean?"

"I knew I couldn't live with myself knowing that I got my men killed. So I called in a series of strikes and ordered that the biggest missile be dropped right on my location."

McCallister stepped back.

"I called in that strike to kill myself, but it missed."

"Brian, I . . . I don't know what to say—"

"Then don't say anything."

For a moment the two of them just stood there.

"Look," McCallister finally muttered. "If you don't want to be Dan Miller's pawn, I get it. But hear me out. The crown prince admitted to you that he intends to kill that journalist, right?"

Rhome nodded.

"He ensnared you, Brian. He made you a liability should you not take the job."

"What are you saying?"

"The ruler of Saudi Arabia revealed to you that he wishes to kill that journalist. If you don't take his job, do you really think he's just going to let you leave the kingdom? What's stopping you from going to the press, what's to stop you from tipping off the agency or the FBI once you reach the States?"

Rhome felt the muscles in his jaw tighten as the realization dawned on him.

McCallister said, "Luckily for you, a new opportunity presented itself just before your meeting with the crown prince. The journalist you are instructed to kill is no longer in Washington, DC; he's fled to Montreal to stay with another dissident, and Lodgepole believes they have a way for you to carry out Dan Miller's plan without bloodshed."

McCallister took out two small items from the briefcase and placed them on the table before taking a seat.

Rhome continued to stand.

For the next five minutes, McCallister explained the new developments in Dan Miller's Hail Mary operation. When he finished, he slid the two items across the table.

"Ultimately, Brian, this is your decision. I'm not going to force you to go. Take these items and head to Montreal, or see what the crown prince has in store for you, should you decline. It's your choice."

Rhome observed the items on the table.

His thoughts floated to his godfather, then to his dead men.

He felt angry, hurt, and betrayed.

Angry for what had been thrust upon him, hurt by who'd been pulling the strings, and betrayed by the person who was supposed to be looking out for him.

His godfather and the members of Lodgepole had placed an unbearable weight on his shoulders. They'd used his situation for their gain.

And now, they were asking for his loyalty, his allegiance—to go on a suicide mission, in order to save the leader of the free world.

Rhome felt like he was going to be sick, then he thought back to an hour before when he'd met with the crown prince.

If everything McCallister had just showed him was true, Raza bin Zaman was the one Rhome should be disgusted with.

Taking a few minutes to organize his thoughts, Rhome finally made his decision and asked, "Jack and Lodgepole actually believe this could work without any bloodshed?"

"Everything is already in motion," McCallister said. "You're the last, most important piece of the puzzle. Everything hinges on you getting on that jet out of Montreal to Switzerland."

"And if I don't succeed?"

McCallister shrugged. "You're our Hail Mary, Brian."

"If I do this," Rhome said. "I'm done for good. You understand me?"

McCallister nodded, and Rhome could see the desperation and guilt in his eyes.

"Once the Saudis' jet clears Canadian airspace, and once you've accomplished what you needed to do, call Jack using Turki Shahidi's phone," McCallister said. "Lodgepole will take it from there."

Rhome stared down at the two items, and without looking at McCallister, he reluctantly grabbed them and exited the room without a word.

Walking across the dark warehouse floor, he stepped out into the alley and then into Steiner's waiting Range Rover.

"Where are we taking you?" Steiner asked.

"Skip the hotel, and drive me straight to the royal airstrip. Tell the crown prince I'll take his job."

CHAPTER FIFTY

ALMOST FIFTEEN HOURS after Jabril Khashiri fled his apartment in Washington, DC, he walked out of the underground Orange Line metro station, and onto the snow-filled streets of Montreal's Snowdon neighborhood.

He carried his suitcase, which contained the USB that Princess Amara had slipped him, plus his external hard drive, the locker key, the fake Canadian passport, and five thousand dollars in cash. Studying the street signs, he started walking north, up Queen Mary Road.

After leaving his apartment that morning, Khashiri had paid cash for a bus ticket to Montreal. What should have been a ten-hour bus ride had taken fifteen because of the snowstorm that was assaulting the East Coast, and the long wait at the Canadian border.

That had been the most stressful part of the trip for Khashiri. Having never used the fake Canadian passport before, he'd been worried it wasn't going to work, but the Canadian Border Service agent cleared him through without a second glance.

With the bus dropping them at the station outside of Montreal, Khashiri had used the metro and took it to Centrale Station, the city's main transportation hub. Grabbing the locker key he'd taken from under his bed the night before, he searched the station until he found locker N348.

Khashiri opened the locker to find a flip phone inside.

Powering on the phone, he immediately received a text message with an address.

Khashiri pocketed the phone, exited the station, walked ten minutes south, and boarded the Orange Line heading toward Snowdon.

Now, standing on the snowy sidewalk in front of a five-story brick apartment building, Khashiri checked the address on the flip phone and matched it with the number above the double glass doors leading into the lobby.

Taking the building's concrete steps two at a time, he was just about to open the front doors, when they swung outward and Umar Abdallah, the twenty-five-year-old infamous Saudi YouTube vlogger, poked his head out.

"Abu Subhi!" Abdallah said, ushering Khashiri into the lobby. "Was there any trouble getting here? Did the passport I got you work?"

"None at all, my good friend. The passport worked flawlessly."

Never in a million years did Khashiri ever think that he would have become close friends with a kid less than half his age. Even after fleeing Saudi Arabia for Canada two years before, Umar Abdallah had the biggest social media presence in the kingdom. With his millions of followers—Abdallah had made a career as an online satirist, poking fun at the Saudi royal family, especially the crown prince. After numerous threats from the royal court, Abdallah had been forced to leave the country in fear for his life. Now, living in Montreal, Abdallah continued to mock the kingdom of Saudi Arabia and its ruler from afar.

Last year, after Khashiri had been fired from his jobs, Abdallah had reached out, and they soon became close friends.

Khashiri patted the young man's cheek. "What would I do without you, Umar?"

"Why did you need to flee this time, Abu Subhi?"

"Not here, my friend."

"Upstairs, then, I have some tea brewing," Abdallah said, grabbing Khashiri's bag for him and pressing the button for the elevator. Getting off at the fourth floor, Abdallah unlocked the door to apartment 406 and led Khashiri inside.

Abdallah put Khashiri's bag down on a sagging brown couch in the sparse living room and then pointed to the IKEA coffee table and the small flat-screen TV mounted on the wall. "I'm sorry, it's not much, Abu Subhi."

Khashiri walked past the couch over to the sliding glass door and took in the snow collecting on the small balcony outside and the street below. "No, it's perfect, Umar, thank you."

Within the first couple of days of Khashiri arriving in Washington, DC, Abdallah had set up an emergency route for Khashiri to get to Montreal should the Saudis ever try to come for him in the United States.

"Do you live here, Umar?"

"No, I live downtown. I've been renting this place for the last two months just in case you needed it."

Abdallah explained that he'd rented the apartment under a fake identity.

Khashiri suddenly got nervous. "Your phone, Umar—did you bring your phone with you?"

Umar took out a flip phone. "Just a burner. My iPhone is back at my apartment."

"Have you ever brought your iPhone here?"

"No, never. Just my laptop."

The vlogger pointed to his black laptop sitting on the kitchen counter.

Khashiri nearly stumbled backward. "You must get rid of it! We must leave this place, now!"

"What's wrong, Abu Subhi?"

"Saud Rahmani is monitoring all our phones and computers—"

Abdallah laughed. "Abu Subhi, that laptop is not my personal laptop. It is encrypted, and I have never accessed the internet in this apartment with it. Why? What is going on?"

"You're sure you've never used the internet on it here?"

"Of course, I'm sure."

"Is there anything on your iPhone or your personal laptop that could lead anyone to this apartment?"

"No, Jabril. Everything was done from internet cafés."

Khashiri's panic somewhat subsided.

"Here," Abdallah said, walking into the kitchen and pouring two cups of steaming hot tea. "Sit down, and tell me what is going on."

Khashiri snatched Abdallah's secure laptop, then grabbed the USB Amara had slipped him the morning before.

Both of them now sitting on the couch, Khashiri told Abdallah how he got the USB and accessed it.

"And what was on it?" Abdallah asked.

Opening the secure laptop, Khashiri inserted the USB, typed in the passcode, and both men gazed at the Dark Sun and RIG files.

"The Dark Sun file is encrypted," Khashiri said. "So I clicked on the RIG file and found this."

Khashiri sat back and let Abdallah read the first couple pages of the RIG file. When he finished, a look of sheer terror overtook his face.

"The crown prince has a Pegasus system? He's been hacking into people's phones and computers?!"

"Yes," Khashiri said. "Yours too."

He pointed to Umar Abdallah's name in the RIG file among the dozens of other Saudi dissidents the crown prince's sidekick, Saud Rahmani, was tracking. "Have you noticed your iPhone and your personal laptop being slower? Hot to the touch?"

"Yes!"

"Mine too."

"And this is why you fled?"

"No," Khashiri said, scrolling down and pointing at the screen.

"Oh my God," Abdallah said. "March ninth is today! Turki Shahidi was going to Washington, DC, to kill you today?!"

"On orders from the crown prince, because of the article I was going to publish on my blog before the accord signing."

"I told you that you shouldn't have started your blog. I told you not to pursue that story in Yemen!"

"I know you did, Umar," Khashiri said. "Now you know why I am so frightened."

Abdallah stood and marched toward the kitchen.

"Where are you going?"

"I need something stronger than tea," Abdallah said, opening the fridge and taking out a can of beer. Cracking it, he took a big swig, then came back into the living room. "What are you going to do with that information?"

"Turki Shahidi was coming to kill me because I was going to publish something about Dark Sun. I believe it has to do with what happened to that Iranian prisoner transport in Yemen. I'm still publishing, but I am going to take it a step further, now."

Khashiri lifted his chin in defiance. He'd been thinking about it during his trip to Montreal.

"I am now going to write an article about this USB, how the crown prince sent his thugs to kill me, to silence me about writing about what happened in Yemen. I will publish everything on my blog, the RIG folder, Pegasus—!"

"No, Jabril. You must be careful. Consider your son. Subhi is at University in Riyadh. The crown prince—"

"The crown prince will never touch my son. He is innocent."

"You of all people cannot be that naive!"

"Subhi will be fine. I will publish, and then go into hiding. Far from you, even. Never staying at one place more than a night."

Draining the last of his beer, Abdallah grabbed his coat from the couch and put it on.

"Now where are you going?!" asked Khashiri.

"To my apartment, to get rid of my phone and computer. I will pick up some more groceries, and then I will stay with you here, so you don't try anything foolish!"

Khashiri watched as Abdallah hurried out of the apartment.

For a moment, he just stared at the door, and then at the table where Abdallah had left his computer and burner phone.

Khashiri reached into his suitcase and took out the external hard drive that stored the article he'd been working on. Next, he took out the scanned photographs of the dead Sudanese children and laid them on the table.

He had everything he needed to finish the most important journalistic piece of his life.

Placing Abdallah's computer on his lap, Khashiri was too excited to realize that the laptop was somewhat overheated.

For the next hour and a half, Khashiri banged away at his article until his eyes started to slacken.

Satisfied with the progress he'd made, he put the laptop back on the table next to the photographs and the two flip phones. Then he grabbed the TV remote, turned on the small flat-screen, and found a news broadcast.

Finding a blanket, he threw it over his body and lay down.

Minutes later, he fell into a deep sleep . . . and did not hear the dead bolt sliding back on the apartment's door. Nor did he see the figure step into the living room and point a pistol directly at his face.

CHAPTER FIFTY-ONE

RHOME WOKE WHEN he felt the Gulfstream's gears lower for landing and sat up in his seat.

Turki Shahidi and Kazem Shurrab had been speaking in hushed tones in the front of the jet's cabin. Now they looked over at him.

"ETA in five minutes; wake yourself up and get ready," Shahidi said.

After leaving the warehouse in Riyadh just over twelve hours ago, Steiner had dropped Rhome off at the royal airstrip, where he had met with Shahidi, Shurrab, and two pilots in the crown prince's Gulfstream.

After takeoff, Rhome had watched Shahidi take a black smartphone from his pocket and make a short call, just like McCallister and the contents in the Hail Mary folder said he would. Rhome had waited until the call was over, before getting out of his seat and going to the lavatory.

Locking himself inside, he took the two items McCallister had given him out of his pocket.

Rhome placed the small aerosol container and a pocket-size leather case containing four syringes under the sink, behind some towels.

After splashing water on his face, he'd headed back into the cabin and slept.

As the Gulfstream made its final approach into Montreal, Rhome took a deep breath and envisioned the success of every facet of the Hail Mary folder's instructions.

As soon as the plane landed, Rhome again watched Shahidi take out the black smartphone, and just as he did when the plane took off, he saw the Saudi enforcer give an update to someone over the line.

When the plane came to a stop in a private hangar, Shahidi pocketed the black phone and handed Rhome and Shurrab Canadian passports.

"Like I said earlier," Shahidi said, "when flying private internationally, customs is light. When they ask about our travels, tell them that we are Canadian businessmen here for a two-hour meeting before we head to Zurich. If they ask anything else, give them this document with your passport."

Rhome opened the passport and saw his face and his new identity on the inside flap, then he looked at the document. It was a confirmation receipt for a conference room at the Montreal Hyatt scheduled for later that night.

"Memorize your passport information, and let's go."

Customs took less than a minute. A black SUV was waiting at the valet in front of the private terminal for them. Shahidi got behind the wheel, Shurrab sat in the passenger's seat. Rhome climbed in the back.

They drove for twenty minutes, before Shahidi pulled into a storage facility and stopped before one of the units. He unlocked the door and slid it open.

Inside were two barrels, two large plastic sheets, two rolled-up carpets, and a black duffel bag.

Shahidi snatched the duffel and told Rhome and Shurrab to grab the carpets and sheets and put them in the trunk of the Suburban. Eyeing the two barrels as Shahidi shut the door, Rhome climbed back into the vehicle.

Shahidi opened the duffel and took out two black jackets, two black hats, two suppressors, and two Glocks and then passed each of the items to Rhome and Shurrab.

Then Shahidi took out a tablet and powered it on.

Rhome got a glimpse of an app that resembled Google Maps on the screen.

Shahidi zoomed in on three multicolored blinking dots all in close proximity to one another. "All three of the two targets' devices are in the apartment."

"Two targets?" Rhome said, feigning confusion.

"Yes, two targets. Our main target has joined another dissident. The crown prince has ordered us to eliminate two birds with one stone."

Shahidi handed the tablet to Shurrab. "Tell me if any of those devices move."

Pulling out of the storage facility, Shahidi drove into the city and arrived in Snowdon fifteen minutes later. A storm had moved in. Large snowflakes were falling over the dark neighborhood.

Shahidi eased the vehicle down a quiet residential street and found an empty parking spot directly in front of a five-story brick building. "Our targets are in apartment 406."

Grabbing the tablet from Shurrab, Shahidi exited the map application, then brought up images of two men.

One was in his midfifties. He sported a salt-and-pepper goatee and wore thin glasses.

The other was midtwenties and had a beard and a full head of black hair.

Handing Rhome the tablet, Shahidi told him to study the faces.

When Rhome gave it back, Shahidi took out his black smartphone and made a call. Five seconds later, Rhome heard the Saudi enforcer say in soft Arabic, "We're in position. About to execute."

Ending the call, Shahidi handed Shurrab an identical phone. "Call me when it's done, and then one of you come down and help me with the carpets and the plastic sheets."

Shurrab pocketed his phone. Rhome donned his black ball cap, put on his black jacket, press-checked the Glock, and screwed on the suppressor before concealing the weapon in his jacket.

Shahidi handed Shurrab an electronic fob and a key. "The fob will get you into the building. The key will open the apartment door. I've cut all the security cameras in the building and all around the block, but still keep a low profile. Now, go."

Rhome and Shurrab exited the vehicle, walked up the front steps, used the fob to scan themselves into the lobby, and took the stairs to the fourth floor.

McCallister's instructions thrumming in his head, Rhome put a hand on the Emirati sniper's shoulder as they stepped into the empty hallway. "I don't care what Shahidi says. There is only one person entering that apartment, and that is me. Give me the key, stay in the hallway, and keep a lookout. When it's done, I'll motion you inside."

For a long moment, the Emirati stared at Rhome, and then he slowly reached into his pocket and handed him the key.

Rhome could feel his heart jackhammering against his cracked rib as he took the key and walked toward the door labeled 406.

I've done my part, he thought to himself. *Jack, you better have done yours.*

Sliding the key into the lock with his left hand, he took out the suppressed Glock with his right and slowly turned the dead bolt over.

Rhome took a deep breath, opened the door, and stepped inside.

———

Umar Abdallah had lived in Montreal for nearly two years, but he still wasn't used to the winters. They were long, dark, and frigid.

Tonight was no different.

Having parked his car around the corner from the building where Khashiri was hiding out, Abdallah shivered and placed his grocery bags on the sidewalk, cursing himself for leaving his gloves in the apartment.

Not only had he left his gloves, but he'd left his burner phone and his secure laptop with Khashiri.

Jabril better not be using my laptop to write his article, Abdallah thought, as he rubbed his hands together, and then he swore out loud when he saw a black SUV pull out of a parking spot directly in front of his building and drive away.

"Dammit, I could have parked right there!"

Grabbing the groceries, he continued down the street and climbed the building's front steps, where he used his key fob to scan himself into the lobby before pressing the button for the elevator.

———

Turki Shahidi had cursed when he caught sight of a young man with grocery bags walking down the sidewalk in his sideview mirror.

He swore again when he realized that the young man was the secondary target, Umar Abdallah, and that he was going to walk right by Shahidi's window and probably make him.

Throwing the SUV in drive, Shahidi had taken his Orion phone from his lap and dialed Shurrab's number as he sped away.

Shurrab answered on the first ring.

"Target two must have left his burner phone and computer in the apartment, he's heading into the lobby as we speak. I am going to pull into the alley. Make sure he is taken care of, then call me back."

———

Rhome entered the apartment and quietly shut the door, his suppressed Glock raised.

Creeping down the short hallway, he noticed the television in the living room was on. Rhome turned left, cleared the small kitchen first, and then stepped back into the hallway and the living room.

The TV cast a blue hue on the large lump of blankets on the couch.

One of the targets seemed fast asleep.

Rhome moved into the bathroom, and then the bedroom, looking for the second target.

But no one else was there.

Shit! Rhome thought.

Mind spinning, he stepped back into the living area, his gun trained on the figure sleeping under the blankets. He looked at the laptop open on the table, and the two flip phones sitting next to it, then something caught his eye: a series of grainy photographs, depicting gory images of deceased kids and teenagers wearing green military uniforms.

Snapping back to reality, remembering why he was there, Rhome focused on the mass of blankets on the couch, aimed his weapon, and fired.

Once.

Twice.

Three times, into the sleeping figure's head.

Moving forward, Rhome ripped the blankets off and examined his handiwork. Then, kneeling down before the body, he reached behind the head, found what he was looking for, and stuffed it under the couch cushion.

Rhome was just about to grab the photographs on the coffee table, when he sensed another presence in the room.

Rhome spun around.

Grocery bags in each of his hands, the second target moved into the living room and stopped cold, his bags falling to the floor.

Before Rhome had time to react, Shurrab snuck up behind the man, raised his weapon, and fired into the back of Umar Abdallah's head.

———

Shahidi pulled the SUV into the alley and parked forty meters behind a U-Haul truck that sat adjacent to the apartment building's rear exit.

He'd no sooner cut his engine, when the door to the exit swung open, and out stepped three people.

In the darkness and the heavily falling snow, Shahidi couldn't make out faces—but one of the individuals was very big, much bigger than Rhome and Shurrab. The other was small and slight.

A woman.

Between the big man and the woman was a third person, short, overweight, and hunched over.

The big man moved quickly to the driver seat of the U-Haul, and the woman opened the passenger's door and helped the overweight man inside before climbing in after him. Watching the U-Haul drive away, Shahidi barely had time to register what he'd just seen because the Orion phone on his lap began to vibrate.

He answered the phone and Shurrab's voice said, "It's done. Do you want help getting the carpets and the plastic wrap?"

The U-Haul's red taillights disappearing out of the alley, Shahidi tried to rationalize what he'd just witnessed. Something felt off.

"Wait there," he said. "I'm coming up."

———

Rhome wiped at the blood splattered on his face and swore at Shurrab.

The Emirati didn't seem to notice as he stood over the body of Umar Abdallah.

Shurrab had that weird black smartphone Shahidi had given him pressed against his ear.

When he lowered the phone, Rhome asked, "Does he want help with the carpets?"

"He said to wait here. He's coming up."

Shit! Rhome thought.

Had something more gone wrong?

The fact that the second target hadn't been in the apartment was bad enough, now why was Shahidi coming up here without the carpets?

Rhome heard the door open and then close. Shahidi stepped into the living room.

The Saudi stared down at Abdallah's body before his attention went to the body on the couch.

Rhome tried to remain cool, calm, and collected as Shahidi moved to the couch and examined Rhome's handiwork.

For a moment, the Saudi enforcer studied the man's blown-out head and the blood seeping into the cushion. Then Shahidi took out a switch-blade and ripped away the left pant leg of the man's jeans, exposing his calf.

Rhome tried to contain his panic as Shahidi scrutinized the brown birthmark on the dead man's leg.

"Good work," Shahidi finally said.

Rhome felt himself relax.

Taking the black smartphone from his pocket, Shahidi motioned to the computer and burner phones, before something else caught his eye on the table.

The Saudi grabbed the photographs of the dead kids and stared at them before crushing them in his hands and stuffing them into his jacket. "Grab the computer and the phones, and meet me in the car."

"You don't want us to take the bodies?" Rhome asked.

"Leave the bodies, I'll take care of them. Go!"

Rhome followed Shurrab out into the hallway and down the stairs to the back alley and into the SUV, wondering the whole time what the hell was going on.

CHAPTER FIFTY-TWO

JACK BRENNER FELT like his heart was coming out of his throat.

Staring into one of the three spotting scopes set up along the floor-to-ceiling windows in the dark, tenth-story high-rise two blocks from the apartment where Umar Abdallah and Jabril Khashiri had been holed up, Brenner heard Ryder's voice come over his earpiece.

"We got Khashiri. Coming to you."

He turned the spotting scope's lens to the street east of the five-story apartment complex and saw the U-Haul heading their way.

"Was Shahidi in the alley?" Brenner asked.

"We believe so," Ryder's voice said.

"Did he make you?"

"Not sure."

"Jack," Dan Miller said to his left. "Shahidi just entered the apartment."

Brenner took his eye off the scope, and looked at Miller, who stood in the darkness next to him, his eyes on his own spotting scope directed at the sliding glass door of the apartment. Behind them, Mike Adams sat next to Elaine Cho—both of them huddled over their laptops at a folding table.

Miller said, "Shahidi is cutting away the jeans. He's looking for the birthmark."

Brenner cursed and directed his scope toward the sliding glass door.

In his thirty-five years working as a spy, Brenner had never participated in an operation as complicated as the one Lodgepole was attempting tonight.

After realizing that Khashiri had fled his apartment in Washington, DC, Nora Ryder had pitched an idea to Lodgepole based on a legendary CIA/Mossad joint extraction dubbed Operation Veiled Cobra, which had gone down successfully in Beirut in 1985.

Ryder's plan was to not only save the lives of Jabril Khashiri and Umar Abdallah, but to also guarantee Lodgepole could get the Dark Sun information from Khashiri and make sure Rhome succeeded with Dan Miller's Hail Mary operation.

"We do what the Mossad and the agency did in Beirut in '85 with Veiled Cobra," Ryder had argued. "Except this will be a little more complicated."

Back in Beirut in 1985, a deep cover Mossad agent had been embedded in Hezbollah. This agent was ordered by Hezbollah leadership to assassinate someone within their organization who had been spying for the CIA. This deep cover Mossad agent, along with the CIA, had then orchestrated a plan to pull out the recently outed CIA asset from his home before the assassination could take place and replace him with a look-alike cadaver.

When the deep cover Mossad agent entered the asset's home, he had riddled the body with bullets, took pictures of the corpse, and had then given those pictures confirming the asset's death to Hezbollah leadership. Not only had this operation saved the CIA asset's life, but it upheld the cover of the Mossad agent embedded deep within Hezbollah.

Ryder's plan was similar, but with a twist.

Back at Lodgepole the day before, Ryder had the idea to confiscate two dead bodies from nearby morgues that somewhat resembled Jabril Khashiri and Umar Abdallah. Her idea was to pull the real Khashiri and Abdallah out of their apartment and replace them with two look-alike cadavers. The plan was to stage the bodies on the couch and in the bed, place blood-splatter packets under their heads, and have McCallister instruct Rhome to shoot at the body's faces to deem them unrecognizable.

"That will never work," Bell had said. "You don't think that Shahidi and whoever else is in that apartment with Rhome will be able to tell he shot two dead bodies? Bodies get cold, they go into rigor."

"Huey and I will rent a U-Haul truck and keep the bodies on dry ice while we drive to Montreal," Ryder said. "Right before Rhome and the rest of RIG arrive, we will use heat pads to warm up the bodies, extract the real Khashiri and Abdallah, and replace them with the cadavers."

"This could actually work," Brenner had said.

And it had.

Sort of.

Within three hours of carrying out Ryder's plan, Lodgepole was able to secure two fresh bodies around the DC area that somewhat resembled Jabril Khashiri and Umar Abdallah.

Adams, having done research on both dissidents, discovered that Khashiri had a large birthmark on his left calf. Lodgepole was able to mimic the birthmark with makeup before the team had split up and left for Canada.

Brenner, Miller, Silva, Bell, Cho, and Adams had Kircher fly them to Montreal earlier that day to get eyes on Umar Abdallah. Upon their arrival, Cho and Adams did some digging into Abdallah's life and uncovered that he had opened a bank account under a false identity two months prior and then had used that account to pay for a one-bedroom apartment in the Snowdon neighborhood. It was then that Bell and Silva located Abdallah and followed him to Snowdon.

Knowing that this was most likely where Khashiri was going to meet Abdallah, Lodgepole had set up shop in a rented high-rise two blocks away, where they could get a view of the apartment, and wait for Khashiri to arrive.

Meanwhile, Huey and Ryder had rented a U-Haul in Maryland and had loaded up the two cadavers, which they laid on dry ice and concealed them with furniture before beginning their ten-hour drive to Montreal.

They were supposed to get to Montreal two hours before Rhome and the rest of RIG were to arrive, but they were delayed in a snowstorm, and by the time Rhome's jet touched down, Ryder and Huey were just getting into the outskirts of the city. It was during the stress and anxiety of thinking Rhome was going to beat Huey and Ryder to the apartment that Lodgepole completely missed Umar Abdallah leaving the building.

When Lodgepole realized Abdallah was gone, Ryder and Huey had already pulled the U-Haul into the back alley.

Notifying them of Abdallah's absence, Brenner had ordered them to enter the apartment, wake up a terrified Khashiri, hold him at gunpoint, and then drag the refrigerator box inside, containing the heated-up cadaver.

By the time Huey and Ryder had the cadaver in place on the couch and had stuffed the refrigerator box in a utility closet, Shahidi was parked out front, and Rhome and Shurrab were coming up the stairs.

It was then that Brenner noticed Umar Abdallah walking down the sidewalk with his groceries, and Shahidi pulling his vehicle into the back alley, where the U-Haul was parked.

Speaking with Huey and Ryder over the comms, Brenner instructed them to get themselves and Khashiri into the U-Haul and back to the high-rise as fast as possible.

Still watching through the spotting scope as Shahidi examined the birthmark on the cadaver's leg, Brenner heard Huey's voice through the earpiece.

"Just parked the U-Haul. Taking elevator to you now."

Brenner watched the Saudi enforcer stand up from the cadaver, then wave Rhome and Shurrab from the room.

"What's Shahidi doing?" Miller said.

Brenner saw Shahidi press a phone to his ear.

"Cho, Adams," Miller said. "Can you intercept that call?"

"Negative," Cho said. "He must be using an Orion phone."

Shahidi hung up, and for a moment, the Saudi just stared out of the sliding glass door, before he pulled a lighter from his pocket and lit the curtains on fire.

"Oh shit!" Miller said, as the curtains engulfed in flame and Shahidi hurried out of the apartment.

Thirty seconds later, Brenner caught sight of Shahidi's black SUV turn out of the alley, then head east for the airport. Pressing his earpiece, Brenner said, "Bell, Silva, tail the SUV, make sure Rhome gets on that jet to Switzerland."

"Copy that, Chief," Bell said.

Hearing sirens in the distance, Brenner put his hand to his forehead, his mind dealing with the ramifications of Rhome being blown, of Hail Mary failing, and what Lodgepole would need to do if that occurred.

Don't think like that, Jack.

Of course, Lodgepole did have a final contingency set in place if Hail Mary failed. Kircher was waiting for them in the jet at the airport to fly everyone directly to Switzerland, where Benedicht Imdorf would get them transportation to Davos before the president of the United States took that stage.

The door to the high-rise burst open, and Ryder and Huey led a scared Jabril Khashiri inside.

"Did it work?" Ryder asked. "Did Shahidi buy it?"

"We don't know," Brenner said, moving over to the Saudi dissident. "Mr. Khashiri, I can't imagine how confused you must be right now, but tonight we saved your life. The crown prince marked you for assassination because of something you were going to publish—"

Shaking like a leaf, Khashiri pointed to the window behind Brenner where smoke was billowing out of the apartment building, "What happened? Where . . . where is Umar?"

"Unfortunately, we weren't able to get Mr. Abdallah out."

"What do you mean?"

"Mr. Khashiri," Miller said. "Listen to me, you need to tell us what you were planning on publishing. What was so important that the crown prince wanted you killed?"

"I . . . I was going to publish about the massacre."

"What massacre?"

"The massacre of a Saudi coalition prisoner transport caravan in Yemen. The prisoner transport that was attacked by Saudi gunships last September."

"Saudi gunships attacked their own caravan?"

"And freed their own prisoners," Khashiri said.

"And who were the prisoners?"

"Quds Force operatives. The Saudis rescued nine Iranian Quds Force operatives." Taking an external hard drive from his pocket, Khashiri held it out before him. "I have all the evidence right here."

CHAPTER FIFTY-THREE

Montreal, Canada
March 9, 4:00 a.m.

TURKI SHAHIDI KEPT the SUV at the speed limit before turning east and stopping on a deserted bridge over the Lachine Channel.

Throwing a rag to Rhome and Shurrab, he ordered them to wipe down their pistols, and then throw them into the channel.

After doing the same with the rolled-up carpets and plastic, Shahidi ordered them back into the SUV and headed toward the airport.

They arrived nine minutes later and moved through security, toward the jet.

Following Shurrab and Shahidi into the Gulfstream, Rhome could barely control his thoughts.

He didn't like the way Shahidi had scrutinized the cadaver.

He didn't like how he'd ordered Shurrab and Rhome down to the SUV.

What had he been doing up there?

As Shahidi drove the SUV out of the alley, Rhome had seen smoke billowing from Khashiri's apartment.

Shahidi's original plan was to remove the bodies discreetly from the building via the rolled-up carpets and plastic and dissolve them in the acid drums at the storage facility.

Instead the Saudi had set the apartment ablaze.

But why?

Rhome's thoughts then went to Jack Brenner and the plan McCallister had detailed to him in Riyadh.

Why had there only been one cadaver in the apartment—why wasn't the other one there?

And why had Lodgepole allowed the second target to enter the building in the first place?

Why hadn't they stopped him?

"Nabil, Jeric! Let's get the hell out of here!" Shahidi yelled in Arabic to his two pilots.

The two men in the cockpit fired up the jet.

Rhome took a seat opposite Shurrab and watched Shahidi take out his black phone.

Back in Riyadh, McCallister had been insistent. *You are not to act until Shahidi calls the crown prince. The whole operation hangs on that one call.*

McCallister had briefed Rhome for nearly five minutes back in Riyadh about this part of the plan. The crown prince was a control freak, a compulsive micromanager. For the Hail Mary operation to succeed, Shahidi needed to give the crown prince the *all clear.* Then Rhome would go into the bathroom and carry out the final step of Dan Miller's plan on the flight to Switzerland.

Rhome took in Shurrab sitting across from him and then looked at Shahidi, who took a seat in the front of the cabin, his black phone still in his hand.

As the jet taxied onto the runway, and the jet's engines came to life, Rhome kept his attention planted on the Saudi enforcer.

Barreling down the tarmac, and lifting into the sky, Rhome counted the minutes as they flew out of Canadian airspace and out over the Atlantic.

Reaching a cruising altitude, one of the pilots poked his head out of the cabin and told them that it would be an eight-hour flight to Zurich.

Make the call, Rhome thought, still staring at Shahidi's phone. *Make the damn call!*

Shahidi acknowledged the pilot, before raising the black phone. But instead of dialing and putting it to his ear, he put it into his pocket.

Shahidi then reached under his seat and something silver flashed in his hand.

Before Rhome had time to react, a pistol was aimed directly at his chest.

But it wasn't Shahidi aiming the pistol.

It was Kazem Shurrab.

Moving toward Rhome, Shahidi held the silver canister and the black syringe pouch Rhome had stashed under the lavatory sink on the flight over.

Rhome froze, looking from the weapon in Shurrab's grip, to the contents in Shahidi's.

"Mahmoud," Shahidi said. "If he moves, shoot him."

"What the hell is going on?" Rhome said, while simultaneously wondering why Shahidi had called Shurrab *Mahmoud.*

"You think I'm dumb, Mr. Rhome?" Shahidi said, holding up the canister and the packet of syringes. "My pilots found these in the lavatory. I told them to search the plane right before we left Mr. Abdallah's apartment."

"What are you talking about?" Rhome said.

"What were you planning to do with these, Mr. Rhome?"

"I've never seen those things in my life."

"You were the only person to use the lavatory in the back of the plane during the flight here."

"Still doesn't mean I know what those things are."

Shahidi scowled. "You take me for a fool? You think I didn't realize that you shot a dead body back at the apartment?"

"I don't—"

With blinding speed, Shahidi struck Rhome on the forehead with the canister.

Rhome's head snapped to the side, as hot blood poured down his face.

He looked from Shahidi to the pistol in Shurrab's hand.

One of the first things Rhome had been taught at the CIA was that in a close-proximity altercation, you always move away from a blade and toward a gun.

Rhome dove for Shurrab's pistol.

Grabbing the barrel of the weapon, Rhome jerked it up, prying it from Shurrab's grip, while simultaneously elbowing the man in the jaw.

The Emirati grunted and pushed Rhome back onto his seat. Still holding the pistol by the barrel, Rhome was repositioning the weapon in his hand, just as Shahidi's boot kicked it from his grasp.

The pistol flew into the air, and Shurrab tackled Rhome to the floor.

Air blowing from his lungs, Shurrab got on top of him and delivered a series of blows to Rhome's broken rib.

Crying out in pain, Rhome saw Shahidi dive for the pistol that had landed under Shurrab's seat.

The Emirati cocked his elbow and delivered a punch to Rhome's nose.

Rhome felt himself go limp.

"Get off him!" Shahidi said.

Shurrab got to his feet, and Rhome gazed up at the muzzle of the pistol Shahidi was aiming at his chest.

"I saw three people get into a U-Haul truck in the alley. One of them was most definitely Jabril Khashiri!" Shahidi said.

"I . . . I don't know—"

Shahidi kicked Rhome in his broken rib.

"Who the fuck is working with you?!"

"I'm not working with anyone."

"LIAR!" yelled Shahidi. Wrenching the black phone from his pocket, he motioned to Shurrab. "Mahmoud, find something to restrain him!"

Shurrab moved to the back of the plane as Rhome peered up at Shahidi, the black phone now pressed to his ear, the silver pistol in his right hand by his side.

Rhome knew he only had one last play.

He kicked violently at Shahidi's knee, knocking him off-balance, the black phone dislodging from his grip. But the pistol remained in his other hand.

Get the gun!

Rhome launched himself at Shahidi. Grabbing the barrel, he yanked it upward.

Shahidi cried out and wrenched the weapon back down. And as if in slow motion, Rhome watched the business end of the pistol slide center mass over his chest, and then he heard a resounding—*BANG!*

A bone-crushing sensation pierced through Rhome's rib cage.

Landing on the floor, his hands went to his heart, and his whole world began to tilt and darken.

He could hear Shahidi screaming, but it sounded distant, like he was yelling from the other end of a long pipe.

Rhome then felt himself slip away.

CHAPTER FIFTY-FOUR

"YOU HAVE EVIDENCE that the Saudis rescued nine Iranian Quds Force operatives?" Jack Brenner said, pointing at the external hard drive in Jabril Khashiri's hand.

Khashiri nodded. "I think it's why the crown prince sent his men to kill me."

Khashiri took out a silver USB from his pocket and showed it to the members of Lodgepole. "This USB was slipped to me yesterday morning at the Middle Eastern Women's Rights Summit. When I opened it, I discovered the crown prince wanted me silenced before I could publish something about Dark Sun. I don't know exactly what Dark Sun is, but it must have something to do with the massacre in Yemen."

"Who gave you that USB?" Cho said.

"Princess Amara."

Cho grabbed the USB and the external hard drive from Khashiri, plugged the USB into her laptop, and asked Khashiri for the password.

After he gave it to her, she looked down at her screen. "The USB is named *Scheherazade*. It's an exact replica of the flash drive Apache gave to Ryder."

"Apache told me he was speaking to a woman over a dark web forum, a woman who called herself Scheherazade," Ryder said. "Apache must have passed her the information he'd stolen!"

"Why would Princess Amara give you this USB?" Miller said.

"I . . . I don't know."

"Chief," Bell's voice said over Brenner's earpiece, "I got a visual on Rhome getting aboard the Gulfstream. It took off a few minutes ago."

Brenner keyed his earpiece. "Good, you and Silva link up with Kircher at the jet. We've got a few developments unfolding here."

Taking out his phone so he wouldn't miss Rhome's call, Brenner instructed Cho to insert Khashiri's hard drive into her laptop, before he motioned to Khashiri. "Tell me everything you know about the nine Iranians."

Khashiri explained that an old source in Yemen had contacted him three weeks prior to tell him that a group of Bedouins last September had witnessed Saudi gunships attack one of their own caravans, kill all the guards, and then unshackle and fly off with nine prisoners. When the Bedouins approached the demolished caravan, they discovered that the guards were young Sudanese soldiers, teenagers and children, hired by the Saudis to fight their proxy war in Yemen. When Khashiri's source caught wind of this months later, he found out that the prisoners were captured Iranian Quds Force operatives, who were scheduled to be moved that night from a Saudi prison in the Yemeni town of Husun As Salasil to the town of Tarim, but who never showed up.

"When my source alerted me to this story," Khashiri said, "I wanted the world to know that the crown prince's soldiers murdered children. Children the Saudi coalition had hired and then slaughtered. I wanted to show the world how much of a monster the crown prince is and ask why his soldiers would free sworn enemies of his kingdom."

Staring at the screen over Cho's shoulder, Brenner observed the pictures and names of the nine Iranians Cho had pulled up from Khashiri's hard drive.

"Does anyone know where these Iranians are now?" Miller asked.

"Six of them have disappeared completely," Khashiri said. "But after sending out their names and photographs to some people I know at immigration and border checkpoints in the Middle East and Africa, I discovered that three of them boarded a cargo ship named the *Nicola* in Tunisia a couple of weeks after they were rescued. The Iranians traveled to Italy under Kazakhstani passports, and workers' visas. The *Nicola's* employee logs indicated that the men were on the ship when it ported in Gioia Tauro, but when it left two days later, they were no-shows."

Brenner felt a weight drop in his stomach. "Any sign of them since?"

"Nothing," Khashiri said. "I wanted to expose all this in my article, especially after finding out what these men's specialties are."

"What specialties?"

"One of the three Iranians who disappeared in Italy is a well-known bomb maker. The six others who disappeared without a trace are snipers."

Brenner felt the weight in his stomach drop to his feet.

"Jesus," Brenner said, locking eyes with Miller. "You don't think—"

"The crown prince is going to use the Iranians to kill President Buchanan," Miller said. "We need to get this information to Bennett and Mansur. Imdorf and the FIS need to be alerted about this immediately!"

"I'm already on it," Cho said.

"Why would the crown prince use Iranians?" Ryder asked.

"It's obvious," Brenner said. "The Saudis' Dark Sun operation framed Iran for the thorium reactors' explosions, now they're going to frame them for killing the president of the United States."

"But what's the end goal?" Ryder said.

"I don't know," Brenner replied, but deep down he knew the answer. Assassinating the leader of the free world would inevitably lead to one outcome.

War.

Realizing what was at stake, Brenner's thoughts went to his godson, and the Hail Mary operation he was hopefully carrying out at this very moment.

Rhome's job once he got on that jet was to wait until Turki Shahidi called the crown prince and alerted him that they were on their way to Switzerland. Once the crown prince was given the all clear, Rhome was to wait until the Gulfstream was put on autopilot before he went to the lavatory and inject himself with one of the syringes that McCallister had given him. The contents of the syringe would counteract the chemical within the aerosol canister Rhome would then deploy in the cabin and cockpit.

With the jet's autopilot on, and the pilots and everyone else unconscious, Rhome would then use another syringe to wake up Turki Shahidi, call Brenner via Shahidi's Orion phone, and then use the eight-hour flight to interrogate the Saudi enforcer on everything he knew about Dark Sun.

Miller had concocted this high-risk plan knowing that the flight to Switzerland gave Lodgepole an eight-hour window to operate in, where the crown prince wouldn't be asking Turki Shahidi for updates.

In the time it took the jet to fly to Switzerland, Rhome would have gotten all the information out of Shahidi in relation to Dark Sun and relayed it in real time to Lodgepole on the ground so they could work with Imdorf, Bennett, and Mansur in Davos to stop the threat against the president.

Right before the jet was to land, Rhome would then use the remaining two syringes and wake the pilots. By the time the jet landed in Zurich, the accord would be under an hour away and Lodgepole would have already figured out the identities of Custer and his conspirators. Imdorf, Bennett, and Mansur knowing the methods in which the Saudis planned on killing President Buchanan would have eliminated the threat, as well as removed any Secret Service agents complicit in the conspiracy. By the time Rhome landed, Buchanan would have already been briefed on Dark Sun and the crown prince's involvement, and it would be up to her to decide what to do next.

"Jack, something's wrong," Adams said, pointing at his laptop that monitored the Gulfstream's flight to Zurich.

"What's wrong?"

"The jet just diverted from its course. It upped its speed to Mach .925, and the pilots registered a new flight plan. They're going to Riyadh, and they're going fast."

The weight that had dropped from Brenner's stomach to his feet now felt like it was dragging him down through the floor.

The energy in the room caused by Khashiri's revelations about the nine Iranians dissipated completely.

"No," Miller said. "No, no, no!"

Brenner felt dizzy—

What went wrong?

Is Brian alive?

Had Shahidi discovered Brian shot a corpse?

"Jack," Miller said, his voice thin. "Jack . . . I'm sorry, I'm so sorry—"

Brenner saw the defeat on his friend's face.

Hail Mary had failed.

Brenner tried to rationalize that thought. He tried to imagine what went wrong. What the Saudis would do to Rhome once they got to Riyadh. Turki Shahidi could be interrogating his godson at that very moment, finding out everything that Lodgepole knew about Dark Sun. Right now, the crown prince could be alerting everyone involved. The method by which Buchanan was to be assassinated could change. He could be moving to a backup plan—

Or maybe the crown prince is calling it off, Brenner thought, then immediately dismissed the idea. Dark Sun was years in the making. Raza bin Zaman had too much at stake.

Brenner was seeing things clearer now than ever before. Raza bin Zaman had been the first to pledge to Buchanan's Global Green Accord, because his motive hadn't been just to stop it.

No.

He wanted to do more. He wanted to set up the Iranians for killing the president of the United States.

The realization hit him like a sledgehammer.

"What do you want us to do, Chief?" Adams said, standing.

"We initiate our final contingency plan," Brenner said. "Mike, call McCallister, and tell him that Brian is blown and that he's heading to Riyadh. Instruct McCallister to do everything to ensure Brian's safety when he lands."

Indicating Cho, Brenner then said, "Get ahold of Bennett and Mansur. Have them tell Imdorf to send the Iranians' information to every security and intelligence service working the ceremony in Davos—"

"Even the Secret Service?" Adams said. "Even though they're compromised?"

"It doesn't matter anymore," Brenner said. "The Iranians are going to be the ones pulling off the assassination. We know for certain that three of them entered Europe." Scrutinizing his watch, Brenner continued, "The world leaders take that stage at seven-thirty tonight, Davos time. The closest airport to Davos is in the town of Thal. Accounting for the eight-hour plane ride, and even if Imdorf can get us choppers from Thal to Davos, we're going to be cutting it close."

"How close?" Huey said.

Cho scrutinized her computer. "If we can be wheels up in thirty minutes, and Imdorf has helicopters waiting for us in Thal, we could get to Davos with twenty minutes to spare."

"Is that going to be enough time, Jack?" Miller said.

"We don't have any other choice, Danny," Brenner said. "Call Kircher, tell him we're on our way to the airport now." Brenner pointed to Khashiri. "You're coming with us. I want you to tell us everything you know about those nine Iranians, and what we can do to find them."

"Wait a minute," Ryder said. "What the hell is the contingency plan?"

Brenner looked at her. "We go to Davos and beg President Buchanan not to take that stage."

CHAPTER FIFTY-FIVE

PRESIDENT ANGELA BUCHANAN sat next to her five-year-old daughter's bed and watched Elise's little chest rise and fall. In the early morning hours, Buchanan wanted to see her children before she headed to Davos for the accord signing.

Having left the twins' room ten minutes earlier, she found herself emotional as she stared down at Elise. Months before, Buchanan had made a promise to herself. A promise that when her time in office was over, she would dedicate all her attention to her children.

They deserved a mother who put them first. Who drove them to school, who attended their soccer games and school plays.

With Bobby gone, and the presidency taking up all her time, she worried that she'd been absent for the most critical part of her children's lives.

A single tear flowed down Buchanan's cheek.

Is it all worth it, Bobby?

Is our dream worth it?

Staring down at her little girl, she heard Bobby's deep voice answer in her head.

Of course it is worth it, my love. Our sacrifice will leave a better world for our children.

A sliver of light slashed across Elise's bed, as a Secret Service PPD agent opened the door.

"It's time, ma'am."

Buchanan smiled sadly, knowing that she wouldn't see her children until after the accord signing, but also understanding that it was time to attend to something that she'd been dreading since yesterday, when the National Security Council dragged her into the Situation Room.

Kissing Elise on the forehead, Buchanan stood and took a moment to collect herself. It was something she always did when changing her role from doting mother to president of the United States.

Straightening her back, and lifting her chin, Buchanan moved out of her younger daughter's room and into the hallway, where Special Agent Edwards and Agent Hewitt, along with the rest of her PPD, waited for her.

Buchanan greeted Edwards, asking, "How is the advance work shaping up in Davos, Mark?"

"Agent Tuck landed there yesterday, ma'am," Edwards said. "She's been working around the clock with UN and Swiss security, as well as prepping the personal protection of the crown prince once he arrives."

"Good," Buchanan said.

As they moved toward the Grand Staircase, Buchanan caught sight of a figure sitting in the shadows on one of the lounge chairs in the hall.

"Katherine?"

Katherine Healey sat rigidly in her seat. She had dark bags under her eyes and was scowling.

"Why aren't you downstairs with everyone?"

Healey stood, slowly. "I cannot go downstairs with you, Angela. Not if you're still going through with this."

"Excuse me?"

"The assassination," Healey said. "I cannot be in the room with you if you proceed with the assassination. It is against everything I stand for. Everything *we* used to stand for, Angela. This goes against all of our ideals, our morals. What would Bobby—"

"Don't you dare, Katherine," Buchanan snapped.

Healey's face pruned.

Both women stared at each other in tense silence, then Buchanan said, "You don't think this decision wasn't difficult for me? You think I want to do this? To take a human life?"

"Then don't!"

"It's my job, Katherine. I am the president of the United States. As commander in chief, I swore an oath to protect the American people. Four hundred and eleven mothers, fathers, sons, and daughters were *murdered* last week on American soil. It is *my* responsibility to make sure that *never* happens again. Now, you can either come downstairs with me, or you can wait for me on *Air Force One*. Either way, my mind is already made up."

Healey shook her head, in disgust. And without saying a word, she stormed off down the hallway.

Watching her go, Buchanan felt a twinge of guilt.

"Ma'am?" Edwards said. "We need to move."

Raising her chin, Buchanan led the way down the stairs toward the Situation Room.

————

Custer stood against the wall in the Situation Room's conference center with the rest of the National Security Council and the dozens of support staff as President Buchanan took a seat at the head of the table.

Unlike his other recent visit to the Situation Room that week, he'd been demoted to sit *seconds* against the wall with the NSC's staffers, but he didn't mind—he felt lucky he'd even been invited to witness such a momentous occasion in American history—an occasion that he'd orchestrated at the behest of his benefactors and beautiful handler.

After Tara Devino had given him his latest instructions, Custer had spent nearly a day reaching out to his lieutenants and others in Washington to pull the strings necessary to convince President Buchanan to assassinate the Iranian Quds Force commander, General Soleimani.

As per Devino's instructions, it was paramount to both Operation Little Bighorn and Dark Sun that Soleimani meet his end before the ceremony in Davos.

Taking his seat, Custer took in the room, his eyes settling on his three lieutenants sitting around the table—each one oblivious to the others and the role they were playing. He looked at Reno, Varnum, and Benteen as they observed the president of the United States.

Buchanan looked terrified at the prospect of what she was going to do—what Custer had instigated her to do.

"General," Buchanan said, indicating General Edward Toole, the chairman of the Joint Chiefs of Staff, "shall we begin?"

"Madam President," Toole said, pointing to a large screen on the north side of the room, "you are looking at live aerial imagery from an MQ-9 Reaper drone that is currently flying at twenty-four thousand feet above Baghdad International Airport. In less than two minutes, a private plane carrying General Soleimani is coming in from Tehran. Yesterday, you signed a Title 10 Memorandum of Notification for the targeted assassination of General Soleimani with the explicit instructions to limit the number of noncombatant fatalities. As per your instruction, it is the consensus of my office that General Soleimani will be targeted when he and his caravan leave the airport's grounds via a private road before entering the city."

"His caravan?" Buchanan said.

"Yes, ma'am, two vehicles," Toole replied. "Our intelligence indicates that he will be traveling with nine other individuals. All are members of his security staff."

"What are you saying, General?" Buchanan asked. "You told me yesterday that Soleimani would be the sole target?"

"Madam President," DNI Winslow interjected, "each member of Soleimani's security detail is a member of the Iranian Quds Force. In the eyes of the American government, every individual who will be in that caravan has been legally deemed an enemy combatant."

Custer watched in delight as the veins in Buchanan's throat pulsed.

"Is there no way to *only* target Soleimani?"

"Unfortunately not, ma'am," General Toole said.

Custer saw Buchanan's hand fly to the ugly greenstone pendant that always hung from her neck. The pendant she habitually caressed when she was nervous.

"Is that going to be a problem, Madam President?" SecDef Lake asked.

Buchanan swallowed hard. "No, it is not a problem. You may proceed."

One minute later, everyone in the Situation Room watched on the screen as Soleimani's plane landed and taxied to a stop on the northern side of the airfield.

The Reaper drone's pilot, based out of Creech Air Force Base in Clark

County, Nevada, zeroed the UAV's telescopic lens in on the plane, as a group of ten men exited and marched toward a Toyota Avalon and a Hyundai Starex.

"We have a positive identification on General Soleimani," Toole said.

Custer watched as the Iranian Quds Force general climbed into the back of the Hyundai, before the two vehicles began driving toward the private road that led out of the airport grounds.

"Thirty seconds until the target reaches the kill zone," Toole said. "Final confirmation, ma'am. Do we have the green light?"

"You . . . you have the green light, General."

General Toole lifted the closed circuit phone from the table in front of him and relayed the order, before saying, "Fifteen seconds until Hellfires deploy, ma'am."

Custer, on the edge of his seat, turned his attention back toward the screen.

"Ten seconds."

"Five seconds."

The Reaper's live feed jolted slightly as seven Hellfire R9X missiles rocketed down from the heavens.

Seconds later, the two vehicles took impact and careened to the side of the road.

Toole lifted the phone to his ear. "It's confirmed, Madam President. Successful strike."

Custer tried to mask his satisfaction. His thoughts floated to his beautiful handler, and what she'd promised him if he'd completed his task.

Trying to keep his excitement at bay, he relished the dire expression on President Buchanan's face.

Then, slowly, Custer looked at Reno, Varnum, and Benteen sitting around the table. He thought of what he'd promised them, and what they'd done for him in return.

In less than twelve hours, Operation Little Bighorn and Dark Sun would be complete. In less than twelve hours, McDougall, his fourth, most loyal lieutenant, would oversee their final task in Davos.

Buchanan slowly put her hands on the table and eased herself out of her seat.

Custer and the rest of the room stood with her.

For a moment, Buchanan was silent. Then she said, "Thank—Thank you, everyone. Now, if you excuse me, I have a plane to catch, and an Accord to sign."

As Buchanan walked out of the room, Custer locked eyes with Reno and gave him a wink.

Filing out of the room a few seconds later with the rest of the staffers, Custer went to the lead drawers near the Situation Room's exit and took out his burner phone.

Stuffing it into his pocket, he moved out of the John F. Kennedy Conference Center, up the stairs, and out of the White House's west entrance.

Climbing into the back of his waiting car, he texted his handler:

Task Complete.

CHAPTER FIFTY-SIX

CLUTCHING HIS ORION phone, the Saudi crown prince, Raza bin Zaman, breathed in the hot, salty air emanating from the waters of the Red Sea and willed himself to relax.

But that was proving difficult.

He checked and then rechecked his Orion phone for any signs of an update, then forced himself to put the device into the pocket in his white *thobe*.

Grabbing the stainless-steel railing that surrounded the bow of his 134-meter megayacht, the *Serene*, he gazed at the whites of his knuckles as they gripped the rail and noticed how much they trembled.

I need to cut back on the Adderall.

In the distance he could hear the faint thrum of a helicopter approaching.

She's right on time, he thought, turning around and taking in the black speck on the horizon.

Before he knew what he was doing, the Orion phone was back in his hand.

No calls.

No messages.

Calm down.

In the thirty minutes since Turki Shahidi called him over the Orion phone, alerting him that Brian Rhome had shot a dead man's body in

Montreal, Raza was finding it harder to keep his compulsions under control.

"Breathe," he said to himself, as his mind replayed what Shahidi had said to him.

This isn't a disaster yet, Dark Sun will still succeed.

After everything, it will still succeed.

Just look what we've accomplished already.

The approaching sound of rotors and the wind from the helicopter's wash pulled Raza back to his senses. Turning, he took in the luxury chopper as it settled down on the helipad on the bow of the *Serene*. And watched as the most beautiful woman he'd ever laid eyes on stepped out and made her way over to him.

As the chopper rose and veered off into the distance, Raza took Tara Devino into his arms and kissed her passionately on the lips.

"I've come with great news, my sweet," Devino said.

"What news?"

"Custer contacted me twenty minutes ago. The Americans did it. President Buchanan killed General Soleimani."

Raza blinked, a flood of emotion overtaking him, his mind going back to that fateful day nine years ago. The day he learned that Ibrahim, his beloved older brother, had been shot down in his F-15 by a SCUD missile during a training exercise in eastern Yemen. A SCUD missile fired by the al-Qaeda terrorist Qasim al-Raymi. A SCUD missile that had been sold to the al-Qaeda terrorist by Quds Force commander, General Soleimani.

When he had come up with the idea for Dark Sun a year and a half before, Raza had ingeniously orchestrated a way to take care of his personal vendettas against the two individuals who murdered his brother. He discovered a way to eliminate these two men, whose deaths would serve as catalysts for Dark Sun's end goal—the annihilation of his true enemy.

"You did it, my sweet," Devino said. "After all these years, you found Ibrahim's killers and brought them to justice."

A sad look crept over Raza's face.

"Are you okay?" Devino asked. "Didn't Custer do well? Isn't this wonderful news?"

"It is."

"Then why do you look so upset?"

Glancing down at his Orion phone again, Raza frowned.

"Are you having second thoughts about this morning?" Devino asked.

Raza shook his head, his mind flashing to the task that needed to be carried out. The task *he* needed to carry out.

"I am having no second thoughts, my sweet. I am ready for what I need to do."

He kissed her once more and remembered all over again how he had fallen in love with her two years ago in Switzerland.

The first time he'd seen her, he'd been utterly infatuated. And that infatuation only multiplied when he'd seen how brilliant and cunning she was. Over the last two years, he'd courted her secretly. Waiting for the day he'd become king, and she his queen.

"Something has happened," Raza finally admitted.

"Something bad?"

"I don't know yet."

"What happened?"

Raza glanced again at his Orion phone, then told her about Brian Rhome faking the assassination of Jabril Khashiri, the dissident journalist who had somehow found out about the nine Iranian Quds force members rescued by Turki Shahidi and Mahmoud Ghorbani back in September, the journalist who wished to publish his disastrous article on his blog before the signing of the Global Green Accord.

"How . . . how is Shahidi so positive that Brian Rhome shot a cadaver?"

"Have you ever met a man more familiar with dead bodies than Turki Shahidi?"

Devino paused, then shook her head. "Do we know anything else?"

"Our pilots found a packet of syringes and a small canister on the plane. Shahidi thinks Rhome was going to try to do something on their way to Switzerland. Instead, Shahidi confronted Rhome and was about to interrogate him, when he accidentally shot the American with a high-powered tranquilizer gun. I instructed Shahidi to fly Rhome back to Riyadh."

"So the plane isn't going to Switzerland?"

"Shahidi will bring Rhome to the Ritz-Carlton, and interrogate him, while Mr. Ghorbani, under his Emirati alias, continues the mission alone."

Devino pondered the new development. "Do . . . do you think that *he* had anything to do with this?"

"He?" Raza asked, confused, then realized who she was talking about. "No, he and his men are locked up in my palace outside of Riyadh. He wouldn't have been able to do anything to harm us."

"Does this change anything? If Jabril Khashiri is alive . . . if he publishes—"

Raza held up a hand. He'd been thinking about this nonstop since Shahidi's call.

"I don't think so. We are merely hours away from the signing. The Iranians are in position. It is too late to change our plans now. What is done is done."

"But what if someone figures out our involvement?"

"No one will," Raza said. "Mr. Ghorbani will go to Davos and tie up all the loose ends. If it ever comes back to us that Shahidi and Ghorbani rescued the Iranians, we will vehemently deny all involvement. After all, who would ever figure out our motive? Who would ever discover that it was me who planned the destruction of the accord?"

"My sweet, I told you to stop hiring more advisers, especially Americans. You are too trusting."

"I need men with his temperament and skill set around me."

Devino gave him a reluctant grin, then held out her hand, palm up.

"What?" Raza asked.

"Your phone."

Raza's grip intensified around the Orion phone.

"My sweet, you need to relax now," she whispered. "No more distractions. Like you said, what is done is done."

"What if Rahmani or Shahidi try to contact me?" Raza said, already feeling the anxiety of being phoneless.

"I will look at the phone every couple of hours," Devino said. "I will let you call the president after your task is complete. But then you must get some sleep, so you can enjoy watching the ceremony tonight."

Raza slowly handed her the Orion phone.

Slipping the phone into her pocket, she reached into another pocket and produced a small vial of clear liquid and handed it to him.

The reality of what he needed to do crashed over him again.

"Do you want me to be with you, my sweet?"

"No," Raza said. "This is my responsibility."

"Then I will wait for you in your room."

Raza stepped around her and walked inside his grand yacht, down a long hallway and toward the members of the king's Royal Guard collected outside the ship's master suite.

The guards bowed when he approached.

"I wish to see my father."

"He has just woken up, Your Highness," the chief Royal Guard said. "The king is having a tough morning."

"Still, I wish to see him before I head to Davos."

"Of course, Your Highness."

Opening the double doors, the crown prince walked into the grand bedroom and quietly locked the doors behind him.

His father, King Zaman, was propped up on the pillows in bed. The old man stared blankly at the television on the far wall.

Pulling a chair to the side of the bed, Raza sat down.

"Father," he said, softly. "Father, can you hear me?"

The eighty-five-year-old king didn't move.

"Father," he repeated. "I'm here to give you your medicine."

Reaching into his pocket, Raza took out the small vial of liquid and put it on the nightstand next to the king's half-finished tea.

For the last year and a half, from the moment Raza bin Zaman had conjured up Dark Sun, he had been slipping small doses of *medicine* into his father's tea. The same *medicine* that wouldn't show up on any toxicology reports. The same *medicine* that had accelerated the king's mental decline, and eventually, his strokes.

Unscrewing the vial, Raza poured its entirety into the tea and swished it around.

He studied the king's clouded eyes, the eyes that had never showed him love. The eyes that only loved Ibrahim, Khalid, and Princess Amara continued to stare blankly ahead.

Moving the cup to the king's lips, Raza said, "This will be painless, Father. Now, drink."

The king slowly gulped down the contents of the cold tea.

Putting the cup down, Raza waited thirty seconds, then watched as his father's chest arched violently toward the ceiling. The muscles in his throat flexed and strained, and a momentary look of terror passed over the king's face before he took his last, gasping breath.

Tears welled in Raza's eyes as he regarded the still king.

Then, with a sudden, sweet understanding that the power and wealth of Saudi Arabia was now in his command, Raza stood and returned the vial to his *thobe* and moved toward the door. Swinging it open, and with as much emotion as he could muster, he shouted at the Royal Guard, "My . . . my father! The king! He is dead!"

Raza let the Royal Guards push him aside and run to their dead monarch.

Raza made a show of collapsing against the wall and down to the floor.

A minute later, the chief of the king's Royal Guard exited the room and knelt by Raza's side.

"Your Highness, are you all right?"

"Call . . . call the Council of Ministers," Raza said. "Alert them to what has happened. They can inform the kingdom of the news. As of now, I am officially in mourning."

"What . . . what of the accord?"

"I said . . ." Raza drew out. "I said that I am in mourning. My people need me in my kingdom. They need me here. My cousin, Princess Amara, can take my spot at the accord. Go, tell the council what has happened."

Raza waited until the man disappeared down the hallway, then got to his feet and headed toward his quarters, a wide smile forming on his face, as he wiped the crocodile tears from his eyes.

CHAPTER FIFTY-SEVEN

PRINCESS AMARA FLOATED in an ether of delirium.

Half conscious on her bed in her dark room within the Saudi ambassador's compound, her mind was fragmented, her body feeling like it weighed a thousand pounds.

Having left the Middle Eastern Women's Rights Summit the morning before, right after her speech, she had been pushed into her limousine by her chief of staff, Wali Mattar, and her two minders. In the limo she had accused them of drugging her food, of kidnapping her children, and holding her against her will.

As she spat her accusations in the back of the limo, she'd gotten physical and launched herself at Mattar. Her two minders had restrained her, pinning her down against the seat, as she fought against them.

In her haze, she remembered that Mattar had pulled a syringe from his jacket and stabbed her in the thigh.

That had been her last full memory.

Now, as she fought for control of her body, her mind went to her children.

To Mimi.

And Ahmed.

She wondered where they were.

If they were safe.

Suddenly, the light went on, and the sounds of heavy footfalls entered her room.

She could hear Mattar talking urgently.

"Help me get her up, and into the chair!" Mattar snapped.

Trying to focus her listless gaze, she felt herself being moved from the bed.

"Should we give her the amphetamines?" another voice asked.

"No," Mattar said. "She will get a dose when we arrive in Switzerland so she can stand on that stage with Buchanan and they can meet their fates together."

Switzerland? Amara thought, as she was placed in a wheelchair. *Stage? Meet our fates together?*

"Is the limo out back?" Mattar asked.

"Yes."

"Good," Mattar said. "Wheel her out, and make sure no one sees her like this!"

Chin slumped over her chest, Amara tried to make sense of what was happening as she was wheeled down the hall, but her mind couldn't comprehend any of it.

Her world began to swim more and more as the drug Mattar had used on her held her like a vise.

And as she was moved onto the elevator, she slipped from consciousness once again.

CHAPTER FIFTY-EIGHT

THE SMELL WAS so sharp, so chemical that Rhome's eyes bulged open, and he screamed himself into consciousness.

Tears leaking from his eyes, he vomited over his naked chest and onto his jeans.

Two figures jumped back.

Someone swore loudly in Arabic, and then a hand slapped him in the face, hard.

Recoiling from the blow, Rhome tried to move his body, but his arms were tied behind his back. He sat in a cold metal chair, his ankles secured together by cord.

His eyes focused on Turki Shahidi and Saud Rahmani. Both men looked venomously at him.

Shahidi still wore the Western attire he'd had on in Montreal.

The memories of Rhome's last conscious moment came flooding back. He recalled the fight on the Gulfstream, tripping Shahidi, then trying desperately to rip the pistol from his grip.

Then he remembered the loud bang, the crushing pain in his chest, and spiraling into darkness.

Rhome gazed at the myriad of black, blue, and purple bruises between his pecs. A red hole sat within the largest bruise—the area where the dart from the gun had struck him.

Rhome then took in his opulent surroundings. The carpet was deep red, the wainscoting on the eggshell-white walls finished in gold trim.

To his right sat a luxurious four-poster bed, and on the nightstand next to the bed was a gold-varnished placard that read:

Ritz-Carlton
Riyadh

Something thrashed on the bed and Rhome recognized the naked, bound, and gagged figures of Luca Steiner and Sergei.

Shahidi crouched down before Rhome.

He held a gold-plated pistol.

Rhome's tongue was swollen and dry. His eyes flitted over Shahidi's right shoulder, down to Rahmani's feet, where a massive water jug sat.

"Water," Rhome croaked.

"Oh, don't you worry, Mr. Rhome," Shahidi said. "You're about to get plenty of water. But first, you are going to tell me why you shot a corpse in Montreal, then you are going to tell me who you are working with."

"I . . . told you . . . I don't know what you are talking about."

Shahidi tapped the gold pistol over Rhome's knee. "I have already interrogated Mr. Steiner and his associate. I know that the CIA forced Mr. Steiner to hire you for the Qasim al-Raymi campaign to penetrate the crown prince's inner circle. I want to know why . . ."

"I don't know—"

"Wrong answer."

Shahidi motioned for Rahmani to bring the water jug. As he did, Shahidi toppled Rhome's chair, and he landed on his back.

Shahidi was on him at once, placing a foul-smelling rag over Rhome's nose and mouth.

"You are thirsty?" Shahidi asked. "Here, have as much water as you like!"

Rhome tried to bite and tear at the rag over his face, whipping his head from left to right. But Shahidi's grip intensified. Rhome tried to scream, but his voice caught as water cascaded through the rag into his mouth and down his nostrils.

Drowning, his brain screaming for oxygen, he started to convulse, and when he was just about to black out, the rag was ripped from his face.

Rhome spewed up hot, snot-filled water.

Hoisting Rhome's chair back into the sitting position, Shahidi yelled, "I KNOW YOU SHOT A DEAD BODY! I SAW TWO PEOPLE TAKE JABRIL KHASHIRI OUT OF THE BACK ENTRANCE!! WHAT DID YOU AND THE CIA HAVE PLANNED?!!"

"Screw you."

Shahidi toppled Rhome over again, but this time, when the rag went back over his face, he was ready.

As the water began again, he took himself to Montana—to the snow-filled mountains behind his cabin, where he had grown up elk hunting. He thought of the backcountry ski trips he used to take with his friends, the campfires they'd make during the nights to stay warm.

He was thirty seconds in when Shahidi jerked him back upright, and Rhome spit the water coming up from his lungs onto his torturer.

Irate with fury, Shahidi pistol-whipped Rhome in the face.

He felt the skin in his left cheek break. When Rhome looked up, Shahidi was ripping the gags from Steiner's and Sergei's mouths.

Pointing the weapon at Sergei's head, Shahidi said, "Mr. Steiner, who told you to hire Brian Rhome for the al-Raymi campaign?!"

"I told you—the CIA!! Two men came to my apartment in Geneva, they threatened me so I'd hire Mr. Rhome. They were going to rat me out to Interpol if I didn't!"

"For your illegal arms deals?!"

"YES!!"

"And why did they want you to hire Mr. Rhome?!"

"They didn't tell me why—"

The sound was so loud, so earth-shattering in the cramped room, that Rhome fell sideways onto the carpet.

The majority of Sergei's head had painted the wall behind the bed.

Shahidi was now pointing the gun at Steiner, who screamed and tried to roll off the mattress.

Shahidi said, "When Mr. Rhome's helicopter landed in Riyadh after our meeting with the crown prince, you picked Mr. Rhome up from the helipad. It was a thirty-minute drive to your hotel. But the security cameras told us that you never arrived. Where did you take him?!"

"THEY MADE ME!!" Steiner yelled. "THEY MADE ME STOP

AT A WAREHOUSE. THEY MADE ME BRING RHOME TO THEM!!"

"WHO?!!"

"THE CIA! THEY MADE ME BRING RHOME TO THE CIA CHIEF OF STATION!"

"William McCallister?!"

"YES!!"

Shahidi lowered his weapon.

"PLEASE—THAT'S ALL I KNOW!"

Making eye contact with Rhome, Shahidi said, "I know that's all you know, Mr. Steiner."

In a flash of gold, Shahidi raised the pistol and fired, blowing a hole the size of an apple in Steiner's chest.

Saud Rahmani wrenched Rhome's chair upright, snarling, "What did McCallister tell you? Why did the CIA insert you—was it about Dark Sun?"

Before Rhome could reply, he heard a crash—a door colliding with the wall.

Shahidi and Rahmani whipped around.

"WHAT IS GOING ON IN HERE!"

Major General Azimi marched into the room, his eyes darting from Rhome shackled on the chair to the gruesome scene on the bed.

Azimi, beet red in the face, pointed a finger at Shahidi. "ARE YOU MAD?!!"

"Leave, old man!"

"You can't do this here!" Azimi said. "This cannot happen in the city! There are guests in the hotel!!"

"We are acting under the crown prince's orders!"

"I just spoke to the crown prince!" Azimi held up a black phone identical to the one that Rhome watched Shahidi use. "He told me he wants this man taken out of the city!"

For a moment, Shahidi didn't say anything. Rhome watched as the Saudi enforcer stared at Azimi, then dug in his pocket and took out his own phone; he dialed and pressed it to his ear.

"The crown prince won't answer," Azimi said. "He's in mourning!"

Still, Shahidi continued to hold the phone to his ear, and then after twenty seconds he lowered it and advanced on Azimi. "And where does the crown prince want Mr. Rhome taken?"

"To Ath Thumamah. To our black site in Ath Thumamah."

Shahidi moved uncomfortably close to Azimi. "So the crown prince calls you, and not me? Why wouldn't he give me these orders directly?"

"How should I know?" Azimi said, not backing down. "His Royal Highness told me to tell you to do whatever was necessary to get the information out of this man, but not here."

For nearly ten seconds, Shahidi continued to stare down the old major general. Then he holstered his pistol and snapped at Rahmani.

"Clean him up, and get him a shirt, then take him down in the service elevator."

Rahmani whistled. Four Saudi National Guardsmen entered the room, and Rahmani repeated Shahidi's orders.

The guardsmen were on Rhome in an instant.

He struggled as they wrestled a shirt over his head. Then they grabbed him and recuffed his wrists behind his back, before lifting his elbows into the air and stress walking him out of the room.

There must have been two dozen guardsmen in the hallway, but that didn't stop Rhome. Following behind Shahidi and Rahmani, he started throwing his body weight and kicking.

"Enough!" Shahidi said, turning around and pistol-whipping Rhome on the head.

Rhome staggered to the carpet.

"CARRY HIM!"

Stunned by the blow, Rhome felt himself being moved into an elevator, down into an empty kitchen, and then outside into an alley.

A dozen Mercedes G-Wagons sat waiting.

"Everyone load up!" Shahidi shouted.

Throwing Rhome into the trunk of one of the G-Wagons, Shahidi hog-tied him, and then placed a blackout hood over his head.

Seconds later, Rhome heard the trunk door close and felt the vehicle speed away.

CHAPTER FIFTY-NINE

RHOME GROANED FROM under the blackout hood.

His shoulders, knees, hips, and ankles screamed at him from being hog-tied so long in the back of the G-Wagon.

How long had they been driving? Ten minutes? An hour?

The vehicle bucked and lurched over uneven terrain. He started going over everything that happened, from Lodgepole's failed Hail Mary operation, to the events in the Ritz.

He recalled everything that Turki Shahidi had said to him.

He knows I'm working for the CIA.

He knows I met with McCallister.

That I shot a dead body.

He just doesn't know why.

Rhome needed to get his story straight before Shahidi took him to wherever the hell they were going.

Then his mind floated to the Global Green Accord signing in Davos, and he felt himself panic.

The accord!

He knew he'd gotten on the jet in Montreal the night before the accord ceremony. He knew it was at least a ten-hour flight from Montreal to Riyadh. It had been dark outside when he was thrown into the G-Wagon. Due to the time that had passed, the accord ceremony could be hours, if not minutes away.

Then something much more pressing hit him.

Something had been missing in the room back at the Ritz, or more like, *someone.*

Rhome flashed to the events in the jet before he'd been tranquilized. He remembered how Kazem Shurrab had held him at gunpoint. How the Emirati had beaten him senseless. Then he remembered that Shahidi had called the man *Mahmoud*.

Where the hell have I heard that name before?

Rhome heard Saud Rahmani's voice from the front of the G-Wagon.

"What the hell is that?"

"What?" Shahidi replied.

"That! The headlights!"

Rhome could hear people shifting their body weight over leather seats.

"Looks like a caravan," Shahidi said.

"Driving all the way out here? At this time of night?"

Rhome could hear Shahidi engage a radio: "Slow down. Everyone slow down."

Rhome felt the vehicle lose speed.

"Did Azimi say anything about anyone being out here?" Rahmani said. "Anyone at Ath Thumamah?"

"No."

"I don't like this."

Shahidi keyed his radio. "Everyone stop!"

Rhome felt the vehicle slam on its brakes.

"They're still coming!" Rahmani said.

"I can see that," Shahidi snapped, then keyed the radio again. "All teams, when those vehicles get to us, wait until they stop. Then get out hard and fast. No one fires a shot without my say."

Rhome could hear someone in the car rack the charging handle of an AK, then Rahmani whimpered, "Turki, what do I do?"

"Stay in the car. If there is an engagement, make yourself as small as possible."

Rhome tried reining in his own thoughts.

"Easy, now," Shahidi said. "Wait until they stop."

Rhome could hear the sound of motors approaching.

"Those are Saudi National Guard jeeps!" Rahmani said.

Shahidi yelled, "Everyone out! Now!"

Rhome heard doors opening, and men around the vehicle yelling loudly in Arabic.

Faraway voices yelled back, but Rhome couldn't understand what they were saying because gunfire broke out from everywhere.

Rahmani screamed. Bullets smashed through the windshield and punched through the leather seats.

Rhome tried to make himself as small as possible, the world around him a symphony of chaos.

Rahmani kept screaming.

And just as fast as it started, the gunfire ceased.

For a moment there was nothing but silence.

Heaving hot, recycled breath beneath the blackout hood, Rhome heard footsteps approaching.

Rahmani let loose a terrified shriek.

Rhome heard the trunk open and felt the cool desert air seep into the vehicle.

Strong hands grabbed at him and yanked him onto the sand.

Someone next to him shouted orders in Arabic, and Rhome winced as he heard a *crack, crack, crack* of single-shot AK fire.

Security rounds, Rhome thought. *Whoever won this fight is not messing around.*

Footsteps sounded, then he heard a large mass thud in the sand next to him.

"Don't shoot! Don't shoot!" Rahmani begged.

Someone cut Rhome's restraints and lifted him onto his knees. The hood was torn from his head. Headlights blinded him, and he clamped his eyes shut.

The hot barrel of a weapon tapped his forehead. Easing an eye open, he looked up into the muzzle of an AK-47 and heard a deep, rumbling voice say, "Are you okay, Mr. Rhome?"

CHAPTER SIXTY

AS THE AK was withdrawn from his forehead, Rhome squinted up at the figure.

Backlit by the headlights, the figure held out a hand and helped Rhome to his feet. And for the first time, he got a good look at the man's face.

"Prince Khalid?"

"Can you walk, Mr. Rhome?" Prince Khalid bin Zaman asked.

"I think."

"Good, we need to hurry."

A sob came from the ground to Rhome's left, and he saw Saud Rahmani huddled in the fetal position at the feet of two of Khalid's men.

Khalid pointed at Rahmani. "Restrain him and get him in a vehicle!"

Khalid led Rhome around the G-Wagon toward a collection of military jeeps.

Two dozen of Turki Shahidi's men lay sprawled out among the vehicles.

Khalid said, "Watch your step."

Rhome stumbled when he realized that he'd nearly walked into the body of Turki Shahidi.

"What . . . what's going on?" Rhome sputtered.

"I'll tell you on the way."

"Where are we going?"

"To Ath Thumamah—"

"I need a phone—I need to call—"

"There's no service out here," Khalid said, opening the door to the lead jeep in the caravan. Helping Rhome into the passenger seat, the prince shut the door, then climbed behind the wheel. Rhome watched Khalid's men carry Saud Rahmani to another jeep.

Khalid spun the vehicle around and tore back up the road, glancing at his watch. "The world leaders are taking the stage in Davos in seventeen minutes. General Azimi is meeting us at Ath Thumamah."

"Seventeen minutes?" Rhome said, rattled by how much time had passed since he'd been shot by the tranquilizer gun on the jet. "General Azimi is working with you?"

"He is."

"How—why?"

"Dark Sun," Khalid said. "Because I discovered some details of Dark Sun."

Khalid explained that four nights ago, he had been angry about losing the ambassadorship title to his cousin, Princess Amara. He explained that he went looking for his brother, the crown prince, at his palace, but he'd instead found Saud Rahmani. The man was drunk, and high on pills, and an argument broke out. In Rahmani's stupor, he told Khalid of an operation he and Shahidi were involved in with the crown prince, and a group of powerful Americans—an operation he'd called Dark Sun.

"Rahmani was on one of his benders," Khalid said. "He was bragging to me how the Saudi intelligence report Princess Amara had given to the Americans was a fake to set up the Iranians. He told me how it was going to be leaked and blamed on the director of the CIA so she'd be fired. I soon figured out that Rahmani was self-medicating because of something that had occurred at work. One of his employees, Abdulmalik Hassen, had stolen two files from him. One of the files was Dark Sun, the other file contained information on a Saudi dissident who was going to publish something about Dark Sun before the accord ceremony. Rahmani was nervous that the crown prince would find out about the stolen files. Apparently, Hassen was also passing information from the royal court to the CIA. Rahmani told me that he and Shahidi would be taking care of Hassen in the morning to retrieve the files before my older brother found out. After Rahmani passed out cold, I fled the palace in a panic, knowing that I needed to alert someone of what I'd heard about Dark Sun."

Khalid explained that he wrote a letter to the CIA station chief in Riyadh.

Rhome looked over at Khalid, remembering his briefing with McCallister the night before he left for Montreal. "You were the man in the burka?"

"I was," Khalid said. "I passed my letter to Abdulmalik Hassen and told him to give the files he'd stolen from Saud Rahmani to his CIA handler. A few hours later, I saw you at the drone base, Mr. Rhome."

Rhome thought back to when he'd met Khalid, remembering how tired and distant the prince had seemed.

"Why didn't you just tell McCallister and Azimi what Rahmani had told you while you were at the drone base?"

"How could I?" Khalid said. "I had no idea if General Azimi was involved or not. And I was surrounded by my brother's most loyal soldiers. It's not like a prince can pull aside a CIA station chief without anyone noticing."

Khalid steered the vehicle around a sharp corner and accelerated out of it.

"After I got back from the drone base, I confronted my brother about what I'd heard, and he immediately arrested me and my men. For the last three days, I have been rotting in a cell below one of my brother's palaces. As it turns out, Azimi had been searching for me. He visited me this morning and told me about my father."

"Your father?"

"My father died this morning, Mr. Rhome."

Rhome didn't know what to say.

Khalid continued, "Azimi told me that my brother was in mourning, that he'd ordered Princess Amara to take his place tonight in Davos. Knowing this was too much of a coincidence, I told Azimi everything I'd heard about Rahmani and Dark Sun. I told him to reach out to William McCallister to see if he got my letter. After leaving me, Azimi got in contact with the CIA station chief, and McCallister told him about you—how an operation the CIA was conducting to interrogate Shahidi had failed, and that you were in trouble and were being flown back to Riyadh.

"A few hours ago, Azimi ordered his most loyal men to break me and my men out of Raza's palace and fly us to Ath Thumamah. It was then that Azimi contacted me and told me about you. That's when we hatched this plan to convince Shahidi and Rahmani to drive you out here and to save you."

Khalid came to a stop in front of a concrete structure, a single light illuminated over its steel door.

Throwing the vehicle in park, he checked his watch. "In ten minutes, the world leaders take that stage. Saud Rahmani knows the entire plan of Dark Sun. We have less than ten minutes to get it out of him."

Rhome followed Khalid out of the vehicle, as the rest of Khalid's men parked behind them. A group dragged Saud Rahmani into the concrete building.

Then one of Khalid's men handed the prince a phone.

"Your Highness," the man said, "General Azimi is on his way. The prisoners inside have been released and are being treated."

"Thank you," Khalid said and handed Rhome the phone. "McCallister told Azimi that the CIA team you were working with is in Davos. Call and alert them that we have Saud Rahmani and that he's very motivated to talk."

Khalid followed his men into the structure and disappeared.

In the cool, desert night air, Rhome gazed down at the phone, took a deep breath, and then dialed his godfather's number.

CHAPTER SIXTY-ONE

JACK BRENNER LOOKED out of the chopper's window as it zoomed over the brilliantly lit town of Davos.

Soaring over the Davos Congress Centre, and the outdoor stage that was constructed on the south side of the building, Brenner could see the tens of thousands of people collected on the lawn before the stage, eagerly awaiting the ceremony that would be starting in roughly fifteen minutes.

Shooting an anxious look at Dan Miller sitting in the chopper next to Huey and Ryder, Brenner thought over everything that had occurred in the hours since Hail Mary had failed.

After determining that his godson had been blown, Brenner and the rest of Lodgepole had alerted McCallister to Hail Mary's failed operation and instructed the chief of station to do everything in his power to ensure Rhome's safety while Lodgepole flew to Switzerland to carry out their contingency plan.

During the beginning of the flight, Lodgepole had worked with Khashiri and confirmed the intelligence he'd told them in Montreal about the nine Iranians having been rescued last September in Yemen. They'd also been able to confirm that three of the Iranians, a bomb maker included, had entered Italy weeks after their rescue and hadn't been seen since.

Having instructed Benedicht Imdorf to send out the names and faces of the nine Iranians to all the security and intelligence services working the ceremony in Davos—the Secret Service included—Brenner had hoped that an agency would be able to provide some sort of lead on the Iranians' locations. But in the end, nothing had come up to suggest their whereabouts.

Almost two hours into the flight, Lodgepole and the rest of the world had received the news that the king of Saudi Arabia had passed away and that President Buchanan had ordered the successful assassination of the Iranian Quds Force commander, General Soleimani.

Moments after the news broke of the two events, the Saudi royal court released a statement that the crown prince, Raza bin Zaman, would no longer attend the accord but would send his cousin, Princess Amara, in his absence.

This had sent shock waves through Lodgepole as their jet headed to Switzerland. Knowing what they knew, they'd come to the consensus that it was too much of a coincidence that the king would die just hours before the accord ceremony, giving Raza bin Zaman an excuse to not stand on that stage.

As for the targeted assassination of General Soleimani, Lodgepole suspected the killing had something to do with Dark Sun, but could not confirm it. Eliminating the Iranian general right before the accord was a gross escalation in the rising tensions between the United States and Iran. If the nine missing Iranians were to pull off something in Davos, it would look like a retaliation for killing their general.

Thirty minutes ago, when Brenner and the rest of Lodgepole landed in the St. Gallen-Altenrhein Airport in the Swiss town of Thal, Benedicht Imdorf had two choppers waiting to fly them the eighty kilometers to Davos.

Brenner unclasped his seat belt as the chopper landed in the field of the Eistraum Davos soccer stadium and wrenched open the door, before stepping out into the snowy field and seeing an identical chopper, carrying Jabril Khashiri, Bell, Silva, Cho, and Adams, settle down next to them.

"Jack!" a voice called.

Well over six feet tall, with blue eyes, and ruffled blond hair, the deputy director of the Swiss Federal Intelligence Service, Benedicht Imdorf, ran over, followed by Amina Bennett and Zahir Mansur.

"President Buchanan's motorcade is arriving at the Davos Congress Centre in three minutes," Imdorf yelled, as he got to the group. "The world leaders take the stage in twelve!"

Leading the Lodgepole members away from the choppers, they fast-walked out of the stadium, as Bennett and Mansur handed every member of Lodgepole FIS credentials, and a red-colored pin that they were told to fasten to their lapels.

"These pins will grant you access to every security checkpoint in town," Imdorf said, as he led them onto a street that flanked the Congress Centre's crowded south lawn. Over the crowd, Brenner could see the grand stage erected in the distance.

Imdorf escorted everyone inside a base of operations tent, and Brenner took in a room packed with Swiss FIS officers huddled over tables with computers and communications gear.

"Everyone in this tent has been briefed on the Iranians, and the threat against President Buchanan," Imdorf said. "What I know, they know. So you can speak freely."

"Do you have a room secured in the Congress Centre, Benedicht?" Dan Miller asked.

"I do," Imdorf replied. "You, Jack, and I will head there momentarily, but first let me give you a situation report. So far, we have no new developments on the three Iranians who entered Italy in October—"

"What about the six snipers?" Miller asked.

"We've been searching all over Europe dating back five months," Imdorf replied. "Border crossings, transportation hubs, but we've found nothing. Neither has any other intelligence agency."

"We need to assume they are here," Brenner said.

"We are," Imdorf replied. "I have every sniper and countersniper team checking in, every minute on the minute. Plus every GeoFence drone in the sky is using their facial recognition software to look for the Iranians."

Brenner could hear the noise of the crowd outside as an announcement was made over a loud speaker that the ceremony would start in ten minutes.

Handing out service pistols and earpieces to Brenner, Miller, and the rest of Lodgepole, Imdorf then said, "Okay, President Buchanan is one minute out. She will be arriving at the east gate."

"Danny and I will intercept," Brenner said. "You get the UN secretary general, and the Swiss president. Where is the secure room we need to bring her?"

"Southeast hallway leading out of the main conference room," Imdorf said. "I'll be waiting for you outside the door."

With that, Imdorf hurried out of the tent, and Brenner addressed the Lodgepole members. "Mr. Khashiri, you stay here. Huey, I'm leaving you in charge. Keep on the comms, we'll reach out with any developments."

"Copy, Chief," Huey said, securing the pistol on his waist.

"All right, Danny," Brenner said. "Let's move."

Running out of the tent and onto the crowded street, Brenner could see the Congress Centre building and the stage three hundred meters away.

Following Miller as they wove through throngs of people and security checkpoints toward the building, Brenner suddenly felt a vibration coming from inside his breast pocket.

Yelling for Miller to stop, he pulled his cell phone out.

"This is Brenner—"

"Jack," a hoarse voice said, over the line. "Jack, it's me. It's Brian—"

CHAPTER SIXTY-TWO

THE IRANIAN QUDS Force engineer crawled to the top of the snow cave and moved aside the balls of snow that he'd clumped together to use for a door.

Making a hole for himself just big enough to fit his spotting scope through, he stared down at the illuminated town of Davos some five kilometers below.

Thankful for the cloudless night, he adjusted the focus of the scope and zeroed in on the stage where his target would stand in exactly ten minutes.

The stage was backdropped by thirty-eight hanging flags, representing each nation whose leader would soon sign the Global Green Accord. As he scanned the stage, he paused to leer at the red, white, and blue flag waving in the middle.

Widening the scope's field of vision, he examined the crowd of thousands already gathered on the Congress Centre's snowy south lawn. Those closest to the stage were held thirty meters back by security teams, fences, and a twenty-foot-tall, four-inch-thick wall of clear, bulletproof glass.

"Cowards," the engineer said, his mind floating to his six other brothers.

He knew they were close. He could almost feel their presence in the valley below. His brothers were some of the best snipers in the world.

Their tools were their rifles—their .50 calibers, and their .338s. He'd seen them in action before. He'd seen them drop moving targets from over two kilometers away.

Though he did not know their exact location in the valley, he knew they had to be close to penetrate that four-inch-thick wall in order to kill their targets.

Widening his lens even more, the engineer saw a few security and press helicopters flying in wide circles over the town. And if he really studied the night sky, he might even be able to spot the drones of the GeoFence. At least the ones that were low enough to see.

The engineer knew that there would also be drones flying at such a high altitude that he would never be able to spot them, even with his powerful scope. Those drones would be models similar to the Reaper and Predator drones the Americans were always flying so close to Persian airspace.

The engineer grinned when he thought of those drones, and the invisible bubble—the GeoFence that surrounded the stage in a one-mile radius.

Invented by the Americans and perfected by United Nation's engineers in the Hague, the GeoFence was constructed and operated by some of the smartest individuals in the world. Not only did it prevent cyberattacks, and other nefarious electronic signals from entering the bubble, it also tracked every cell phone, computer, GPS, and any other electronic device within its boundary—and even had the ability to fry every bit of technology within its range.

On paper, it was impossible to penetrate the United Nations' GeoFence. Like the GeoFence that surrounded the White House, the UN GeoFence was constantly monitored by small drones that moved around within its perimeter. These drones not only served as relay devices to extend the depth, width, and length of the GeoFence if need be, but also carried with them highly specialized cameras with thermal and x-ray capabilities.

It was these thermal cameras the engineer feared most. They were the reason why he and his two brothers—disguised as backcountry skiers—had hauled their own drone up this mountain so far away from their target the morning before.

Since then they'd been hiding in the snow cave they'd dug for themselves, waiting for their moment to strike.

From behind the engineer in the snow cave, the bomb maker asked, "How does it look?"

"It is about to begin."

"And the wind?" asked the pilot.

"Nonexistent, brother," the engineer replied. "It is a great night to fly."

With the closest airport in the Swiss village of Thal, some eighty kilometers to the north—most of the world leaders had taken helicopters from St. Gallen-Altenrhein to Davos.

But not all of them, the engineer thought. *Not the arrogant Americans.*

Still gazing through the scope, he saw the thirty-vehicle caravan coming from Zurich into Davos from the south. The engineer noted that President Buchanan's motorcade driving toward the Congress Centre was replete with law enforcement Suburbans that drove in front of and behind the two identical armored limousines, each so aptly named the *Beast*.

Not wanting to display his body heat any longer, the engineer pulled back his spotting scope and then resealed the hole with the snowballs before sliding down into the tight cavern they'd carved out of the snowy mountain.

Landing in the small room, he gazed at his two brothers in the lantern light, the drone sitting at their feet.

The engineer noted the worry on the pilot's face.

"What's wrong, brother?"

The pilot frowned. "How do we know the motherboard you installed in the drone will break the GeoFence?"

"You do not trust Allah?" the engineer said. "You do not trust General Soleimani or Colonel Ghorbani?"

"I . . . I do, but—"

"But what?"

"But how do *they* know it will work?"

The engineer pulled a cord and his computer tablet from his rucksack. Connecting the tablet with the cord, he stuck its other end into the drone's motherboard housing unit.

The tablet's screen flickered, displaying an ever revolving series of code. Knowing that the bomb maker and the pilot would never understand the code, the engineer turned the screen toward them nonetheless. "This motherboard comes straight from the Americans. Straight from the inner sanctum of the Secret Service. This is the exact motherboard that sits inside all the other drones flying within the GeoFence." Addressing the pilot, the engineer said, "All you have to do is fly the drone to the edge of the GeoFence. As soon as it penetrates the bubble, the GeoFence will detect it and lock onto it. But it will not attack it, nor will it send off any alarms; instead it will recognize the drone as one of its own, one of the dozens flying within the bubble."

"But how will the drone detect our target?" the pilot asked.

"It will chase a benign radio signal carried by someone close to our target. The drone will follow that signal until facial recognition kicks in."

The pilot looked skeptical.

"The technology is foolproof, brother," the engineer insisted. "There is no human error to deal with. Just perfect code."

At last the pilot's shoulders relaxed. "If you are confident in the technology, then so am I."

The engineer patted the pilot on the arm. "Why don't you shut your eyes for a few minutes, brother. Soon, we will need you at your best."

The pilot agreed with the engineer and lay back on his skis and his heavy parka that leaned against the snow cave wall.

Glancing in the direction of the bomb maker, the engineer locked eyes with him. "Now, brother, all you and I have to do is wait."

CHAPTER SIXTY-THREE

"BRIAN!" JACK BRENNER said over the phone. "Brian, are you all right? What happened?"

Rhome could hear a large crowd in the background of Brenner's static-filled connection.

"Jack, you need to listen to me. I've got Saud Rahmani in my possession—"

"You've got Rahmani?!"

"Yes, what do you need me to do?"

"We . . . in Davos. President . . . about . . . to take stage."

More static came over the line, as Brenner's voice cut out.

"Jack!"

"GeoFence . . . messing with . . . phone . . . will call back . . . on Danny's!"

The line went dead.

"Shit!" Rhome said, pacing in the darkness before the Saudi black site building. He heard the chug of a helicopter approach. Looking to the south, he watched as it came in close, circled the building, and then landed fifty yards away. Major General Azimi climbed out of the chopper and ran toward him.

"Are you okay, Mr. Rhome?"

"I'm fine," Rhome said, and he told the general that Khalid and Saud

Rahmani were inside. As Azimi hurried into the structure, Rhome's phone rang.

"Brian, can you hear me?" Brenner said. "I'm with Lodgepole. We're in Davos. The Saudis broke nine Iranian Quds operatives out of a Yemeni prison back in September. Six of them are snipers. One is a bomb maker. We suspect they are in Davos!"

Rhome felt his pulse quicken.

Brenner said, "Force Rahmani to tell you where the Iranians are, and how they plan on assassinating President Buchanan. If any member of the Secret Service or any other individuals on the ground in Davos are involved, get their identities. Then call me back on this number."

"Copy," Rhome said. "Stay by your phone."

Cutting the call, Rhome sprinted into the facility.

Davos, Switzerland
Congress Centre
March 9, 7:20 p.m.

Princess Amara stood in the crowded high-ceiling conference room surrounded by her security detail and clasped her hands together, trying to keep calm.

The vast room—the same room that held the Davos Economic Forum every year—now contained the press, security, aides, and staff of the other world leaders mingling around her.

"The president of the United States will be arriving in one minute," the master of ceremonies said over a loudspeaker.

Excited murmurs broke out over the room.

Having come to consciousness on a private jet some two and a half hours before, Amara had found herself sitting across from Wali Mattar and her two minders.

"We are about to land in Zurich," Mattar had said.

"Zurich?"

"Yes, an American Secret Service detail will be waiting for us. They will drive us to Davos for the accord signing."

It was then that Mattar told her of the Saudi king's death, and how the crown prince was in mourning, so he'd sent Amara to sign the Global Green Accord in his stead.

With no time to mourn her uncle's death, Amara was then given a cosmetic bag and a light green *abaya* and a cream-colored *hijab*.

"Go in the lavatory and put these clothes on and do your makeup," Mattar said. "We will be landing shortly."

Her mind still clouded and groggy, Amara had done as she was told and it wasn't until she was finishing the last of her makeup when her memories of the last week started to come back to her.

As she stared at her reflection in the lavatory mirror, she thought of her children, and of Farid, her chief of security, and the USB and the note he'd smuggled to her in the snow globe. Then she thought of Jabril Khashiri and the scene that had played out at the Middle Eastern Women's Rights Summit and the fight she'd had with Mattar in the limousine, when she'd confronted him about drugging her.

But the memory that had struck her like a mallet was the last memory she'd had before waking up in the jet. The memory of Mattar and her minders putting her in the wheelchair in her room at the ambassador compound and what they'd said:

Should we give her the amphetamines?

No. She will get a dose when we arrive in Switzerland so she can stand on that stage with Buchanan and they can meet their fates together.

Having completed her makeup and getting dressed, Amara, now armed with that memory, had stormed out of the jet's lavatory and challenged Mr. Mattar.

"Why am I really being sent to Davos?!" she'd yelled at him. "What do you have planned for me and President Buchanan on that stage?!"

The ferocity in which Amara approached her chief of staff had caused her minders to grab her and hold her back.

"Princess," Mattar said, taking a syringe from his pocket, "do not make me inject you with this drug again—"

"He killed the king, didn't he?" Amara shouted. "The crown prince killed the king, so I can stand on that stage. Why?!"

"Princess, I don't know what you are talking about."

"Bullshit!" Amara cried. "I heard what you said back in DC. How me and the American president would meet our fates on that stage!"

This had caused Mattar to frown.

Amara said, "As soon as we land, I will tell my American Secret Service detail what you said. I will tell them that you are planning to kill me and the president!"

At this point, Mattar laughed. "No, Princess, you won't."

"And why wouldn't I?!"

"Because they are working for us."

Amara had recoiled at that. "They . . . they can't all be working for you."

"Just the important ones," Mattar said, taking a step closer with the needle. "Now let's calm you back down."

Mattar sank the needle into her shoulder and depressed the plunger. Instantly, the drug took hold of her, but not enough to slip her out of consciousness.

When the plane landed in Zurich, she was escorted out onto the tarmac and was met by a group of American Secret Service agents led by a large woman—the same woman who'd taken Amara to the White House a few days before when she'd briefed President Buchanan on the Saudi intelligence report.

Reintroducing herself to Amara as Agent Tuck, the Secret Service agent explained that she would be leading Amara's security element for the duration of the accord ceremony that night.

Escorting Amara, Mattar, and her two minders into the back of a Suburban, they began their hour-and-forty-five-minute trip to Davos.

In her fog during the drive, Amara tried to fight the drug and figure out a way to get out of her situation.

Knowing that anyone in the Secret Service could be compromised, it wasn't until they were just outside of Davos that the princess realized the only way to circumvent the threat to her and President Buchanan's lives was to go straight to Buchanan herself before they got on that stage.

Now, standing in the crowded room surrounded by Tuck, her Secret Service detail, Mattar, and her two minders, Amara turned her attention to the grand hall leading into the room.

Applause broke out a moment later, and Amara watched as President Buchanan entered.

Knowing this moment could be her only shot, she made a beeline directly toward the leader of the free world.

————

Davos, Switzerland
Congress Centre
March 9, 7:20 p.m.

Sitting in the back of one of the two presidential limos, President Buchanan finished making some last-minute adjustments to the speech she would soon be giving after the UN secretary-general welcomed all the world leaders onstage.

From what Buchanan had been told, the UN secretary-general would talk for five minutes, then hand the podium over to her. She would then give her twenty-five-minute address before she and Princess Amara would be the first to sign the Global Green Accord.

Buchanan's motorcade sped into Davos, past thousands of eager onlookers who cheered her arrival.

Dressed in a baby-blue designer overcoat for the outdoor event, Buchanan took a deep breath as the limo pulled up to the east entrance of the Davos Congress Centre. Throngs of journalists waited for her, pushed back by hundreds of security personnel manning the barriers.

She saw Special Agent Edwards climb out of the front seat of the limo as Agent Hewitt and the four agents in her personal protective detail surrounded her door.

Our moment has finally arrived, Bobby, she thought, clutching the greenstone pendant.

We finally did it, after all these years, we finally did it.

As Edwards opened the door for her, Buchanan was met by a blast of cheers and bright flashes as hundreds of cameras captured her arrival.

Stepping into the cold night, Buchanan waved to the onlookers as Edwards, Hewitt, and her detail escorted her up the Congress Centre's stairs, and into a long white-marble hallway.

"You'll assemble in the main conference room with the rest of the world leaders, ma'am," Edwards said, fidgeting with his earpiece. "Then we'll walk down to the stage-right corridor where you and the Swiss president will lead the rest of the leaders behind the UN secretary-general onto the stage."

"Thank you," Buchanan said, and she noticed that Edwards was still wrestling with his earpiece. "What's wrong, Mark?"

"My comms are acting up, ma'am. Nothing to worry about."

Taking a left out of the grand hall, Buchanan was led into a high-ceiling conference room and was met with rapturous applause as both the press, sequestered on the north wall, and the thirty-seven other world leaders and their aides cheered her arrival.

Buchanan waved at everyone, then greeted the German chancellor followed by the president of France.

Moving farther into the room, she heard a familiar voice say, "Madam President?"

Buchanan turned to see her chief of staff, Katherine Healey.

Healey stood there meekly. "The speechwriters have made your final changes, it's being sent to the teleprompters now."

"Thank you, Katherine," Buchanan said and realized she hadn't seen her old friend since their argument in the White House earlier that day.

"Ma'am, I . . . I also want to apologize for this morning. It wasn't my place to challenge you."

"It's exactly your place to challenge me, Katherine. I would not be here if it wasn't for you."

"Thank you, ma'am. And congratulations again."

As Healey walked away through the crowd, Buchanan's eyes settled on the very person she wanted to see before the ceremony began.

Moving toward her, Princess Amara was followed by a contingent of Secret Service agents, led by Agent Tuck and Amara's personal security.

On Buchanan's immediate left, Edwards continued to mess with his earpiece.

"Madam Ambassador," Buchanan said and frowned when she scrutinized Amara's appearance.

The princess's usual cheerful face was sallow, her eyes sunken and bloodshot.

"Are you okay, Princess?"

Amara nervously eyed Tuck and her security detail. "I'm . . . fine, Madam President. Just . . . having a rough day, all things considered. I was wondering if I could have a word?"

Buchanan put a hand to her mouth. "How insensitive of me. I'm so sorry to hear about your uncle, Princess. Your cousin called me earlier with the terrible news about the king. If there is anything I can do, please let me know." Buchanan then indicated the Secret Service agents around Amara. "How is your security working out?"

Amara shot another nervous glance at the individuals around her. "They're fine, Madam President, but I was wondering if—"

"Ma'am," Edwards said, cutting off Amara.

"What is it, Mark?" Buchanan snapped.

His hand still on his earpiece, Edwards leaned in. "I'm going to have to step away for a minute to change comms, ma'am. Agent Hewitt will relieve me. I shouldn't be long, then I will escort you to the stage."

Edwards motioned to the stage-right corridor.

"Yes, fine," Buchanan said, watching Hewitt approach and Edwards walk away.

Turning her attention back to Amara, she took the princess by her hands and gave them a small squeeze. "Don't be nervous, Princess. This is a day we will remember for the rest of our lives. Together, we will change the world. Now, if you excuse me, I need to make my introductions."

With that, Buchanan stepped around Amara and made her way toward the prime minister of India.

———

Special Agent Edwards cursed as he moved away from President Buchanan and into the hallway heading toward the Secret Service checkpoint at the east entrance of the Congress Centre.

After a year and a half of careful planning for this very night. After a year and a half of overseeing and orchestrating the Secret Service's presence in Davos, all the coordination and advance work and time he had put in to make sure that President Buchanan's attendance would go off without a hitch, Special Agent Mark Edwards had to now suffer the embarrassment of having a defective earpiece for what should be the most momentous occasion of his career.

From the moment he'd put the earpiece on when *Air Force One* had landed in Zurich almost two hours ago, he'd noticed that it was somewhat glitchy.

I should have changed the damn thing in the Beast, he thought, as he got to the group of Secret Service agents manning the east entrance above the two parked presidential limos.

Gazing down at the primary limo, the one that Buchanan had arrived in, that was facing south, Edwards's eyes then went to the secondary limo across the street, just fifty yards beyond, that was parked facing north. He sighed when he thought back to all the hoops he'd had to jump through to ensure that both vehicles stayed parked at the east entrance of the Congress Centre for the duration of the ceremony.

One thing that got hammered into the minds of every Secret Service agent during their training was to make sure their principal, in his case, the president of the United States, had the most efficient evacuation routes.

As special agent in charge of the president, Edwards's main role was evacuation. His job was to stand over the left shoulder of the president at all times and take her out of *any* situation that he deemed a threat.

Tonight, the primary evacuation route of President Buchanan was the Beast parked outside of the east entrance, facing south toward Zurich.

If for any reason that egress route was compromised, he would take his principal to the secondary route—the Beast parked facing north toward the town of Thal.

But an emergency egress route is not going to be necessary, Edwards thought.

In his twenty-plus years as a Secret Service agent, Mark Edwards had never witnessed an event as secure as Davos was tonight. The three rings of protection surrounding the world leaders extended miles in every direction. There were more security personnel in the town than all the guests, onlookers, and attendees combined.

For the last couple of months, every threat that had been made

against the US president and the Global Green Accord ceremony had
been meticulously investigated.

Every building, room, hallway, street, sewage tunnel, and crevice in
the town had been searched dozens of times a day in the weeks preceding
the event. All line-of-sight shooting lanes were locked down by sniper
and countersniper teams. Plus the drones in the sky and the GeoFence
surrounding the area monitored everything. The only aspect Edwards
had initially worried about when planning the Secret Service's protection of the president in Davos was that Buchanan had insisted that the
signing take place outside. But that worry had ended when UN security
staff had decided on placing a twenty-foot-high, four-inch-thick wall of
bulletproof glass in front of the stage. They also allowed a Secret Service
counterassault team to assemble on the left side of the stage, whose main
role was to assist Edwards, Agent Hewitt, and the PPD in getting their
principal to safety.

Having gone over hundreds of new threats made against the president
and the accord in the last few hours, Edwards had seen only one threat that
had initially caused him alarm. The deputy director of the Swiss Federal
Intelligence Service, Benedicht Imdorf, had released the names and pro-
files of nine Iranian Quds Force operatives suspected of entering Europe
back in October. With Agent Tuck having arrived in Switzerland before
him to prepare for the Saudi contingents arrival, Edwards had ordered her
to evaluate and coordinate a threat assessment with the Swiss FIS.

Just before landing in Zurich, Tuck and her team had alerted Edwards and the rest of Secret Service command that the threat level of the
nine Iranians being in the area was a *soft* threat level at most.

Only three of the Iranians had been documented entering Italy five
months before, and there was no evidence to suggest their presence any-
where close to the accord ceremony.

Tuck had informed him, though, that erring on the side of caution,
she had uploaded the nine Iranians' faces to the GeoFence's facial recognition drones.

If they were in the area, they would be spotted and taken care of
immediately.

Coming up to the Secret Service checkpoint, Edwards stopped in
front of a young agent, who said, "We heard you needed new comms?"

Grabbing an earpiece from the man, Edwards took out his defunct set and exchanged devices.

Fitting it into his ear, he tested it, and satisfied, he took one last glance at the two presidential limos below him, when he felt a strong hand grip his shoulder, and a familiar voice say, "Mark, we need to speak with you, right now!"

CHAPTER SIXTY-FOUR

JACK BRENNER MOVED his hand off Special Agent Edwards's shoulder and took a step back, standing next to Dan Miller.

"Jack?" Edwards said. "Danny?"

"Mark," Brenner heaved, trying to catch his breath from sprinting up the road and into the Congress Centre after his call with Rhome.

"What are you two doing here?" Edwards asked. "What's going on?"

"Mark, please, we need to talk," Miller said.

Edwards and the Secret Service agents behind him stared at the pair with perplexed looks.

"Where's the president?" Brenner asked.

"In the conference room, she's taking the stage in eight minutes."

"We need to speak with her."

"What are you talking about, Jack?" Edwards said, muting his earpiece. "What's going on?"

Brenner dropped his voice, so the Secret Service agents behind Edwards couldn't hear. "Deputy Director Benedicht Imdorf has a secure room set up in the southeast hall. You need to take the president to that room now. The UN secretary-general and the Swiss president are already on their way there."

"Excuse me?"

"Mark, listen. You are going to have to trust us that there is a credible and immediate threat to President Buchanan's life—"

Edwards reached for his comms, but Miller grabbed his arm. "It needs to be an off-the-record movement. No other agents outside of the PPD can know about it. Meet us in the room in one minute. You will see Benedicht Imdorf outside the door. Do not have *any* other agents come into that room. Just you and the president, understand?"

Edwards silently appraised the men and their frantic states. "Okay."

"Good," Miller said.

Collecting his breath, Brenner watched Edwards hurry down the hallway toward the conference room and then followed Miller as they rushed to the southeast hall.

———

Edwards jogged into the conference room, Dan Miller's and Jack Brenner's words seared in his mind.

There was something about their panic-stricken faces that had spooked him.

Spotting his principal, who was speaking with the prime minister of India, Edwards hurried over and grabbed Agent Hewitt. "Charlie, I need an off-the-record movement to a room in the southeast hall."

Hewitt looked at him, confused.

Twenty yards away, Agent Tuck stood next to Princess Amara. Tuck's eyes met his.

Hewitt whispered, "POTUS is taking the stage soon—"

"I only need her for ninety seconds."

"Okay, I'll call the sight agent to sweep the room."

"No. It's already been swept and secured. Tell your guys to stand guard outside."

"What's going on, Mark?"

Edwards ignored him and stepped between Buchanan and the prime minister of India.

"Ma'am," Edwards said, putting a hand on the small of Buchanan's back, "you need to come with me."

Not waiting for a reply, Edwards led his principal toward the southeast hallway.

"What do you think you are doing, Mark?" Buchanan said.

I'm not exactly sure, Edwards thought, but he didn't need to think.

The fear on Dan Miller's and Jack Brenner's faces told him all he needed to know.

The PPD and Agent Hewitt hot on their tail, Edwards shot one more glance at Tuck across the room, whose face was lined with concern, and then moved into the southeast hallway where Benedicht Imdorf was waiting outside of a door.

When they got to him, Imdorf let them inside.

CHAPTER SIXTY-FIVE

STANDING IN FRONT of Dan Miller, Jack Brenner gazed past the confused UN secretary-general and the Swiss president as Special Agent Edwards escorted President Buchanan into the small sitting room.

Benedicht Imdorf came in last, locking the door behind him.

"What the hell is going on?" Buchanan spat.

"I would like to know the same thing!" said the Swiss president. "Benedicht, what is the meaning of this?"

Edwards locked eyes with Brenner. "You gentlemen have ninety seconds."

"The ceremony is about to begin," the UN secretary-general said. "Why are we in this room?"

Brenner said, "All of you need to shut up, and listen to me."

"And who the hell are you?" the secretary-general asked.

"My name is Jack Brenner, and this is my colleague, Dan Miller; we're former members of the Central Intelligence Agency." Putting his attention on Buchanan, Brenner continued, "We have brought you into this room, Madam President, to tell you that you *cannot* take that stage."

"Are you mad?!" the secretary-general said.

"I don't have time to explain the specifics," Brenner said. "But we have reason to believe that there are nine unaccounted for Iranian Quds Force operatives somewhere in the vicinity, six of whom are snipers, one a known bomb maker. We believe they are going to make an attempt on President Buchanan's life."

Edwards glared at Imdorf. "My agency already received this threat and deemed it *soft*. So why am I hearing about this again, and behind closed doors?"

"It's not a soft threat," Miller said. "And you are hearing this again behind closed doors because we have reason to believe that the Secret Service is compromised, Mark."

"What did you just say?!"

"Benedicht was instructed to release the information in hopes that another agency could identify and locate the Iranians. We got creative in meeting you all in here, to tell you that this threat is *very* credible and real."

Brenner interjected, "Madam President, a task force in the CIA unearthed a plot against you. A plot that is overwhelming in scope and could potentially involve individuals close to you. The fact that Special Agent Edwards, or yourself, was not informed of this earlier was because we had no way to get to you without anyone knowing—without any of your Secret Service agents knowing."

"Are you saying that you suspected my involvement?" Edwards asked.

"We suspected *everyone's* involvement," Miller said. "We launched an operation to derail this plot against you, Madam President. Earlier today, that operation failed. Now we are doing the only thing we can do, by approaching each of you and begging you to not take that stage. To give us more time. There is a known Iranian bomb maker out there somewhere, and six highly accomplished snipers. We don't know where they are, but we might soon. So please, listen to me when I say this. Give us an hour—"

"Absolutely not," the secretary-general said. "The security in Davos is impregnable. There is no way a bomb is near that stage. And there is no way for a sniper to break that bulletproof glass!"

"The glass is not impenetrable," Imdorf said. "It could be broken by numerous, high-velocity rounds hitting the same spot multiple times. It is unlikely that the glass would puncture, but it could under the correct circumstances."

"How many bullets would that take?" the Swiss president asked.

"A fifty-caliber could potentially weaken the glass," Edwards said. "If another couple of rounds were to hit the exact area of impact, it *could* go through. But we're talking about multiple rounds hitting the same *exact spot.*"

Brenner was glad Edwards was taking this seriously.

"But how difficult could that be?" Buchanan asked.

"Incredibly difficult, ma'am. But not impossible," Edwards replied.

"And the likelihood of a bomb being in the area?"

"Impossible," Edwards said. "The area has been swept continuously for months. The likelihood of a bomb being in the vicinity and being detonated is nearly zero."

"And the Iranians?" Buchanan asked. "Could they be here without us knowing?"

Edwards shook his head slowly. "The Iranians' faces have all been uploaded into the GeoFence's facial recognition drones. If they're in the area, they would've already been found."

Brenner noted that there was some uncertainty in Edwards's voice.

"Well, that settles it!" the secretary-general said.

"Please, Madam President," Miller said. "All we are asking for is an hour. Push the ceremony back an hour, and let us find these bastards."

Buchanan clasped the greenstone pendant around her neck, deep in thought. Outside, a thunderous roar came from the crowd.

"We need to go," the secretary-general said.

"Thirty minutes, Madam President," Miller said. "Give us thirty minutes—"

"No," Buchanan said.

"Ma'am," Edwards interjected. "Maybe we *should* delay the ceremony."

"Absolutely not," Buchanan said. "And you cannot override my decision. I have been waiting for this moment for nearly half of my life. I trust the GeoFence's facial recognition technology, and the structural integrity of that wall. If we knew for certain that the Iranians were in the area, that would be a different story. But so far you've shown me zero evidence of their presence. There have been enough hiccups this week that have threatened the continuation of this ceremony, and I won't let anything else get in the way of me standing on that stage and signing that accord. That is my final decision."

Buchanan made for the door.

For a short beat, Edwards's eyes stared into Brenner's, and the old spymaster could see the concern on his face.

As the Swiss president and the UN secretary-general followed Buchanan, Brenner said to Edwards, "Stay close to her, Mark. Don't trust anyone. Just stay close to her."

CHAPTER SIXTY-SIX

RHOME RAN DOWN the long hallway deep into the underground facility, and through a door that opened up into a narrow cellblock.

Ahead, he could see Prince Khalid's men tending to dozens of freed prisoners.

Rhome stopped short when he saw General Azimi kneeling over a man in his early sixties who was sitting with two terrified young children in his lap.

Azimi looked up at Rhome and said, "Saud Rahmani and the crown prince locked up Princess Amara's children and her staff in this facility, like they were dogs!"

Rhome observed the children and felt an anger flare up in him. "Where's Rahmani?"

"This way," Azimi said, leading Rhome through the cellblock to a door that opened into a foul-smelling concrete chamber.

The chamber's floor was concave. A giant drain sat in the center of it. To Rhome's left stood a table filled with various devices of persuasion; below the table was a white bucket, with the word *salt* written on it in Arabic.

In the middle of the room, a naked Saud Rahmani hung from his wrists by a rusty chain bolted to the ceiling.

Rhome stopped behind Azimi at the edge of the concave floor and noticed that there were four high-powered water cannons in each corner of the room. Each cannon was manned by one of Khalid's men and aimed directly at Rahmani, whose body was already beet red and bleeding, water and blood dripping from his feet toward the drain.

"How dare you hold the princess's children in this hellhole!" Azimi yelled, charging toward Rahmani.

Khalid, who stood before the hanging man, stopped the general's advance.

"Ahmed and Mimi will be fine," Khalid said, holding Azimi back. "We will make sure this piece of shit is punished."

"We don't have time for this!" Rhome yelled, glancing at the clock displayed on the phone Khalid had given him. "The world leaders take the stage in eight minutes."

Having studied enhanced interrogations at the Farm, Rhome knew that getting answers out of a subject had a great deal to do with psychology. You had to start small, catch your subject in a lie, then increase the consequences for lying.

Rhome said, "We know the crown prince broke out Iranian Quds Force operatives in Yemen last September so they could be sent to Davos to assassinate the American president. How many Iranians are in Davos?"

"FUCK YOU!!" screamed Rahmani.

"Hit him with the hoses," Rhome said.

Khalid pulled Rhome and Azimi back and then raised his hand as the cannons pummeled freezing water onto Rahmani's exposed skin.

The man screamed in agony.

When the cannons stopped, Rhome looked down at his phone.

Seven minutes.

Rhome took in the man's battered flesh. "How many Iranians are there?!"

"I don't know!"

"Hit him again."

After the cannons finished their deluge, Rhome repeated his question but Rahmani refused to reply. After two more rounds of the hoses, Rahmani screamed, "SIX. THERE ARE SIX IRANIANS!"

"Wrong answer," Rhome said and delivered a punch to Rahmani's diaphragm. "HOW MANY!!"

"NINE!!" Rahmani finally sobbed.

"HOW ARE THEY GOING TO KILL THE PRESIDENT?!"

"SNIPERS!!" wailed Rahmani. "They're all snipers!"

"ALL NINE OF THEM?"

"YES!"

"WRONG ANSWER!" Rhome yelled. "HIT HIM AGAIN. ONE MINUTE THIS TIME!!"

The cannons bellowed for a full sixty seconds, then stopped.

Glancing at his phone, Rhome saw he now had three minutes to work with. He needed answers now.

Walking over to the white bucket under the table, Rhome brought it over to Rahmani. The man was on the verge of passing out.

Scooping a handful of salt from the bucket, Rhome threw it on the man's raw skin.

Rahmani screamed bloody murder.

"I KNOW SIX OF THE NINE IRANIANS ARE SNIPERS. WHERE ARE THEY TAKING THEIR SHOTS?!" Rhome yelled.

Reaching into the bucket again, Rhome pulled out another handful of salt.

"NOO!!" screamed Rahmani, then said, "The snipers are in two teams of three! One team is on the Vaillant Arena across from the park. Their target is the president. The other is on the roof of the Steigenberger Grand Hotel and they're targeting Princess Amara!"

"And how are they coordinating their shots?! How do they plan on penetrating the bulletproof glass and getting past the countersniper teams?!"

For thirty seconds Rahmani sobbed his answers.

Salt still in his hand, Rhome waited for Rahmani to finish, then got in his face and hissed, "I know there are others involved in Davos. Secret Service agents, people close to the president. I want names."

Rahmani sputtered, "H-How—"

"GIVE ME THE NAMES!"

Looking at the salt in Rhome's hand, Rahmani said, "There is only one, but I don't know their real name. Just that they're a Secret Service agent who goes by the code name McDougall."

"McDougall?"

"Yes!"

Rhome was just about to press the man harder, when Khalid stepped in. "What about the other three Iranians, what's their role?"

"I . . . I don't know!!" shrieked Rahmani. "The crown prince kept that a secret between him and Turki Shahidi!!"

Rhome cocked his arm, and Rahmani flailed. "PLEASE THAT'S ALL I KNOW!!"

Dumping the salt on the floor, Rhome raised his phone.

"You won't get service in here, Mr. Rhome," Khalid said.

Rhome swore and pointed at Rahmani. "If you haven't told us the identity of McDougall and the locations of the other three Iranians, and what they have planned, by the time I get back, you'll be begging me to bring back the cannons and the salt."

Turning on his heel, Rhome sprinted out of the facility, dialing Brenner's number as he went.

CHAPTER SIXTY-SEVEN

PRINCESS AMARA STOOD in the conference room and stared at the southeast hallway as the UN secretary-general, the Swiss president, and President Buchanan came back into the room.

Over the loudspeakers, the master of ceremonies alerted the world leaders that it was time to line up in the stage-right corridor for the main event.

Amara felt an unbelievable panic consume her, as she thought of what could be awaiting her and the president on that stage.

She was still surrounded by Mattar, her two minders, and her Secret Service detail, when Agent Tuck motioned to the corridor. "It's time, Princess."

Wali Mattar's words still ringing in her ears, about the Secret Service's complicity, Amara's eyes skirted from Tuck to the agents around her.

Any of them could be involved.

But what choice do I have?

Amara decided to take a gamble.

"A-Agent Tuck, I need to tell you something."

The big agent cocked her head at the nervousness in Amara's voice.

Leaning in, Amara whispered, "I can't go on that stage. The president can't—"

A strong hand suddenly gripped Amara's bicep.

"No need to get cold feet, Princess," Mattar said into her ear and led her toward the corridor.

"No, please! I can't—"

"Think of your children, Princess," Mattar said, out of earshot of everyone else. "Think of Ahmed and Mimi. Think of what the crown prince will do to them if you don't get on that stage."

Amara choked back a sob.

"I promise we won't touch a hair on their little heads if you cooperate."

Still gripping her arm tightly, Mattar escorted Amara into the corridor and let go of her when they stopped behind President Buchanan.

Turning, the president gave Amara a comforting grin.

The crowd outside cheered. Then the master of ceremonies announced the world leaders onto the stage.

———

Brenner clutched the secure phone that he'd spoken to Rhome on ten minutes before and followed Benedicht Imdorf and Dan Miller into the grand conference room.

Outside, the crowd pulsed as the world leaders took the stage.

In front of Brenner, a barricade of security personnel blocked the stage-left and stage-right hallways that led outside. In between the two hallways, among the security, were a collection of monitors showing a live feed of the event.

As Brenner, Miller, and Imdorf moved to the monitors, Brenner examined the screens and saw President Buchanan, Princess Amara, and the Swiss president take their seats along with the other world leaders, as the UN secretary-general stood before the podium.

Brenner glanced at his phone.

"What the hell is taking Rhome so long?" Miller said.

"I don't know," Brenner said, then asked Imdorf, "Sniper and countersniper teams all checking in?"

"Everyone accounted for," Imdorf replied, his hand on his earpiece.

On the screens, the UN secretary-general began his introductory speech.

Come on, Brian, Brenner thought. *Come on!*

As one minute turned to two, Brenner finally felt the phone vibrate.

Brenner answered, "Brian?!"

"Jack," Rhome's voice said, "there are two sniper teams. Three men in each. One team is on the roof of the Steigenberger Grand Hotel and is targeting Princess Amara. The other is on the roof of the Vaillant Arena. Their target is President Buchanan. Two shooters in each group, one spotter. One is on a fifty-caliber, the other on a .338. They're going to use two rounds from the fifty to punch through the glass, then the .338s for the kill shot. The shots are coordinated to take place as soon as Buchanan gets to the podium for her speech. The Iranian snipers will be overtaking the countersniper teams on the stadium and on the roof of the hotel thirty seconds before the shots are made!"

"And the other three Iranians? The bomb maker?" Brenner asked.

"Don't know yet."

"Who else is involved?!"

"A Secret Service agent who goes by the code name McDougall."

"Do you know McDougall's identity?"

"Negative," Rhome said. "Stay by your phone."

Brenner hung up and gave the information to Imdorf, who relayed it over his earpiece.

As Imdorf spoke into his comms, Miller asked Brenner, "And where are the other three Iranians?"

"We don't know."

CHAPTER SIXTY-EIGHT

"IT'S TIME," THE engineer said, glancing at his watch, an identical copy of which was given to all eight of his brothers before they'd left on their respective missions. The watches were synced to one another to the thousandth of a second.

If the engineer's math was correct, it would take the drone exactly one minute and thirty-nine seconds from the time it left the snow cave until it reached the GeoFence's perimeter.

Handing the pilot the tablet and the joystick he would use to fly the drone northwest toward Davos, the engineer said, "Don't be nervous. You have practiced with this exact drone all winter. You can operate it with your eyes closed. Plus, Allah flies with you tonight."

Having cleared the chunks of snow from the cave's entrance, and triple-checking that it was wide enough, the engineer powered on the drone and its eight rotors began to whirl.

The engineer checked his watch.

"Thirty seconds."

The pilot pulled back slightly on the joystick. The drone rose a foot into the air, a forty-pound spherical bomb of plastic explosives and ball bearings attached below.

"Ten seconds."

Cocking the joystick to the left, the drone slowly made its way out of the chamber and up the wide chute toward the opening.

"Five seconds."

It was hovering at the entrance, and the engineer watched the pilot's face as he stared at the tablet's screen with total concentration.

"Three, two, one!"

The pilot pushed the joystick hard to the left, and the drone blew out of the snow cave and into the night.

CHAPTER SIXTY-NINE

RHOME SPRINTED INTO the chamber and stopped short. "What's going on?!"

Saud Rahmani was on the ground, Khalid and his men kneeling over him.

"When we started questioning him again, he started seizing!" General Azimi said. "We can't wake him up!"

Rahmani's face was bone white, his lips purple.

"Should we try to warm him?" Khalid asked.

"No, fuck that," Rhome said, moving over to the table on the far side of the room. His hands danced over the drills, pliers, and scalpels before hovering over a plastic case. He opened the case, exposing a row of filled syringes. Reading the labels in Arabic, he found the one marked *Adrenaline*.

Grabbing it, he ran over to Rahmani's lifeless body and sank the needle into his heart and depressed the plunger.

Rahmani's body nearly left the ground, and he gasped for air.

Rhome grabbed the man by his scalp. "THE OTHER THREE IRANIANS, WHAT ARE THEY PLANNING?!"

Rahmani's eyes rolled backward. Rhome slapped him hard across the face and repeated his question.

Rahmani mumbled something.

"What?!" Rhome said.

"Bomb . . . drone."

"They're using a bomb on a drone?!"

"Y . . . Yes."

"And McDougall? Who the hell is McDougall and what is his role in the plan?!"

Rahmani's body started to tremble and his eyes fluttered shut.

Rhome stood. "Wake him back up, and find out who McDougall is!"

The phone was already at Rhome's ear as he dashed outside.

CHAPTER SEVENTY

IN THE SWISS FIS tent, Nora Ryder paced in front of the monitors showing the UN secretary-general giving his introductory speech onstage.

To Ryder's right, Huey, Jabril Khashiri, and the rest of Lodgepole stood among a group of Imdorf's most trusted FIS officers—everyone's eyes glued to the screens.

Then Ryder heard Imdorf's voice crackle over her earpiece.

Everyone else in the tent simultaneously touched their comms.

"Two Iranian sniper teams. One on the roof of the Steigenberger Grand Hotel, the second, on the roof of Vaillant Arena! They are impersonating our countersniper teams. The shots will take place as soon as President Buchanan takes the podium. All units converge on those locations!"

"Where are those buildings?!" Huey asked.

One of the FIS officers said, "The Steigenberger is on the other side of town. Vaillant Arena is one hundred meters to our south!"

Huey said, "Tell your officers near the Steigenberger to get on that rooftop; Ryder, Mansur, Bennett, on me. We'll take Vaillant."

Ryder made sure her pistol was secured in its holster as they ran out onto the crowded street toward the stadium's entrance. Three Swiss FIS officers were already waiting for them and escorted them into the lobby.

"The roof is seven stories up," one of the FIS officers said, pointing to a stairwell door.

Removing his pistol, Huey barged through the door and up the stairs. Ryder, hot on Huey's heels, could hear Bennett, Mansur, and the FIS officers behind her.

Cresting the sixth landing, Ryder heard Imdorf's voice over her comms, "The UN secretary-general has just finished his speech, President Buchanan is about to take the podium!"

Then an urgent voice with a Swiss accent cut over the comms, "Iranian sniper team on the Steigenberger has been eliminated!"

Stepping onto the seventh-floor landing, Ryder came up behind Huey as he tried to open the metal door to the roof.

"It's locked!" he yelled, then threw his weight into it.

It wouldn't budge.

"Imdorf!" Huey said, through his comms. "Can any of the countersniper teams get eyes on the Vaillant's roof? Any of the security choppers?"

"Negative on the countersniper teams. Security chopper is twenty seconds out!"

"Fuck this," Huey said.

Pointing his pistol at the lock, he shot off three rounds.

The lock popping out, Huey launched his shoulder into the door and staggered onto the rooftop.

Gun raised, Ryder hit the roof second, and immediately heard the sound of suppressed small arms fire as Huey was jerked violently backward. Ryder caught a glimpse of a man wearing a black ski mask kneeling on the roof over the bodies of the dead countersniper team.

The kneeling man's pistol swung from Huey to Ryder.

As Huey continued to fall, Ryder aimed over the Ground Branch operator's right shoulder and squeezed off three rounds into the kneeling man's chest.

Jumping over Huey, she was just about to skirt an air-conditioning unit, when three concussive blasts boomed over the rooftop.

———

Sitting onstage between Buchanan and the Swiss president, Princess Amara looked through the wall of security glass at the crowd before her as the UN secretary-general finished his speech and introduced the American president to the world.

Her breathing clipped and staggered, Amara saw Buchanan get to her feet and move toward the podium, as the crowd went wild.

Shaking uncontrollably, Amara clenched the fabric of her *abaya* and realized the Swiss president was asking her if she was okay.

Ignoring the man, Amara eyed the Secret Service agents standing offstage to her right.

I need to do something! Amara thought.

I can't just sit here, I need to—

"Ladies and gentlemen, citizens of the world!" Buchanan's voice echoed over the crowd to ecstatic applause.

Amara whipped her head around, her gaze planted on Buchanan, who had both her palms raised in the air.

As Amara took in the scene, she saw something that made her blood run cold.

The bulletproof glass directly in front of Buchanan spider-webbed and cracked.

Before she knew what she was doing, Amara jumped to her feet and dove for the president as the glass shattered backward and something scarlet flared from Buchanan's right shoulder, spinning her like a top.

———

Vaillant Arena Roof

Pistol out in front of her, Nora Ryder circumvented the air-conditioning unit, before stopping dead in her tracks.

Two prone figures wearing black ski masks lay behind two high-powered rifles, their barrels smoking.

Below, screams erupted from the crowd.

Suddenly, both men turned and, spotting Ryder, reached for their pistols on their beltlines.

Her body reacting for her, Ryder took aim and mashed down on her trigger.

CHAPTER SEVENTY-ONE

ON THE SECURITY monitors, Jack Brenner saw the glass wall in front of President Buchanan burst backward, glass showering her face. Then, almost simultaneously, something collided with the president's right shoulder, swinging her sideways.

As Buchanan fell, Princess Amara caught her midair, then tumbled to the ground.

Chaos broke out in the room around Brenner.

On the monitors, he watched Special Agent Edwards grab the president and rush her offstage.

Seconds later, a wave of security agents blew out of the stage-right and stage-left exits, hauling their country's leaders away from the threat outside.

In the confusion, Brenner saw the Secret Service CAT agents, and the PPD, led by Agent Hewitt, blow into the room and sprint to the grand hallway. In the middle of the group, Edwards held the limp, bloodied form of President Buchanan in his arms.

Twenty yards behind the scrum of agents was Agent Tuck, cradling Princess Amara.

Something in the deepest recesses of Brenner's brain told him to follow the wounded president.

Forcing his way through the mob of people and into the hallway, Brenner could hear Miller shouting after him.

Now, halfway down the grand hallway, he could see the top of Hewitt's and Edwards's heads, as they and the other Secret Service agents knocked people aside and ran down the staircase toward the closest of the two presidential limos.

At this point, Agent Tuck, who was still holding Amara, was a good five feet in front of Brenner, and forty yards from the staircase.

As the cluster of agents ran with the president down the stairs, Hewitt frantically opened the door to the armored limo.

It was then that the whole world dissolved into slow motion, and Brenner became aware of two things occurring simultaneously.

The first was the movement of Agent Tuck, who had stopped running in front of him, and dropped Princess Amara to the ground, before diving for cover herself.

This would have alarmed Brenner had it not been for the blur of movement coming in from the sky at the east entrance.

In horror, he saw a drone carrying a spherical device the size of a beachball zoom over the top of the limo and hover two feet over Hewitt's and Edwards's heads as they tried to get the president into the vehicle.

His body registering the threat before his brain, Brenner threw himself to the ground as the loudest noise he'd ever experienced ripped through the crowded marble hallway.

CHAPTER SEVENTY-TWO

CUSTER HAD BEEN waiting for this moment for a year and a half, but never in his wildest dreams did he think it would play out as miraculously as it was playing out right now on the big screen.

Having seen the bulletproof glass shatter into President Buchanan's face, and the flash of red spew from her right shoulder, Custer had jumped from his seat in the White House's Family Theater and then looked at the dumbfounded expression of his most important lieutenant sitting next to him.

Following his handler's orders, Custer made sure the day before that he and Reno would not only be alone in the same room together while they watched the accord ceremony, but that they would watch from the White House, considering the steps the Secret Service would surely take once they heard what had occurred in Davos.

His attention darting from the terror on Reno's face to the pandemonium unfurling on the screen, Custer watched as Buchanan and Princess Amara were scooped up by Special Agent Edwards and Agent Tuck and taken off the stage.

Reno rounded on Custer. "What have you done!"

Custer locked eyes with his lieutenant. "I have done what I promised I'd do a year and a half ago. Now, listen to me. At any moment, the Secret Service are going to come in here and rush you down to the bunker, and then they are going to collect your National Security

Council and bring them down with you." Custer grabbed the man's arm to emphasize his point. "Once you are secured and safely down there, you are going to instruct the Secret Service to bring *me* down as well. Is that clear?"

Reno's face went pale.

Custer shook the man's arm. "Is that clear, sir? Or do I have to remind you again of the tapes I have recorded of your involvement?"

Reno's body shook, and he stammered, "I-I-It's clear!"

"Good," Custer said, pointing back to the screen. "Now, watch."

The news broadcast had pulled back from the stage, and now showed an aerial helicopter view of the Congress Centre as an off-screen anchor tried to rationalize what had just happened.

Then Custer saw it.

A spec darted fast out of the sky and headed toward the Centre's east entrance.

For a moment, nothing happened, then the entrance exploded in a brilliant flash of light.

"OH MY GOD!!" Reno yelled.

A wave of triumph overcame Custer. "I fulfilled my promise to you, sir. I got rid of Buchanan and destroyed her accord. It's now time for you to fulfill your promise to me."

"You didn't say you would kill her!"

The double doors to the Family Theater blew open, and a swarm of Secret Service agents came into the dark room, their weapons drawn.

"Mr. Vice President!" the lead agent said to Reno. "We're taking you to a secure location."

Vice President Michael Dunn continued to stare at Custer in disbelief, as the Secret Service agents pushed Custer aside, swarmed their principal, and lifted him into the air.

"Remember your promise to me, Mr. Vice President!" Custer yelled, as Dunn was being whisked from the room. "Remember your promise!"

As the doors snapped shut behind them, Custer's attention went back to the destruction on the screen.

President Buchanan was surely dead.

The Global Green Accord was destroyed.

Now, it was time to initiate the final step of Dark Sun and Operation Little Bighorn.

Reaching down, Custer grabbed the tumbler of bourbon sitting next to his seat.

Lifting the glass into the air, he toasted his good fortune, and what was to come.

CHAPTER SEVENTY-THREE

JACK BRENNER ROLLED onto his back and tried to blink, but his eyes were so filled with soot, and his ears rang so loudly, he couldn't hear his own groans.

He winced as he rubbed his eyes.

Opening them, he gazed up through blackened smoke.

The ringing in his ears dampened, and then as if someone turned the volume back on, he heard screams coming from all around.

Propping himself up on an elbow, he blinked, and like a crashing wave, the memory of what had just occurred roared back.

Panning his head, he saw the hundreds of figures sprawled in the smoky hallway. Most of them lay still, their bodies contorted and disfigured, but others wailed and thrashed in pain.

Someone let out a groan directly in front of him, and he saw Agent Tuck, getting a disheveled Princess Amara to her feet.

"Are you two okay?" Brenner asked, as he slowly stood up.

Tuck, and the princess, their eyes bloodshot and their pupils dilated, both nodded.

Brenner then examined the devastation and yelled, "Danny? Benedicht?"

"Jack!"

Turning, Brenner observed Miller's broad frame standing twenty yards behind him, helping up Benedicht Imdorf.

Both men seemed shell-shocked, but fine.

As screams continued to permeate throughout the hall, Brenner realized that Tuck was helping Princess Amara through the injured and the dead toward the stairway and the closest presidential limo.

A feeling of absolute dread came over Brenner.

The president!

Brenner hurried forward, stopped at the top of the stairway, and took in the blackened crater at its base, and the presidential limo, which looked like a charred version of itself.

It was then that he realized the scope of the destruction.

Not only were the Secret Service CAT agents and the PPD vaporized, but every unarmored vehicle in a forty-yard radius was completely destroyed, the president's motorcade, and everyone who had been around it, cut down by the blast.

Brenner thought of the hundreds of journalists and security personnel who had stood at the base of the stairs.

Hearing sirens blaring in the distance, Brenner noticed that the secondary presidential limo still sat across the street, looking virtually untouched.

As he walked down the staircase, he joined Agent Tuck and Princess Amara, both of whom stood over the blast site, staring in shock at the scorched limo in front of them.

As Brenner came up next to Tuck, something caught his attention in the rubble at his feet—a flash of green within the gray, black, and red.

Kneeling down, he pushed aside the chunks of debris and picked up a green rock.

He knew this rock.

It was the Maori carving, speckled with dark mica, that always hung from a fine gold necklace around President Buchanan's neck.

Both Tuck and Amara saw the pendant in Brenner's hand, and he heard the princess whimper, "I . . . I tried to stop it. I—"

But Amara never finished her sentence, because the door to the back of the presidential limo jostled slightly, and then opened.

Special Agent Edwards stumbled out of the vehicle and landed in a heap on the ground, blood oozing from a gash on his head.

"Help," Edwards croaked as he pointed back to the open door. "She's still alive. The president is still alive!"

Before Brenner, Tuck, or Amara could move, Dan Miller brushed by them and ducked into the limo, materializing five seconds later with an unconscious and bloodied President Buchanan in his arms.

"She needs a hospital, now!" Miller said. And the urgency in his voice seemed to knock everyone out of their stupors. "Benedicht! Where is the hospital?!"

Imdorf came to a stop before the limo. "It's in town, near the tram—"

"No!" Brenner said. "She *can't* stay in Davos."

"Why not?" Miller asked.

"We don't know if another attack is coming," Brenner said, helping Edwards to his feet. "The Secret Service is compromised; we need to close the bubble around the president and go dark."

Tuck, who was still standing next to Brenner, shot him an expression of bewilderment.

"What do you want to do?" Imdorf asked.

Brenner pointed to the secondary presidential limo parked on the other side of the street. "We'll take the backup limo and haul ass north. Benedicht, wrangle as many doctors as you can and have them meet Lodgepole at the helicopters in the Eistraum stadium. I'll alert Cho and Adams to have the pilots rendezvous with us at the five-kilometer marker up Route 28."

Brenner, acutely aware of the president's condition and their need for secrecy and haste, said to Tuck and Amara, "You two can come with us. Danny, you're driving."

CHAPTER SEVENTY-FOUR

BRIAN RHOME PACED in front of the Saudi black site, the phone held out in front of him.

"Come on, Jack!"

He'd been trying to get ahold of his godfather for the past couple of minutes, but the call wouldn't go through.

Checking the clock on the phone, he realized President Buchanan and the rest of the world leaders had taken the stage over thirteen minutes ago.

It was all Rhome could do to not assume the worst.

Continuing to frantically pace, Rhome swore and tried to get the phone to connect, when he heard the door to the building squeal open behind him.

Khalid stepped out into the night.

"What happened?" Khalid asked.

"I don't know," Rhome said. "My calls aren't going through."

"Rahmani just gave us a name."

Rhome stopped pacing. "McDougall's?"

"Yes."

"Who is it?!"

When Khalid told him the person's name and rank in the Secret Service, Rhome couldn't believe it.

He'd never heard of the individual before, but he knew of the rank.

"You've got to be fucking kidding me."

The sound of ringing suddenly came over the phone's speaker.

The call connected.

A second later, he heard his godfather's voice.

CHAPTER SEVENTY-FIVE

One Mile North of Davos
March 9, 7:44 p.m.

SITTING IN THE back of the secondary limo next to Princess Amara, Jack Brenner felt helpless as he watched Special Agent Mark Edwards and Agent Tuck trying to stanch the bleeding coming out of the unconscious President Buchanan's right shoulder.

The limo, driven by Dan Miller, hauled ass up Route 28 toward Thal.

It had been a madhouse getting out of Davos, but Miller had taken advantage of the limo's weight and armored capabilities and had torn through every security checkpoint and roadblock until they'd gotten on the highway.

Given the speed with which Miller was driving, Brenner determined it would be less than four minutes until they'd come to a stop at the five-kilometer marker.

Having gotten off the phone with Cho a minute before, she'd alerted Brenner that they just secured three doctors on the helicopters and were heading their way now.

She'd also alerted him that a team of surgeons were being collected in Thal and an operating room was being prepared for President Buchanan.

Brenner, his attention still focused on Tuck and Edwards, saw the Secret Service special agent in charge take off his jacket and throw it on the seat next to him before he stripped his leather harness holding his service weapon to get at his white-collared shirt.

His holstered weapon landing on the seat next to Amara, Edwards then ripped off his shirt and used it as a compress to stop the flow of blood coming out of Buchanan's shoulder.

C'mon, Danny! Drive! Brenner thought, just as he felt his phone vibrate in his hand.

Seeing the number, Brenner answered, "Brian!"

"Jack!" Rhome's voice said. "The other three Iranians are using a bomb on a drone—"

"I know," Brenner said. "It went off, Brian. Buchanan was shot. Then the bomb went off, we're getting her out of Davos now to get medical attention, but it's not looking good."

Silence descended over the line for a long beat, then Rhome, his voice grated, said, "I've got a name, Jack. I've got McDougall's identity."

When Rhome said the name a second later, Brenner froze, and looked up at the two Secret Service agents still huddled over the president.

"You're positive about this, Brian?"

"One hundred percent."

The fear and confusion that had consumed Brenner since the bomb exploded was immediately replaced by something more primal and resolute.

Dropping his voice, Brenner said, "You still have Saud Rahmani?"

"We do."

"Good. Now, get the names," Brenner whispered. "Get the names of Custer, and everyone else involved in the United States. Then get the password from Rahmani to decrypt the Dark Sun file."

"Done."

"Once you do that, find the crown prince's current location. I need you to do something for me."

For the next thirty seconds, Brenner spoke and when he finished, he said, "Do you think that's possible?"

"Shouldn't be a problem."

"Good, I'll send McCallister your way with everything you'll need. Now, go deal with Rahmani."

"Copy that," Rhome said and cut the call.

Brenner lowered the phone and stared at Tuck and Edwards, who continued to work on Buchanan. Then slowly, Brenner reached for the pistol at his beltline that Imdorf had given him back at the FIS tent.

Amara noted the movement as Brenner pulled out the weapon and pointed it in Edwards's and Tuck's direction.

"McDougall!" Brenner shouted.

Both Edwards and Tuck froze.

"Turn around slowly, with your hands up!" Brenner said.

His reflexes still dulled from the bomb blast, Brenner didn't have time to react when he saw Tuck throw Edwards to the limo floor, pull her service weapon, and point it directly at President Buchanan's chest.

"You shoot me, I shoot her," Tuck said, her voice loud.

"Drop your weapon, Eunice!" Brenner said, his pistol aimed at the back of Tuck's neck.

"Not a fucking chance, Jack," Tuck said, her gun still planted on Buchanan's lifeless form.

"What the hell are you doing, Agent Tuck!" Edwards yelled, lying on his back on the limo's floorboard.

"Shut up, Mark!" Tuck said, then in one fluid motion, she grabbed Buchanan around the waist with her massive arm, spun, and then lifted the unconscious president onto her lap, before pointing the pistol back at Brenner.

Tuck had made the movement so quick and efficient, Brenner had zero time to deliver a clean kill.

Now, with Buchanan's lifeless form draped over Tuck, Brenner had no shot.

Never lowering his weapon, Brenner said, "It's over, Eunice. We have the names of Custer and everyone involved. We know all about Dark Sun. In seconds, Danny will be meeting those helicopters up the road, and you will come face-to-face with a highly trained CIA task force who will not hesitate to put you down."

"That's not going to happen, Jack."

"And how do you figure that?" Brenner asked.

"Because I am going to kill everyone in this limo."

"And how are you going to explain everyone dying of a gunshot wound when the ballistics are traced to your gun?"

"I'll say it was you," Tuck said. "I'll say that you are McDougall. I'll say you took my service weapon—shot everyone in cold blood. I was able to wrestle the gun from you—"

"You don't get it, do you, Eunice?" Brenner said, trying to keep his voice under control. "My task force *knows* you are McDougall. The jig is up. We have all the evidence. Whether we live or die, or whatever lies you try to spout, they know who you are. It's over."

Brenner saw Tuck's pistol quiver in her hand.

"Why did you do it, Eunice?" Brenner said, trying to buy some time.

A snarl formed on Tuck's lips. "Because she was destroying our country, and Custer was in a position to stop her. *I* was in a position to stop her."

"So you conspired to kill the very person you pledged to protect?" Brenner said. "You are a disgrace to your oath, Eunice."

"I was doing my patriotic duty, Jack," Tuck said.

"Well, you failed."

As the words escaped Brenner's lips, he saw the barrel of Tuck's gun go from him to President Buchanan's head. Realizing that he had inadvertently backed the agent into a corner with no way out, he heard Tuck say, "The snipers were supposed to kill Buchanan and Princess Amara, and if that didn't do the trick, the drone was supposed to take care of the rest. If that failed, then I was the final backstop. I was always willing to die for this cause, Jack."

In a panic, Brenner watched as Tuck applied pressure to the trigger and then a second later, he heard the earth-shattering report of a gunshot rip through the back of the limo.

CHAPTER SEVENTY-SIX

BRENNER JUMPED IN his seat as the gunshot went off.

Miller, who had unmistakably heard the discharge, slammed on the brakes, causing everyone to fall forward.

A large splatter of blood caked the limo's back window, where Tuck's head had once been.

Instantly, Mark Edwards jumped up and grabbed President Buchanan.

The limo now having come to a complete stop, Brenner saw Princess Amara holding Edwards's service pistol in her shaking hands.

"Princess," Brenner said, extending a palm, "give me the gun."

Amara, whose finger was still on the trigger, continued to aim the weapon at Tuck's lifeless body.

"Princess, please," Brenner said, calmly.

Brenner moved slowly toward her and gingerly took the weapon from her grasp as the limo's back door was wrenched open.

A pistol, held by a beefy hand, extended inside.

"What the fuck is going on in here?!" Miller shouted.

"It's okay, Danny!" Brenner yelled. "Everything is fine, we need to get to those choppers!"

"We're here," Miller said. "Choppers are thirty seconds out!"

Miller finally poked his head into the limo and recoiled when he saw the state of Tuck's body.

"She was McDougall, Danny," Brenner said. "Now, help us get Buchanan outside."

Brenner, Miller, Edwards, and Amara all helped carry the president onto the road, just as the two helicopters touched down in front of them.

Cho, Adams, and Huey got out of one of the choppers.

Huey held his left arm with his right, and Brenner saw that his tan shirt was covered in blood.

Ryder and a team of doctors came out of the other chopper, and together, everyone helped secure Buchanan to a backboard, as the doctors ran an IV line into her arm and put an oxygen mask over her face.

"Trauma team is waiting in Thal," Cho shouted to Brenner over the rotor wash.

In front of them, the doctors lifted the backboard and hurried to the first chopper. As Edwards followed, Brenner reached out and grabbed the special agent in charge by the arm. "Mark, you need to keep the bubble around the president closed."

"How's that possible, Jack?" Edwards said. "The Secret Service is going to want to know her condition and whereabouts."

"We still don't have the identities of everyone involved, Mark," Brenner said. "But we will soon. Tell the Secret Service of her condition, but don't give them her location. Not yet."

Edwards nodded, then ran to the first chopper.

As the bird lifted and took off toward Thal, Brenner and the rest of Lodgepole climbed on the second chopper. And when they got inside, Brenner leaned over and spoke into Cho's ear, "Elaine, I need you to get me a secure line to Elizabeth Hastings, immediately."

CHAPTER SEVENTY-SEVEN

SITTING IN THE White House's Family Theater, Custer continued to stare at the news playing out on the big screen.

Even twenty minutes after the bomb went off, there were no new updates on President Buchanan or what was occurring on the ground in Davos.

Knowing the bomb would never have detonated if the facial recognition technology didn't locate its target within five feet of the drone, Custer was confident that Buchanan had not survived, and if she had, he knew that his lieutenant, McDougall, would do everything in her power to make sure the job got done.

Taking his last sip of bourbon, he saw the door to the Family Theater crack open and a Secret Service agent step inside. "Sir, the vice president is requesting your presence in the basement."

Custer eased himself to his feet and told the agent to lead the way.

Stepping into the East Wing, Custer followed the agent as he took him down a dead-end hallway where a collection of Secret Service agents waited before a bookcase.

The agent leading Custer moved past his fellow agents and slid the bookcase aside, exposing an elevator door.

Custer, being a self-proclaimed student of American history, knew all about the underground bunker that sat five stories below the White House. Having been constructed by FDR during WWII, the PEOC, or the Presidential Emergency Operations Center, was considered to be the most secure facility in the world. Built to protect the president from an array of doomsday scenarios, the PEOC, or the *Basement* as it was known to the Secret Service, held two years' worth of food and supplies, as well as bunk rooms and a conference center that was an exact replica and had the same capabilities as the conference center in the Situation Room.

Never having been down to the PEOC before, Custer tried to mask his excitement when the Secret Service agent led him into the elevator, shut the door, and then hit the button that sent them fifty feet into the earth.

As the elevator descended, Custer envisioned what he was about to do next.

If all went well, he would be back aboveground in less than fifteen minutes, and in less than twenty, he would notify his handler and tell her that the final facet of Dark Sun and Operation Little Bighorn had succeeded.

Custer felt the elevator stop, and the doors opened, exposing a dimly lit concrete hallway.

Following the agent down the tunnel, Custer saw a collection of people congregated in front of a circular blast door ahead.

"This is the last of them," the agent said to another Secret Service agent standing before the door.

Eyeing the people around him, Custer took in the members of the National Security Council. He saw his lieutenants, Varnum and Benteen. Both men, like everyone else standing before the blast door, seemed to be in shock.

The Secret Service agent put his face to the iris scanner before typing in a code on the door and then pulling it outward.

After everyone was led inside a small anteroom, the Secret Service agent escorted them into a conference center.

Sitting at the end of the long table in the room, Vice President Dunn looked like hell.

The television monitors in the room depicted the havoc continuing to play out in Davos.

When the doors shut, and everyone took their seats, Custer took the chair at the other end of the table, opposite Dunn, and made eye contact with the vice president.

The expression on Dunn's face was something between disgust and trepidation.

After a moment, Dunn ripped his attention off Custer and said, "We've received word through the Secret Service that President Buchanan is in critical condition and her prognosis seems grim. She's being taken to an undisclosed location as we speak. As of this moment, I am officially the acting president of the United States."

The silence that descended over the room became deafening.

After what seemed like minutes, Dunn finally said, "What information have we heard coming out of Davos?"

The chairman of the Joint Chiefs of Staff, General Edward Toole, cleared his throat and opened a file in front of him. "Mr. Vice President, UN Security has secured the bodies of six individuals they believe carried out the sniper attacks. All of them have been positively identified as Iranian Quds Force members."

"Iranians?" Dunn said, taken aback.

"Yes, sir," Toole said. "Hours ago, the Swiss Federal Intelligence Service put out an APB on nine suspected Quds members who they believed entered Europe last October."

"What is the Iranian government saying?" Dunn asked.

"Nothing yet, sir."

"You said there were nine Iranians, six are dead. Where are the other three? Were they the ones flying that drone?"

"We aren't entirely sure," Secretary of State Newman replied. "Their whereabouts are currently unknown."

"Sir," Toole said. "My office has drawn up a series of responses. I suggest we send in the Eighty-Second Airborne Division into the Persian Gulf, as well as look into targeting the nuclear facilities that the Iranians—"

"Mr. Vice President, if I may?" Custer interrupted.

Toole and the rest of the room stared at Custer. Then Dunn snapped, "Yes, what is it?"

"I feel like I need to say something, sir."

General Toole and a few other members of the NSC leaned back in their seats and crossed their arms in annoyance.

Custer noticed their irritation and said, "I know I'm not a national security expert, nor do I wish to overstep my bounds, but I feel like I need to get something off my chest before you all begin."

Custer leaned forward. "Mr. Vice President, the actions you take now and in the coming days will not only define your vice presidency, but if President Buchanan dies, your presidency. Now, I do not wish to speak ill of our critically injured president, but I believe what just occurred in Davos is a direct result of the weakness and inaction President Buchanan displayed recently with the Iranians. She did *nothing* for nearly nine days after the reactors melted down. And though she did finally carry out her response against General Soleimani this morning, I believe the damage was already done, sir. The Iranians took advantage of our passivity and they struck. They critically injured our president. And if your intelligence is sound, they will have ended up killing her. They *killed* our commander in chief, sir. That action alone is the most *deliberate* act of war that has *ever* happened to our great nation."

"What are you saying?" Dunn asked.

"I am saying, sir, that the world, our enemies and our allies included, are going to be looking at you, and *your* actions. You need to set a new precedent, sir. You need to show the world that if you fuck with America, America will fuck you back ten times harder."

The room again went quiet.

"What are you proposing?" SecDef Lake asked.

"I'm proposing an eye for an eye. They probably killed our leader. Now, I propose we kill theirs. I say we strike their president, their ayatollah and their supreme leader."

Noting the alarm on Dunn's face, Custer stared straight into his eyes. Dunn knew that Custer held the recordings of his role in Operation Little Bighorn. Recordings of the vice president fervently agreeing to do *anything* to stop President Buchanan and her Global Green Accord. Recordings of Michael Dunn agreeing to obtain the travel routes of the graphite rods that would go into the thorium molten salt reactors.

Noting the vice president's fear, and understanding the power Custer held over him, Custer said, "I'm not dull enough to think that such a decision could be carried out so hastily, Mr. Vice President. It took Bush and Cheney days of sitting in this very room before they drew up plans

of retaliation after the towers fell. All I am saying is to *consider* my proposal, and remember where your loyalties lie."

Standing, Custer said, "Now, if you excuse me, I should go to the
Hill and be with my colleagues. God knows the weeks we have ahead
of us."

Opening the conference room door, Custer gripped the handle and
shot one last glance at Dunn, and then with a satisfied expression on
his face, he stepped out into the anteroom and asked the Secret Service
agents to escort him back upstairs.

Custer's role in Dark Sun and Operation Little Bighorn was complete.

President Buchanan was surely going to die.

Her accord was destroyed.

And now, after strong-arming the vice president of the United States
to kill the leaders of Iran, the world would teeter on the precipice of war.

The industries that Buchanan had worked so hard to destroy would
now come soaring back.

What had the crown prince, Raza bin Zaman, said a year and a half
ago, when he'd first pitched his plan to Custer?

You can't run a war without oil.

CHAPTER SEVENTY-EIGHT

"HURRY!" THE ENGINEER said, as his two brothers struggled to ski toward the road below. "We're almost there!"

They'd left the snow cave almost three hours after the bomb had detonated and put on their boots and skis. Using their night-vision goggles, they climbed over the mountain ridge and began their descent to the road a few kilometers below.

The engineer had received a phone message minutes after the explosion that gave him a set of coordinates and the description of the vehicle that would extract them.

Having grown up in the Alborz Mountains in northern Iran, the engineer was an expert skier, but his brothers were floundering. He had to wait for them numerous times, their descent getting slower and slower as they got down to the tree line. Even the engineer had to admit that it was difficult to ski during the night through such dense trees, even with the assistance of the NODs.

As he waited, he pulled out his GPS and realized that the vehicle that would be picking them up was only a few hundred meters away.

A minute later the bomb maker and the pilot came to a stop right behind him.

"We are nearly home free," the engineer said. "Soon we will be back with our families. We will be welcomed as heroes."

He could still hear the sirens and the helicopters in the valley over the ridge, but now with over eight kilometers between them and Davos, he knew it was unlikely that anyone would be searching the alpine wilderness so far away from town.

He pointed through the trees. "The car will be waiting for us there."

Five minutes later, they came to a stop on the edge of a trailhead parking lot.

In the shadows, the three Iranians took off their skis and examined the single black van that sat in the lot.

"Stay here," the engineer said.

Making sure he had easy access to his pistol, the engineer stepped awkwardly in his ski boots toward the van.

When he was ten feet away, the driver's door opened, and the light inside turned on, exposing a man with sharp features and a closely cropped black beard.

As the man stepped out of the van, the engineer gripped his pistol tightly within his jacket pocket.

"Brother?" the man said in Farsi. "Is that you?"

Though he did not recognize the man's face, he recalled the shape of his body, and the intonation of his voice.

Relaxing the grip on his pistol, the engineer said, "Colonel Ghorbani?"

"Yes, brother."

Waving over the bomb maker and the pilot, the engineer embraced his beloved colonel.

Letting go, he stared at Mahmoud Ghorbani through the night-vision goggles. "What have you done to your face, Colonel?"

"My part of the mission required it," Ghorbani said, gazing at the bomb maker and the pilot who came up beside the engineer. "You three have done spectacularly well. You've done exactly what Allah asked of you."

A sense of pride coursed through the engineer.

"Are you three ready to go home?"

"Yes, Colonel," the engineer said, and just as he was about to express his gratitude to his former leader, he cried out instead as Ghorbani pulled a suppressed pistol from his jacket with lightning speed.

Two bright plumes of light discharged from Ghorbani's weapon, and he heard the familiar *thwack* of a bullet hitting human flesh.

He watched his two brothers fall to the snow, and he then turned to see the pistol aiming directly at his head before the muzzle flashed a third and final time.

CHAPTER SEVENTY-NINE

WILLIAM MCCALLISTER SAT in the fuselage of the UH-60 Black Hawk, his eyes peering through the dim green interior light at the six bearded men wearing black BDUs.

On each man's lap sat an HK 416D assault rifle.

The men wore no insignias on their clothing or dog tags around their necks.

In the eyes of the American government these men did not exist, nor did their elite unit.

They were members of the CIA's Ground Branch, more specifically, Omega Team.

"Two minutes out, gents," the pilot said over McCallister's headset.

Pulling a black duffel bag onto his lap, McCallister looked over at the sixty-five-year-old paramilitary operations officer sitting across from him. "What the hell are you smiling at, Walt?"

Pulling a tin of Copenhagen Long Cut from his pocket, the man placed a mound of it in his bottom lip and continued to grin at McCallister.

"Sitting behind a desk these last fifteen years made you fat, Willy."

"Shut up, Walt," McCallister said, patting his round stomach, returning the smile.

Not only was the man sitting across from McCallister the longest-serving operator in the CIA's Ground Branch, but he was also the

longest-serving active combat soldier who'd ever served for the United States of America.

"You miss it?" Walt asked, tauntingly.

"Every fucking day."

Taking a small notepad and pencil from his chest rig, Walt made a show of writing down McCallister's name and putting a check next to it.

"You're still fucking doing that?"

"That's two checks for the swear jar," Walt replied, with a wink. "And of course I am. It freaks out the new guys."

Chuckling, McCallister regarded the dark sand flying by below and then his expression turned grim, as he remembered why he was on this chopper, and what had happened in the last five hours.

Like mostly everyone else in the world, McCallister had watched in distress from his office in Riyadh as the United States president had been shot, and then later blown up.

Roughly an hour after the attack, he'd received a call from Jack Brenner.

In the thirty-five years he'd known the man, he'd never heard Brenner that upset.

The former director of the Special Activities Center told him what had happened in Davos, and how Lodgepole had been unable to stop the attack.

He told McCallister that Rhome had been saved by Prince Khalid and his men. McCallister was grateful that General Azimi was able to convince Turki Shahidi and Saud Rahmani to take Rhome to Ath Thumamah, where an ambush had been set and Rhome rescued.

McCallister was then surprised to learn that Turki Shahidi had been killed in the ambush, and that Saud Rahmani had been taken alive and interrogated. But Rhome had been unable to extract the information from the Saudi in time to stop the attack.

After that, Brenner had ordered McCallister to get a Ground Branch team into Saudi Arabia. Brenner had a plan for McCallister, a plan that included meeting Rhome in Ath Thumamah.

As the helicopter dipped toward a sparsely lit structure in the middle of the desert, McCallister could make out a series of military jeeps and two helicopters sitting out front.

When the Black Hawk landed, McCallister and the rest of Omega Team climbed out and hurried over to the concrete building.

As they approached, McCallister noticed a man sitting against the wall, smoking a cigarette.

The man's left hand had dried blood on it that extended up to his forearm, where it met a giant black snarling wolf tattoo.

"Brian?"

Rhome flicked his cigarette and stood. "What took you guys so long?"

"Had to fly them in from Djibouti," McCallister said, looking worriedly at the blood on Rhome's arm.

Rhome caught him looking. "It's not mine."

"That's what I was afraid of."

Rhome pulled a piece of paper from his pocket and handed it to McCallister.

"That's the password for the encrypted Dark Sun file," Rhome said. "And the names of everyone involved."

Placing the black duffel at his feet, McCallister opened the folded piece of paper and stared at the twenty-character passcode, and then read the five names in disbelief.

"Jesus Christ," he said.

"Get those to Jack as soon as possible; I haven't been able to reach him in the last few hours," Rhome said. Then he picked up the duffel McCallister had brought for him, unzipped it, and looked inside. Satisfied, Rhome said, "Do you have the location of the boat?"

McCallister handed Rhome a piece of paper. "It's anchored in the Red Sea at these coordinates. The helicopter with the party favors is leaving Jeddah in a few hours."

Rhome studied the coordinates, then stuffed the paper into his pocket.

"Lobo," Walt said, coming up beside McCallister. "You look terrible, man."

"Fuck you, Walt," Rhome said and cracked a grin when the old paramilitary operations officer took out his pencil and notepad.

After greeting the five other operators, Rhome walked inside to change.

Still holding the paper in his hand, McCallister wished the Ground Branch team luck and then stepped away to try and get ahold of Jack Brenner.

CHAPTER EIGHTY

STANDING ON THE bow of the *Serene*, the crown prince, Raza bin Zaman, scanned the calm, blue waters of the Red Sea and felt a sense of completion and accomplishment overcome him.

After a year and a half of planning, of patience, and careful orchestration, it's finally done, he thought; then he glanced at the Orion phone in his hand and felt a tinge of annoyance break up his good mood.

It had been nearly twelve hours since he'd heard anything from his two right-hand men, Turki Shahidi and Saud Rahmani.

Before Raza administered the final dose of *medicine* to his father yesterday, Tara Devino had taken his Orion phone from him so he could focus on his task. After leaving his father's room, he had spent the rest of the day with Devino relaxing and indulging in matters of the flesh.

In between their bouts of lovemaking, Devino let Raza call President Buchanan to alert her of his father's death and that he wouldn't be attending the accord ceremony.

Other than that call, Devino hadn't let Raza use his phone until this morning when they had woken up after spending the night in bed together and watched the destruction play out in Davos.

Having finally regained possession of his Orion phone a few hours ago, he had been concerned to see that he only had two missed calls from Turki Shahidi from the night before.

In the first call, Shahidi had left him a voice mail telling him that the

Rapid Intervention Group had arrived back in Riyadh, and that Shahidi would be meeting Rahmani at the Ritz-Carlton to interrogate Brian Rhome, while Mahmoud Ghorbani flew straight to Davos.

The second call had been an hour later, but Shahidi left no voice mail.

Those calls had occurred half a day ago, and Raza still couldn't get in touch with either Shahidi or Rahmani.

This, of course, was most unusual.

Never before had his two men been out of contact for so long.

So what the hell was going on?

Raza wanted to know what they discovered at the Ritz during Brian Rhome's interrogation. He wanted to know why the American had shot a corpse in Montreal.

It doesn't matter anymore, Raza thought to himself. *Dark Sun succeeded. President Buchanan will surely die, if she isn't dead already. The accord is destroyed.*

Hours before, Tara Devino had received word from Custer that he had succeeded in threatening the vice president of the United States to assassinate the leaders of Iran. Soon, Raza would watch from the sidelines as America destroyed Saudi Arabia's greatest enemy.

The enemy that killed my brother.

Once Iran's leaders were dead, a war would most certainly be launched. A war that would need oil to power its ships, tanks, and planes.

Raza thought back to the day he created Dark Sun. The day he recruited Custer in Riyadh during that bipartisan delegation.

Custer had been on board right away. He'd seen the genius in Raza's plan—and had even added some genius of his own.

It had been Custer's idea to bring other powerful Americans into the fold. Individuals who privately hated President Buchanan. Individuals who wanted her out of office and her accord stopped by any means necessary.

Custer had told Raza that these individuals would be left in the dark, their roles compartmented from each other and the final goal.

And when all was said and done, Raza bin Zaman would have the new president of the United States, Michael Dunn, and his senior leaders in his pocket.

He would have control over them while they waged war with Iran.

With the Saudi Council of Ministers taking their vote later that after-noon, Raza was hours away from becoming the new king of Saudi Arabia.

Dark Sun had succeeded.

So let yourself celebrate, he thought.

Turning around, Raza gazed over his helipad at the open-air lounge where Tara Devino sat on a couch before the bar and snorted a line of cocaine from a small mirror on the table.

Giddy with anticipation of the party that was about to be thrown, Raza moved over to the lounge and thought, *How did I get so lucky with her?*

It had been Devino's idea to bring in the party favors—the drugs and the high-class Eastern European escorts—for the day.

Walking into the open-air lounge, Raza watched Mahmoud Ghorbani enter from the door near the bar.

"Mahmoud," Raza said. "Are you ready for today?"

Ghorbani had arrived thirty minutes before, after tying up the loose ends in Davos. The Saudi sleeper agent who his father, the late king, had inserted into Iran as a teenager grinned and joined Devino on the couch.

Activating Ghorbani for Dark Sun had been Raza's idea. He needed a man he could trust. A man who could carry out the switching of the graphite rods. A loyal soldier who wouldn't mind getting plastic surgery so he could slip undetected through any country he pleased.

It had been Ghorbani's idea to rescue and manipulate his old Quds Force brothers to carry out the assassination in Davos. And it had been Ghorbani's idea to participate in the Yemen raid to oversee the potential advisers Raza wanted to hire for the Rapid Intervention Group.

Without Ghorbani, Dark Sun would have never succeeded.

Taking the rolled-up bill from Devino, Ghorbani leaned over the table and snorted a long line, before wiping his nose and asking, "Can I make you a drink, Your Highness?"

"A Bloody Mary," Raza said, and then sat down next to Devino.

Coming back with three Bloody Marys, Ghorbani handed one to the crown prince and another to Devino. "When are the girls arriving, Your Highness?"

Glancing out to sea, Raza pointed at the fast-approaching speck growing larger on the horizon. "I would say within the minute."

Both men watched as the helicopter carrying the party favors landed on the helipad on the bow of the *Serene*.

"My love," Devino said, holding up the small mirror containing narrow white lines. "Have some, it's incredible."

Raza was just about to grab the mirror, when he said, "Oh, I almost forgot to turn on the music. Can't have a party without music!"

Reaching for the iPad on the table, Raza turned on the surround sound and cranked a techno mix. Then, looking over at the helicopter, he noticed that the dozen, long-legged, bikini-clad women who had climbed out were not making their way toward the open-air lounge. Instead, they stood huddled in front of the chopper's door.

"Mahmoud!" Raza yelled over the blaring music. "Tell them to get their asses over here!"

Grabbing the mirror from Devino, Raza took a rolled-up bill and placed it under his large nose and was just about to snort a line of the white powder when the mirror shattered in his hand.

Confused, Raza looked down and noticed that blood was shooting out of the orifices where three of his fingers had once been.

Confusion turning to terror, he saw Ghorbani draw his pistol just as the gun was blown from his hand.

A moment later, two scarlet holes cut through the man's white linen shirt, sending him backward onto the table.

Devino let out a scream.

Standing, Raza reached with his good hand for the pistol he had hidden under his *thobe* and then buckled forward as the most searing pain he had ever experienced in his life erupted from his left knee.

Dropping his pistol, he pitched onto the ground.

Looking up at the escorts still collected around the helicopter, he saw a man dressed in a black T-shirt and a black ski mask materialize from the throng of women. The man walked forward, his suppressed pistol aimed straight at Raza.

Raising his nearly fingerless hand, Raza wailed, "NO!"

Clearing the bow of the ship, the man kicked Raza's pistol aside, then bent over and grabbed the crown prince by the scruff of his *thobe*. It was then that Raza recognized the snarling wolf tattoo on the man's forearm.

Hurling Raza onto the couch next to Devino, the man pointed his weapon at the crown prince's chest, then tore the mask from his face.

"CUT THE MUSIC," Brian Rhome yelled.

Devino touched the iPad's screen, and the music stopped.

Looking over at the escorts and the helicopter, Rhome motioned for them to leave.

After the chopper took off, Raza sputtered, "Are . . . are you a fool? I have two dozen of my best guards on this ship. They will be here any second."

Raza motioned to the security camera in the corner of the lounge and grew terrified when Rhome didn't react.

"Your security team isn't an issue anymore," Rhome said, and then he jerked his head at the door near the bar.

Raza saw six bearded men, dressed nearly the same as Rhome but holding large machine guns, step into the lounge.

Raza gaped at the men and then felt his pulse quicken as his younger brother, Khalid, stepped in after them.

"WHAT IS GOING ON HERE?!" Raza yelled.

"Hello, brother," Khalid said.

"YOU!" Raza spat, and he made to stand, but the bullet wound in his knee wouldn't allow it.

"How did you—"

"General Azimi got me out," Khalid said.

Raza's attention went back to Rhome as he took off the black rucksack he was wearing and pulled out a camera and an expandable stand.

The six bearded men aimed their weapons at Raza while Rhome connected the camera to the top of the tripod.

Raza screamed, "I will have all of you beheaded in Deera Square!"

"No, you won't," Khalid said.

"I AM THE KING!" Raza yelled.

"You killed the king," Khalid replied. "And you're not king yet."

Raza looked from Khalid to the camera. "What are you doing with that?!"

"I'm filming a confession," Rhome said. "A confession for the world to see."

In a panic, the crown prince watched as Brian Rhome pressed record.

CHAPTER EIGHTY-ONE

WALKING THROUGH THE Cabinet Room, Garrett Moretti once again could not believe his luck.

In a few short months, he had gone from being his father-in-law's chief of staff to becoming the acting director of the CIA.

Now, having heard through the grapevine in the last twenty-four hours that President Buchanan would surely not survive her injuries, it was all but certain that Moretti's father-in-law, Michael Dunn, would become president and appoint Moretti for the role of full-time CIA director.

Not only would Moretti be in charge of the world's most powerful intelligence agency, but he would be stepping into the role as a *wartime* director, a war that would certainly begin after his father-in-law carried out the assassinations of Iran's leaders in the coming days.

Moving through the Cabinet Room, Moretti stepped into the presidential secretary's office and continued to wonder why he'd been called to the White House by the FBI director for a closed-door meeting.

Maybe they want my guidance on how to deal with Iran, he thought, as the president's secretary opened the door for him and motioned him into the Oval.

Walking into the most powerful office in the world, his good mood evaporated when he recognized the individuals sitting on the couches in the room.

The door snapping shut behind him, Moretti saw the wild gray hair of the former director of the CIA, Elizabeth Hastings, and the two men sitting on either side of her and stopped dead in his tracks.

"What the hell is *she* doing here?" Moretti asked, looking at Vice President Michael Dunn slumped behind the Resolute desk.

When his father-in-law made no attempt to answer, Moretti turned his attention to the two men sitting on either side of Hastings.

Both Jack Brenner and Dan Miller glared at him.

Avoiding their threatening gazes, Moretti then took in the other individuals in the room.

Peter Coolidge, the national security adviser, stood at the far wall of the Oval next to the bust of George Washington. Next to Coolidge was Secretary of Defense James Lake, General Edward Toole, and Secretary of State Allison Newman.

"We're glad you could make it, Mr. Moretti," FBI director James Burke said, standing from the couch.

"Michael?" Moretti said, again addressing his father-in-law. "What's going on?"

Behind him, the door to the Oval opened, and the director of national intelligence, Johnathan Winslow, entered, followed by three Secret Service agents. Each agent carried a folding chair.

"Where do you want them, ma'am?" the biggest agent asked.

Hastings stood from her seat and pointed to the middle of the room.

The three agents unfolded the chairs and placed them before the Resolute desk.

The biggest Secret Service agent spoke again, "All recording devices in the Oval have been shut off at your request, and the room will be locked down as long as you need it. Oh, and I almost forgot."

Sticking his hand into his jacket, the agent pulled out a black smartphone and handed it to Hastings. "Winslow had this on him, just like you said he would."

"Thank you, Agent Rogers," Hastings said. "We shouldn't be long."

After the agents left the room, Hastings pointed to the three chairs and said, "Each of you sit down, now."

Moretti shook his head in confusion. "Elizabeth—"

"Sit, Garrett!"

Recoiling at Hastings's sharp tone, Moretti followed Winslow's lead and took a seat in one of the chairs.

"Now you, *Mr. Vice President*!" Hastings said.

Moretti was surprised how his father-in-law followed Hastings's directions like a scolded child.

Dunn sat down next to Moretti, and Moretti whispered, "What's happening, Michael?"

"Shut up, Garrett," Dunn snapped.

Hastings placed a black folder on the Resolute desk, then extended an open palm toward the men. "Your phones, please, gentlemen."

Moretti reached into his pocket and took out his secure CIA-issued BlackBerry.

"Your *other* phone, Garrett."

Moretti got nervous when he realized what she was talking about. Looking over, he watched Vice President Dunn reach into his pocket and hand Hastings an identical phone to the one that Custer had given Moretti a few months back.

Reaching into his own pocket, Moretti handed the strange black smartphone to the former director of the CIA, who placed it next to the other two on the desk.

Hastings glowered at the men, then said, "Last night, I got an interesting call from two of my former colleagues. A call, I can say with confidence, that I never expected to get. During this call, Jack Brenner and Dan Miller gave me the most appalling and outright disgusting intelligence briefing of my entire career. A briefing that provided explicit evidence that you three gentlemen, both wittingly and unwittingly, participated in a conspiracy with the crown prince of Saudi Arabia and an individual who calls himself Custer, a conspiracy that involved assassinating President Buchanan and stopping last night's Global Green Accord, all with the end goal of starting a war with Iran."

"What the hell are you talking about, Elizabeth!" Moretti cried, trying to get out of his seat.

"Don't you fucking move, Mr. Moretti," Hastings said. "I'll get to you in a minute!"

Dumbstruck, Moretti eyeballed his father-in-law and DNI Winslow, who both had an expression of distress on their faces.

Hastings continued, "We know everything, gentlemen, from your relationships with Custer, to your private views of President Buchanan and her Global Green Accord. We know what Custer promised each of you, and what you did for him in return. He made you think you were all patriots, that you were saving this country by stopping Buchanan and her accord."

"He didn't tell me he was working with the Saudis!" Winslow said. "He never told me he was trying to kill Buchanan! This was supposed to be about stopping the accord!"

"I know that," Hastings said. "And you blindly agreed to help him, Johnathan. You agreed to collude with a man to undermine a sitting president. A president who appointed you to be her director of national intelligence. You blindly agreed to commit treason."

"Treason?!" Winslow whimpered. "I was only thinking about the country."

"You were only thinking about yourself!" Hastings yelled, picking up the black folder from the desk and holding it in the air. "We know about your code names—Reno, Benteen, and Varnum—names Custer gave you all to keep your identities a secret. We know Custer kept you all compartmented from each other, how he had you do favors for him in exchange for promises."

Hastings stared at Winslow. "Tell me, *Benteen*, and don't lie, because I know the truth. Tell me what you did for Custer and the promise he gave you in return."

"I . . . I got him the UN GeoFence schematics."

"And in return?"

"He . . . he told me he would make me secretary of state once Buchanan was out of office."

"And you never once considered *why* Custer wanted those GeoFence schematics?"

"I . . . I didn't know—"

"Then you are dumber than you look," Hastings said, then gazed at Dunn. "And what did you do for Custer, *Mr. Vice President?*"

"I didn't intend for any of this to happen—"

"Answer my question, Michael."

"I . . . I gave him the travel routes of the graphite rods coming out of India."

"The graphite rods that caused the meltdowns in the reactors," Hastings said. "You were complicit in killing thousands!"

"I didn't know, Elizabeth!" Dunn pleaded.

"And in return?!" Hastings asked.

"Custer said he would make sure Buchanan was thrown out of office, that I would get the presidency . . ."

"Well, I hope all that blood on your hands was worth it," Hastings said and opened the black folder. "Other than you three, there was another coconspirator. An individual who went by the code name McDougall. A coconspirator who planted a homing device last night in Davos in Special Agent Mark Edwards's earpiece. A coconspirator who provided Custer with the motherboard that was given to the Saudis to put in that drone. That coconspirator was Agent Eunice Tuck."

Moretti's jaw dropped.

Hastings continued, "Custer promised Tuck the number one job at the Secret Service if she succeeded." Closing the folder, Hastings stared at Moretti. "Garrett, as you have probably deduced by now, you were merely a pawn in Custer's scheme. Custer only manipulated you to get rid of me. He had you give me a copy of that Saudi intelligence report, so he could frame me for the leak."

"I told you, I had nothing to do with this!"

"I know, Garrett," Hastings said. "You are just a power-hungry fool. A fool Custer manipulated to get what he wanted."

Placing the black folder down, Hastings looked at all three men. "Gentlemen, this conspiracy has all been a ploy to get the United States to start a war with Iran to ensure the world never moved away from fossil fuels, a ploy that almost worked, had it not been for some quick thinking by my old colleagues."

Hastings nodded in appreciation to Dan Miller and Jack Brenner.

"I was also made aware of what happened yesterday in the bunker," Hastings said. "How Custer strong-armed Vice President Dunn to target Iran's leadership. Luckily, we were able to provide back-door evidence to the Iranian Supreme Council to de-escalate the situation. That international crisis has been averted. Now we just have to deal with this crisis on the domestic front."

"You don't have the authority, Elizabeth," Dunn snapped.

"You're completely right, Michael," Hastings said. "I don't have that authority, but *she* does."

Hastings pressed a button under the Resolute desk, and the door on the left side of the Oval opened.

Moretti turned to see President Angela Buchanan sitting in a wheelchair, being pushed in by Special Agent Mark Edwards.

Moretti almost fell out of his seat.

"Madam President!" Dunn cried and jumped up.

Beaten and bruised, a sling holding her right arm, President Buchanan stood slowly from her wheelchair, and with a defiant expression on her face, she said, "Save it, Michael."

Dunn froze and sank back down.

Limping behind Hastings, President Buchanan gave her a curt nod, sat down behind the Resolute desk, and glared at the men.

Then raising her good arm, she said, "Director Burke, if you please?"

FBI director Burke walked over to her and gave her three pieces of paper.

Buchanan took the papers. "You three gentlemen are an embarrassment to your country, and the titles you hold. In my hands are your letters of resignation that you will sign right now. After you give your signatures, each of you will be taken into federal custody. I have spoken to my colleagues, my counterpart in Iran, and Prince Khalid in Saudi Arabia. We have come to the conclusion that what really happened last night in Davos, and the conspiracy each of you participated in, be kept a secret. As far as the public will be made aware, the nine Iranian Quds Force members were acting alone. I have decided that a secret commission be set up in the coming months to hand out sentences to each of you, based on your levels of complicity. Tomorrow, the press will be alerted of your resignations."

"How can you do this!" Dunn yelled. "I am the vice president of the United States!"

"But you are not above the law," Buchanan said. "You are a traitor to this office, and to this country. If any of you fail to sign your resignations, we will leak *everything* to the press right now. The whole damn thing!"

"You wouldn't," Dunn snarled.

"You want to try me, Michael?"

Moretti watched his father-in-law's hands flex and then unflex.

"We are giving you the option to avoid public scrutiny," Buchanan said. "It would be better for the country, and the world, if they never find out what really happened. And in the coming weeks, when the world leaders decide to come back and sign the Global Green Accord, we will do so in solidarity. But fail to sign those letters and we will blow this whole thing sky-high."

Dunn's head sank.

"But what about Custer?" Winslow said. "What's going to happen to him?"

Buchanan looked to Hastings.

Hastings, her face stern, said, "You leave Custer to me."

CHAPTER EIGHTY-TWO

CUSTER STEPPED OUT of his Audi RS7 and onto the gravel roundabout in front of Elizabeth Hastings's house, a bottle of Blanton's bourbon in his hand.

Taking in the FBI agents in their blue field jackets, Custer wondered how Hastings had convinced the feds to let her throw a dinner party while she was still technically under house arrest.

His old friend had called him that afternoon, inviting him over for dinner and cigars.

Never one to shy away from a good time, Custer accepted.

Walking toward Hastings's front door, he immediately felt a pang of guilt for what he'd done to her, how he had set her up after their last dinner party, a few weeks before. How he'd faked getting too drunk and had spent the night in one of her guest rooms, only to wait until she was asleep to then install software on her home computer that would make it look like she'd leaked the Saudi intelligence report.

Pushing that minor guilt aside, Custer put on his best smile.

No need to worry about that now, he thought, moving to the front door, and wondering what was currently happening at the White House in regard to Vice President Dunn carrying out the retaliation on Iran's leadership.

Custer envisioned waking up in the morning and seeing the headlines in the papers about Iran's leaders' assassinations and the impending war.

Greeting the FBI agents on Hastings's front deck, he rang the doorbell.

Ten seconds later, the door was opened by a young man wearing jeans, a black T-shirt, and a chef's apron. The man's head was shaved, and his beard a little too unruly for someone who was most certainly the help.

Grimacing as he saw the snarling wolf tattoo on the man's arm, Custer stepped inside, took off his jacket, and handed it to the man.

"Where's Elizabeth?"

"On the deck out back," the man replied.

Walking through the former CIA director's living room, and then past the dining room, Custer smelled something savory cooking in the kitchen, before stepping outside and finding Elizabeth Hastings sitting on her deck before her stone fireplace, smoking a Cuban cigar.

"Lizzie," Custer said, "I do hope you have one of those for me?"

"Richard!" Hastings replied, getting to her feet. "You're early, and of course I have one for you."

Hastings gave Senator Richard Lancaster a warm hug, before Lancaster handed her the bottle of Blanton's. "Did you get a butler?"

"He's just the chef," Hastings said. "I convinced FBI director Burke to hire him for the night so you and I could have a nice dinner."

"Your power over people, Lizzie, even in your darkest hour, will never cease to amaze me."

"Oh, Richard, you're too much," Hastings said, then waved over the chef.

"Brian, pour two glasses of bourbon for us and bring out a cigar for the senator."

The chef nodded and said, "Dinner will be ready in five minutes, ma'am."

"Thank you."

Lancaster watched the young man leave, then said quietly, "I have some exciting news to share, Lizzie."

"Really?" Hastings said, sitting back down before the fire and indicating Lancaster do the same. "And what news is that?"

Coming back outside, the chef handed Lancaster and Hastings each a glass of the Blanton's and then gave Lancaster a clipped Cuban cigar and a matchbox.

Grabbing both items from the chef, Lancaster lit his cigar, and waited for the man to leave, before saying, "Rumors have been circulating around the beltway that Buchanan is still in critical condition. I spoke to Vice President Dunn this morning, and he told me that if Buchanan doesn't survive he will be appointing *me* to be his running mate for his reelection this November."

"Oh, Richard," Hastings said. "That is amazing!"

Though he had not heard from his lieutenant, McDougall, since the events in Davos, Custer knew that she would do everything in her power to make sure Buchanan died. Whether that happened today, or tomorrow, it didn't matter. McDougall was a true believer to the cause, and Custer knew she would get the job done.

Raising their glasses, they cheered Lancaster's good fortune before taking a sip.

"Lizzie, as vice president, I will make sure that President Dunn does everything in his power to pardon you."

"You would do that for me?"

"Of course I would. You are the closest thing I have to a sister. I would do anything for you."

Taking a nip of his bourbon, Lancaster heard the chef come out onto the deck and declare that dinner was served.

"Can I take this cigar inside?" Lancaster asked.

"Of course," Hastings said.

Lancaster grabbed his bourbon and followed Hastings into the dining room, where two plates of steak were sitting at each end of the table. Taking his seat, Lancaster laughed at the bottle of ketchup next to his plate.

"Oh, Lizzie, you always knew how to charm me."

"Richard, I've known you for over fifty years. I know how much you enjoy steak and ketchup."

Putting down his cigar in the ashtray next to his bourbon glass, Lancaster picked up his knife and fork, then his attention caught on an oil painting on the wall above Hastings's head.

"Is that—?"

Hastings, who was just about to bite into her own steak, turned and considered the painting. "Oh, that? It's just one of the prints I got in the divorce. I decided to hang it this afternoon, right after I invited you for dinner."

Staring at the oil print of Edgar S. Paxson's famous depiction of *Custer's Last Stand*, Lancaster felt a strange sense of foreboding in his chest, starting with a sharp pain between his ribs.

Wincing, he said, "I had no idea Declan had such a fine taste in art."

"It's one of the original prints," Hastings said. "And to be quite honest, one of the most satisfying things I got in the divorce because it really pissed Declan off."

Peeling his attention off the painting, Lancaster thought over everything that had transpired in the last year and a half, from the moment Raza bin Zaman pitched his idea for Dark Sun, and how Lancaster had worked secretly with the crown prince to perfect his plan. He thought over how he launched Operation Little Bighorn in the United States. How he got Reno, Benteen, Varnum, and McDougall to carry out his and the crown prince's every wish. He thought of how he used Senator Declan Brandt, Elizabeth's old husband—the boisterous fool—to be his voice in convincing President Buchanan to carry out the assassination of General Soleimani.

A year and a half ago, right before Buchanan's Green Initiative was about to be passed, the crown prince had asked Lancaster to be the only one on his side of the aisle to vote in favor of her ludicrous bill. The crown prince wanted Lancaster to be able to confide in Buchanan, to get close to her, to make it look like he was a champion of her policies. Together, both Raza bin Zaman and Senator Lancaster seemed like they were Buchanan's most ardent supporters, when in reality, they were working behind a cloak of deception to effect an outcome of a series of events that could never be linked back to them.

While cozying up to Buchanan, Lancaster used Brandt to be his true voice. To be the one who pushed his true agenda. But unlike his other four lieutenants, Lancaster decided early on that Brandt was too much of a wild card to participate in Operation Little Bighorn, so Lancaster kept him out of the loop and manipulated him from the sidelines.

Coughing slightly, Lancaster tried to ignore the stabbing sensation in his chest, and the numbness that was creeping down his left arm.

Picking up the ketchup bottle, he smothered the steak before cutting himself a piece and plopping it into his mouth. As he swallowed, he put a hand to his chest, the stabbing sensation turning into a crushing feeling.

"Are you okay, Richard?" Hastings asked.

Lancaster took a sip of his bourbon, then put it down, his vision going wobbly.

"Richard?"

Lancaster blinked and realized that the room was spinning.

"Lizzie," he said. "I . . . I think something is wrong . . . I think I'm having a heart attack!"

Hastings hurried to his side.

"Lizzie, I think you need to call an ambulance!"

Hastings yelled, "Brian! Come in here!"

His vision now swirling, Lancaster watched as the chef walked calmly into the room.

Hastings said, "I think he's having a heart attack!"

The chef took his time moving over to Lancaster. "This doesn't look like a heart attack, ma'am."

Gazing confused at the chef, Lancaster took in the man's unflustered eyes.

"If I were to guess," the chef said, "I'd say this was the effect of a specific toxin that mimics the symptoms of a heart attack, a toxin that when inhaled at high temperatures is incredibly lethal."

Sweat now pouring down his face, Lancaster stared at his smoldering cigar in the ashtray. "What . . . what did you just say?"

Hastings said, "It does look like the effect of a toxin, doesn't it?"

Lancaster's bulging eyes met Hastings's ice-cold stare, before he lost his balance and fell to the floor.

Flipping him on his back, the chef and Hastings stood above him, Edgar S. Paxson's painting of *Custer's Last Stand* visible on the wall over their shoulders.

Lancaster gasped for air, his chest feeling on the verge of imploding.

Hastings crouched down. "You really thought I didn't know that you framed me? You really believed Dark Sun and Operation Little Bighorn would succeed, *Custer*?"

Gaping at his old friend, Lancaster sputtered, "W-What? How?"

"It's over, Senator," the chef said. "We've got the crown prince on tape. He confessed to everything."

"And we sent the tape to the Iranians," Hastings added. "And all your lieutenants have been arrested, and Dunn removed from office. President Buchanan is alive and well; she'll announce their resignations tomorrow. You failed, Richard."

Lancaster felt something hot come up his throat and gurgled.

"Try not to fight it, Richard," Hastings said. "It will all be over soon."

Squatting next to Hastings, the chef contemplated Lancaster and said, "Quite the code names you gave yourself and your operation, Senator. Didn't you know George Armstrong and his boys lost?"

Lancaster gasped, and his vision tunneled as he felt a cataclysmic shift deep within his chest.

And as his eyes began to flutter, the last thing that Senator Richard Lancaster saw on earth was the Edgar S. Paxson painting, showing Custer dying at the Battle of the Little Bighorn.

EPILOGUE

BRIAN RHOME STOOD on the frozen sand of City Beach and stared at the icy, crystal blue water of Whitefish Lake.

It was that time of year in northern Montana when the weather fluctuated between flat-out blizzards and bluebird thirty-degree days.

Fortunately, today was the latter.

Rhome looked down at the vial in his right hand containing Mack's ashes. The ashes he hadn't been able to let go of since last September.

Clutching the vial, he turned around and regarded the four individuals leaning against the black Suburban watching him.

Jack Brenner and Huey Oliver stood in the middle of the other two men men who ran the Third Option Foundation, former Ground Branch warriors who selflessly dedicated the second chapter of their lives to helping and supporting the families of their fallen brothers.

Rhome turned back around and walked toward the edge of the icy lake, feeling his throat constrict as he squatted down, still holding the vial of Mack's ashes.

"Sorry this took so long to do, brother," Rhome said, his eyes misting over. "I haven't been myself for a long time, but I'm finally getting better. I promise I'm going to be there for Kelsey and the girls as long as they need me. I'm going to finally take some responsibility, Mack."

Rhome unscrewed the vial's cap and squinted down at Mack's gray ashes, and his tears began to run.

He heard his old friends' voice in his head, *If they ever get me, scatter my ashes in Whitefish Lake . . .*

Rhome took a deep breath, and then threw the ashes into the air, watching as the cold wind blew them out over the water and ice.

Remembering the motto that his old friend lived by, Rhome said, "Only dead fish swim with the current. Rest easy, buddy."

Screwing the lid back onto the vial, Rhome stuffed it back into his pocket and walked toward Brenner, Huey, and the two other men waiting for him at the SUV.

Matilda wagged her tail excitedly as Rhome approached, and Brenner handed Rhome her leash. Mrs. Jorgensson was visiting a relative in Idaho and had asked Rhome to look after the Saint Bernard for the weekend, so when Brenner and Huey flew to Bozeman the day before to drive to Whitefish with Rhome, Matilda tagged along.

"You good, Lobo?" Huey asked, his arm in a sling, recovering from the bullet wounds he sustained in Davos.

"I'm good."

Brenner put a hand on Rhome's shoulder. "Do you want us to drive you to the house?"

"I'll walk, it's just up the road."

Brenner released his grip on his godson's shoulder. "We're going for a beer at the Great Northern. Swing by after; President Buchanan wanted me to talk to you about the future of Lodgepole."

"Jack, I told you, I was done."

"I know what you told me," Brenner said. "It's just a talk. Not a commitment."

Rhome took in his godfather's tired eyes. "All right, I'll drop by after I go to the house."

Rhome's godfather, Huey, and the two Third Option Foundation guys got back into the Suburban and drove south toward the bridge over the train tracks leading them into downtown Whitefish.

After the vehicle disappeared, Rhome and Matilda started walking north up Lakeside Boulevard, until they hit Washington Avenue.

Standing at the end of the street, he looked down at the red house with the swing set on the front lawn, and Rhome realized that he was shaking.

Then after what felt like hours, he finally mustered up the courage, led the Saint Bernard down the street, and stopped before Mack's house.

Mack's old F-150 was parked in the driveway outside, and just as Rhome was about to walk to the front door, he saw movement on the other side of the kitchen window and froze.

Five seconds later, Kelsey Mackenzie's slim figure appeared on the other side of the screen door. She wore jeans and a light sweater, her tangle of blond hair tied in a bun.

Rhome saw Mack's widow's hand go to her mouth.

Rhome tried to say something but stopped when he saw three little blond girls peer out behind their mother.

Katherine, Tessa, and Grace, all miniature versions of their mom, stared at Rhome.

Then Katherine, the oldest, not yet seven, wrapped an arm around Kelsey's leg and said, "Who's that, Mommy?"

Rhome could see Kelsey Mackenzie's face begin to quiver.

He took a step onto the front lawn and felt his mouth go dry.

He'd spent months thinking about this very moment, when he'd finally summed up the courage to stand on this very lawn.

What he'd do.

What he'd say.

"Kels, I'm . . . I'm so sorry—"

Rhome could see mascara-stained tears moving down Kelsey's cheeks, before she said, "Stay inside, girls."

Opening the screen door, Kelsey stepped out onto the front stoop, and for a long beat, they just stared at each other.

"Where the hell have you been?" she finally said.

"I've . . . I've been trying to figure things out, but I'm here now," Rhome said, wiping the tears falling down his face. "I'm so sorry, Kels—"

Kelsey Mackenzie marched down the snowy front steps toward Rhome and Matilda, then stopped right in front of them.

For a moment, Rhome thought she was going to strike him.

But instead, she threw herself forward and wrapped her arms around his neck and sobbed.

They held each other and cried, until Matilda whined and nudged her large snout at Rhome's side.

Releasing their embrace, Kelsey wiped at her tears and looked down. "Who is this?"

"This is Matilda, my neighbor's dog."

Over Kelsey's shoulder, Rhome could see Mack's daughters still standing behind the screen door.

"Girls," Kelsey said. "Come out here and say hello to your godfather."

Mack's three young daughters filed shyly out of the house and stood on the stoop, staring at him.

"They're so big now," Rhome said.

"Well, what's it been, two years?"

"At least."

Matilda panted in excitement from seeing the three girls.

"Can we pet your dog?" Mack's youngest daughter, Grace, asked.

"Of course," Rhome said, unclipping the dog's leash. "Matilda, go say hi."

The big Saint Bernard stood up, her bushy tail wagging wildly as she marched over to the girls, who squealed in delight as they pet her massive head.

Beaming at the girls' reaction, Kelsey asked Rhome, "Did you two come up by yourselves?"

"Jack and Huey flew into Bozeman yesterday. We drove up this morning, then met the TOF guys in Kalispell. They're at the Great Northern right now having beers."

"Of course they are," Kelsey said with a laugh, wiping the last remnants of tears from her face. "Thank you for coming, it means a lot."

"I'm sorry it took so long."

As his attention shifted from Kelsey to the girls now playing in the snow with Matilda, Rhome peered out at the lake.

A bald eagle flew languidly over the water, its wings riding the thermals that rose up toward the surrounding mountains, and the heavens beyond.

And at once an unfamiliar wave of emotions flowed through him.

They weren't emotions he was accustomed to—the survivor's guilt, the pity, the self-reproach.

No.

These emotions were different.

These were feelings of gratitude.

Of forgiveness.

Forgiveness of himself.

Staring at the beautiful landscape around him, hearing the happy squeals of Mack's girls on the lawn behind him, and Kelsey's laughter as she joined in playing with Matilda, Brian Rhome—for the first time in a long time—caught himself genuinely smiling.

Maybe now, after everything he'd been through—after losing so much, *all* would finally be okay.

ACKNOWLEDGMENTS

Completing this book was the most difficult and exhilarating thing I've ever done in my life and it wouldn't have been possible if not for the amazing support system around me.

First off, I would like to thank my wonderful wife, Mariafe, to whom this book is dedicated, for putting up with me this last year during all the highs and lows—all the times I battled imposter syndrome, and for encouraging me forward when I thought finishing this novel was impossible.

I would also like to thank my parents, Mark and Betsy, who not only gave my wife and me their basement to live in during the pandemic, but allowed us to bring along our moody English setter, Arlo, and our crazy Saint Bernard puppy, Matilda, as well.

As my readers can see, Matilda made her way into this book and Arlo did not, but that will hopefully change in the next book—that is, if Arlo is in a good mood and will allow it!

As I said in the acknowledgments section of my debut novel, *Sleeping Bear*, it takes a village to write a book, and that's still true.

To Emily Bestler, thank you so much for all the hard work you did whipping the manuscript into shape and for making my dreams a reality. It means the world.

To Lara Jones, for keeping me on track and holding everything together. I swear, I will get better at responding to your emails in a timely manner, and using less exclamation points!!!

To David Brown, you are the most hilarious and the best publicist in the business.

To everyone at Simon & Schuster and Atria Books and for all you do behind the scenes, thank you.

To my superagents, Meg Ruley and Rebecca Scherer, whose meticulous early reading of the manuscript made it so much better. Thank you both again, and to everyone at the Jane Rotrosen Agency, thank you for working so hard.

To my early readers Walker Adams and Alex Marker, thank you for all your keen insight. And to Del, thank you for your help and friendship. I can't wait to see what happens with *A Patient Man*. And yes, I know personal cell phones can't be used within the halls of Langley, but hey, that's why I love writing fiction!

To my cousin Allegra—who thinks I am the funniest person in the world—thank you for all your Gen-Z prowess and for helping me with social media. I swear I'll get better.

To C. E. Albanese, thank you so much for helping me on all things Secret Service. I'm sure I messed something up, and you can tell me all about it next time I'm on *The Crew Reviews* podcast!

Lastly, I would like to say this: In the past decade of my life, I've had the privilege of becoming close friends with individuals who had careers similar to certain characters in this novel. Individuals who dedicated their lives to working in the shadows and making our country safer than it was yesterday. Though I won't say your names, I want to thank all of you for the countless hours you've helped me with this book, as well as introducing me to the great and selfless people at the Third Option Foundation, which I respect so much. Because *Wolf Trap* is a work of fiction, the portrayal of the Third Option Foundation in the novel isn't exactly how the foundation operates in real life. There are no big bearded men out in the middle of the night tracking down individuals and leaving calling cards, nor would the CIA in any way, shape, or form direct TOF to track someone down to provide psychological evaluations or psychological support.

That was simply artistic license I took in writing this work of fiction.

Instead, the Third Option Foundation is so much more. As a 501(c)(3) tax-exempt national nonprofit organization, TOF and its programs work to remove the barriers and stigma surrounding behavioral health support by providing robust care systems for those in need.

Operating under the motto "Quietly helping those who quietly serve," TOF seeks to heal, help, and honor the CIA's Special Operations community and their families by providing crucial survivorship assistance and resiliency programs to heal the wounded, help the families of those they've lost, and support those who are still serving.

If you are interested in learning more about this incredible foundation and how you could potentially help, please check out their website at: thirdoptionfoundation.org.